Elemental Spirits

Building a Magical Practice in an Animistic World

About the Author

Jaq D Hawkins currently has four books in publication in the Mind, Body, Spirit category and is the author of the popular *Spirits of the Elements* series, now combined in the single volume, *Elemental Spirits*. She also has five Fantasy fiction novels in print and E-book.

She began both writing and spellcraft at an early age, performing her first ritual at fourteen, and has studied various aspects of the magical arts for over sixty years.

She lives in the English Midlands with her partner and a selection of cats.

Information on all Mind, Body, Spirit titles as well as her fiction titles can be found through her website at www.jaqdhawkins.co.uk.

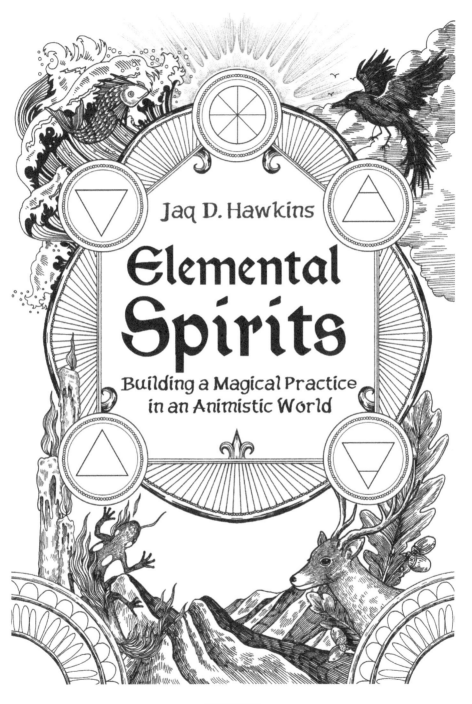

Jaq D. Hawkins

Elemental Spirits

Building a Magical Practice in an Animistic World

Chicago, Illinois

Paperback ISBN: 978-1-959883-56-2
Library of Congress Control Number on file.

Published by:
Crossed Crow Books, LLC
6934 N Glenwood Ave, Suite C
Chicago, IL 60626
www.crossedcrowbooks.com

Printed in the United States of America.
IBI

More by the Author

Chaos Witch (Independently Published, 2022)
Echoes of Ganesha (Independently Published, 2019)
The Chaonomicon (Chaos Monkey Press, 2017)

Contents

INTRODUCTION ~ 1

CHAPTER 1
AN ANIMIST VIEW ~ 4

The Nature of Earth. 5
The Nature of Air. 8
The Nature of Fire 12
The Nature of Water 16
The Nature of Aether. 22

CHAPTER 2
FOLKLORE ~ 25

Earth Spirits 26
Air Spirits 29
Fire Spirits. 31
Water Spirits 34
Aetherial Spirits. 39

CHAPTER 3
TUNING IN TO LOCATION SPIRITS ~ 45

Places to Find Earth Spirits. 47
Places to Find Air Spirits. 49
Places to Find Fire Spirits 52
Places to Find Water Spirits. 55
Places to Find Aetherial Spirits 59

CHAPTER 4

SPIRITUAL PERCEPTION ~ 61

To See Earth Spirits 62
To See Air Spirits 66
To See Fire Spirits. 68
To See Water Spirits 70
To See Aetherial Spirits. 75

CHAPTER 5

FOLK MAGIC ~ 77

Working with Earth Elementals. 77
Working with Air Elementals 82
Working with Fire Elementals. 88
Working with Water Elementals 93
Working with Aetherial Elementals. 99

CHAPTER 6

FORMAL RITUAL ~ 102

Calling Quarters 103
Earth Rituals Out of Doors 110
Air Rituals Out of Doors. 111
Fire Rituals Out of Doors 111
Water Rituals Out of Doors. 112
Earth Spirits for a Specific Task. 113
Air Spirits for a Specific Task. 114
Fire Spirits for a Specific Task 114
Water Spirits for a Specific Task 115
Aetherial Spirits in Formal Ritual 117

CHAPTER 7

TRADITIONAL SYMBOLS AND MAGICAL CORRESPONDENCES ∼ 119

Astrological Correspondences 121
Alchemical Correspondences 123
Associations Between Creatures, Plants, and Colours. . . . 125
Numerology. 132
Incense Correspondences. 135
Magic Squares 142

CHAPTER 8

PRODUCING ELEMENT-BASED THOUGHT-FORMS OR SERVITORS ∼ 145

Creating a Thought-Form Elemental or Servitor 146
Sustaining a Thought-Form 147
Earth Thought-Forms or Servitors 148
Air Thought-Forms or Servitors. 149
Fire Thought-Forms or Servitors 151
Water Thought-Forms or Servitors. 152
Aetherial Thought-Forms or Servitors 156

CHAPTER 9

DIVINATION ∼ 158

Divination with Earth Spirits. 159
Divination with Air Spirits 162
Divination with Fire Spirits. 163
Divination with Water Spirits 165
Divination with Aetherial Spirits. 167

CHAPTER 10
TREES, BIRD LORE, HOLY WELLS, AND DANCING WITH THE FIRE ～ 171

Tree Lore. 171
Bird Lore. 177
Holy Wells. 180
Dancing with the Fire 188

CHAPTER 11
EXAMPLE SPELLS AND METHODS ～ 192

A Sample Opening Ritual 192
Calling Quarter Guardians 195
The Middle Bit 198
Earth Elemental Spells 199
Air Elemental Spells 204
Fire Elemental Spells. 210
Water Elemental Spells 214
Simple Folk Spells and Other Magic 224
Aether 244

CHAPTER 12
LIVING WITH ELEMENTAL SPIRITS ～ 246

Bibliography and Recommended Reading *250*

Introduction

IN THE YEARS BETWEEN 1998 AND 2001, I wrote five books called *The Spirits of the Elements Series*. The books enjoyed a certain popularity and were sold by a small speciality publisher who dealt in occult material, which went out of business when the owner died. Writing the series was, in itself, an interesting experience. Any writer learns while writing, both through research and because putting ideas down in writing has a way of bringing out information hidden in the dark recesses of the psyche. When you write about spiritual entities, they tend to take notice and, in the case of nature spirits, add certain playful influences to the life of the writer. I learned more about nature spirits by writing about them than I had learned in my entire life before.

The purpose of this book is not to repeat what I have written in past books, but to expand on the knowledge and personal experience that has accrued over many years and write a book that would be of use for both beginners and more experienced magic users. The magical community has become more sophisticated over time, even though there will always be those who are new to magic. This book will be kept accessible to those just starting out, but I hope to keep the tone suitable for the responsible adult magician.

When I speak of elemental spirits, the reference may refer to a wide spectrum of spiritual essences as well as more individualised spirits of different kinds. I'm basically an Alchemist and an Animist. I believe that everything that exists has a spiritual nature, including things that are manufactured. Everything is made from basic elements that begin in nature, after all. Obviously, a more direct connection with the spirit of an element is to be found in an unadulterated natural source of that element, but constructions can take on their own spiritual nature over time as well.

Just look at the feeling of spiritual presence one finds in old churches, temples, cathedrals, or other places that have become associated with spiritual practices.

Belief in Victorian-like fairies is not required to work in the world of elemental spirits, and, in fact, I deal more with the essences of natural elements like stones, winds, flames, and bodies of water than with personifications of the "wee folk."

However, I like to keep my belief parameters flexible, allowing for that grey area between fancy and reality that makes all things possible. It is a particularly effective approach when working magic. Cold, hard scientific facts can be very limiting.

I also tend to visualise elemental spirits more in the style of the artist Brian Froud or in the imagery one finds in some Fantasy films where a rock suddenly animates and begins to speak to the characters. Pretty fairy images are all very well, but a spirit does tend to resemble the physical embodiment of its nature. However one chooses to perceive elemental spirits, the important aspect is to create a connection between oneself and the elementals.

The test of any concept of magic, of course, is whether it works. If I recite silly rhymes to imaginary weather fairies and a heat wave ends with unexpected rainstorms, I have a result. How "real" the weather fairies are is inconsequential. They are sufficiently real to bring in the rain clouds, and that will do nicely. That my scientific brain says there is no such animal as a weather fairy or that it is yet another coincidence of an unpredictable and naturally chaotic system makes no difference to the consistent result. Logic says that as the consistency of the result is real, the method of achieving the result, however nonsensical, must therefore be genuine.

When I first started actively practicing magic at the age of fourteen, I had no thoughts of spirits. Yet, on my first spell, I spoke to a flower, addressing the essence of the flower therein. It was a divination spell that had to slightly bend physics to give me a correct answer. No doubt there is some perfectly plausible explanation for the accurate result.

No matter. The magician Austin Osman Spare purported the value of free belief and many magicians since have found the technique useful. Perhaps magic(k) sometimes wanders too far into the world of academia to seek acknowledgement and we should step back to the folk magic roots that allow the magic to work even when it doesn't make logical or scientific sense.

Our enlightened society looks too hard for explanations. Sometimes magic requires that little pushing of parameters that comes with uncertainty. This is a particularly difficult skill for the most educated magicians to cultivate, yet, in fact, there are many university-educated individuals actively practicing magic(k) in the acceptance that sometimes science doesn't know how it works, it simply does.

We are not here for explanations or scientific justification. This tome exists to guide the reader in the methods of working with elemental spirits. The "whys" and "wherefores" are put aside in favour of the *how*. As long as it works, the rest doesn't matter.

As an aside, I generally spell the word "magic" without the added "k," although I have sometimes included it in parentheses in references to ceremonial or formal ritual magic. Someone I like and respect once said in a review that I spell it "wrong," but I must disagree. The "k" was instituted by Aleister Crowley to differentiate real magic from stage magic, but many good books on magic were written long before then and the added "k" has never been in universal use.

Crowley's practices have no direct significance to my style of magic, which is largely based in nature and natural systems, so I don't use his "k" as it just doesn't sit well. Apart from that, his methods of commanding spirits are at odds with my methods of working in co-operation with them. I do not have the stringent religious background that set Crowley in conflict with demons.

There are no demons (in the Christian sense) in an Animist world, though the word *daemon* is an old term for a nature spirit.

Noun (in ancient Greek belief): A divinity or supernatural being of a nature between gods and humans (Knowles).

Religious reformers have hijacked many words throughout history. We need take no notice of them. Beliefs about the nature of elemental spirits have coloured folklore throughout recorded history and in all cultures. In Chapter Two, we will look at some examples of the names and characteristics that have been attributed to elemental spirits in the past.

Our primary concern, however, is with the present and how we can work in harmony with the spirits of nature and of everything that exists, as we recognise our own spiritual nature and how we fit into the gestalt universe of elemental spirits.

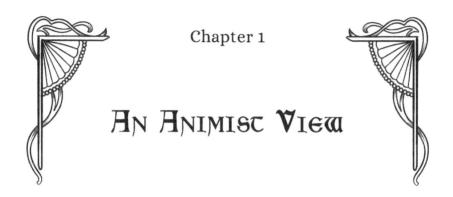

Chapter 1

An Animist View

Elemental spirits have played a role in human belief and history since time immemorial, particularly among people who practice some form of magic(k). From folk magic to Alchemy and ritual magic, some acknowledgement of elemental spirituality occurs in most beliefs and magical systems.

I approach this subject matter from an Animistic viewpoint. I feel some form of spiritual essence in everything. In some nature religions, the Earth itself is deified. It gives life, food, and a firmament on which to base our existence. It comes naturally to attach attributes of the Alchemical elements to nature spirits because the spirits themselves attach to things in nature. The spirit of a lake is obviously a Water spirit, the spirit of a windstorm an Air spirit, a Fire spirit inhabits a flame, and Earth spirits are the guardians of trees, rocks, and all the material objects we see around us.

Humans create correspondences between things, and some magical systems rely on the resonance of these correspondences, but nature flows from one element into another. We can create models of "systems" to help us better understand the workings of nature, and physicists might have a higher grasp of that which can be weighed, measured, and categorised, but belief in spiritual essences persists even in well-educated minds. Once you've actually seen an elemental spirit, no amount of knowledge of molecular biology or other sciences can negate the evidence of that first-hand experience.

For the purposes of this book, I will examine the elements individually for the most part. However, we must keep in mind that in the natural world (and even in magic), elements do not work in isolation but as a whole.

THE NATURE OF EARTH

Humans tend to personify the Earth spirits and perceive them as the "wee folk" or fairies. Most of the nature spirits that come to mind when we think of fairies (by whatever cultural names we know them by) are Earth spirits. Fairies of flowers, rocks, plants, trees, and many other associations with the material are Earth spirits. The *terra firma* on which we stand and spend our lives is as essential to our survival as the air we breathe.

Earth is the solid building block of all that is in the physical world, which is why Earth, as an Alchemical element, represents the material existence of all things. Earth provides a foundation on which plants and trees can grow. In magical correspondences, Earth represents health, prosperity, and mundane concerns, as well as the spiritual foundation of the magic itself. In ritual or ceremonial magic, it represents the body of the magician, which acts as a physical temple where the construction of the magic takes place.

Without Earth, we have nothing on which to construct. Without our bodies, we have nothing in which to personalise our soul. Some might say that would be an advantage and I am sure there is plenty of scope for astral magic, but as long as we are contained within our bodies, we shall continue to have a natural Earth temple within which we may perform magic to affect our very Earthly environment. If we are honest with ourselves, much of the magic that is done by witches and magicians is very much directed at affecting something on the Earthly plane.

Therein lies understanding of the magic of the Earth element. Without a solid basis, there can be no magic. The mundane world that many spiritually minded people try to rise above is an integral part of the lofty ideals of spirituality that some might try to ignore but can never really overcome. In nature, there is no quest to overcome the material world. It is very much a part of nature, and the instinctive reaction for any living thing to a need within the material world is to seek satisfaction of that need within the natural rhythms of nature.

A hungry animal will seek food. A thirsty plant will reach through the Earth with its roots to seek water. Religions that strive to overcome the material for the spiritual are attempting to deny the solid basis of flesh and Earthly needs. This is unnatural not only for humans and other animals but also for the balance of the universe as we know it. There is balance in nature, which is reflected in the balance between the Alchemical elements. It is only humankind's arrogance that strives to deny the basis of the natural world.

In magic, the Earth element is commonly invoked for purposes associated with the material or the planet itself. These include healing spells, prosperity spells, planetary healings, and any number of purposes that involve the physical world. Many magical systems invoke some aspect of divinity that rules over these Earthly purposes as part of these spells. Some directly invoke the nature spirits themselves.

How much a nature spirit actually co-operates with such an invocation is another matter. One is far more likely to create a thoughtform elemental in response to a nature spirit invocation than to attract a spirit out of its natural habitat.

To experience an actual nature spirit, one must visit the natural habitat of that spirit. Those of us who believe in an Animist philosophy recognise that every tree, every stone, and all things in nature are inhabited and looked after by resident spirits. Several books have been written about nature spirits by their various names, but most notable are those about the Findhorn community in Scotland where people have reported directly communing with nature spirits.

Books of folklore might give some conflicting information, but the consensus is that the growing things of the Earth are cared for by nature spirits, often referred to as fairies in English-speaking countries, which are not normally visible to the human eye. However, these are not the only "fairies" that are historically reported. There are many legends of tricky or even severely nasty forms of fairies who do mischief to humans. They are often depicted as less attractive to the eye than the pretty images of flower fairies that we have inherited from the Victorians.

Many a traveller has been afraid to enter a remote forest for fear of the spirits who might seek to protect their habitat from the ravages of humankind. Most of the legendary bogies and brownies, hobgoblins, and even house fairies are associated with the Earth element.

Spirits of standing stones, also called *dolmens,* are particularly strong and easy for the sensitive person to perceive because their habitat is something that is used to amplify the magical currents of the Earth itself in the form of electromagnetic energy. Standing stone spirits can be powerful allies if given proper respect, yet visitors to Stonehenge after dark have reported an uneasy feeling there at night. The stones know how to protect themselves, as was illustrated in a story about religious fanatics trying to pull down a group of stones until their leader was crushed by one falling atop him.

The Earth has a way of cleansing and renewing itself that can be frightening to humans who get in the way of natural phenomena like earthquakes or volcanic eruptions. These events demonstrate the power of the primordial chaos of destruction and renewal. As someone once quipped to me, "Nature eats its own."

The power of the Earth, particularly amplified in some way, is a tremendous force to reckon with. While we might view natural disasters as catastrophes when human life is lost, for the Earth it is also a representation of the creative principle. New land formations come about as a result of Earth movements or lava flow. Nutrients from deep within the Earth's crust are brought forth to feed new life, and the inner energies of the Earth are released for purposes that have nothing to do with the human dwellings and lives that might get swept away should they fall into the path of one of these Earthly power surges.

Some forces are beyond human ability to harness or control, and the best we can do is try to get out of the way. Ancient human societies who have come into regular contact with these Earth forces have often believed in spirits or deities who might bring earthquakes or who are the ruling spirit of a volcano. Though we no longer throw virgin sacrifices into a rumbling volcano, anyone close to this sort of natural phenomenon might find it easy to personify the destructive force behind it.

Certain temples and standing stones are evidence of humankind's attempts to try to focus a manageable amount of this natural energy, with success depending on the level of understanding put into these manmade amplifiers. Study of shapes and constructions, like the pyramids, have led to speculation about how certain contours or locations might be conducive to amplification of Earth energies.

The stone circles in Britain and some parts of Europe have given rise to much speculation as to their original purposes. While the observatory

theory might be the most widely accepted, there is a lot of evidence that suggests that the placement of these stone monuments actually serves to amplify the Earth's electromagnetic energy (Hitching). Carefully shaped Earth mounds, like Glastonbury Tor in Southwest England and the Great Serpent Mound in Ohio, are also subject to speculation about amplified Earth energies, associations with Earth spirits, and any number of stories and legends that suggest that there is much more to them than creative sculpting.

The Earth itself was deified as Gaia, the mother goddess, in ancient Greek mythology. It is an association that modern Pagans still recognise. Many Native American tribes and other Indigenous cultures around the planet have similar traditions of worshipping the Earth in some form. The Earth gives forth life because it brings forth growing food that allows humans and other animals to survive.

Her helpers, the "wee folk" who care for the growing things and have become known to us as *fairies, devas,* and many other names, are Earth spirits. In understanding the spirits we associate with the things of Earth and the solid foundations of natural magic, we bring ourselves closer to understanding the balance in the universe and the importance of the solid building blocks behind the creative principle we call Earth.

THE NATURE OF AIR

Air is one of the most essential elements of life as we know it and is, in fact, the one single element that we cannot live without, even for a few moments. Without air, there would be no life. How interesting it is, then, that Air rules intellect and inspiration.

Air can be creative, breathing life into the plants and animals of the Earth, or it can be very destructive as anyone who has survived a hurricane or tornado knows well. The spirits who are represented by this element reflect this dual nature in many ways.

The spirit of a storm may be seen as destructive by someone who has lost a home or loved one through its force, yet the same storm is often a cleansing process for nature as a whole and even serves to transport any number of seeds and other natural particles from one place to another, making life for another species more possible. Like all of the elements, it is a double-edged sword.

Spirits of Air are many and varied. Very few of them are as familiar to us as the Earth spirits who are more often depicted in various art forms, but they surround us in their various guises just the same. Apart from the obvious spirits of winds and storms, as well as smaller whirlwinds and such, there are the spirits who appear in smoke for divination, spirits of high places, and spirits of communication, like the Irish Banshee that screeches its message into the wind for all to hear.

These are all forms of Air spirits. There are those who believe that certain birds are also Air spirits in solid form, the messengers of the gods.

As an element, Air rules intellect, thought, the first steps toward creation, movement, pure visualisation, spells involving travel, instruction, freedom, obtaining knowledge, discovering lost items, and uncovering lies. It is the element of dreams and plans, goals, and inventions.

As a magical element, Air feeds the mind and spirit. Without inspiration, our own species would stagnate and eventually die. Without imagination and invention, humankind would have no purpose in the scheme of nature to justify the existence of our species.

Many might argue that our tendency to invent modern devices is at the root of all of nature's ills, but like the winds in the storm, technology can be used for creation as well as destruction. We carry within us the potential to use our unique abilities in conjunction with the natural world.

Imagination is the creative principle behind all magic. It is the spark that ignites the power and the inspiration that gives it purpose. Air spells would be appropriate for gaining inspiration, helping with study, visualisation, seeking or blessing travel, spells to obtain freedom or to discover lost items, and seeking the improbable.

Air is the symbiotic element of nature. We breathe oxygen along with other animals and expel carbon dioxide, which in turn is breathed in by members of the plant kingdom that expel oxygen. This give-and-take principle places us within the rhythms of nature in an inescapable pattern of sharing and mutual dependency.

In astrology, it is the Air signs who are least concerned with material possessions, timekeeping, or other material worries. It is through freely giving of ourselves that we find freedom from worldly concerns, which in turn frees our imaginations and creative abilities.

Air spirits live in a world of movement. We only become consciously aware of air if it moves about us, or if it is taken away from us. This concept bears contemplation. Humans who do not progress in some way will stagnate and experience a form of depression that could be likened to living death. We must imagine, we must learn, and we must move through the chapters of our lives, or we will sink into despair.

Nature renews itself with the seasons. The differences between one season and another are most observable within the Air element. Air temperatures change, winds and storms follow seasonal patterns, and the colours of the visible sky tell us much of what we need to know about the time of season we are experiencing.

The exact changes will be very different from one location to another, but the weather patterns of any specific place can be determined through the information we are able to perceive from the air.

It is the Air spirits whom we must consult if we wish to have any influence over our local weather patterns. Yet, there are many other purposes for which we might wish to invite the assistance of Air spirits. Safety while flying in an aeroplane springs to mind. Travelling through the realm of these spirits in a modern technological contraption that disrupts the natural air currents as well as spewing pollution and large amounts of unpleasant noise is intrusive, to say the least.

For this reason, I will not fly without good reason and will opt for train travel instead wherever possible. I have, in fact, not travelled by air since a trip to Japan in 2005. In the days when I did travel more frequently as a matter of necessity, I always tried to project my reasons for invading their element to any Air spirits who might be interested, particularly during plane landings, thanking the Air spirits for their kind assistance for safe landing after touchdown.

Air spirits can be most elusive to visual perception, as they are intangible by nature and can only usually be perceived through their own movement. They can all too easily be overlooked when seeking elemental spirit contact, yet are potentially very gratifying spirits to know well.

A friendly Air spirit who is willing to conjure up a breeze on a hot day at a moment's notice can be a useful ally. By the same token, an Air spirit who has been offended would not be the best of companions while crossing a suspension bridge.

Air spirits can carry messages and are frequently the bearers of omens for those who are able to listen to them. Air is also the element of pure joy. The spiritual "lift" that one feels upon being struck by inspiration for a creative idea or the solution to a difficult problem is very much a

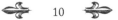

product of the Air element. Inspiration and imagination are the most magical qualities of Air.

Air currents are one of the major areas of study among chaos scientists who seek to understand the naturally chaotic patterns in nature. Their job is not an easy one. Air is the most unpredictable element, even more so than Fire, and one must use caution when employing it in magic.

The Butterfly Effect,[1] which has become part of twenty-first-century common knowledge, is something that should be borne in mind when performing spells based on the Air element. The slightest influence on the initial conditions of a spell—even a stray thought during its performance—can have far-reaching effects on the direction the spell will take once it is released.

Air is change. Constantly moving and unpredictable, air can be pushed one way or another but never entirely controlled.

The spirit of a light breeze comes into being simultaneously with the movement of the air, lives in a moment of pure joy, then dissipates to nothingness as the air disperses. In a moment of spiritual life, it has experienced the magic of creation, danced the dance of life, and is gone. Yet it will come into being randomly over and over as the gentle breezes come and go.

This is the magic of Air. Intangible, yet it is pure creative power. It is a positive force, existing without conscience or capacity for menace, yet all too dangerous for its lack of personal attachment to anyone or anything. What is a village to a hurricane-force wind? The joy is in the blowing and in the movement of creative patterns. The destruction in its wake is part of the cycle of renewal. Through the destruction of old trees, new seeds can reach the sunlight.

Air is impersonal. An Air spirit might take an interest in a human for a moment, but the moment is fleeting. If one wishes to employ the services of an Air spirit, one must first attract its attention, then perform one's spell and be done with it before the spirit becomes distracted and is away. Cast a spell with an Air spirit and you literally cast your fate to the wind.

---

1   The Butterfly Effect is an illustration of sensitive dependence on initial conditions. The analogy is that a butterfly flapping its wings in Hong Kong can create tiny air currents that affect other air currents and escalate until it results in a storm over New York.

Air spirits live for the moment, within their own sphere of influence with no regard for others, even of their own kind. The forces of Air can gather with dramatic results, but it is done spontaneously in the spirit of play. There is no forethought and no concern for consequences.

Imagination is spontaneous, a spark that happens without warning and is not easily forced. Such is the realm of Air. Working with pure creative spirit has infinite potential in magic and, for some purposes, might be the only force that is sufficient for the task. The key is not to try to force the spirit to your will, but to learn the nature of the spirit and how best to direct it towards your goal. Then, prepare to respond to changes that you didn't expect and to deal with whatever consequences might fall if it all goes horribly wrong.

Air is the element of music, poetry, and literature. It is in the arts that we are able to free our imaginative spirit and in our reactions to colour and to music that we respond to the deepest emotions within ourselves wherein lies the potential for powerful magic.

THE NATURE OF FIRE

The molten lava that seethes forth from an active volcano gives us imagery of the primordial chaos that lies unformed in the centre of the world we know, both physical and spiritual. Fire is chaos and chaos gives rise to order. It is only the form of the result that is unknown. Fire rules catastrophic change, will, and passion as well as purification, fear, anger, jealousy, and ecstatic trance.

Fire is the element of action, of passion, and of transmutation. Fire is the element of inner ecstasy: that sensation that comes when the magic flows in pure unity with ultimate intent.

Fire rules all forms of magic because magic is a process of activated change. Sexuality and passion, the sacred Fire of sex, and the spark of divinity that shines within all living things are all associated with Fire. Yet the intensity of passion that lies behind the spirit of Fire far transcends the basic primal urges that initiate reproduction. To quote Samuel Johnson, *"Love is only one of many passions"* (63).

The passion of Fire encompasses all that represents drive, life force, progression, fortitude, and the inner experience of the Divine Fire. Where Air represents intellectual inspiration, Fire represents the spark of action that brings inspiration into manifestation.

Fire is often symbolised by the Sun. It is depicted in churches with sunburst images to represent the Fire of God. Many religious texts speak of inner experience of the Fire, or of the Divine Light. During the Crusades, the Christians imported symbols for the Islamic Fire and incorporated the Persian Ahura Mazda into their own version of God, which also carries influences from Babylonian, Assyrian, and Sumerian Sun cults.

Fire is symbolised as light, as well as the spiritual light that is spoken of in *The Tibetan Book of the Dead*. Most Shamanic religions believe in some version of the idea that at death, the soul inhabits a spiritual body that preserves the Fire, or light of being. At birth, the soul is given the "spark" of life as its material beginning. Conversely, the Buddhist Nirvana is described as "blowing out the Fire of desire."

On a practical level, fire provides heat, light, and the ability to cook, but can also bring total devastation if uncontrolled. Here on planet Earth, the Sun is the source of light and warmth. It is the generator of life. Without it, we would die. It is no wonder that the Sun in some form of representation is central to many forms of religion.

Practicality and folklore come together in many traditions and even in superstitions regarding Fire. In crofting communities, one of the accepted duties of the woman of the house (traditional keeper of the continuity of the family) was to get up in the morning to bring the fire back to life, then to meditate on the hearth and home. This is a form of folk magic that still survives in some remote communities.

The lighting of bonfires on hilltops has historically been used as an early warning system during times of war in Britain, yet is also associated with the Fire festivals such as Midsummer and Lughnasadh (*Laa Lunys* in Manx).

Leaping over a fire is an old fertility rite, as is the driving of cattle between two fires. This is also a purifying ritual.

Christian women less than a century ago still kept a consecrated candle burning during and after the birth of a child until the infant was baptised to keep the fairies from stealing the infant. This is connected to underworld associations with Fire as well as the Christian belief that fairies were lost souls of the dead or fallen Angels.

On the Isle of Man, it is considered unlucky to lend fire or even tinder and flint on New Year's Day, or sometimes on the sixth of January, which is an older date for the New Year.

Fire is the reformative element, as in the fire from whence the Phoenix rises again and again. It is also the element of consummation and purpose.

Fire continues until all resources are exhausted. Fire is a powerful element, which can be used for positive or negative results, and one that can easily get out of hand if not carefully contained. Fire magic can be frightening, yet fear itself can be a powerful tool in magic.

Spirits of Fire come in many forms. The most obvious is the spirit of a flame, whether it is a small candle flame or that of a raging forest fire, but there are also the possessive spirits of passion and will, the Spirit of the Dance, spirits of hot places, of light, and of chemical reaction. Fire spirits have purpose, and they continue so long as there is fuel for that purpose. Fire never just gives up.

A Fire spirit does not necessarily have to take form in actual flame, but might well perform its purpose within the edges of physical ignition. The spirit of Fire can be summoned through the most primal forms of magic: drumming or dance, for example, which easily leads to ecstatic trance.

The focus of a Fire spirit ritual might be a flame of a candle, campfire, hearth fire, or bonfire, but the habitat of the spirit lies in Spirit, the infinite potential that knows no time or space. The realm of a flame spirit lies just beyond the level of manifestation.

Any fire safety official can confirm that fire can ignite spontaneously from sufficient heat and fuel. In a similar manner, a Fire spirit can spontaneously manifest as a burst of flame, as an action, or even as a burst of illumination. This is different from the inspiration that might be brought about by an Air spirit. It is a sudden awakening of knowledge of the mysteries. This is the basis of religious ecstasy.

Fire has many underworld associations, including most underworld gods and goddesses and the principle of death in the cycle of death and rebirth. The worship of these old gods has historically been connected to the act of animal and human sacrifice, though such practices are not used in modern Western Paganism. Yet, the principle of life force magic works in many ways, and leaving behind the barbaric customs of another age does not separate us from access to this very potent spiritual force.

Becoming fully aware of how to contain the spirit of Fire is comparable to learning to understand our own human drives and passions. Just as we learn to control our most primal urges and actions when we are children in order to operate within the bounds of social acceptability, we are able to learn to contain the spirits of Fire within parameters once we comprehend their basic nature.

Fire is the driving force behind Spirit. It is the energy that inspires us to carry on despite obstacles and delays, or to pursue that which might seem unobtainable. Fire spirits are living spirits. Just as the more commonly perceived Earth spirits live within plants and rocks, Fire spirits live within the potential for flame. This potential reaches far beyond the flame itself and can be insubstantial.

In magic, the Fire element is often invoked for intents involving action. Fire spells might be used when other spells have proven insufficiently powerful or active. If the purpose is important enough, the magician will brave the obvious dangers.

I am very aware that many of my writings on magic are riddled with warnings and cautions, especially when writing about fire. Although there is always a need for vigilance and circumspection when using magic of any kind, I will not hesitate to encourage the reader to embrace the power of Fire, with suitable precautions.

Fire spirits are often depicted in art as demons or inhabitants of subterranean underworld communities. Cartoons show us little flames with mischievous expressions on their fiery faces, spreading their kind prolifically in the scene, or as little demonic creatures from Christian mythologies, which multiply rapidly and inundate the situation to the chagrin of a main character who is suffering the consequences of incaution.

This sort of depiction is not entirely fictional. Fire spreads easily, the Fire spirits giving rise to many more of their kind so long as there is fuel to feed upon. Yet it can be contained.

Magic that utilises strong emotions, including anger, fear, and obsession, can be a useful tool, as the Fire spirits attracted to or created by these emotions are as strong as the emotions themselves and are not as easily squelched as a visible flame. Fire spirits are independent spirits, separate from the magician who creates them every bit as much as the spirit of a candle flame is apart from the human who struck the match.

Fire is transmutative. The same force that can create terrifying destruction in a building can melt sand into pure, clear glass. It can destroy infection as efficiently as it can destroy a forest. From destruction comes new life, as is illustrated by the Phoenix. From the flames of purifying transmutation comes the gold of Alchemy. From the chemical reaction in a nuclear explosion comes wanton destruction, yet from a smaller explosion of air and fuel in the combustion engine comes the power to run a machine.

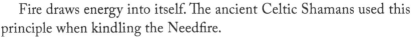

Fire draws energy into itself. The ancient Celtic Shamans used this principle when kindling the Needfire.

When we appreciate the eternal balance of creation and destruction and the essential need of one for the other, then we can comprehend the nature of the spirits of the creative, the destructive, the transmutative, and driving force that we know as Fire.

THE NATURE OF WATER

Water is the element of the subconscious. This is the realm where magic transmutes intent into new possibilities, where they may take active form. The "appropriate state of mind" for magic is essentially a psychological state wherein we are opened to the messages of the subconscious and can meld that which comes from the depths of our minds to conscious thought (and even to communication with the world of Spirit), or to sublimate our wishes into that subconscious realm where the magic is allowed to form into a vibrational force that can affect conditions outside of ourselves.

Water is associated with the deep blue of the ocean, with the direction West, and with the autumn season. It is also associated with symbolism in all its forms, especially with the world of dreams. Water rules purification, the unknown, love, and other emotions. Fluid, flowing from one shape or level to another, it is ever-changing, but the changes of Water are very different in nature from the sudden, sometimes devastating ravages of Fire.

Water can cause destruction in the landscape and in the lives of those who happen to get in the way of a flash flood or tsunami, yet the nature of the disaster is of a fluid, cleansing sort rather than the consumptive power of fire. The book *The Living Stream* states that *"Fire cleanses with violence, but Water with gentleness"* (Rattue).

Those who have been "cleansed" by a typhoon or tsunami might be tempted to disagree. Author James Rattue also tells us that Water is "other" and that it *"emerges in a miraculous way from the earth, for it is neither living, not inanimate; it possesses life, yet is not itself alive, and unlike fire, can never fully be domesticated."* As an Animist, I perceive Water as possessing spirit, perhaps more alive than Rattue perceives.

The power of the raging sea, the gentle magic associated with holy wells, and the meditative nature of pools and ponds represent the diversity of the nature of Water.

Water, in and of itself, is not violently destructive. It is only when it is whipped up by air, thrown about by the earth, boiled by fire, or unnaturally contained and then released by humans that the very weight of its fluid mass becomes a danger to those in its path. Water conceals both dangerous creatures such as sharks and helpful creatures like dolphins, who have been known to rescue shipwrecked sailors and take them to land.

Those who drown generally do so through exhaustion or hypothermia because they have been caught in underwater plants or have got themselves into a situation where they have lost the strength to swim.

Sailors of days gone by who prayed to Neptune or Poseidon to give them safe journey over the sea might have been well advised to consult Air and Earth deities as well. Without the interference of winds or undersea earthquakes, the sea would be ever calm, moving only in relation to the gravitational pull of the Moon. The spirit of Water is essentially calm, and it will always return to a calm state once it ceases to be disturbed by external phenomena.

Water is associated with absorption and germination. Pleasure, friendship, marriage, fertility, love, happiness, healing, sleep, dreaming, and psychic acts are all identified with Water. Water is believed to give access to the world of spirits, and many a tale is told of hidden "ways" to the Land of Faery at the bottom of a lake or well.

Water worship has been widespread throughout civilizations as early as 6000–4000 BC, as is evidenced by Water symbols found on goddess and other statues that date from those periods, especially in civilizations around southeastern Europe and northern Africa—like Ancient Rome, Greece, and Ancient Egypt—and cities like Babylon and Troy. Evidence of Water worship is also found among Indigenous peoples from Africa, Australia, and the Americas.

On a physical level, water covers 71% of our planet and encompasses 60% of our body mass. We must have water to live. We can survive for days or even months without food, but without water, we last only a couple of days at best. Water conducts electricity, reverberates sound, and absorbs electromagnetic energy. Perhaps this is why some tales tell of certain spirits that cannot cross water.

Water represents the feminine, as does the Moon. How appropriate, then, that the effects of the Moon's gravitational pull are most easily observed in the element of Water: the tides of the oceans (or even something as small as a glass of water), and the mood swings that we experience at the time of the full moon.

Spiritual meditation is associated with the calm Waters of the soul. Water is generally associated with calm, and indeed will calm itself if left unaffected by other elements. It is only when we add winds or earthquakes at sea that water becomes a raging hurricane or a wall of destruction. Interaction with fire might bring a rolling boil, or with rocks in a river to become a raging torrent. Left to itself, a pool of water will develop life and illustrate the cycle of creation and natural putrefaction, yet the calm pool also reacts to the gravitational forces of the Moon. Water reacts to all that occurs around it, reflecting phenomena as our emotions reflect all that occurs in our lives.

There is an old English saying that *"all things begin and end with the sea."* The sea is one of the most powerful forces in nature (perhaps even the most powerful force on the planet).

Magic itself reacts deeply to the use of powerful emotions. In any form of Water magic, the Moon's phase is particularly important in relation to the rhythm of the tides in the location where the spell is to be performed, even if the location is landlocked.

Scientists have done experiments with shellfish in which they observed the changes in their natural rhythms when the shellfish were moved from one location to another. In one experiment, a group of mussels were taken to a location in the midwestern United States where there is no ocean, yet the shells opened and close in rhythm with the times tides would have occurred had there been an ocean present (Brown).

Water is deep and mysterious, infinitely associated with magic and elemental spirits in folklore. The Mermaid is perhaps the most widely known of folkloric Water creatures, but there are malicious Water spirits who would entice an unwary human to a Watery death and benevolent Water spirits who present the gift of magic to those deemed worthy. (The Lady of the Lake from Arthurian legends is among these.)

The strange creatures that live in Water capture the imagination. Those that we can easily see like fishes and Water mammals are fascinating. Those we cannot see in the depths of the ocean or lochs give rise to fantastic tales of giant squids, lost aquatic dinosaurs, or serpents of diverse sorts. Water expands the imagination like a mirror that makes

all things look larger and indistinct. It is this very distortion that can lead to new vistas of imagination…or to madness.

Water is essential to all magic as a cleanser. Many magical and religious traditions require the practitioner to bathe before commencing ritual or an act of magic. Most also require cleansing or purification of ritual objects.

Water encompasses creativity in an emotional sense. While artistic inspiration is associated with Air, it is our emotions that are touched by a moving poem, a piece of music, or a painting that speaks to us. We react with emotion to an old tale or to a work of modern fiction because it feeds the spirit of imagination on an emotive level. Whether the story, poem, or work of art is created by ourselves or another, Water moves us fluidly from the creative world of air into the responsive realm of Water.

It is said of the world of Faery that as long as the stories are still told, the old ways are not forgotten. Water reflects the realm of Spirit, and it is within our emotions that the Water spirits become a thing of reality through storytelling.

Water is an element that can easily be experienced first-hand. Unlike Fire, one can choose to immerse oneself in the element, though it is more common that spells are performed at the seaside or the edge of a pond, river, or stream. Warm water creates the ultimate enfoldment in the nurturing Waters of life and can contribute to a sense of empowerment in whatever magic one chooses to perform within this sphere of natural magic. Water spells might even be performed in the bath.

Seeking Water spirits in nature, however, involves going outside. Sources of water are more likely to be cold unless you live somewhere temperate. While the discipline involved in immersing oneself in chilly waters can be exhilarating and add a strong emotional reaction to your magic, safety should always come first and foremost.

Indoor water supplies will naturally contain some form of Water spirit, but these are transient spirits who lack the aged solidity of water sources found in nature. Even human-made ponds are likely to have been established for some time, and the proximity of newly made wells and ponds to nature very quickly attracts the attention of elementals to the location.

A newly established Water spirit that inhabits such a place will spontaneously merge with local spirits of dew and other natural moisture to form a spirit that is both old and new. The newness will soon fade as the water gives life to micro-organisms, algae, and small plants. Water is the giver of life, which associates it with the feminine principle of creation.

This does not render the position of Water spirits in the home as unimportant—far from it. What the spirit in a freshly poured glass of water lacks in the sense of timelessness, it gains in the vitality of freshness. Despite the unnatural processes that humans subject their water supplies to in order to clean out impurities and bacteria, the Water itself maintains the life-giving spirit that is its essential self. It may lack some of the natural minerals that we must replace from elsewhere, but it is still fresh water. It is essential to life.

Water must move and change to maintain this life-giving property. Water that does not move or produce some form of life stagnates and becomes poison. One might ask why this does not happen in ponds or wells where water seems to stay constant rather than moving as in a river or ocean. This is because the water in these places creates its own ecosystem and the cycles of life maintain the integrity of the water.

Just as water must move and change to live, so do we humans who so much consist of Water. We are driven by emotional needs as much as by physical needs. Even the most seemingly emotionless scientist is driven by a passion for discovery. We are driven by nature to grow, to learn, and to discover. Those who lose their zest for life very quickly shrivel into nothingness.

It is that which we sometimes call the "human spirit"—the need to do something more than merely to exist—that can lead a downtrodden person back to the world of the living, or another person into the realms of art and science where there is much to discover or to create.

The importance of emotion to our species has led to some very deep and dark recesses of imagination when it comes to Water spirits in folklore. Besides the mysterious creatures of the deep, many tales tell of underwater kingdoms of fairies or other creatures, often including beautiful maidens who bring magical gifts to mortals on the land. Perhaps the best known of these is the Lady of the Lake from the Arthurian legends, who provides the sword Excalibur to Arthur to aid his quest to unify the peoples of England. She then receives it back into her keeping upon Arthur's death, to keep it safe until his return in a reincarnated form.

Water conceals many hazards yet is infinitely inviting and comfortable to swim in if appropriate safety precautions are observed. The buoyancy of water magically frees us of the limitations of gravity, and therein lies an important lesson in dealing with Water magic. Water can seep through some very stringent limitations, like damp penetrating an otherwise solid wall. This can be good in that a spell involving a Water spirit might slip through some very obstructive conditions.

On the other hand, one must remember that the Water spell might just as easily spread beyond the boundaries that have been set for it. Usually, this need not be a major problem, depending on the nature of the spell. However, the magic user who works with Water should always be aware that there is likely to be some bleed-through and should anticipate the possibility of having to contend with some mopping up.

The spirit of a body of Water is relatively easy to perceive. Water has a powerful effect on human emotions by doing nothing more than being present. Most people naturally find peace at the side of a still pool or encouragement from a trip to the seaside unless they come to the Water's edge in a state of despair. Those who are drowning in emotion might seek to drown in the very element that could help them to find a less tragic sense of peace. Water inspires the depths of emotion, but those depths can turn to the sweet or the bitter.

Those who visit a particular place of Water on a regular basis will form a natural bond with the attendant Water spirit. Many people both famous and obscure have found serenity at the side of a pond near their home or at the site of a holy well. Henry David Thoreau wrote about Walden Pond in his relation of his voyage of spiritual discovery in his book, simply titled *Walden; or, Life in the Woods.*

Holy wells in particular are known for recurrent magic, particularly healing or wish fulfilment. Those who live near such a well might find themselves drawn to the well on occasion if they are sensitive to elemental emanations, just as others will visit their pond or nearby seaside. The Water, symbolic of the deep unconscious, entices the consciousness and demands the release of stresses and troubles. It lures the natural intuitive mind, allowing solutions to become clear or psychic abilities to surface. Water runs deep within us both physically and spiritually, although sometimes it will demand its sacrifice. This, too, is illustrated in folklore.

THE NATURE OF AETHER

Aether is the element of Spirit. It encompasses the basis for all of the other elements (Earth, Air, Fire, and Water) and is believed by magicians to be the fabric of existence through which magic transmits. It is the stuff of which Aristotle called "First Matter," or the primal source, sometimes called the "first element" or "primary body" (Blackburn).

This is a reference to the source of All, that which must exist in order that all else may come into being. It is, in essence, the primordial chaos of creation itself. Aristotle considered this element to be pure and incorruptible, unaffected by change and decay.

In a realm of pure Spirit, the qualities of visible elements combine and diffract like coloured light viewed as separate bands through a prism, but with Spirit the prism works both directions, bringing the qualities of any one element into the whole of Spirit as easily as it diffracts the single aspect from the whole. The element of Aether represents magic and Spirit and the mystery of how one relates to the other.

Magic performed through the element of Aether may include practices that call on forms of Spirit like ancestral, Angelic, or even demonic spirits, but is generated through one's own spiritual essence. Aetherial magic is magic of the self, of the magician, and of the magician's relationship to the world of Spirit as an interrelated whole. While the form the magic takes might be steered by the beliefs held by the magician, the end result will always affect the magician's personal spirit.

Aether is represented by various symbols from different cultures. Perhaps the most apt is the lemniscate, which represents eternity.

Aetherial spells might be used for nearly any purpose but are most appropriate for forms of magic like self-transformation, spirit contact, reaching higher consciousness, or searching Akashic records[2] and benevolent magic bestowed on another. It might also be used for malefic magic,

---

2   In theosophy and anthroposophy, the Akashic records are a compendium of all human events, thoughts, words, emotions, and intent ever to have occurred in the past, present, or future.

but this is extremely dangerous as the magic of Spirit must flow through the magician's own spiritual essence; the most experienced magicians who are capable of making use of this area of magic will usually realise that there are less risky ways to go about the purposes that might have brought this sort of magic to mind.

Beliefs about Aetherial spirits are many and varied. Some believe in Angels of various sorts, some believe in a race of fairies. Some believe they are being watched over by their ancestor's spirits. Some believe in a pantheon of gods and goddesses or a supreme spirit who rules over all. In most cases, there is found a belief that petitioning the assistance of these spirits can be of benefit.

It is not my purpose in this book to dictate belief or theology to the reader who might have their own ideas of the form that Spirit takes, but I hope to take the spectrum of beliefs into account in my suggestions of how to work with various forms of spirits.

Like the more physical elements, Aether is self-cleansing and self-balancing. Those who seek to abuse the world of Spirit quickly find that the "wave" will correct itself, depleting the magical resources of one who seeks to use this form of magic for base intent, or cycling the negative energy back onto its originator. Too much positive energy can have a similar effect, as more than any of the physical elements, Aether demands balance.

The power of Aether, or Spirit, is the ultimate force. A person who "has spirit" can overcome any obstacle, survive any catastrophe. A person who "lacks spirit" can succumb to depression at the slightest difficulty or give in to circumstances without making any effort to improve conditions. In extreme cases, the person might even fall into psychosis in order to escape the responsibility of "self."

The ability to work this form of magic has the potential to accomplish seemingly impossible goals and naturally attracts what some people call "luck." The magic of Spirit is infinite in its potential where all possibilities exist, and even the improbable might happen if the right combination of factors are employed. Learning to focus and direct this infinite potential is the stuff of Aether and of magic itself.

Creation and destruction take on new meaning when applied to the realm of Aether and is far more frightening than the physical disruptions of earthquakes, severe storms, fires, or tsunamis. Spirit is transformed through tearing down old conditions, concepts, and habits to recreate

into the new. This can manifest through what is known as the "dark night of the soul," the complete devastation and transformation that characterises the changes that starting on a magical path can bring.

It is through tearing down old concepts and beliefs in the arena of Spirit that the magician becomes able to face their own strengths, weaknesses, and darker side, and to hopefully emerge from the test spiritually stronger and, more importantly, aware of nuances of their own inner nature. This is the rebirth of Aether, the awakening of one's individual spiritual nature.

In learning to understand those spiritual entities that we associate with Aether or the world of Spirit itself, we seek to understand the balance of the universe and the nature of Spirit as it applies to our own human spirits.

Chapter 2

fOLKLORE

*"All nature spirits are not the same as fairies;
nor are all fairies nature spirits."*
—Lewis Spence

ESTABLISHING A DEFINITIVE SEPARATION of elemental spirits from the fairies of folklore and legend is a tricky business, as our ancestors put names to many of the spiritual entities they believed in, and once you put a name to something, you give it power. Something subtle changes if you call a tree spirit a *dryad* or perceive the spirit of a rock as some species of gnome.

To further complicate the issue, we have epic legends that tell us of fairy peoples like the Tuatha Dé Danann of Irish origin. Tales of this nature have given us a perception of a race of fairies who go on rades: marches across the countryside that humans might observe as passing fairy lights. It is said that if one actually sees the fairies, they might decide to take the observer along with them, never to return.

Some legends of "wee people" may come from circumstances where there is a logical explanation. There is anthropological evidence that suggests that a race of dark-skinned little people might have lived on the high dune known as Skara Brae on the Orkney mainland in the north of Scotland several centuries ago.

These people would have been invaded and pushed into hiding by the Vikings who settled in the area. The need to survive could easily drive such a race of people to scavenge food in whatever way they were able, including stealing supplies from the invading settlers.

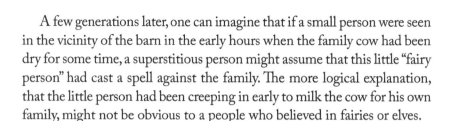
A few generations later, one can imagine that if a small person were seen in the vicinity of the barn in the early hours when the family cow had been dry for some time, a superstitious person might assume that this little "fairy person" had cast a spell against the family. The more logical explanation, that the little person had been creeping in early to milk the cow for his own family, might not be obvious to a people who believed in fairies or elves.

However, potential explanations of this kind are few and far between. It seems that all countries have some folklore about "the wee people" that defy logical explanation. They are known by various names: fairies, elves, gnomes, and many more.

No matter how many examples I provide of spirits in folklore, there will be readers who know of other names of entities that should have been included. However, this is not intended as a dictionary of folkloric spirit names and attributes, but as an overview of the perceptions that our ancestors have put on elemental spirits in their various guises so that we may form a particular perspective.

In an Animistic view, it is only natural to perceive that every plant, tree, and even rock has an attendant spirit. Concepts of more powerful or lesser spirits are largely a human projection in our efforts to understand the nature of spirits of those things we can see and touch.

While there are still people who hold literal belief in many of the following examples from folklore, my own perception lies somewhere between that belief and a reconciliation of these fairies with the spirits of nature. Many themes repeat by different names.

With that in mind, let's take a look at some of the better-known spirits of folklore and consider how they might fit into a perception of elemental attributes.

EARTH SPIRITS

In the past few decades, much of the superstition inherent in our culture has given way to an understanding of the balance in the natural world that we share with plants, animals, and many things that are unseen.

To those who believe in nature religions, this balance is illustrated by the four alchemical elements: Earth, Air, Fire, and Water. For some, this must also include the fifth element of Spirit, known as Aether.

Many of the most widely known forms of elemental spirits—fairies, bogies, brownies, and other house fairies—are easily associated with

the Earth element. Originally, personalities were attributed to these traditional spirits by country peoples who had believed in them for centuries and felt they were part of life with which they must reckon in their daily routines.

A few samples of some of those which most often appear in books about old fairy lore follow:

BROWNIE (BRITISH): These go by regional names: *Bwca* in Wales, *Bodach* in the Highlands of Scotland, and *Fenoderee* on the Isle of Man. They are house spirits who come out at night and perform various chores. They are often left gifts of cream and cake spread with honey by the humans who inhabit their adopted homes. It is considered wise to stay in favour with the house Brownie, lest they change character and become a troublesome Boggart.

DWARVES (SAXON): Dwarves are depicted as short, muscular, and bearded. They are another mining spirit, but are also reputed to work in metals and to fashion very fine weapons and jewellery. Some legends say that they cannot come into the daylight, or that they turn into toads during the daytime.

FIR DARRIG (IRISH): One of the practical joking nature spirits. It is considered wise to humour them.

GHILLIE DHU (SCOTTISH): Ghillie Dhu is a type of solitary fairy who inhabits birch thickets in Scotland. Their clothing is made from leaves and moss.

GOBLIN OR BOGIE (BRITISH): This is a general term used for ugly fairies, but also a specific term used for small, malicious beings. Some goblins are shapeshifters and will appear as animals. They are a tricky breed who will lure human victims to their own destruction.

KOBOLDS AND KNOCKERS (CORNISH), WICHTLEIN (GERMAN), AND COBLYNAU (WELSH): These are names for mining spirits. Kobolds and Knockers are troublemakers who will undo the day's work for the human miners. The Wichlein are harbingers of impending doom who announce the approaching death of a miner by tapping three times. The Coblynau,

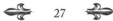

on the other hand, are harmless spirits who imitate the human miners and are actually considered to be good luck. The classic Jack-in-the-box was modelled after the common Kobold.

LEPRECHAUN (IRISH): Most people have heard of these. They are specifically Irish and particularly known for hiding pots of gold. One children's legend tells us that we can find the pot of gold at the end of the rainbow, but an older version requires that we catch the Leprechaun and force him to turn over his gold in return for his freedom. Some tales also claim that the Leprechaun must grant three wishes to the lucky human who caught him. Oddly, there seldom seem to be female Leprechauns. A less widely known aspect of the Leprechaun is the change that comes over him at night, when he becomes the Cluricaun, raids cellars, and rides drunkenly on the backs of sheep.

PIXIES OR PISKIES (CORNISH): These have become a popular focus of the tourist trade in Devon and Cornwall. Pixies are sometimes called *Urchins*. They take the form of hedgehogs and can be either mischievous or agreeable. Some may steal horses or take wild night rides on the wild Dartmoor ponies, while others might work hard threshing corn at night for rewards of bread and cheese.

PHOOKA OR PÚKA (IRISH): The Phooka is a shapeshifter who might take the form of a dog, horse, bull, or even a goat or eagle. He offers a lift to the unwary traveller, then takes him on a wild ride across rough country before dumping him unceremoniously in a ditch or mire. The Phooka enjoys a good laugh from doing this.

SPRIGGANS (BRITISH): Spriggans are reputed to be rather nasty and unattractive spirits (possibly the ghosts of old giants) who are known for thieving and for stealing babies, leaving a changeling of their own in exchange. They can be bargained with or even repulsed by Holy Water, or by turning one's clothing inside out. They are capable of robbing human houses, blighting crops, bringing whirlwinds, and other destructive acts.

TROLL (SCANDINAVIAN): Trolls are generally unattractive, bad-tempered, muscular beings who cause mischief. They dislike daylight and sometimes live under bridges in order to catch travellers to eat for their dinner.

Traditional fairies are only one type of Earth spirit, but they hold as much reality to those who believe in them and encounter them as the less fanciful elemental spirits that inhabit the natural world. It can be easy to forget while enjoying pretty depictions of fairies from Victorian art that all of the old legends about elemental spirits repeatedly warn against trespassing on fairy ground or offending the "wee folk" in any way.

Fairies are not necessarily mischievous or nasty by nature; they simply have their own social rules and ignorance of these can have disastrous results for an unwary trespasser. A more modern perception of Earth spirits comes to us from writings about a garden inhabited by nature spirits in Findhorn, Scotland. Several books have been written about the human residents of the original caravan park where vegetables grew to amazing size on rocky, inhospitable ground. These tell us that every plant and each vegetable has an attendant deva to look after it.

AIR SPIRITS

The various types of spirits perceived as Air spirits tend to be elusive and inconstant in form. They are able to move among us unnoticed and are less often depicted in art than other elements, though they are gaining popularity in stories. Folklore includes a few classical or legendary forms of Air spirits. Some of these are as follows:

BANSHEE (IRISH): A solitary woman, described as very pale with long, streaming hair and fiery red eyes. She is seen or heard only momentarily. Her cry portends a death in the family. Only the old Irish families have a Banshee. Sometimes she communicates her message through the light tap of a robin at the door.

DOOINNEY-O*íe* (IRISH): Also referred to as the "Night-Man," Dooinney-O*íe is a* kindly spirit who warns of storms either by shouting or appearing in misty form to give warning, or by the blowing of a horn. In the Isle of Man, a similar spirit is known as a *Howlaa*. This spirit warns by howling and is never seen.

ELLEFOLK (SCANDINAVIAN): The Ellefolk travel through air, fire, wood, water, and stone. They can even ride sunbeams through keyholes. Both male and female Ellefolk foretell the future, love dancing, and are such masters of the musical arts that a few notes of their music can cause a human to lose their reason. They have great power over humans and are related to dancing Fire spirits in that their elfin dance is a great temptation to men, who step inside the fairy circle and dance until they go mad.

HEDLEY KOW (BRITISH): A mischievous bogie who haunts the village of Hedley, near Ebchester. He ends his frolics with a horse laugh at the expense of his victims. Kow love to disrupt life in the farmhouse by imitating the voice of servant girl's lovers, giving cream to the cat, unravelling knitting, misleading unwary travellers, and generally scaring people.

LEANAN-SÍDHE (IRISH): In the Isle of Man, she is known as a blood-sucking vampire, but in Ireland, she is the muse of the poet.

NIGHT-ELF (EUROPEAN): The Night-Elf oppresses sleepers. They are known by many names in different cultures: *Stendel, Cauchemar, Nachtmart, Inciut, Marui, Toggeli,* and *Emgue.* They enter houses through keyholes or knots in wood and ride on the chest of sleepers who fight to awaken from the elfish nightmare.

SERVAN (SWISS): Lost objects are stolen by the Servan. He pulls covers off beds and performs similar mischiefs, but also helps with the housework.

TENGU (JAPANESE): Playful but occasionally malicious spirits. They live in treetops and are depicted as small birdlike men, hatched from eggs.

WIND FOLLETTI (ITALIAN): These travel in wind twirls. They turn winds destructive and unleash rain and snow. Known by many names, *folletti* is a general term. They are most numerous and dangerous in Sicily.

Apart from this sampling of Air spirits from legend and superstition, there are also beliefs in Air spirits who take the form of certain birds such as the mistle thrush, who spreads mistletoe and is sacred around the Winter Solstice. Several species of birds are considered in different cultures to be the messengers of the gods. A segment on bird lore is included in Chapter Ten.

Bees are also reportedly messengers of the gods. It is said that they have a particular fondness for wild thyme and, consequently, this herb can be used to see fairies. The tops are gathered from somewhere where fairies are reported to have been seen or perceived and made into a brew for this purpose. Primroses are said to have the same power, although they are eaten rather than brewed. (I advise against this, as primroses have high toxicity and can cause stomach upset or even skin burns. They are definitely toxic to pets.)

One superstition says that to touch a fairy rock with a posy of the correct number of primroses opens a door to Faeryland, while to do so with the wrong number opens the door to doom, which should be warning enough!

In *The Middle Kingdom*, D.A. MacManus describes some curious features of the "Fairy Wind." This is essentially a name for small whirlwinds, also known as dust devils, which occur especially during the hot weather in dry, sandy climates, including in MacManus's experiences in Ireland.

They are described as "little whirlwinds which draw the dust up into the air in rapidly twirling spirals that move across the country at varying speeds," which "sometimes assume fantastic shapes" (MacManus). He goes on to describe winds that resemble large figures with outstretched menacing arms, which residents of particularly sandy districts of India assume to be Genies.

In fiction and art, Air spirits have been increasing in popularity since the mid-nineteenth century. While Victorian depictions of fairies have become increasingly popular, we are seeing more and more examples of mythological flying beasts in films and drawings. Flying horses and cats have become part of the modern artistic consciousness for those who enjoy pushing the boundaries of imagination. The movie *The NeverEnding Story* brought a dragon-like flying dog into fantasy consciousness and a popular animated series, *The Adventures of Unico,* has made characters of the four winds.

FIRE SPIRITS

Whenever I think of Fire spirits, I can't help thinking of the cartoon imagery of little sparks of flame that can burn at the wick of a candle or combine into a larger, sometimes raging, fire. In folklore, Fire spirits can appear in many guises. The fairy horses of the Tuatha Dé Danann, for example, are made of "fire and flame," not of heavy Earth, and are therefore reputed to travel as fast as a brush fire wafted by a heavy wind. They have a broad chest, large eyes that reflect Fire, and quivering nostrils.

Such an intimidating presence is easy to associate with the element of Fire. Some other examples of traditional Fire spirits are as follows:

BASILISK (WESTERN EUROPEAN, FRENCH): The Basilisk is a mythological creature with a glance powerful enough to kill a human. One legend claims that it was created by an Alchemist from the Alchemical Fire. It lives in the vicinity of springs and fountains, which might suggest a Water spirit connection, but I've included it under Fire because of its Alchemical Fire associations.

DJINN (ARABIC): Properly called *Jinnee* or *Jinneeyeh* for the female, anglicised to *Genie*. The Djinn may be good or evil. They are very long-lived, have magical powers, and are formed from Fire without smoke. They can mate with humans and produce offspring who will have the attributes of both.

DRAGON (MULTICULTURAL): Dragons come in many forms, most of which are associated with Fire. Dragons and serpents are an archetype that represents the cycle of creation and destruction and the Kundalini spirit of sex and magic. Their serpent associations cross into other elements, such as the sea serpent (Water) and the Chinese dragon, which is associated with both Fire and Air. Generally, the fire-breathing dragons of fairytales come to mind first for those in the West.

DRAKE (ENGLISH, GERMAN, FRENCH, SCANDINAVIAN): These travel through the air as a flaming ball or fiery stripe but are a house spirit. They develop an intense relationship with the master or mistress of the house and bring gifts of gold and grain. In return, the master or mistress must provide gifts of food and reverence. To insult the Drake endangers the existence of the house it lives in. They smell of sulphur and it is considered wise to get under cover when they pass. They can take a variety of shapes and forms and are known by the names *Grak* or *Drachen,* as well as *Fire-Drakes.*

FEE (FRENCH): Sometimes called *Fates (Fêtes),* this is a general term for fairies in French. The Fee were originally associated with fertility, and fertility results from sexual passion, which is associated with Fire. The Fee should not be stopped from borrowing things, which they do frequently, and are dangerous to dance with. An unwary human who is caught into their whirlwinds of dance will die of exhaustion.

FIREPLACE FOLLETTI (ITALIAN): These hypnotise young brides with their burning eyes, which fill the brides with melancholy and despair.

INCUBUS/SUCCUBUS (MULTICULTURAL): A seductive spirit who comes to humans at night to copulate. The Incubus is a male spirit, and the Succubus, a female. Old legends claim that they bring nightmares, but this is likely an interpretation decided by a sexually repressed society. Incubi and Succubi respond to human lust, need, and desire.

LAMIA (GREEK): In Greek mythology, Lamia is the mother of some illegitimate children of Zeus who are slain by Hera. She mates with a dragon and is a bad housekeeper. Lamia appear as large, uncouth women, and slay children in revenge for the loss of their own.

RARASH (EAST EUROPEAN): This spirit lives on a farm and appears as a hen or small boy. It is associated with the hearth fire and brings gifts to the farmer, stolen from neighbours.

TYLWYTH TEG (WELSH): Dancing fairies who live underground (with underworld associations) and wear bright colours, chiefly red. They come forth on moonlit nights and dance in circles, sometimes enticing unwary travellers into their dance where they play tricks on them. Salamander (multicultural, Alchemical): The Salamander is the Fire form recognised by most Wiccan religions in ritual, but originally comes from Alchemical elemental correspondences as assigned by Paracelsus. Salamanders are desert creatures in the flesh and are age-old representatives of underworld Fire. This is partially a serpent association and is also inspired by the fact that Salamanders hide under rocks to escape the hot sun.

Tylwyth Teg are also called *Verry Volk* in Gower (near Swansea, Wales).

VOUIVRE (FRENCH): A snake-elf that appears beside fountains, much like the Basilisk, and has a diamond in its forehead that protects it. The diamond is kept out of sight while the Vouivre is drinking or bathing. A man who captures the diamond will gain tremendous power and wisdom. Robbed of its treasure, the Vouivre will pine away and die. Again, we have a serpent association with a spirit who lives near water. There are many such examples of Fire spirits living close to water, which might suggest a natural control over the rampant temperament of Fire as an element.

Sometimes, serpentine associations take the form of a worm, and there are legends in various parts of the world about worm-like creatures that are seen by humans. One of these is the Mongolian Death Worm, a large worm-like creature that reportedly lives in the sands of the Gobi Desert, swimming through its sandy ocean as though it were a serpent in the sea. It suddenly bursts forth through the dunes to attack its victims, usually camels, which it kills with an electric charge or poison. The locals call it the *Orgoi Horhoi.*

Those who claim to have seen it say that the camels can smell it and will react to the danger just before its appearance. Like many such creatures, it has never been photographed or proven to actually exist, but there are enough individual sightings—as well as dead camels—to merit attention.

This creature, real or not, has become part of the folklore of the region and is believed by some to be a demonic sort of spirit. The Mongolian Shamans believe that the spirit attacks only those who are a threat to their nation, but that it attacks in dreams. Oddly, there have been injuries on explorers who have investigated the sightings, after having had vivid dreams of the creature. Its appearances most often seem to occur in areas where a particularly poisonous plant called *goiho* grows.

One film worth noting in this context is *Backdraft*, a film about firefighters and the nature of the beast that they continually encounter. There are subtle references to and intelligence behind the Fire itself, especially when a convicted arsonist, played by Donald Sutherland, cryptically asks the main character, *"Did the fire look at you?"*

WATER SPIRITS

Water spirits in folklore are often changeable and moody. Water holds much of the symbolism that is of central importance to fairy lore. It has a dual nature: that which creates life and provides nourishment, and that which can take life.

Like the rivers, pools, and other bodies of water that they inhabit, the Water elementals are known for the dual qualities of abundance and treachery. The names and forms of these Water creatures are far too numerous to list completely in a single chapter, but there are some recurring "types" that seem to repeat in different cultures by many names.

Alastair MacGregor, in his book on Scots folklore, *The Peat-Fire Flame,* gives several accounts of one of these basic types: the seal women. These Water spirits typically discard their fishtail garments and come ashore to marry a human and beget children, then are eventually drawn back to the sea. They abandon the human husband and their children to return to their Watery world, never to be seen again.

The feminine aspect of Water arises in several general themes of Water fairy lore. Water spirits who appear as beautiful women are among the best-known legends, including the classical mermaid or *Loreleii*, which are closely related to the legend of the Morgan.

The Morgan in legend is an eternally young sea fairy whose passion leads her to seduce mortals, although her need for human love is never satisfied. This drives her to despair and she rises to the surface at night to brush her fine hair and sing her plaintive song, which often draws sailors towards her. They are subsequently shipwrecked on the rocks, similar to the Greek Sirens, but instead of leading all of the sailors to their destruction, the Morgan "takes" one to be her husband.

Water maidens recur as spirits of magical wells or of lakes and pools, who sometimes bear gifts or grant wishes. The most well-known of these is undoubtedly the Lady of the Lake of Arthurian legend, who rises from her lake to present the magical sword Excalibur to the once and future king of legend. Other female lake spirits cross into the realm of animal shapeshifting and take the form of waterfowl, particularly swans.

Other animals associated with Water spirits include the Salmon of Wisdom, who swims in the Pool of Inspiration and Foreknowledge. The symbolism of this wise fish spills over into some of the Celtic fairy folk tales, where "little people" are reported to wear salmon-skin caps.

Celtic peoples are known to have had a staunch reverence for Water spirits. Many treasures have been found in lakes, which are considered to provide inviolable protection. Offerings, including coins, jewellery, and valuable weapons, were frequently made to the spirits of Watery places.

Water spirits have been reported to appear to human observers in a variety of odd guises. I personally have no doubt that some Water spirits can and will intentionally take on an expected form above or near water that can be perceived by humans in order to elicit a reaction.

More commonly, Water spirits will take their form within the water, needing no substantial form to observe their human subject, yet sometimes allowing themselves to be observed for a fleeting moment. It is easy in such a situation to dismiss a face, a curious fish, or any number of other manifestations as no more than a trick of reflected light or passing water creatures of the more mundane sort.

Some Water spirits appear on land in the vicinity of water, including toad elementals, Water horses and bulls, and, oddly, Black Dogs. Sightings of Black Dogs are still reported in or near certain rivers, just as "white lady" ghosts recur in the vicinity of wells.

In general, Water spirits or attendant animals who dwell in or near rivers and streams tend to be less dangerous than their counterparts who live in the seas and lakes, although someone who has been nearly drowned by a Kelpie from the river is unlikely to dwell on a comparison with a Leviathan or a Sea Nymph.

Certain trees are also associated with Water spirit activity, especially alder, one of the catkin-bearing trees. Alder is resistant to wet rot and ancient lake dwellers were dependent upon it. In fairy lore, some Water spirits and mysterious white horses issue from magical gateways hidden amongst clumps of alder.

Faerie islands are closely associated with Water spirits. The Irish in particular have many faerie islands inherent in their folklore. These islands are often the home of fairies, gods, or even the dead in the later Christian associations of fairies as spirits of the dead.

Faerie islands are generally thought to be utopias of happiness, peace, and plenty, where it is always spring and there is no aging, disease, or work. Some of them are inhabited by weird and monstrous beasts. Some faerie islands float while others are submerged, rising above the surface only at night or periodically, such as every seven years. They can never be found when looked for, but only happened upon at times of need or when one's presence is desired by a Water maiden.

Following is a small sampling of some of the better-known Water spirits of legend and folklore:

ALVEN (DUTCH): Alven is an insubstantial spirit who glides over water in rivers and streams and can also glide through currents. It is a very powerful spirit who controls many bodies of water, particularly the River Elbe. Alven are shape changers, another common theme of Water spirits.

ASRAI (BRITISH): Full moon night is called *Asrai night* when these spirits come to the surface of the Water to look at the Moon once every century. A single ray of sunlight will melt them into a pool of Water. They are benevolent and shy, live deep underwater in lake bottoms or in the sea, and appear as small, beautiful women with long green hair.

BEAN-NIGHE (GAELIC): A type of banshee who haunts the rivers and streams of Scotland and Ireland, washing the blood-stained garments of those who are about to die. They are reputed to be the ghosts of women who died in childbirth and are fated to perform their task until the time when they would normally have died.

CABYLL-USHTEY (MANX): A Water horse known to steal cattle or maidens.

GLASTIG (SCOTTISH): This Water fairy is part seductive woman, part goat. The goat attributes are hidden under her green dress. She lures men to dance with her before feeding vampire-like on their blood, but she can also tend to children or old people or herd cattle for farmers.

GWAGGED ANNWN (WELSH): Lake maidens who are tall, blonde, and immortal. They live in rich palaces under lakes and come to land to dance, hunt, or stroll near the lake. There is sometimes an association with the Arthurian Lady of the Lake.

KELPIE (SCOTTISH): The Kelpie is often seen in the form of a horse. It haunts rivers and streams and allows unsuspecting travellers to mount him, then dashes into the water and dunks or drowns them. The term is associated with the Each-Uisge, which is a malevolent Water horse. The Highland Water horse haunts the sea and sea lochs, changes shape often, and takes victims into water and devours them, leaving their liver to float home. Kelpies are similar to the Tarbh-Uisge, a Water bull that can be either malevolent or benevolent. The terms *Kelpie* or *Each-Uisge* are sometimes used to describe what is known in Northern England as a *Water Dobbie*.

One of the most common beliefs regarding Dobbies is that one may be protected from them by keeping a dobbie-stone in the house. This is a piece of limestone that has a hole worn by Water through the middle. It is said that these stones ward off witches and evil spirits, especially Dobbies.

Right: Dobbie-stone, also known as a hag stone.

LADY OF THE LAKE (BRITISH): Romanticised through the Arthurian legends, the Lady of the Lake is claimed by some sources to originally be Le Fata Morgana, a Water fairy who raised storms at sea. This gives rise to speculation as to the polarity of the Lady of the Lake with Morgan LeFay in the legends.

LEVIATHAN (HEBREW): Originally depicted in the Christian Bible as a crocodile or the great python of Egyptian monuments, Leviathans are seen in common usage as any large, scaly sea monster. They are sometimes referred to as the Water aspect of the Christian devil.

MERMAID (MULTICULTURAL): Half human woman, half fish. In some versions, they entice humans with their song and cause shipwrecking storms. In others, they rescue drowning sailors and bring them safely to land. Still more legends claim that they desire human legs and husbands, and in tales like *The Little Mermaid*, there is a way to obtain this goal, but at a terrible price. Mermaids sometimes inhabit streams, pools, or lakes, as well as the sea. Mermen also appear in some tales.

MERROW (IRISH): Merrow are merpeople who wear red-feathered caps that help propel them to their Watery homes. The females are beautiful and sometimes marry human men because the males are very ugly but good-natured. Both sometimes come ashore as little hornless cattle.

NEREIDES (MEDITERRANEAN): In some tales, these travel in whirlwinds through Air but live in rivers, springs, wells, as well as some mountain locations and caves. In Greek mythology, they are the daughters of the sea god Nereus who attended Neptune. They ride on seahorses.

NIXEN AND WATER MEN (GERMAN AND NORSE): These are freshwater spirits who guard the way to Elfland. They seduce young girls and take them to their underwater homes (a counterpart to the Water maiden theme). The Nix appear on the surface of the water, singing and playing the harp, raising storms and warning of drownings. They teach humans the art of fiddling if they are given gifts of white or black goats. The unwary human may find that they won't be able to stop fiddling from such a gift until someone cuts the strings.

SHELLYCOAT (SCOTTISH): So named because he wears shells on his coat that clatter when he moves. He takes pleasure in leading travellers astray (a frequent theme among Water spirits).

SELKIES (SCOTTISH): Selkies live in the seas around Orkney and Shetland and resemble seals. A female Selkie is able to shed her seal skin and come ashore as a beautiful maiden. If a mortal man finds her skin and hides it, she can be forced to become his wife, but if she ever finds the hidden skin, she will immediately return to the sea. Male Selkies raise storms and overturn boats to avenge seal slaughter.

URISK (SCOTTISH): A solitary fairy who haunts lonely pools. He will seek out human company, but his appearance terrifies those he approaches.

WATER LEAPER (WELSH): A Water spirit who preys on Welsh fishermen.

Some tales of magic speak of magical mist, fog, or dew. It is an old English folk custom to wash one's face in the morning dew on the first day of May to achieve fair skin.

AETHERIAL SPIRITS

Some forms of spirit don't attach to anything of the material world. These include some forms of ghosts and fairies. This is an area where belief and religions will disagree amongst one another about the names and features of some forms of spirits, yet there are also factors that different beliefs will generally hold in common.

Many people have some form of encounter with an Aetherial spirit at some time in their lives: visitations from newly deceased loved ones, Angelic beings, sightings of the "wee folk," or some form of "divine guidance."

Sometimes one hears of encounters with "darker" spirits: Black Dogs, "demonic" entities, or other malicious spirits. Often those who take up magic but have a deeply ingrained religious background will conjure such dark spirits from their own deeply ingrained fears, though they take on a certain amount of reality.

Magicians and witches live in a world of the spiritual. Even the most pragmatic and scientific-minded magician must take spiritual essences into account, whatever their personal explanations for them might be.

The artist and magician Austin Osman Spare used to encounter spirits regularly, often allowing his artwork to be guided extensively by them. Many Pagan religions and new age beliefs include some form of spirit guides. The world of Spirit is very closely entwined with the world of magic. Although not all magic users "call" spirits to assist in magical operations, most will "banish" to clear away any residual spiritual essences at the end of a ritual.

Folklore is rife with stories of encounters with spiritual entities, including the following.

ANGELS

Angels, guardian or otherwise, have become reinterpreted over time, and beliefs concerning them can differ greatly from one set of beliefs to another. The word *Angel* comes from the Greek *Angelos*, which means "messenger," and the Christian idea of Angels comes largely from passages in the Bible that speak of divine messages which are brought to humans by Angels. Some are depicted as powerful beings who help individuals or turn the tide of wars.

Angel magic relies on these beings to perform acts of service to human magicians. This is an area primarily associated with Dr. John Dee and Enochian Magic. Dee wrote extensively on the hierarchies of Angels and the ruling Angels of various correspondences.

Angels also have a place in New Age thought and have been associated as higher spirits in the realms of nature spirits.

FAIRIES

Apart from the common folklore fairies that one might interpret as Earth spirits, beliefs concerning fairies include other sources for them. Christian legends claim that they are spirits of mortals who have died or Fallen Angels. The story is that when the Fallen Angels were cast out of Heaven, God commanded them, *"You will go to take up your abodes in crevices, under the Earth, in mounds, or soil, or rocks"*(Evans Wentz).

Most fairy beliefs actually predate Christian invasions of the countries where belief in them continues despite the changes brought by religious predominance, particularly in Britain and Western Europe. They live

in legends of a beautiful race that marches in armies, doing battle and performing magic, dancing and drinking, and participating in various revelries in a land of their own where time and space runs differently than in the ordinary world of humans. They go by many names and titles, but the best known in the UK and Ireland are Queen Maeve and the Tuatha Dé Danann.

Superstitions regarding fairies include the belief that eating or drinking of their fare will entrap a human in the Land of Faery, where time runs so differently that a day of revelry can result in the human emerging back into his own world many years later. Another belief is that they cannot bear the touch of iron or salt. In some pre-Christian religions, it was believed that people were taken in death not by Angels, but by fairies.

GHOSTS

Ghosts are the disembodied spirits of the dead. Occasionally, such a spirit will visit a loved one at the moment of death, but more often those who are seen are shadow bodies of those who have passed on. Belief systems vary on this point, but many allow that several stages of death occur as the essence of a person passes to whatever afterlife awaits.

The shadow bodies therefore contain very little of the consciousness of the original person and can become like sleepwalking spirits, who are sometimes witnessed repeating a pattern of events that occurred shortly before death.

There are many stories of ghosts who periodically appear in a specific building or walking along a particular road, repeating a route or haunting a location where their living self once dwelt. There are also animal ghosts, like Black Dogs and large cat creatures like the Beast of Bodmin Moor.

GODS

As with the spirits of the four basic elements, Aetherial spirits are known by many different names in different cultures. Those cultures also attach variations of personality to whatever entities they recognise, though some common themes crop up repeatedly. This is especially true in the higher spirit realms of gods and goddesses.

Many of these expect certain modes of behaviour from the humans who worship them or with whom they might come into contact. They generally demand respect and sometimes obedience or even offerings. The penalties for neglecting these demands can be formidable, and those who seek to come into contact with these spirits must allow for these requirements.

Many gods and goddesses are ancient and well-established in their personalities and requirements. To seek assistance from such an entity is to enter a realm within which *they* make the rules. I recommend studying the nature of any god forms one wishes to approach very carefully, especially when asking for favours.

To an extent, entities of pure Spirit will accommodate our perceptions of them, but very old forms become established through the perceptions of many people over time and cannot be easily adapted by any single witch or magician. For example, I sometimes come across someone mentioning on a social network that they've offered alcohol to Ganesha, which always makes me cringe. Ganesha comes from the Hindu religion and might well take offence at such an offering.

Another example is the Ancient Egyptian gods, who are not going to change their nature to please modern adherents. These have long-established temperaments and requirements, and it is wise to consider the intricacies of their nature before involving one of them in an act of magic.

GUARDIANS OR WATCHERS

Guardian spirits include things such as house spirits, guardian Angels, or Watchers, which are called into ritual in some traditions. Their purpose, as the names suggest, is to protect in some way. While some of these spirits might be thought-forms, they are just as often likely to be natural spirits, either of a place or in some way attached to a person.

Animal familiars can be included among this type of spirits, as a person's affinity to an animal familiar will naturally attract a spirit with the qualities of that creature. While this might be most prevalent in Shamanic cultures where belief in totem animals is an accepted part of the structure of their religion, it can also be true for those who seek to embrace similar beliefs as an "animal familiar." It is the acceptance of guardian spirits in any form that allows their effectiveness.

POLTERGEISTS

More often than not, a poltergeist is a thought-form spirit. They are tricky house spirits who make things fly around or disrupt electronic equipment. Sometimes they quietly move things around at night, including the furniture, to be found out of place in the morning by the human residents who are often upset by the nocturnal goings on.

Unlike the thought-form spirits that we intentionally create, a poltergeist is very likely to have been manifested without the conscious knowledge of its originator. Observers of paranormal activity have noted that they often become active in households where a girl is just reaching puberty.

This is a sufficiently common phenomenon that it was depicted on an episode of *The Waltons* television series in 1978, titled "The Changeling." Based on these modern folkloric ideals, the hormonal changes in pubescent girls can become electromagnetically active in such a way that television and radio reception can be affected by the presence of the girl in a room. In more extreme cases, things have been seen to move, sometimes as if they were thrown by an unseen entity.

This form of thought-form activity can escalate through disruptive emotions, such as anger or fear. Poltergeist activity can be triggered by the stress of moving house, leading to an assumption that the family has been attacked by "ghosts" in their new home when in fact a family member is generating the disturbance unknowingly.

The activity generates fear, the fear increases the emotional disturbance, and the family becomes locked in an unbearable circle of increasing activity. Enough of this cyclic energy can cause the disruptive energy to form into an independent entity, unconstrained by any controls. It has manifested out of wild energy like a cyclone manifests in crosswinds and will continue to behave indeterminately, feeding on the very emotions from which it first manifested.

One wonders how many "haunted houses" are actually the hub of wild emotions turned thought-form. There are exceptions where an actual ghost with a sense of humour might move things around a house and, by definition, the playful spirit is a poltergeist. However, the nastier the activity, the more likely it is an uncontrolled thought-form gone berserk.

These spirits are reasonably easy to eradicate through grounding techniques, including exorcisms. The energy can dissemble as readily as it assembled itself. The effort required will depend on the accumulated strength of the entity and whether some of it might have dissipated through entropy if the house has been empty for a time.

A partially dissipated thought-form can gain renewed vigour if someone new moves into the house and begins to react to little anomalies that start to happen, thereby setting off the cycle again. I always recommend "cleansing" a house of residual spirits when moving in, as this will suffice to avoid any leftover poltergeist manifestations in all but the most severe cases.

Vampyres or Demonic Spirits

Vampires have an extensive history in folklore, but here I choose to address the demonic spirit form of *vampyre,* differentiating with an alternate spelling. Spirits that fall into this category might include the Incubus and Succubus, referred to under "Fire."

A vampyre spirit takes something from the human or in some way seeks to have control over another spirit. They are sometimes thought-form spirits, conjured by their own victims. Certain mental conditions (like bipolar disorder) can make someone prone to attacks from this sort of spirit. They can often lead one to believe that a psychic attack is coming from an external source—perhaps from a trusted friend or someone with whom the victim has had an argument—when, in fact, the victim's energy is being drained by their own unbalanced mental forces.

A demon, on the other hand, can be a helpful spirit who does the bidding of one who summons it, or a malicious spirit.

The dividing line between a demonic spirit and other forms of Aetherial spirits can be largely one of interpretation, as people have been taught through religion and media to think of the word "demon" in relation to evil spirits, yet alter the spelling slightly and you have *daemon,* an old word for a plant spirit.

Chapter 3

Tuning in to
Location Spirits

"Nullus enim locus sine genio est."
("For no place is without its presiding spirit.")

—Servius

THE SPIRIT OF A SPECIFIC PLACE is the easiest thing for anyone with even a scrap of sensitivity to sense. It is not unusual for even the most mundane person with no interest in magic or spirituality whatsoever to feel either relaxed or intimidated by a particular location for no discernible reason.

From an Animist point of view, the cause becomes obvious. The collective spirits of the elements that make up the location are projecting their emotions toward visitors, whether those emotions are welcoming, meditative, or hostile. Sometimes the "vibes" can be very strong, such as in a place of worship where a spiritual feeling overwhelms even the atheist or agnostic visitor or, at the opposite end of the spectrum, a frightening sense of malevolence in a place thought of as "haunted" or "demonically possessed."

In human perception, we often tend to personify the spirit of a place as a single entity. This is a common misconception. Places in nature are made up of multiple elements in combination. For example, a forest is made up of trees, rocks, other plants, the air within the shade of the forest, animals who live within the environment, and any rivers or streams that might pass through the forest. This also includes the surrounding terrain (perhaps open meadows or mountains). All will have some effect on the spirit of the forest.

A forest is not a contained entity, yet it has a mutable border that is defined by the line of trees that begin or end the forest. Many forests in history have become places of superstition, either embraced as magical by people living in settlements nearby or avoided as "haunted."

Forests have a hidden quality that creates a sense of mystery. Animals who live in the shade of trees are often the kind who become food for predators, so staying out of sight for survival is easily emotionally imprinted onto a forest environment. If a forest is next to an open field where exposure is a danger, the forest becomes a place of sanctuary and sustenance.

It isn't only the animal wildlife who contribute to the emotional imprint of this environment. The trees themselves thrive through close proximity, lending each other shade and a solid barrier against the wind as well as intertwined root systems that serve as communication between them. The other growing things also depend on some protection from direct sunlight and other aspects of what feels like an enclosed atmosphere.

Conversely, the spirit of a high cliff would thrive on the sense of freedom that comes from open spaces and riding the winds without fear. This sort of place spirit is most aligned with the Air element and has inspired many humans to take up sports like hang gliding and sky diving, even using a wingsuit despite the danger to the fragile human body.

How one defines "spirit" can get in the way of understanding the nature of a gestalt place spirit. While it is easy to perceive the spirit of a place as a personified entity in and of itself, in fact, the spirit of a place is a conglomeration of the combined elementals who make up the constituent parts of a place, perhaps even caring for and protecting it, as well as the energies of all who visit there.

To fully understand the nature of a place spirit, one must be able to conceive of a spirit that is a whole, made up of component spirits of the various elements of the location.

Having said that, there are certain places that can put us in awe of a dominant element.

PLACES TO FIND EARTH SPIRITS

Stonehenge is a place where many tourists visit to sense the wonder of an ancient and very Earthy magical place. The spirit of Stonehenge has inspired many archaeologists, nature worshippers, and all sorts of people to take an interest in the history and meaning of the stone monument. The spirit of Stonehenge is made up of the spirits of the individual stones, the spirit of the land itself, the wind spirits who incessantly whistle through the stones, and so on, down to the spirits of the grass and plants that cover the area.

Over the years, the spirit of Stonehenge has been altered to accommodate the energies put into it by all of the tourists and curiosity seekers who visit to such an extent that, by day at least, it hardly resembles the spirit that once attracted so much attention in the first place. Yet there are those who have been there at night who sense an altered spirit of another kind: a menacing, protective spirit that would shield the stone monument from the energies of so many intruders.

Another well-known magical place in England, Brimham Rocks in Yorkshire, has a very different spirit despite the number of tourists who visit there. There are no ropes to keep visitors off the rocks, which in itself differentiates the place from the impression at Stonehenge where the human-made barriers and guards create a feeling of restriction.

Magical places are not the only places that have resident spirits. Every place or object, natural or human-made, is attended by spirits in some form or other. Places where one might perceive Earth spirits include the obvious forests, deserts, and mountains, as well as less obvious places like your kitchen, home garden, or even your office or other workplace. The sorts of spirits that one will encounter in these places vary accordingly.

Ancient sites are easily associated with resident spirits. Graveyards or burial mounds are historically associated with anything from a general "feeling" about the place to strong beliefs in sacred spirits who guard the area. Visitors to many places of worship have noted a calm feeling about these places, whether it is an indoor church, an outdoor grove, or another form of temple.

The act of reverence creates a spiritual energy in these places, and psychically sensitive people easily pick up on that calming energy. Just as a place like Stonehenge is affected by both its ancient history and the throngs of tourists who visit it today, an office computer or a child's toy absorbs the energy of the attention it receives and begins to take on a spirit of its own.

At a basic level, human-made objects and places are constructed from materials that once came from the natural world, and these materials affect places (like an office, for example) where the first impression is largely shaped by human inhabitants. Yet, on a subtle level, it is also affected by a place spirit made up of the items contained in the office, living or inanimate. A single green plant can have a significant positive effect on such a place.

Natural places are the best for attempting to sense elemental spirits. More intense Earth spirit energies may be found at stone circles and other magical places, but any out-of-the-way place where nature can thrive undisturbed by human interference is likely to be conducive to Earth spirit encounters.

An awareness of the nature of place spirits can be a real benefit when deciding what sort of spirit one would like to have ruling one's own special places. A place outdoors to meditate or conduct rituals might be chosen according to a natural affinity with the spirit of a place, or with a little work and awareness of natural laws of nature, a friendly spirit can actually be encouraged into a place.

While I would seriously discourage anyone from randomly attempting to change the spirit of a natural place where resident spirits are already in attendance, a particularly nasty feeling place can be vastly improved through human efforts with the intention of co-operating with the nature spirits.

For example, if you know a place where humans have dumped rubbish and the plants have mostly died, it is worth considering that you have the power to alter the spirits of the place by cleaning it up and planting healthy growing things. If this is followed up by caring for the new plants, a relationship between you and the place spirits—as well as the individual spirits of whatever you have planted—will naturally grow, and you will have created your own special place.

This can also be done at home, both inside the home or with a magical garden. All of the little things that one collects and keeps either at home or at a workplace will affect the spirit of the place, even more so if these things are alive, like plants and certain kinds of stones. The spirit of a human dwelling is very much affected by the energies of the people who live or work there, so if your home has an uncomfortable feeling to it, it might be worth trying to gain some insights into what sort of energies the residents are sending out.

Magical gardens are a personal favourite form of spirit magic for me, as it is possible to form very close human/elemental relationships in such a garden. I am not defining a magical garden as a garden where specifically medicinal herbs are grown, but as one where, whatever you choose to grow, magic is used in the process, and building a relationship with the garden spirits is a part of the project. This can be done just as effectively in a few pots as in a large plot of land. My own preference is for a small plot of land, like a small planting area set aside from a patio or back garden. This allows for close intimacy with the flower spirits or whatever you might choose to grow.

The first time I had such a small garden, I used it as an outdoor temple and decorated it with a small stone circle and fairy statuary to designate a focal point for performing magic. I would get up every morning and go outside first thing to sprinkle a little water on the plants while chanting incantations for their growth and inviting fairies in to help. This little ritual formed a close bond between myself and the spirits of the garden, and not only did flowers grow in less-than-ideal circumstances, but the magic I performed there worked more easily than I think it might have done in an indoor temple.

PLACES TO FIND AIR SPIRITS

Attempting to determine specific places where one might find Air spirits might at first seem to be an exercise in redundancy. After all, Air is everywhere on the surface of our planet and Air spirits flit about within their element…everywhere. However, while one might learn to be aware of the surrounding Air spirits who form a natural aspect of our daily lives, there are times when one might wish to specifically commune with Air spirits for a particular purpose, such as performing appropriate magic, meditation, or communication of some form. Then the need to seek an especially powerful form of Air spirit arises.

Most ancient or tribal religions believe in some form of sky spirit that is generally very powerful. This is an obvious and ultimate Air spirit, one that rules over the entire sky above us and therefore encompasses everything in our world's atmosphere. Closer to home are the more specific location spirits, such as the spirits of high places and the winds of open plains.

Air spirits of a place can be complicated to classify within our perceptions of the elements because nature is not so clear-cut. The symbiotic nature of elements in nature is such that a sacred place (or even just a high place on a rocky outcrop or cliff) involves an Earth spirit, who is guardian of the rocks, cliff, or mountain, meeting the world of the Air spirit. High places are likely to attract wild birds to nest and they, too, have spiritual associations with Air.

Some very powerful wind spirits can be found at a seashore, where Water meets Earth and Air simultaneously. It is a place where winds move the world through its paces. Air currents change the character of the world around us in deeply mysterious ways, which is why the seashore is a favourite place for many people to visit for walks, quiet meditation, or any number of contemplative pursuits.

There is a magical quality to the seashore that comes of the meeting of three elements. It creates a plaintive feeling in the soul and pulls the human spirit into deep thought. It is no wonder that a campfire on the beach can bring so much comfort, as the addition of the fourth basic element forms a completion of sorts: a balancing of spiritual forces.

Every movement of air has its attendant spirit. A breeze or an air current that moves a cloud or a wind of any magnitude are all directed by an Air spirit, which is actually a gestalt spirit consisting of countless individual Air spirits who come together like a group of cells that form an intelligent being. This is why large storms like hurricanes and tornados often seem to behave in ways that can be perceived as having direction, even intelligence, and can therefore be affected by magical operations with an appeal to the ruling spirit.

It is the Air spirits who give a place what we call "atmosphere." This is not just a play on words. There are several influences that contribute to our subconscious reaction to the feeling of a place; we might react to the projected "vibes" of Earth spirits in a room who inhabit objects or to the emotions projected from other people in the room. However, it is the Air spirits who we are most likely to respond most strongly to on the subconscious level.

Just as Earth spirits can become a part of one's home through the natural or material objects we bring in, Air spirits will constantly change

the character of a room as fresh or foul air passes through. Air spirits are very sensitive and will react to the thoughts and motivations of people who come and go within their space. If a room or building is continually used for a specific purpose, the Air spirits will reflect it in the "feel" of that place.

This is easily detectable in places like churches or prisons, which reflect a specific atmosphere of calm or stress. Places which are seldom visited by humans or where no human has been can seem very strange when they are discovered because the impressions come entirely from the natural world and feel very alien to most human observers.

Just as the spirits of Earth are able to become attached to human-made objects, Air spirits can inhabit artificially created spaces. An easy example is a balloon. Air that is blown or pumped into a balloon is contained to a large extent, though the balloon will deflate eventually, and this containment creates a place spirit that is just as enduring as any other location spirit.

One of my favourite childhood films provides a rather good illustration of befriending a contained Air spirit. It is a French film called *The Red Balloon*. The main characters are a little boy and his large red balloon, which seems to have an intelligence of its own and shares several adventures with the boy. It is in French, which I don't speak, but I found that understanding the words was unnecessary to follow the story. It is a classic and I recommend it to anyone who has missed it, adult or child. At the time of writing, it can be found on DVD and several streaming platforms.

I would generally question the idea of intentionally trying to contain an Air spirit. Like Water, Air becomes stale if it does not move and change. The sort of relationship that one might wish to form with Air spirits can be done with those who naturally occur in one's home. It is a matter of becoming consciously aware of their presence and making an effort to form a bond, rather than taking them for granted and joking about them when the cat tries to chase them.

An Air spirit within a home temple, for example, could be actively invited and cultivated, possibly even named, thereby creating form for the spirit.

In the days when I used to fly (in an airplane, not on a broom), I used to chant a spell to the Air spirits and apologise for intruding into their element in a transport which dumps pollution and upsets the Air currents. I have since stopped travelling by airplane, partly because airlines have made it such an uncomfortable experience but also because I do not want to contribute to the world's pollution problems.

Those who are into sports like hang gliding, however, put themselves in a position where they could commune with the Air spirits in glorious ways without adding pollutants to the atmosphere of the planet. I have never been brave enough to try these sports, but I can appreciate the freedom of flight and the pure joy that goes with it.

Much of what defines a place for an Air spirit requires a shift in our concept of boundaries. For example, if one steps through a doorway into a building, where does the Air spirit of the outside separate from the Air spirit within the place we have entered? When the door opens, the Air intermingles freely and there is a transitional area between what we see as "outside" and what we perceive as "inside."

All things in nature move and change, and boundaries are not recognised by nature spirits in the same way that humans define them. Once we become familiar with the sorts of spirits that we can define by elemental classification in our own minds, it becomes necessary to think of the world of elemental spirits as a whole and to largely leave these concepts of boundaries behind us. The associations with individual elements are very useful for learning about nature spirits and increases our awareness of the various sorts of nature spirits and their relationship to nature in all its guises.

PLACES TO FIND FIRE SPIRITS

One might speculate that a place to find a Fire spirit is obvious: in a flame. It is true that flames, large or small, will certainly be attended by a Fire spirit, but there is more to Fire than just flame.

Anywhere where there is heat has the potential for detecting a Fire spirit. This includes deserts, volcanic areas (especially in the interior of an active volcano), and places as common as a warm room. Any warm place has increased potential for an actual fire if conditions are right: heat plus fuel plus oxygen equals fire. It is within the heat element of this combination where the Fire spirit potential waits, ever patiently seeking the addition of the other two components to spark forth into life.

For this to happen, the heat must reach a sufficient level to ignite the available fuel. Many a house f ire has begun because an increase of heat

from sunlight through glass refraction shining on the back of an upholstered piece of furniture provided the conditions conducive to smouldering towards flame. This is why you keep your crystal ball covered!

Places where fire tends to recur, like a bonfire pit, hearth, or candle wick, will be watched over by a perpetually reincarnating Fire spirit. As fire is frequently created in these places, the location itself develops an attendant Fire spirit who traverses between the state of potential and actual flame spirit. Like a spirit of an Earth locality, these spirits become associated with their location as caretakers of the flame, ever renewed.

Like other elemental spirits, these place spirits are generally made up of a gestalt of many Fire spirits that come together in a common cause: that of giving the Fire perpetual life. This is particularly true of larger fires, such as the hearth fire that is forever changing its size and intensity, never quite the same from one moment to the next, yet still existing as a continual fire until it is allowed to fade from lack of fuel, only to be rekindled again and again.

To an extent, a tension is formed between the Earth and Fire spirits because of the potential destruction if the Fire should get out of control, while a more playful feeling energy emerges between the Air and Fire spirits. The combination of the various elemental energies can be electrifying or terrifying. A ritual space where a bonfire occurs regularly very quickly attunes to the tribal instincts among attendant humans, bringing out the need for rhythmic music and dancing.

There is an inherent connection between the Fire element and the dance. Dancing stirs up a spirit of passion within the human soul: not necessarily sexual passion, but something that lies far deeper in the primal human spirit. Ecstatic dance has the potential for stirring strong magic, and places where dance regularly occurs maintain this spiritual energy.

Stage dance can stir these same energies despite the precision of learned movements. A professional dancer learns the moves for their routine until they can perform it almost without thinking, setting a spirit of fervour loose within their movements that is every bit as strong as a freeform ecstatic dance. This will translate to the members of an audience as a feeling of excitement and anticipation that is perceptible even to the most mundane attendee of the theatre.

This sort of impression of Fire energies can affect a location long after the dancing has stopped. To the more spiritually aware visitor to stone monuments and other historical places, it is not difficult to sense which places have a history of Pagan dance rituals. Any place where strong emotions have been repeatedly expressed is likely to maintain a certain intensity that associates Fire with its location spirit.

This includes places of ancient sacrificial rituals (animal or human) like the Coliseum in Rome, which has been described as having an intimidating energy. Places that have provided positive inspiration, such as Mount Olympus, project a positive, uplifting energy that is also associated with Fire.

Some places become associated with Fire spirits through natural phenomena, such as places that have been struck by lightning. The oak tree is sacred to the Celts because it attracts lightning. Places with volcanic activity resulting in natural hot springs or geysers inspired awe from various peoples historically and still capture the imaginations of modern visitors. The La Brea Tar Pits in Los Angeles are still a major tourist attraction and even played a significant role in the film *Volcano*, which depicted a lava fissure from beneath the hot tar of the pits. This scenario is still at least a remote possibility!

These places of natural heat or attraction for electrical activity have their attendant Fire spirits, along with whatever other nature spirits might inhabit the local trees, rocks, ponds, or other features of nature that might be present.

More than the usual amount of caution is required when dealing with Fire spirits in a location, as their natural drive to consume can easily lead them out of control. Containing the space might not be sufficient. Fire can jump. Fire can spontaneously combust under the right conditions. Fire has a fierce desire to live and to expand. This is where forming a relationship with the spirit of the Fire can benefit magic that needs to transcend an obstruction, but ordinary fire safety rules should always be meticulously observed.

Fire is an infinitely mutable element. It can be used for destruction, purification, change, and some forms of creation. A Fire spirit who is attuned to a cooking source or a campfire can be employed to infuse food with Fire energies while cooking. How many times have witches been portrayed with a cauldron bubbling over a hearth fire, the potion within being infused with ingredients for a spell? And let's not forget the blacksmith's art, forging strong weapons from directly within the fire.

Again, I advise caution and practical fire safety. Fire is excitable, and a Fire spirit who is stimulated through ritual can, without any malicious

intent whatsoever, extend itself beyond the intended parameters and create a very real hazard.

Wherever Fire spirits are to be found, they can be perceived by the excitement and intensity that they inspire within our own human spirit. We are more closely related to spirits of Fire than many of us realise. Fire, as an element, holds the spark of life. Our bodies may be made of Earth, but the spirit that gives us drive and fortitude to live despite hardships and obstacles is of Fire.

Places that are attended by Fire spirits are easily distinguishable by a feeling of energy or power that inspires the stronger emotions, either in an uplifting response or one of alarm. The spirits of Fire can be embraced with understanding rather than feared for their destructive potential. Remember that destruction is nature's process for renewal. It is human nature to fear the unknown, therefore the key to embracing the Fire is to know it.

PLACES TO FIND WATER SPIRITS

Water spirits are often perceived as "place guardians." While Water as an element is similar to Air and Fire in that the actual substance (and therefore the attendant spirits) of the element is ever-changing, creating a larger mass from infinite minute components, the overall body of Water maintains an apparent attendant spirit that is little affected by the constantly changing quantities of actual fluid by evaporation or source water. Quite often, trying to determine the feeding source of a body of water can be difficult or impossible and is frequently left to assumption.

These place guardians can vary widely in temperament. The guardian spirit of an ocean is a formidable concept, represented by magnificent gods like the Roman Neptune or Greek Poseidon. A guardian spirit of a lake or river where people have drowned may be assessed as malevolent, pulling victims under the surface by way of sacrifice, yet the actual Water spirits could be blameless of human misfortune…or not.

One should never be too dismissive of the origins of local folktales, especially when drownings reoccur often in the same locality without a more obvious cause. It might be the perfectly logical result of an underwater hazard, but then again, one must remember that the fishes must eat to continue the biological ecosystem that keeps a source of water "alive." Who is to say whether a Water spirit might in some instances have turned predator?

The Water spirits that inhabit the natural world are sometimes not so far removed from the fanciful creatures of folklore. The spirits of Water might sometimes imitate these forms, teasing the human observer and maintaining the mystery that lies beneath the unseen. There is much evidence that Water spirits attending specific bodies of water are able to travel over land near the source of water, hence the stories of well guardians and animal or ghostly custodians of pools, lakes, and rivers. Water is rather unique in that a spirit is not always tied to the actual element. They might appear within the water as some form of swimming creature, yet might also appear on land, patrolling the surrounding area of their special Watery place.

Spirits of specific locations of water can be cultivated, as seen in the stories surrounding many human-made ponds and wells. Many tales are told of guardian spirits appearing in the peripheral vision of an observer, who finds no one there when they look directly at the place where they thought they saw someone.

Most Watery spirits in art will be depicted as the swimming form, hence pictures and paintings of mermaids and Neptune-like guardians, sometimes sitting on rocks so that they occupy Earth and Air environments, near but not necessarily within the water. Indigenous cultures will sometimes refer to a source of stagnant water as being possessed by evil spirits, yet this is what happens if the ecosystem within the Water dies.

Whether a particular Water spirit is regarded as benevolent or malevolent is rather dependent on the experiences of those who encounter the source of water. In the end, Water spirits are like magic: neither good nor evil in essence.

One cannot help but respond to the emotional lure that Water has on us. It draws us like a magnet attracts metal, enticing us into the depths of the world of water and its hidden treasures or hazards. Occasionally, someone is repelled by larger bodies of water and reacts with fear.

As with Earth and Fire entities, we tend to perceive the size of spirits of Watery places as something that changes with the volume of water. Ocean and tsunami deities are depicted as large leviathans while pool and pond spirits are perceived as small and gentle, yet it is the lake, pond, and river spirits who most often become associated with sacrifice

by drowning the occasional swimmer or drawing the sacrificial victim into its watery depths in an apparent suicide.

Like Fire and Air, the actual element of Water flows from one place to another while the location spirits of both places maintain their individual, if fluctuating, structure and identity. When a river flows into a lake, the river has its own guardian spirit, as does the lake. If there is a waterfall involved in the transition, the waterfall will be attended by yet another individual keeper.

The spirits of the Water molecules change their nature as they flow from one to another, much like the individual cells of our brains each have their own electrical charge but make up a communal thought process within their own sphere of the brain.

There is a natural affinity—almost a melding of spirits—between a Water spirit and a human who encounters it. This is not surprising considering the amount of water (approximately 60%) that comprises our physical being. It is part of the reason that we respond to places of water on an emotional level, either by being drawn into it or reacting emotionally, sometimes with unexplained fear to a particular place like the proverbial dark pool. It is a natural response to reach out our emotions to a water spirit whom we encounter.

Some places of water are believed to be "gateways" to the otherworld. In fiction and folklore, these are often depicted as underwater places where humans can exist magically, sometimes conditionally on staying in physical contact with a mermaid or other Water creature. All places of water are inherently magical, and we instinctively respond to them as such. There are Water spirits present in any source of the element, including rain puddles, condensation on a window, or the mist in the air.

The Water spirit of a place is obvious when speaking of a lake or other body of water, but places that are not primarily of Water are also affected by the spirits of Water that come from seepage. The wet rot in the walls of a house will affect the overall feel of the place, far beyond the physical dampness that one might experience. Many "haunted" houses obtain their sinister atmosphere from dampness in the walls, as the spirits of what is essentially stagnant water project their dark emotions into the general ambience of the house.

The tendency of Water spirits to draw the human spirit towards them also contributes to the eerie feeling of such a place, as the human visitor to the house might not be aware that there is dampness within or find themselves enticed into the unknown. The impression of being enveloped into this Watery essence is not unlike drowning, yet there is no physical danger, only the warning signals in the mind that alert us to its potential.

In general, our emotional response to Water is calming rather than sinister. One has only to add a bottled water cooler to an office to promote an atmosphere of clean efficiency into an otherwise average room. Our subconscious response to the processed and purified water, contained and electrically cooled, is one of calm and apparent control of our environment.

It is the Water in a place like the Glastonbury Well Gardens that gives the place its feeling of spirituality far beyond what we feel from the resident plant life or the effects of human visitors. Gently running water alone brings a feeling of calm that defies explanation.

Water is affected by human presence just as are the other elements, yet the cleansing nature of Water tends to wash away most of the vibratory influences of visitors very quickly. The Water spirit of a place maintains its inherent Spirit when other elements are changed by contact with all who touch them. This creates a very old feeling to the spirits of Water and especially to places of Water. Even a fairly recently constructed pond develops this "old" feeling in a very short time. It is a trait that is unique to the Water element.

The change in atmosphere at Stonehenge at night is partly due to the evening mists. It is that old and ancient feeling that is transmitted through Water that washes away the jumble of vibrations that are left by the daily hordes of tourists. If the tourists stopped visiting the place for just a few days, the nightly cleansing by both the winds of Air and the Watery mists would likely return the feel of foreboding power that this place had when it was first discovered.

The spirit of a place of Water is not affected by having some of its quantity taken away. People have sought the ater of sacred wells, fonts, and pools for centuries, yet these places are not less potent for the samples that are consumed or taken away. Water renews itself, sometimes mysteriously.

The spirit of a place of Water can, however, be affected by that which is put into the water. Pollution of any sort can turn a Water spirit malevolent, yet the nature of such a spirit can be changed again with the cleansing of the place. Life added to a source of water can have a very positive effect. Contributing fish to a depleted lake or newly made pond is like giving the gift of life to the spirit of the place and has very positive effects, though a small pond will require cleaning the natural biological effluvia.

PLACES TO FIND AETHERIAL SPIRITS

Many people believe that Spirit can be found more easily in certain places, whether it is in a church, temple, or in a fairy mist. Places of worship of any kind naturally attract Aetherial spirits. It is not unusual for such places to retain these spirits long after they fall into disuse, even centuries later.

Places where strong emotions have been repeatedly raised, especially those where animal or human sacrifices once occurred, can leave a particularly strong impression. If you were to visit an old Aztec temple, for example, a sensitive person would pick up excitable or disturbing energies lurking under the calm atmosphere of a place where plants have overgrown and reclaimed what was once constructed by men.

Visitors to these places have described a feeling of something that lies dormant, just waiting to be reawakened. The gods who were historically worshipped at these temples were given blood sacrifices in ways that are not pretty to contemplate, and the feeling of expectation of more of the same remains.

Conversely, a church where tranquil, reverent forms of worship once took place tends to retain a benevolent, calming sort of spirit, even long after the building itself has been deconsecrated by appropriate clergy.

Ghosts and Watchers can often become attached to a specific location. Who among us has never encountered a "haunted house" in our childhood? Angelic spirits are periodically observed in places like Lourdes in France, where such a spirit has been observed by multiple visitors, and in the castle ruins of *Monségur*, where a "white lady" has been similarly observed.

The form and perception of these sorts of spirits are largely formed by the expectations of observers or worshippers, but the benevolent quality of an Angelic spirit is inherent in the spirit itself, just as some ghosts can project malice or disinterest (or even sometimes benevolence) according to its nature.

The world of Spirit exists everywhere but manifests more strongly in certain places. One thing I've observed is that civilisation does not negate spirit. The same "calm" that some people find in country walks can be found in cities, especially for those who are accustomed to urban surroundings. "Tuning in" to Spirit can be done while walking the streets of London or Los Angeles, sitting on a bench in Amsterdam, or riding a Metro train in Paris. San Francisco has a very strong feeling of Spirit that probably harks back to the gold rush days but was significantly affected by the cultural revolution in the late 1960s. The spirit of every city is unique.

Hauntings in buildings can be caused by human spirits who have left an imprint on the location, most often because of sudden and unexpected death, or they can be attracted to a particular house by experiments with séances or other forms of spirit evocation.

Some places, like Peel Castle on the Isle of Man, are known for harbouring malevolent spirits, in this case, the Moddey Dhoo, which is a Black Dog spirit. Theories differ as to why this occurs, but once the spirit attaches to a place, they do tend to stay.

Some places become associated with fairies, especially fairy hills or mounds. These spirits can be very territorial and it is wise to leave their special places unmolested. Occasionally, an ordinary place can become covered in a fairy mist that can even create a temporary change in the landscape that will revert to normal when the mist passes. Such a mist is not always thick and obvious. The one time I encountered one, a dull greyness was the only indicator that I had stepped outside of the ordinary sunny day that had surrounded me a moment before.

We humans, though we inhabit a physical form, are also creatures of Spirit and can form connections with other Aetherial spirits of various realms. Our own homes reflect the sort of spiritual energies we project, especially if a home temple or altar is constructed. It is the realisation of our own spiritual nature that leads to an understanding of the nature of magic in the realm of Spirit.

Becoming aware of ourselves as "of Spirit" can change how we see the world around us and our perspective of what is important. It can even lead to the ability to see other Aetherial entities in the places and realms of Spirit.

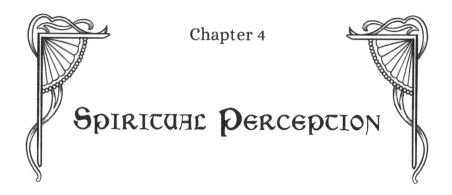

Chapter 4

Spiritual Perception

ACTUAL VISUAL PERCEPTION OF NATURE SPIRITS is uncommon but not unknown. They are not physically perceived with the eye in the same way as solid objects. There are two kinds of receptors in the eyeball called rods and cones. The rods perceive line and definition, while the cones perceive colour. The combined messages are sent to the brain, and we "see" things as a whole, with a defined shape and colour.

Seeing nature spirits requires a shift in perception because the rods in our eyes perceive nothing from them. It is the cones that can perceive spiritual essence. This is probably why fairies are often depicted in art as brightly coloured and fanciful little creatures. To an extent, their shape is determined by what we expect it to be. It is also because they are perceived with the cones—in the colour spectrum, on the edges of normal vision range—that they become elusive when we try to look directly at them.

To see fairies or nature spirits, one must try to catch a glimpse with the corner of the eye. Generally, our reflex is to try to look directly at the movement we've perceived in peripheral vision only to find nothing there. It is no wonder that people who catch a glimpse of fairies wonder if it was ever there at all!

Some amount of psychic perception is helpful when attempting to see any form of spiritual beings. There is a knack to combining the psychic and the physical perception to form a whole. Most people sense their presence long before visual perception, though surprise glimpses are not unusual.

Some people like to indulge in meditative preparation to attune to their psychic senses before attempting to seek out visual perception of nature spirits or fairies. This might include the use of essential oils, calming music, or a preferred form of meditation. These trappings will make no difference to the entities themselves, but anything that helps shift our own perception is potentially useful.

TO SEE EARTH SPIRITS

Going out into nature—perhaps the woods or another place rich with growing things —will put you in an environment where elemental spirits are plentiful. The suggested method for trying to visually perceive them takes a lot of patience and dedication for the average person. To begin with, choose a place where you can sit comfortably for a long time and can easily return to many times. Ideally, it should be accessible but unlikely to be disturbed by other people who might happen by. The occasional passerby can be ignored, but it's best to keep interruptions to a minimum. You will have to visit this place frequently, possibly in all sorts of weather, so keep this in mind when making your choice.

Go to your chosen place and just sit and listen. This is very important. If you have ever tried to approach or befriend a wild animal, you will know that their natural first reaction to an intruder is to run away. Nature spirits have a similar reaction, albeit with more curiosity, and it's much easier for them to hide.

Practice some form of silent meditation, even if it is only to sit, watch, and listen. When you decide you've had enough, go home. I recommend eating something at this point to ground yourself, even if you don't feel you've done anything unusual. Bread and jam is good for this.

Return to the place as often as you can to just sit and listen. (I did say this takes patience.) You will reach a point where the place feels very familiar and even takes on a personal feeling as your own special place. There is also a possibility that you will experience a stage where the place feels hostile and uncomfortable. If this happens, you must decide whether to persevere or to choose a different place. You may be tested, or the resident spirits might be intentionally trying to intimidate and scare you away.

There is also a possibility that you're reacting to your own vulnerability in leaving your psychic senses open. Either way, this stage will very likely pass, unless the resident spirits really are completely unwilling to have humans invading their territory. If you choose to persevere, just keep going back until the place welcomes you. You'll know what I mean when it happens.

This is the time to begin actually looking with your peripheral vision. Regard the familiar rocks, trees, and plants with new eyes, allowing yourself to perceive colour auras surrounding each of them. Look through and around the familiar objects, then shift your gaze slightly so that you can see it with your peripheral vision. Whatever you think you see is probably really there, but the reflex to try to get a better look is almost impossible to avoid. Try again. Don't push yourself too hard, especially the first time. You can come back and try again.

You may recognise birds or animals who frequent the area. Mostly it's best to leave them alone, but if you want to speak to them softly, without moving, they might begin to accept you as a part of the place.

One note if you live someplace like the Sierra Nevada mountains, use some practical sense and avoid places where bears or mountain lions are likely to appear. I can make no guarantees that potentially dangerous animals will respond to your calming meditation. If they choose to see you as an intruder, you could be lunch. The same warning applies to places where poisonous snakes, insects, or spiders are often found. Apply common sense when choosing your location.

Tradition dictates leaving something as a gift to the fairies. A little milk (perhaps poured into a half shell), a crumbled biscuit ("cookie" to the Americans), or cake is nice and doesn't leave anything unnatural to spoil the nature spot. Never leave objects or items that nature cannot absorb. That includes the strips of cloth one often sees tied to trees in certain places. There are places where these are appropriate, if they are cotton and have no man-made fibres, but they should never be left at unspoiled locations in nature.

Persistence will pay off with this method eventually, whether it takes two visits or two hundred. The important thing is to believe what you see, because you will see it better another time if you know it's really

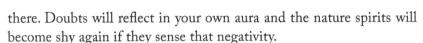
there. Doubts will reflect in your own aura and the nature spirits will become shy again if they sense that negativity.

Remember that there are different kinds of nature spirits in this place, and you will probably catch glimpses of different ones at different times, though you might see several in succession which could make your eyes flit about and possibly cause dizziness. Nature spirits are perfectly capable of doing this intentionally, rather like a game. It is a natural survival method for them as it easily confuses the unprepared human invader.

The appropriate reaction is to simply enjoy the game and smile at your own confusion. If you good-naturedly concede defeat and leave your offering, you might well begin to establish a positive rapport.

If a single nature spirit repeatedly appears and disappears behind an object, it is worth staying a while. It could be that you have aroused curiosity from a particular entity. It takes a lot of patience to sit and wait for such a creature to decide to show itself, or perhaps to run away after all, but once you have gained the attention of a particular nature spirit, it is likely to take an interest in you on future visits.

You must never try to chase or hunt for these wild entities. They will come to you in their own good time…or not. If quite a long time passes and no interest is forthcoming, you might want to try a different place.

IN THE GARDEN

Within your own garden, there are probably many Earth spirits who are already familiar with your presence, even if you only walk by the garden rather than taking an active interest in gardening yourself. However, they are more likely to take an interest in you if you have actively taken an interest in them, and particularly if you don't mind getting your hands dirty and take a first-hand role in nurturing the garden yourself, or at least interacting with it regularly.

If you live in a home with an established garden, you can begin by spending a little time with the garden every day, even if it's only a few minutes to sprinkle a handful of water. Personally caring for the garden and taking an interest in what grows there, naturally or because you planted it yourself, will build a close relationship to the nature spirits who certainly inhabit it.

The method for seeing nature spirits in your own garden is much the same as in the wild. The main difference is that in the garden they are used to your presence and will be more likely to show themselves more quickly.

Growing your own magical garden from scratch is ideal, as this allows you to choose what you want to grow and naturally build familiarity with the individual plants and creatures in the garden. It can as easily be done in pots if you have limited space as in a patch of garden attached to a house. The size of your garden doesn't matter from a magical perspective, but you must care for it on a daily basis and, above all, never neglect it to the extent that it dries up and dies.

If you have the sort of lifestyle that makes caring for a planted garden difficult, you might want to create a rock garden instead. Rock spirits are very Earthy creatures and very magical beings. This sort of garden might even be preferred by a magician who is looking for a way to work closely with elemental energies.

If space allows, a rock garden within a flower, herb, or vegetable garden can be very attractive as a focal point and provide a natural Earth altar within a garden temple.

Rock gardens can take many forms. Most of us have seen adverts for the traditional Japanese rock gardens sold as a kit: a square container that holds sand with one or more large rocks and a rake to form patterns in the sand around the rocks. They make a good meditation tool, but if this is a desired form, I recommend making your own, or at least using rocks you've collected somewhere in nature.

The choice of rocks for any kind of rock garden is important. Rocks with a high quartz content have measurable electromagnetic energy and are very good for rock circles. Rocks that you collect from places you visit will develop their own personal significance.

However, one must *never* bring harm to magical stones by chipping away pieces of them. If you visit a site with dolmen stones, loose pieces on the ground are fair game but damaging the erected stones to take away a piece will result in very negative energies from the stone.

Collected rocks can also be arranged indoors as an Earth altar. Designs are open to the far reaches of imagination! Looking for the resident spirits of stones is the same as any spirit in nature, but rock spirits tend not to wander far from their stone abode. This can make them a little more difficult to see, though it can be achieved with patience.

TO SEE AIR SPIRITS

Air spirits are particularly difficult to actually see not only because air itself is invisible, but also because the movements of most Air spirits are so quick and constant that one can never be sure whether there was anything there or not when the eye does catch a glimpse of one. More often than not, it is the material objects they move that tell us that Air spirits are present.

Despite this, Air spirits can be glimpsed spontaneously. The slight movement you thought you saw in the corner, then looked to see nothing there, might have been a trick of the eye, but maybe not. Passing Air spirits easily attract the fringes of vision at times when we are specifically looking at something else, like the page of a book or a television screen, or when we are in a state of contemplation and have left our eyes a little unfocused.

Pets chase Air spirits frequently, either in the house or outside. The invisible object that has suddenly caught the attention of your dog or cat could be a speck of dust with a light reflection, or it might be that the animal's acute senses have caught sight of a passing Air spirit and are considering whether or not to pursue it.

Animals see elemental spirits more easily than humans, although cats will generally leave Earth spirits alone. These are part of their surroundings that are accepted much as the resident humans are accepted, while the Air spirits are more like an intruding mouse and like to flit about in a manner that triggers the cat's hunting instinct.

Spirits of things like tornados or dust devils are easier to see because there is more form to the spirit so long as the storm or Air movement continues to exist. I do not recommend trying to attract the attention of tornados in particular for obvious reasons. Storm chasers may find them fascinating, but the dangers are substantial.

It may be difficult to visually perceive the spirit of still air or a passing breeze, but like all elemental spirits, Air spirits can be invited into a ritual setting where they can more easily be distinguished through incense smoke or other moveable trappings.

There is a method of intentionally unfocusing the eyes until you see tiny points of light that I've used when calling up a cool breeze on

a hot day. It's fairly easy with a little practice. I was able to teach it to my daughter when she was only eight years old. While outside, face a direction (usually North-ish, unless you live in the Southern Hemisphere) where cool air could come from. Look into an open expanse of sky and let the focus of your eyes blur just a little. Look for the little points of light. As soon as you see them, visualise them rushing towards your face. It usually manifests right after you release your concentration.

If you work with trance states, you might be able to tune into Air spirits anywhere by slipping into a light trance and using your peripheral vision to seek out the flitting shapes within the aura of things around you. Using the unfocusing method described above, you may even be able to discern moving shapes immediately in front of your vision.

Do not concentrate *too* hard. Practice will teach you the balance between focused attention and straining too hard-to-see definition.

Air spirits are curious by nature and not as cautious as Earth spirits, so it's likely that some will take an interest in your experiments and might even perform tricks for you.

Once you've established mutual perception, you might be happy only to effectively introduce yourself or you might want to ask for favours, like the cool breeze previously mentioned. If you are within your temple space, you might want to try sending a message to someone. While thought-form Air spirits are best for this, there is no harm in testing whether resident Air spirits would be willing to co-operate. Similarly, these spirits can be helpful for finding lost articles. Wild spirits are unlikely to complete such a task.

Learning to recognise the presence of Air spirits is a means unto itself. It becomes easier to do each time it is done, and it increases your overall awareness of the world of Spirit. Having attracted their attention within a familiar environment will also increase the degree of co-operation you are likely to receive when a time comes that you do ask for their assistance.

Forests and gardens are good places to look for Air spirits by looking between things. While this is a more Earthy setting, the symbiotic exchange of oxygen and carbon dioxide is a natural environment for Air spirits. It's entirely likely that you will catch a movement of these spirits before seeing any sign of the resident Earth spirits.

TO SEE FIRE SPIRITS

The most "visible" Fire spirits are usually those who can be observed in flames. There are rare exceptions. A friend of mine once described to me several "small naked black men in a friend's garden" that she had observed dancing. She later learned that the site had once been an ancient Indigenous initiation centre. Were these residual Fire spirits manifesting as a result of ritual dance ceremonies that once occurred on the site? That one is open to speculation.

One thing to bear in mind when attempting to see flame spirits is the potential for eye damage. One should *never* stare directly into a candle flame, for example: not for divination, nor any reason. When seeking visions from Fire, it's preferable to look just above the flame. In larger fires like a campfire, hearth, or bonfire, images have been known to form within the flames themselves, but the more concentrated the light source, the more danger there is for eye damage.

Fire spirits are usually particularly agreeable when it comes to communicating with human observers. The changing nature of the element gives plenty of scope for the imagination to formulate images of the spirit, or for the spirit to present itself in a form of its own choosing. Naturally, one should always use caution when seeking Fire spirits and to be meticulous about containing any actual flames.

A different form of Fire spirit might be observed during ritual dance or in places where this has frequently occurred. Most aren't as corporeal as the little men referred to above, but can be perceived through movement, as if they exist between the movements of the dancers. Again, the peripheral vision detects them where a direct gaze will not. This sort of spirit arises during the dance and disappears into its potential state soon after the dancing stops, though repeated dancing in the same place strengthens its external manifestation. This is how it's possible to catch a glimpse of a residual Fire spirit of the dance in a location that is no longer used.

Some Fire spirits in nature can be terrifying, like the spirits of uncontrolled fires. The bystander who encounters such a spirit might well be in danger from the fire itself, which is not a situation I would advise seeking out. If caught in a crisis situation, it couldn't hurt to petition the Fire spirit to pass you by or let you through, but Fire spirits are erratic and generally unconcerned with human problems. A wildfire is to a Fire spirit like a feeding frenzy is to a shark. Don't bank your life on benevolence.

People who fight fires for a living are in a position to meet Fire spirits on a regular basis. A psychic firefighter has an opportunity to get to *know* the Fire, and in doing so could have a better chance to tame the beast. The physics of fire's behaviour are taught as part of their training, but the instinctive ability to predict the movements of the fire comes through experience.

If you invite a Fire spirit to show itself within a well-controlled, contained fire, these spirits can be uniquely co-operative. They can be enticed to help with predicting the future, far-seeing the present in another location, or persuaded to assist in acts of magic. Remember that Fire represents action. For Fire spirits, the joy is in the doing. Little thought goes into reasons or consequences.

Once again, fire safety caution is strongly advised as freeing the spirit to perform a magical act must not also free the flame itself.

Seeing a flame spirit may happen spontaneously but can be done intentionally by unfocusing the eyes and looking at the spaces above and around the actual flame, where the heat appears to make objects waver to human vision. The Fire spirit might test you, causing you to feel irrational fear that makes you look away. If you stare too intently, remember to blink several times to re-wet your eyes.

You can develop a relationship with a Fire spirit by rekindling the fire in the same place repeatedly, either a hearth fire at home or a place outside that is cleared for a pit fire. Once you invite and make contact with a Fire spirit, you can call it again the next time you light the fire in the same location. Name the spirit, or let it name itself, and you can call it from its potential state every time you provide fresh fuel and spark.

The spirit of Fire works in conjunction with the human spirit in that the life force is fed by the very presence of a Fire spirit. This is why dance therapy is often a very successful form of treatment for certain medical conditions. The human spirit is naturally drawn to fire, harmonising in a symbiotic exchange of energy that is not unlike the melding of flame that occurs when two sources of flame meet and combine into a single, much larger fire.

Encounters with Fire spirits can be invigorating, yet, once again, there is potential for danger. There are some people who are unable to reconcile the feeling of communing with the spirit of Fire with the separation of their own life force and these people can be seduced into the allure that leads to arson, losing control to an addiction much like alcohol or drug addiction. The power of the spirit of Fire should never be taken for granted.

TO SEE WATER SPIRITS

Whatever our individual lifestyles may be, we are very much ruled by our emotional natures (even the most self-controlled among us). It is by tapping into the psychic abilities that naturally accompany the emotional side of our nature that we can learn to develop psychic vision. It is also the nature of Water, which draws out our emotions, and, therefore, our aptitude for spiritual vision, that often makes Water spirits the easiest to see.

Water spirits present a rather unique enigma to visual perception in that they are often seen in the reflection of light on or near water. This makes them more easily seen, even to the extent that spontaneous sightings are legendary, yet it also lends an elusive quality to the sighting, leaving the observer unsure whether anything was actually seen or if it was only a trick of the light.

The cone receptors in the eye can more easily perceive the colourful spectrum of spiritual light when it is amplified by water reflections, but the forms move and waver and, in most cases, are all too quickly gone before one can adequately discern and assimilate what has been observed. It is often left to imperfect memory and belief to interpret a fleeting image in motion.

Water spirits are generally bold creatures, unafraid to be seen by humans, yet enjoy the game of hide and seek much as their counterparts among the other elements often play. Many of them are shape changers and might appear as aquatic animals of some sort.

Some of them—particularly spirits of pools, peat bogs, and certain seas—actively seek to attract humans for their own purposes. One should be careful of these. There are some Water spirits who seek to consume the life force of humans, and these might possibly have learned in times gone by to expect the occasional sacrifice.

Apart from the obvious bodies of water and their vicinities, Water spirits might be observed in mirrors, fog, rain, dew, or snowbanks. Mirrors and fog are particularly good mediums for scrying.

This is one of the reasons that a scrying mirror is traditionally washed with a mixture of vinegar and water before each use. The mirror, a reflective surface much like water in a pool, attracts a similar sort of spirit, but the magical washing brings the actual element in contact with the surface. This will help the working if the assistance of a Water spirit is desired.

Apart from accidental sightings of Water spirits, there are ways one can practice going about observing these spirits. Some of them are the stuff of superstition and folklore; others are a matter of common sense and understanding of the world of nature spirits.

One example of a superstition of how to go about observing sea spirits is to take a holed stone to the ocean at night, close one eye, and look out to sea through the hole with the other eye. This method is based on using a stone that has formed a hole through natural water erosion, preferably one found at the seashore, as the stone would have an affinity with the seawater that eroded through it, and the hole would provide a focus point for observing the spirit. I cannot say that I have ever personally tried this method, but I keep an open mind to any possibilities.

Another method from folklore is to watch the reflection of the full moon on the ocean or other body of water. The Moon is closely attuned to the natural waters of the Earth through gravitational pull and is representative of feminine intuition.

Besides creating a dance of light and shadow within which the intuitive eye can perceive shapes, the light will actually attract the creatures of water, both physical and spiritual. If you ever observe dolphins playing in their natural habitat at night, you will see them leap and frolic in the streak of moonlight on the water.

My aunt once told me a story of her own encounter with sea creatures in the ocean at night. She was living in Hawaii at the time, and night swims were not unusual. One night, she was out for a swim and the moonlight attracted various fishes into her vicinity. My aunt had a spiritual streak and found it easy to commune with local wildlife.

Then, among the other sea creatures, she saw the distinctive fin of a shark very near her. She was sensible enough to know that splashing around would be likely to identify herself as prey and, instead, followed her instinct to stroke the shark. Like the other fishes, the shark swam close to her and allowed the unusual intimacy, offering no threat. I never advise seeking out situations of potential danger, but this was a good example of responding in a spiritual manner to a situation that had presented itself.

Most creatures of the deep attracted by moonlight stay under the surface. Water spirits share the playful nature of the dolphin and, like most spirits, are more attracted to the soft light of the Moon than to the harsh glare of the daytime Sun. Many a sailor throughout history has reported seeing figures, like ghostly ladies, walking on the surface of the water in the streak of light given off by the Moon. It might be that some of these ghostly ladies were created at the bottom of a rum barrel, but many others have appeared to the sober and sane observer.

Those who read books of folklore will find many examples worldwide of stories about sightings of Water spirits in various forms, as well as superstitions regarding them. Some of these have been altered by later religious influence, such as the Manx superstition that a child whose eye touches water in baptism has no chance of becoming second-sighted.

On a more practical level, the key is to remember that any source of water, even dew on the grass, is a potential wellspring of Water spirit activity. One only has to learn the knack for catching a glimpse of movement on the edges of a reflection of light and shadow in the Water, then to trust the evidence of one's own visual perception.

As with Earth spirits, it is possible to cultivate a relationship with the spirit of a specific source of water, such as a pond or other small body of water. Ponds breed a spirit of calm, though the same could be said of a gently trickling stream. It is best if the chosen place is unlikely to be invaded by passers-by, and water safety should always be observed. Apart from weeds and other water hazards, some places like Australia might have wildlife hidden within otherwise calm bodies of water and I don't fancy trying to explain to a crocodile that I just came to meditate with the Water spirits.

Just as with Earth spirits, the method for attuning to the spirits of your chosen body of water is to begin by just sitting and listening for the first few visits. Visit as often as possible, but do nothing to disturb anything in the location. The local wildlife, as well as the location's spirits, will become accustomed to your presence eventually, and the place will begin to feel very natural and welcoming. Always eat something as a natural form of grounding after each visit, but it is best to do so *after* leaving the place. Nothing should be left behind, except perhaps a biodegradable offering.

Once the seeker's presence becomes accepted and welcomed by the location spirit, it is time to deal directly with the source of water. Gazing across the surface of a pond or the edges of a stream might lead to immediate sightings or might only begin by peripheral glimpses of reflection and movement.

Depending on the form of the water, it might be possible to enter into the element and repeat the attuning exercise within the water itself, but, again, the seeker is advised to consider safety. Very cold water or fast currents are real dangers, as are underwater reeds and plants that can entangle one's feet. Also, some places are prone to sudden flooding. Consider any of these potential dangers as well as the weather when entering water, especially when alone.

Water spirits are most easily seen between extremes of light and darkness, so dawn and dusk are the best times to look for them. Any source of water will have some light reflection, even on a dark night. Bright sunlight reflected off of water can be blinding. To seek visual perception of a spirit within the water takes some practice to filter out the movements of nature over what might seem to be a very calm surface.

Ripples in the water or insects flying about can draw visual attention. A lake or pond can hold an astounding amount of movement that distracts the eye, but with practice, one can learn to differentiate between the ethereal flitting of a Water spirit and the ordinary movements of aquatic and insect life, which catch the eye too easily as do the reflections of birds flying overhead. The contrast becomes easier to differentiate once the first spirit sighting occurs.

Beneath the surface, there is much less distraction from flitting bugs, frogs, and blowing leaves. If the body of water is safe for swimming or snorkelling, fishes, large or small, are much more easily identified, but visibility might be very poor depending on the clarity of the water and the degree of light available. A diving mask can be very useful for clarifying vision under the surface, though they tend to block peripheral vision.

The natural distortion of vision that occurs without a mask in water can be an advantage. There is no need to unfocus the eyes underwater and the natural tendency to move the eyes about in search of clear vision is ideal for seeking peripheral vision of Water spirits.

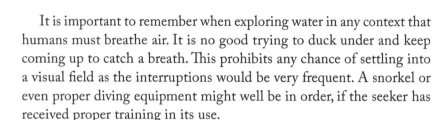

It is important to remember when exploring water in any context that humans must breathe air. It is no good trying to duck under and keep coming up to catch a breath. This prohibits any chance of settling into a visual field as the interruptions would be very frequent. A snorkel or even proper diving equipment might well be in order, if the seeker has received proper training in its use.

Divers are taught to never dive alone, but to go with a buddy. You might be able to find someone who shares your interest in Water spirits who would be prepared to attend a diving course with you for the purpose. Diving alone is definitely not advised and can be very dangerous.

Another thing to keep in mind is that this is *their* realm. You are the intruder. The Water spirits might welcome you, but they might just as easily resent the intrusion, even if the location spirits above the water have accepted you. There are many stories in folklore about drownings due to resentful Water spirits.

Don't forget to leave an offering for the Water spirits, as well as for the Earth spirits of the location. A little cake sprinkled on the surface of the water is ideal, as it helps to feed the fishes. Just a little given to a nearby tree completes the offering.

One more thing to consider is that the place should not be unduly interfered with. If your chosen place is a domestic pond, cleaning it periodically is perfectly acceptable and should please the resident spirits. If, on the other hand, it is a wild stream or pool, it is best left to nature unless it is overcrowded with dead leaves or has been polluted. In general, nature knows how to look after itself.

Those who live near a fast-moving river or the ocean might naturally wish to seek Water spirits in these places, despite the suggestion that a calmer location is easiest. The fact of living near such a water source creates an exception and the same general methods can be adapted.

Living in constant proximity to these more active watery places creates an attunement that compensates for the potentially violent nature of the moving water. Having lived near an ocean at some times in my life, I am well aware that waves or torrents that might seem intimidating to visitors to the area can actually have a very calming effect on a local resident who will have assimilated the natural rhythms of the ocean or river.

Water, calm as it might seem in its undisturbed state, is a very powerful element, and the spirits of Water can be more formidable than one might remember while gazing into a calm pool. I advise respecting them.

TO SEE AETHERIAL SPIRITS

Aetherial spirits stand apart from those of the other four elements in that they are more often detected in spontaneous sightings, perhaps more by those with psychic ability (knowingly or unknowingly), but sometimes by people who cannot see spiritual presences in any other circumstance. This would apply to someone who sees the "ghost" of a recently dead relative who makes a visitation to impart information.

Children and animals are more likely to see Aetherial spirits than adults in general, yet some spectres appear repeatedly to all comers in specific locations. Angelic visions and demonic manifestations have been reported to reoccur to specific observers or in a chosen place, which is then dubbed as holy, haunted, or possessed accordingly. Interestingly, these manifestations may happen visually, audibly, or through a "sense of presence" equally, and yet will usually be described as an appearance.

Fleeting glimpses of Aetherial spirits are most common, but some spirits have been observed strolling leisurely down a corridor for several minutes or down a road where their physical form died. Others have manifested in holy places or have actually followed a person for an extended period of time.

An experience was related to me first-hand by someone who had been followed by a Black Dog spirit through a park. When the dog drew alarmingly close, the person stopped, cast a circle of protection around himself, and stayed in it throughout the night. This was someone who was experienced in spirit magic, which leads to speculation of whether involvement in this sort of magic might attract spirits, or whether the dog would have been equally inclined to follow a non-occultist.

Those who go looking for encounters with Aetherial spirits are well advised to do their research beforehand to be very sure of exactly what they wish to encounter, as well as how to deal with malevolent spirits should they attract something other than what they intend to find.

Stepping into the world of Spirit opens the senses to all manner of presences. There is good reason why only the priestly castes in many cultures are allowed to communicate with Spirit, having had the proper training.

As with the other elemental spirits, if you wish to seek out Aetherial spirits, you should try to do so somewhere that you will be uninterrupted if possible, though if your quest takes you to a holy place like Glastonbury

Tor, Lourdes, or certain stone circles, it will likely be populated with other seekers. These people generally mind their own business and make room for others, all politely ignoring each other in their respective quests. It is not disruptive in the way that a bystander happening upon a private ritual might be.

If you ever have a chance to visit the Isle of Man, there is a strong fairy culture there and sightings of pure light fairies are not unknown. I saw some myself in Groudle Glen, a place particularly known for fairy activity. What I saw were diamond-shaped blue lights, dancing along the path in front of us. My daughter saw them as well, though other people along with us did not. I tried to reproduce what I actually saw and the resulting image is below.

Many spirit forms will take on an appearance that the observer expects to see. This is especially prevalent with fairies, Angels, and demonic spirits. Ghosts will usually resemble the previously living person, as the connection to that form maintains a pattern on the astral levels for some time.

Inviting a spirit to manifest is something that is best preceded with forethought. Dealing with potentially powerful spirit entities or inviting them into your home or temple can bring unpredictable consequences and is not advised for the inexperienced. Some forms of spirit, even if not malicious, can be mischievous.

People who are stressed or enduring unusual hardship are more open to psychic impressions and therefore prone to spontaneous spiritual sightings. There are many legendary stories of travellers in adverse weather conditions who come across shelter in an inn with convivial people where they are given food, drink, and warmth, then return to the location a month or two later to find that the inn they sheltered in has been gone for more than a hundred years.

The ability to see spirits of any kind is something that becomes easier with practice. Whether it is done through ritual or observation, the eye can be trained to detect the insubstantial and elusive substance which exists in the world of Spirit.

Chapter 5

FOLK MAGIC

MOST OF US HAVE ANCESTORS who have practiced some version of natural magic or folk magic. Even those with strict religious taboos against sorcery have some form of superstitions or beliefs that accommodate dealing with nature spirits in some guise.

Asking a nature spirit for assistance in an act of magic is very different from seeking spiritual intervention through formal ritual, and success depends greatly on the voluntary participation of the spirits in question. Nature spirits are not generally invoked but can be invited to join a ritual.

A "ritual" in this context can be anything from a simple act of folk magic to a full-blown circle, perhaps held in the woods or other natural settings outdoors. Even spirits who inhabit your back garden live in nature's realms, and it would be unrealistic to expect them to come indoors to join your ritual, though house spirits are another matter.

WORKING WITH EARTH ELEMENTALS

If you have made an Earth temple or altar either in your home or in your garden, you might wish to invite nature spirits into your constructed place for them. The spirits of the plants and stones will be there in the garden whether we invite them or not, but by intentionally inviting them, we are welcoming them and establishing a connection through which we hope to nurture them. This can be done just through friendly thoughts, by doing basic incantations, or in full ritual.

If you do want to perform indoor rituals involving Earth spirits, you are more likely to get co-operation from house spirits, though there is no harm in inviting outside spirits to join you. Just don't be disappointed if they decline.

You may wish to cultivate relationships with specific Earth entities with a view towards including them in your ritual practices that are ruled by Earth, such as business, money, employment, prosperity, stability, and fertility. I personally tend to keep both an indoor temple and an outdoor one in the garden, which are attended by different spirits.

Purposes that have to do with financial concerns are unlikely to be meaningful to the spirits in the garden, unless a reason they can appreciate is supplied, but purposes like fertility and healing are closer to nature. For these, I would be more inclined to perform the ritual out of doors.

Folk magic is a term used to describe the daily magics that we have had handed down to us through superstitions of our forebears, as well as the newer versions that are continually taught by children to each other in school. The human species has a natural inclination towards developing little rituals to affect the world around us in magical ways, and children often demonstrate this in their games.

We are familiar with superstitions that require that we touch wood, step over cracks in the pavement, or avoid walking under ladders. These simple superstitions are based in folk magic and many once had practical reasons behind them. If we become more consciously aware of the magical roots of these superstitions and of the uses of folk magic in general, then we can transcend the inclination to *pooh-pooh* these little habits and apply the concepts of magic behind them to the things we do in everyday life.

Involving Earth spirits in our everyday magics is a matter of understanding the nature of the spirits themselves, as well as the form of magic we wish to perform. We can consciously involve Earth spirits in things like growing plants, harvesting, and cooking, as well as folk spells that are found in stone, image, tree, and knot magic.

For example, a typical knot magic spell would involve focusing on a specific desire while tying knots in a cord, which might be subsequently buried or kept in a special place. This sort of spell might actually frighten an Earth spirit, as binding spells in general are anathema to a nature spirit's sense of freedom.

However, by understanding that this is indeed the case, we can put more thought into the construction of the spell and look for a way in which the Earth spirit can play a part willingly without fear. In this case, the first thing to do is to consider the intent of the spell. If it is a spell for prosperity or any financial issue, abandon the idea of a knot spell and do a coin spell instead.

A Coin Spell

A coin spell is ideal for money and general prosperity spells, although this is a tricky area of magic and success is partially reliant on whether the practitioner believes that it will work. As in all spells, the magic actually takes place in the subtle workings of the subconscious mind, and allowing doubt to intervene can trip you up.

Inviting an Earth elemental to help might well make the difference, as this takes the magic beyond the magician and into a realm where magic is a commonplace occurrence.

Specific spells can be found in many variations, but here is a basic one that incorporates the help of an Earth elemental:

First, you must establish a relationship with a specific spirit or with the spirits of a specific place. A garden temple or a rock spirit kept indoors are good choices. You will also need a coin (preferably shiny and silver), some herbs, and a container. Camomile and pennyroyal are good choices for the herbs. Be sure to check the correspondences of any herbs you choose.

The container can be a small glass or earthenware jar, or a small bag made of natural fabric (cotton is best for this as it is biodegradable). You can also add anything else that you feel will add a personal touch or appropriate energies to your intent, such as a small green stone. Lodestones are particularly appropriate for a spell intended to draw something towards you.

Gather these things in the place you have chosen to perform the spell. Be sure to choose a time when you will not be interrupted. Perform some form of calming meditation and contemplate the purpose of the spell. Then you are ready to invite your Earth elemental(s) to join in the magic.

Having reached a conducive state of mind yourself, project that state of mind to the elemental(s) with whom you wish to communicate. The most effective manner of accomplishing this is to do it verbally, remembering that words have power. You can simply speak to flowers, stones, or any object that you associate with the chosen elemental(s), or you can reach magical gnosis through chanting words in rhyme.

Apart from the hypnotic effect that this has on the subconscious mind of the magic user, the fact is that nature spirits enjoy the music of the rhyme and will naturally be attracted to the sound of a soft voice in ritual chant. Again, you want to be sure that you have insured privacy as best you can because you might feel silly chanting fairy invitations over your garden if the neighbours happen by. Stopping in mid-chant out of embarrassment could shatter the mood for the day. Alternatively, you can lower your voice to a murmur until the intruder has passed.

Using words that might sound twee or silly is highly recommended as nature spirits respond well to the feeling of fun in them, even if the intent of the ritual is very serious. You will want to begin with a verse or two that has been predetermined, then follow it up with more spontaneous verses to help focus your intent.

If you don't feel you are creative enough to make up verses on the spot, try it anyway. If it doesn't go smoothly, practice more. You might surprise yourself. Don't put too much pressure on yourself, especially over the assumption that words at the end of a sentence must rhyme exactly. It is more important to allow the thoughts to flow into words and create the magic in the process.

If repeated often enough, the opening verses can become a mantra for you that will release the creative spirit of ritual, or they can form a connection with the elemental spirit(s) that you are addressing. Exact wording doesn't matter as much as always remembering to consider the meanings of words used in magic of any kind, and the possible ways it might go wrong if translated differently than you intended.

Having reached an appropriate mind state and invited the elemental spirits to participate, the coin spell is "charged" by adding something personal to the coin and herbs, such as wrapping three strands of your own hair around the other items three times (three is a traditional number). Do not tie knots. If you have short or no hair, you can use a thread that has been soaked with any of your bodily fluids, keeping in mind associations with your intended purpose.

I would do this in the middle of the spell, while chanting and working the purpose of the spell into the words of the chant. If it is a spell for money, words that express the reason for the need are most effective. You are asking spiritual entities to help you attain this goal, so stating

your reasons will get a better response than just asking for wealth for no apparent reason that an Earth elemental could appreciate.

The mental process involved in creating the words spontaneously during this part of the spell is essential to the magic. Since you will likely be working alone or with someone spiritually very close to you for this, it doesn't matter if the words come out sounding silly.

Put the items into your container and close the spell either with an original verse or by repeating the first one over again. If you are going to bury the container, you should do so during the closing chant. If, alternatively, you plan to put it away somewhere, you should secure the lid at this time, then put it in the chosen place without speaking to anyone on the way.

A KNOT SPELL

If you have decided that a knot spell is appropriate for your purpose after all, you will still need to be careful not to offend your elemental. Secure knots are primarily used for binding, and I do not recommend them in general when working with elemental spirits, although there are exceptions to every rule.

An appropriate purpose for a knot spell that is Earth-spirit-friendly would be if you wanted to incorporate something new into your life, perhaps personal change, better luck in general, stability in some aspect of your life, or anything else that would be appropriate to the Earth element. With a little imagination, this could even still be used to promote prosperity as a trend woven into your life.

The key word there was *woven*. You will need something to weave, plait, or otherwise tie together without tying secure knots. Three strands of a vine growing in the garden (not cut!) such as ivy is wonderful for this, as long as you are extremely careful not to harm the plant. If you do not have something appropriate growing in the garden or prefer to do this indoors, you can use corn husks, straw, or anything natural that the Earth elemental might be able to relate to. If you make corn dollies, this skill can certainly be used here.

If you wish to invite a rock spirit into this spell, you might be able to use ribbons to decorate the rock as long as you do not bind it. Placing the ribbons under the rock and allowing the ribbons to hang over the edge of a table or shelf works well to get the initial weave started.

Once you have chosen your place and medium for the spell, decide on an opening rhyme that would be appropriate for the Earth elemental you wish to invite and for the spell's intent. As in the coin spell, there are three parts to the ritual after the calming meditation, starting with the chant for the opening invitation, followed by the weaving or plaiting as the chant continues. Do not tie a secure knot when you finish but leave your medium in a position where it will be undisturbed, at least for some time, while you finish off the spell with a closing chant.

OTHER FORMS OF BASIC EARTH SPELLS

One of the most basic forms of "folk magic" is to simply bury an image or object representative of the need in a plot of virgin ground or at the base of a standing stone or tree. You can invite the local elemental to help this basic spell with their own magic while performing the task.

Acting out a purpose while asking a stone or tree spirit for assistance is also a popular method, like asking a holed stone for fertility while a woman crawls through.

An image representing your desire can be drawn in dirt and the local spirits invited to assist. This sort of magic is basically sympathetic magic and methods can be developed through your own imagination as well as those we hear about from folklore, like stirring a cauldron (or pot of soup) while chanting a rhyme relevant to the purpose of the magic. Making Earth spirits a part of one's daily life in these small ways has a spiritually calming effect on most people.

WORKING WITH AIR ELEMENTALS

To invite an Air spirit into an act of nature magic can be exhilarating in the same way that having the wind in your face while riding in an open car or standing in the wind in an open space can bring a feeling of elation. The natural playfulness and curiosity of Air spirits make the likelihood of a response to an invitation into a magical act very high, so long as the right approach is used.

Part of the key to this is to remember that nature spirits must be *invited*, never commanded. I can't repeat that too many times. They will co-operate because they want to, not because they feel compelled to. A magic user who tries to force an elemental free spirit is begging for trouble, as the spirit will certainly rebel against any attempt at compulsion, and the possibility of a spell backfiring is significantly increased if such an elemental spirit decides an arrogant magician needs to be taught a lesson.

The physics of nature applies to any spell, regardless of the form the magic takes. For example, one is far more likely to accomplish calling up a breeze outdoors (where there are natural air movements to work with) than indoors, where even an open window only allows a limited influx of fresh air. A little common sense applied will help to determine the probability factor for any intended act of magic.

Air spirits can be cultivated in a similar manner as Earth spirits. However, it is good to remember that not only is an Air spirit's attention span very short as a general rule, but Air elementals are in a constant state of change, and the cultivation of one in a specific place or for a specific purpose, perhaps as a temple spirit, would require frequent attention in order to perpetuate familiarity with the spirit.

This attention could take an easy form, like entering the space on a daily basis and performing a simple incantation to sustain contact with the Air elemental in the case of a temple spirit, or if one wishes to maintain an Air elemental for a specific purpose, spending a few minutes a day "charging" the spell would serve the purpose.

The sensitive magician will realise that the continuity of the spirit is tenuous, and that any neglect of this daily maintenance is likely to result in the total dissipation of whatever magical energies have been invested in forming a connection with the elemental spirit.

Spells that might be appropriate for employing Air spirits include any magic involving travel, instruction, freedom, obtaining knowledge, discovering lost items, uncovering lies, or developing psychic abilities. Spells to encourage inspiration or imagination in any way are also appropriate to Air.

Any of these purposes might be approached in a spontaneous manner with a spell invented on the spot, which would appeal to the nature of an Air spirit. Most divinations are also appropriate to the Air element to some degree, even if the medium of divination is associated with another element.

Specifically, Air divinations are strongly based on intuition. Air spells might also be used to aid concentration or for visualisation magic. Air spells include singing spells and sweeping spells, both of which are very effective forms of folk magic, as well as others.

A lot of the folk magic having to do with Air concerns weather prediction, as you might expect from traditions developed by rural communities. Weather magic can be surprisingly easy so long as one makes the effort to work *with* the elements rather than trying to work against them.

Air spells might involve an action, such as placing something into the air in some manner, perhaps dropping it off a high place, so that the object connects physically with the element. It might involve writing a desire on paper which is burnt at the end of a charging ritual and the ashes blown into the air. Sigil magic is doubly connected to Air, as it involves writing (albeit in symbols) as well as sending the desire into the air in this way as a popular finish to the magic.

Another Air spell might include shouting the desire into a high wind or performing an incantation to travel on the breeze. It can also involve using body movements as a form of writing in a slow dance, although dance magic itself pertains to Fire. Many Air spells are done in conjunction with other elements.

One very traditional form of folk magic that involves Air and Earth is to sing a spell while knitting, which is a form of knot magic, or performing some other craft while singing or chanting, thereby permeating the finished item with the energy of the spell. With a little imagination, this could be applied to any craft one does with the hands: decoupage, needlework of any kind, drawing, painting, woodwork, and certainly jewellery making. Talismanic jewellery has a long tradition.

Divinations often involve an Earth-based medium, yet intuition and communication must necessarily come into any form of divination and those are Air traits. Spells done on the seashore are likely to include Air and Water, possibly Earth as well, and, if fires are allowed on the beach, perhaps all four elements working in conjunction.

The tenuous Air element often benefits from the combined energies of another element in order to sustain form or intent. One that does not require input from other elements is the simple incantation. The ability to bring results from an incantation without any other action or symbols being employed is pure Air magic, and an area where inviting Air spirits into the ritual can be of great benefit.

This also applies to visualisation magic. The art of visualising an outcome (or just forming an intent in the mind and watching the results unfold) is a form of Air magic, not unlike writing the spell in some

manner. There is a fine line between folk magic and formal ritual magic, the subject of the next chapter, when employing this form of spell.

If we wish to consciously involve Air spirits in our daily magics, the place to begin is to become aware of the Air spirits naturally present in the home, temple, garden, or other outdoor location where we might wish to perform acts of magic. Take a moment to quiet the mind and become aware of the of the quiet hum and feeling of spirit life that is present around us at all times.

Sending a thought of greeting to the Air spirits is likely to attract their attention, resulting in an immediate feeling of well-being within oneself. This is the inner confirmation of their presence that must be trusted before you can proceed further.

Once this contact is established, you might want to attempt visual perception as described in Chapter Four, or you may wish to invite them to assist you in some task you are performing on either a magical or mundane level. You might even wish to just play with them, or they might lead you into their games themselves.

Air spells can be used for a variety of general purposes besides those that are specific to Air. Air spirits, ironically, are actually very helpful for aiding concentration on any subject, despite their own flighty nature.

SINGING SPELLS

For some people, singing comes naturally. They walk around humming, whistling, or singing to themselves unconsciously while performing their daily tasks. Others may have a special interest in music and will sing more consciously or even perform. Then there are those of us who know we have terrible voices and wouldn't be caught singing "Happy Birthday" in public. Any of these people are capable of singing spells. Tone deafness is only a minor obstacle.

Singing or humming has a special magical quality of its own that helps to establish an awareness of spiritual energies. It is hypnotic to a degree and a natural aid to focusing the will. It can be done in any location and needs no materials, although doing something with the hands (as in the knitting spell mentioned earlier) further concentrates one's attention and naturally leads one into a light trance state.

Singing by itself can become a means to trance with a little practice. The rhyme and metre of setting words to a tune, however simple, create the desired focus. This can be the sole element in an act of natural magic, employed in conjunction with hand or body movements (as in Kahuna magic), or focused on an object to be used for the ritual. This might be a sigil, a stone of appropriate kind or colour, or any other object associated with the subject of the spell.

The words themselves can be constructed as in any rhyming chant. The meanings should be clear enough that no unwanted surprise reinterpretation will occur, but otherwise are open to any level of creativity. If you're a lousy poet, it doesn't really matter. The meaning behind the words is what will shape the spell. They should include a definitive mention of the intent of the ritual and may include an invitation for the Air spirits to join you or to take part in some way.

If this does not come naturally at first, don't worry. You might need to start slowly by putting yourself into a conducive state of mind, then projecting your invitation to the Air spirits silently at first. It is just a small step to move from thought to verbal expression.

The trick is to relax rather than try to force yourself and to allow the thoughts to flow into words in their own time. This process will create the magic. Just as in rhyming chants, it can be helpful to establish a couple of predetermined opening verses that can be followed by spontaneous expression.

For example, when I used to travel by air, my verses as I entered the plane started out with:

"Spirits of the Air and sky,
protect me now as I must fly...."

A simple rhyme followed by spontaneous words to explain the reason why I must invade Air space in a machine that is so disruptive to air quality and natural air movements. My verses varied in poetic quality and sometimes didn't rhyme all that well, but they did the job.

In both singing and chanting spells, regular repetition maintains energy. Repeating the spell in some form on a regular basis until the intent manifests is important. Repeatedly chanting or singing a spell at a particular time each day, or even at irregular intervals, feeds the energy of the spell and sublimates the intent in the mind as the words become automatic and expressed more and more unconsciously. Failing to continue could allow the spell to dissipate.

OTHER AIR SPELLS

Most religions include some form of prayer to a spiritual deity (or deities), essence, or ancestor among their practices. This is a simple form of just asking for whatever it is you desire. When petitioning a spiritual entity, it is important to present your reasoning for your request with good intentions and expectations for success without falling into arrogance or a demanding attitude.

The request must be presented with confidence, not desperation. What is known as "lust for result" actually dissipates the magic and can result in failure.

Air magic can be used to rid yourself of things or to bring things to you. The basic methods to incorporate into a spell to rid yourself of something might include blowing away ashes from a burnt sigil or other effigy or dropping something that represents the unwanted energy off a high place in an attitude of throwing away bad rubbish. But don't litter!

Usually, this would apply to a personal trait you wish to discard or something like bad luck or limitations that are making life difficult. It is not generally advisable to use the effigy of a person for this, as tragic consequences could result, and then you're in a realm of dark magic which should never be approached casually. If you want out of a bad relationship, a preferable method is to use a photograph of you together, cut between the two people, and slowly move the unwanted person further and further away in daily spells or even send their half somewhere far away.

To bring something into your life, such as a wanted trait or talent, opportunity, better luck in general, or a specific energy towards a goal, one simple method is to visualise the wanted energy and literally breathe it in with the Air spirits. You can invite the Air spirits to strengthen you as you breathe deeply to raise your energy and attune your "vibrations" to the desired goal.

One particularly powerful spell I've used with great success is a writing spell. Any sheet of paper and writing instrument is all you need for this. Start at any corner of the paper and write, preferably in a personal alphabet known only to yourself, describing what you want to occur. No need for poetry on this one. Write in a clockwise circle around the edge of the paper and continue spiralling inward. A sentence or two per day will keep building the energy of the spell until it manifests. If

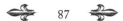

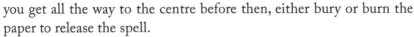

you get all the way to the centre before then, either bury or burn the paper to release the spell.

Imagination is a strong element in Air spells. It takes a certain amount of creativity to construct spells of any kind, but imagination is actually ruled by Air. Visualising a goal is an act of magic in itself and a factor in any more elaborate spells. Imagining an outcome is the first step to attainment.

Making Air spirits a part of your daily life in various ways has a spiritually uplifting effect on most people. Simply being aware of them as you live and breathe creates a certain magical aura that easily becomes a source of magical energy when need arises and is a strong factor in the feeling of presence that many people sense when they encounter a practicing magician.

Working with Air spirits taps into the source of primordial magic: the power of creation itself. Use it wisely!

WORKING WITH FIRE ELEMENTALS

Fire spirits, much like Air spirits, are very spontaneous by nature. It follows that Fire magic is also conducive to spontaneity in several different ways. One might be suddenly compelled to perform an act of magic, which by its very driving force could then be classified as Fire magic. A specific spell involving the element of Fire can easily move in an unexpected direction, which brings a certain element of danger, yet is an extremely powerful force presuming the magic user is able to keep the progression balanced and under control.

A Fire spell could cause something to happen spontaneously. The relative stability of the result is dependent on the relationship between the magic user and the Fire spirit involved, as well as the care taken to set up the spell properly and be specific about the intent. Fire spells that do not specifically call upon the assistance of Fire spirits will attract them anyway, so it is just as well to become familiar with their nature and to invite their participation in one's Fire spells from the start.

Spells that involve energy, authority, sex, healing, destruction, purification, or spiritual evolution are associated with Fire.

Fire spells might also include divination or love spells. Fire spells are specific to action, change, progression, and passion. Magic itself is the process of change (in conformity with Will, as the infamous magician

Aleister Crowley phrased it), so abstinence from the use of Fire spells and spirits in order to avoid the inherent dangers is an effectively futile gesture.

Fire spirits are naturally attracted to any spell that involves action or change. By embracing the power of Fire, the magic user can determine the parameters of the magic.

Fire, despite all its dangers, can be contained. Indoor spells are easily contained within a hearth or candle flame. Outdoors, a safely prepared bonfire, campfire, or even a barbeque provides adequate containment if actual flame is required or likely to occur. Repeated use of a designated fire pit can provide a location for attendant Fire spirits to recur.

Not all Fire spells require flame. Fire energy can be roused through such methods as ecstatic dance or strong emotions, but extreme caution is recommended in any Fire spell. Sufficiently strong magic can cross a line and result in spontaneous ignition, as learned the hard way many years ago when such a spell resulted in my house burning down. There was no source of flame involved in the spell and the fire department never determined the cause.

Fire can be frightening, yet this, too, can be used in magic. Fear, although very unstable, is no less powerful in effects than other strong emotions like anger, jealousy, or passion, and can be a source of great control in situations where fear must be overcome. Firewalking, for example, is an act of magic that directly confronts the natural fear of fire in order to walk the hot coals. The sense of elation, another strong emotion, that accompanies the accomplishment is intensely magical and could be channelled into an act of directed magic.

Fear can also be put to magical use in crisis situations where spontaneous magic is the only option. The magician who is experienced in the use of Fire magic and the nature of Fire spirits can rely on this powerful force when need arises. Spontaneous Fire magic is very chaotic, but it is also very effective.

On a material level, the spirit of a large fire is no different in nature than the spirit of a candle flame, just as the spirit of a small pebble is really not very different from the spirit of a large boulder. The source of fuel determines the material lifespan of the Fire spirit.

Fire spirits are very powerful spirits, and their potential is not to be used haphazardly, but need to be contained within strict parameters. Even allowing oneself to be effectively "possessed" by the spirit of Fire, or passion, can be kept contained within acceptable boundaries by a competent magic user.

Whether one works with possessive Fire spirits, potential or manifest flame spirits, Kundalini, or even Fire spirits of legend and mythology, the laws of nature are much the same. Fire spirits are intense and impersonal, and the wise magic user will respect their destructive potential. Yet, no magic is as invigorating as Fire magic, and the spirits of this element are exuberant rather than malicious.

Fire has a long history in world religions that associate it with spiritual light, including the Pagan Romans, in Christian and Jewish mysticism, and in Tantric Hinduism, among many others.

Determining where the line should be placed between folk magic and ritual magic can be difficult where the element of Fire is concerned. Practices like using drumming and rhythm in dance magic date back to tribal magic, yet the same methods might also be used in formal ritual.

Fire has been the subject of superstition throughout history. It naturally follows that it has been a medium used in many basic forms of folk magic. Fuming or burning an image, herb, or other flammable object—such as smudging, a practice used by Indigenous peoples of North America—is commonly used in magic, especially for purification or cleansing rituals. The use of candles is one of the most basic methods in a wide spectrum of magical practices.

Preparing an object to be burnt and the ashes scattered is popular in modern times for sigil magic but has a long tradition with burning effigies and other items. In some ancient cultures, this even includes sacrifices, as was dramatically illustrated in the film *The Wicker Man*.

A paradox of human nature arises in the use of Fire spells. Fire, more than any other element, has historically inspired fear and awe. This very emotional response adds power to the spell, yet it is in understanding the element of Fire that we learn its parameters and lose much of the fear that our ancestors felt, thereby gaining more control of the element as well as the magic we create through it.

However, overconfidence can weaken the force of the magic. Fire, as I've said, is spontaneous. The potential for the unexpected is always present and should never be forgotten. A healthy dose of caution not only keeps us alert to the very real chaotic nature of this potentially very destructive element but also reminds us that it can too easily get out of control and revives our respect for its inherent devastating power.

An Air and Fire Knot Ritual

In the previous section, I suggested a knot spell that involved knitting in front of a hearth fire. A variation on that spell is to use a piece of cotton string and tie knots into it while singing your spell, then give it over to the hearth fire to release the magic.

A group version could be done while dancing around a bonfire or campfire with a fairly long piece of cotton string. Natural fibres are always best! Open the spell and light the bonfire or campfire (or ensure it is already strongly burning during the opening ritual). The participants will dance in a circle around the fire, chanting the intent. This chant would be decided in advance.

The string will be passed from one person to another, with each person tying a knot and passing it to the person behind them in the circle. When everyone has tied a knot, or it has passed through the circle an agreed number of times for smaller groups (three or seven is traditional), the person presiding over the ritual stops the dance and commits the string to the fire. Then, the spell is closed.

Woods for Fuel

Bonfire magic has traditions dating back hundreds of years in the British Isles. Some have to do with what types of wood to burn. Certain trees are traditionally burnt at the quarter festivals. The nine woods of the Beltane, Samhain, and Midsummer fires are ash, apple, birch, yew, hazel, rowan, willow, pine, and blackthorn. The Maypole was traditionally made of hawthorn. The Yule log, burnt at Midwinter, was traditionally made of ash.

Oak should never be used because it is the King of the Woods. Neither should alder, which is sacred to Bran, nor elder, which is sacred to Hella, goddess of the Underworld.

Reaching into the Spirit of Fire

Inviting a Fire spirit into a spell is a little different than working with other elemental spirits. The potentially destructive power of Fire is all too apparent to a sensitive magic user and requires an ability to balance "on the edge" of chaotic energies.

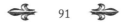

As in other elemental spells, one begins by gathering the items that are intended for use in the spell. These may be many or few, or perhaps even none at all. Some more experienced magic users prefer to work without "props" and might not even feel the need for a source of flame, as the potential for fire exists at all times within our oxygen-rich atmosphere.

A witch or magician can provide the spark and fuel a Fire elemental from within. However, one must be wary of backlash when working from within. There is good reason for externalising Fire symbols with implements of magic.

As with all magic, it is important to ensure that you will not be interrupted during the spell. This is essential when working with Fire spirits. One begins by calming or meditating as with other spells and contemplating the purpose of the spell, but in a Fire spell, the calm is quickly followed by a stirring of fiery energies.

To reach a spirit of Fire, you must stir the Fire within yourself. The purpose of the spell will usually provide an avenue of approach. Strong, intense, and wild emotions must be called up; passion and anger are the strongest, but not hatred, as it is a weak and uncontrolled emotion. Passion and anger also have some potential to run out of control, but it is the ability to stir these emotions and yet keep them intensely restrained that will determine the success of the operation.

Stirring these emotions is done through an internal psychodrama (a willing of the specific emotion to arise). A state of passion or anger can be roused through external stimuli such as sexual stimulation or pain infliction if working with a partner. An appropriate trance state can also be stimulated through dramatic, hypnotic methods such as drumming and dancing freeform around a source of flame, an altar, or just the centre of the ritual space. Visualising memories that stir the chosen emotion can be amplified with these methods.

When a sufficiently powerful emotional state is achieved, it is projected to the spirit of the Fire if a flame or representative object has been used. A focus point for this energy is advised. A sigil drawn on paper will do nicely.

The conducive state for projecting this energy is intense, powerful, and possibly even frenzied. This is the nature of a Fire spirit. Like other elemental spells, an invitation to a Fire spirit to participate in the magic can be done verbally through chanting or song. Chanting is advised, as the beauty of music could dilute the intensity that you've worked up.

Pre-prepared lines to repeat over and over work best for this element. A stanza of four carefully worded lines to chant are easy to remember and create a natural rhythm. Fire spirits respond to the strength behind the words more than to the words themselves. However, as in any spell, be very careful about the choice of words and any alternative meanings. Your own subconscious is directing the spell, and you wouldn't want the intensity of Fire energy to go astray.

You may wish to add other ingredients to your working. Strands of hair or a prepared sigil can be "fed" to the Fire. A statement of intent could also be written on paper before or during the spell and burned by the source of flame, if one is used. The trouble with this is that you should try to make sure the entire paper is burned, leaving no small bits. You could get your fingers burnt in the attempt, literally, figuratively, or both. Keeping a pair of ritual tweezers can be very useful here.

Hopefully, you will have thought out your intent and potential consequences before beginning any Fire spell, even a spontaneous one. According to folklore, inappropriate love spells last for seven years with the results getting progressively worse, and spells that are performed in a state of passion or anger can all too easily be regrettable when your emotions have calmed again.

Fire is a necessary element in the balance of nature. Despite its all-consuming nature, we use it in our daily lives to keep warm, to cook food, and to enjoy those things for which we feel passion. We cannot escape the stronger emotions; we can only learn to contain and direct them as one contains a source of flame.

WORKING WITH WATER ELEMENTALS

Water represents intuition. Water spells are based on the emotions and often performed on the intuitive level. The symbol most often associated with Water is the cup or chalice, which holds hidden depths. Within those depths of hidden knowledge lie the secrets of the interrelation of all elements, among other things.

Invoking or evoking Water spirits can be a rather tricky business, as they are difficult to grasp or contain in any manner. In general, one can only give direction to a Water spell or spirit, knowing that the eventual outcome will ultimately be unpredictable in its detail.

Bringing a Water spirit into an act of natural magic is not at all difficult. In fact, if one performs magic near any body of water, it is highly likely that the spirits of that body of water will participate, invited or not.

Water, by its very nature, seduces and lures the human spirit into a magical state of mind. It has a natural calming effect that is very conducive to entering a trance state. The simple act of having a bath or shower can relax tension. Any form of meditation or contemplation performed near a large body of water is assisted by the enticement of calm that exudes from the water itself. Imagine then, how much more effective an act of magic might be if its performance is enhanced by a deliberate invitation to the Water spirits and an active request for them to participate.

Water spirits exist anywhere that water might be found, indoors or outdoors. Water spells performed indoors might be performed with common water from the tap, which can be drunk or used for cooking in kitchen spells. Water in the bath or shower can be used for cleansing or other Water-related spells. An incantation to obtain a state of total relaxation performed during a shower can be very effective indeed! A spontaneous spell done while relaxing in the bath can be just as effective as one that has been planned and set up in advance.

Some magic users like to keep a source of water indoors to use for ritual purposes, such as an indoor electric fountain or a bowl of water for scrying or other spells. Water from sacred wells can be kept bottled and ready for use in one's working space or temple.

Outdoors, there are even more possibilities. It is not unusual to feel inspired to perform an act of magic when in the vicinity of a stream, river, pond, or the seaside. Water spirit spells can also be very useful when swimming, especially if difficulties should arise, though I don't advise relying on Water spirits to compensate for unsafe swimming conditions. Remember that they are known to take their sacrifices.

Having said that, I would not hesitate to petition the local Water spirits if an unforeseen situation should arise. Sinking bogs, tangled weeds under the surface of a lake, or finding oneself lost at sea are all to be avoided if possible, but if thrust into such a scenario, it could do no harm to petition the local Water spirits for assistance.

Many tales are told of sailors who have been rescued by dolphins after a shipwreck and taken to an island or floating object. Some more

fantastic tales claim similar rescues by mermaids, though these are usually explained away as hallucinations. Keep in mind that mermaids also have a reputation for claiming the lives of those lost at sea.

Water spells are commonly used for cleansing and purification, accessing the subconscious, and stabilizing the emotions. Water is fluid, constantly changing, and these qualities must be kept in mind when performing Water spells of any kind.

Water is representative of pleasure, friendship, marriage, fertility, happiness, healing, sleep, dreaming, and psychic acts. Spells that concern any of these things might well be appropriate for the Water element. Some, such as fertility and healing, might also require or be appropriate to another element working in conjunction, depending on the intended approach.

There is an old folk belief that water is particularly powerful when the morning Sun first shines on it. This may be the basis for the name *Brightwell* that adorns many places and ancient wells. A simple spell can be performed by mentally projecting a sigil onto the reflection of either the Sun or the Moon on the water's surface, allowing oneself to relax into the meditative state that is all too easy to get lost in.

This state is very conducive to sleep, which could be inconvenient outdoors, but a form of the same method can be performed indoors over a bowl of water positioned to catch the moonlight through the window. The spirit of the Water can be called to aid in the purpose, but it is recommended that this form of spell is restricted to calmer purposes, as a very active spell or one that involves strong emotions could be disturbing or even offensive to the Water spirit.

WATER SPELLS IN FOLK MAGIC

Water is, perhaps, the most commonly used element in folk magic. It is often used in its cleansing capacity, both physically and symbolically. Old superstitions reflect practical health precautions such as the belief that one should never drink water that has stood in a glass overnight. It is believed that such water would then be possessed by demonic forces, or that fairies would have taken the essence from the water as they are believed to do with milk and food offerings.

In fact, these superstitions date from a time when water left standing might become contaminated with typhoid or influenza germs in days when such diseases were epidemic and often incurable by the medicines known at the time.

Some other superstitions regarding water are less dire in origin and intent. One classic belief mentioned earlier is that if, on the first day of May, one rubs the morning dew into one's face, it will keep the skin looking young.

Stone magic can be mixed with Water magic by dipping stones in water to conduct their magical properties, followed by drinking the water. Not all stones are suitable for this so do your research! Some gemstones can be damaged by water or even make the water toxic.

A form of sigil magic is performed by using an object to symbolise a desire, which is then tossed or placed into water. A similar folk spell is to draw a symbol to represent something one wishes to "cleanse away" from one's life on a stone or other object, then toss it into the water—preferably a running source—to wash away the affliction. In modern Pagan practices, water is often used symbolically in Earth cleansing rituals.

Water itself does not have to be present for all magical workings but can be symbolised by things that are given to us by the sea or other natural bodies of water. It is a common belief that a shell placed at the entrance of a house ensures that good luck will enter it.

Shells are frequently used in ritual of many sorts and have always held fascination for our species, not least of all because the natural fractal spiral patterns of some shells, like conches, appeals to our most primal connection to the patterns of the universe. Conch shells also produce a loud *trump* when blown into, which makes a great opening to a sea-related ritual.

Much of weather lore concerns the warning signals for rain. The following rhyme is from tree lore and is considered a seasonal guide or predictor of rainfall. It is based on the order in which trees blossom for the season:

> *"Ash before Oak,*
> *We're in for a soak.*
> *Oak before Ash,*
> *We're in for a splash."*

MAGIC BY THE SEASIDE

Magic of the ocean has old roots. Fishermen and sailors have given us centuries of folk beliefs, legends, and folktales. Much of the ways of the sea are based on the physical effects of the tides, which are closely linked to the phases of the Moon. Tides work in approximately twelve-hour cycles but are correlated to the twenty-eight-day cycles of the Moon as well.

An incoming tide (referred to as flow) correlates to a waxing Moon, while the outgoing tide (ebb) correlates to the waning Moon, though both ebb and flow occur twice a day in physical terms. In the Charles Dickens novel *David Copperfield,* the character Mr. Jarvis dies as the tide goes out, illustrating a common fisherman's belief that the spirit goes out with the tide.

Magical tools may be brought along for acts of sea magic, or objects can be gathered at the seaside for spontaneous ritual. Quite often, no implements are required at all for this sort of magic, as the ocean and its relation to the spirit of the magic user can be quite sufficient.

High tide is a good time for sea magic because it correlates symbolically to the full moon, while low tide correlates to the new moon phase. Although there are situations where a new moon is appropriate in magic, the low tide is a time of low power. It can, however, be a good time for meditation, introspection, and seeking information from past lives. The time of strongest power would be when the high tide coincides with an actual full moon.

In any given seaside location, there are two high tides and two low tides in a twenty-four-hour period. You can chart the times for these tides from information given in local papers, libraries, or sport and fishing shops. From a practical point of view, it is particularly important to be aware of tides if you are performing your ritual on a stretch of beach, as you could find your altar suddenly swallowed up in the flow or even find yourself trapped against a rocky cliff side as the beach disappears beneath the rising tide.

One must remember that time frequently runs differently when in ritual trance. More than one person has suddenly found the waves swirling around their ankles unexpectedly while their thoughts were distracted. If you plan to use the time of an incoming tide to build power in your ritual, be sure you know exactly how far the tide will come up on your chosen beach! Some can disappear completely.

Despite its salt, sand, and other apparent "impurities," the sea is very good for cleansing, purifying, and trance rituals. One simple spell for spiritual cleansing in the sea is to let small waves splash over you and make a simple statement, such as, *"I am renewed."* As always, water safety is paramount. This sort of ritual should be saved for a familiar beach where you are used to swimming; potential riptides need to be considered, too.

An easy way to obtain trance is to sit on the beach and listen to the natural rhythms of the waves crashing. This can be done with eyes closed (again, know your tides!). A different sort of trance state can be achieved by watching the reflection of the full moon on the ocean and projecting a magical wish into the wavering forms in the reflection of light. With some practice, one can learn to use the release of energy in the crashing waves to magnify power for any spell.

A basic sigil spell can be performed by writing the need or a symbol that represents the desire into wet sand near the tide line during flow and chanting a simple ritual incantation over the space as the tide washes the image away, but remember that the tide is in waxing phase, so you'll want to use this for a positive spell that brings something into your life (rather than something to wash away).

CHANTING A WATER SPELL

One of the oldest images of witchcraft is that of a woman (usually a hag) chanting while stirring some sort of brew in a cauldron. This is, in fact, a very effective spell method, although the folktale images and cartoons have distorted it.

Water stirred in a pot on its own creates a visual vortex, a focal point that can lead to magical trance. A cooking spell that wishes goodness to come from the food might only involve a light trance, but other spells, whether performed in the traditional cauldron or a common saucepan, can use the method for much deeper levels of trance which might be required for more difficult magic.

Symbolic ingredients can be added to the water during the course of the spell, especially herbs that might be used for their specific scents as well as symbolism. Items that symbolise the spell's objective are certainly appropriate. I have yet to meet a witch or magician who actually uses eye of newt, toe of frog, or bat wings as in the cartoons and on *The Addams*

Family, but these are actually code names for certain herbs. Eye of newt, for example, is mustard seed.

Hopefully, I don't have to caution anyone that breathing in the fumes of poisonous ingredients on the simmer can be deadly, or that fire safety must be maintained when cooking despite trance states. Use common sense!

The cauldron method is good for charging binding spells, luck spells, and many other purposes that might involve submersing a talisman or symbolic construction of some form into the "magical stew." Again, know your materials and whether submersion would damage them.

Water spells can have terrific force behind them if one evokes the more potentially violent aspects of Water, but, in general, working with Water spirits brings a serene tranquillity into an act of magic. However, the magic user must be wary of slipping into depression if there is prolonged work exclusively with Water. If this should begin to occur, an uplifting ritual involving Air or Fire is strongly recommended. Most often, balancing the elements is best, but there are always exceptions where a focus on a specific element is appropriate to the purpose.

Water promotes spiritual cleansing. Often, it is the emotions that are subject to this process. The spirits of Water reflect this association with emotion in their nature and are generally inclined to react when they are called, and sometimes when they are not. Water draws the practitioner of magic deep into the realms of their own strong emotions, sometimes into places of darkness where many fear to tread. It is this quality of Water spirit magic that begs for the controls that are present in an act of formal ritual.

WORKING WITH AETHERIAL ELEMENTALS

In day-to-day magics, one usually thinks of directing interaction with spiritual entities towards spirits of the basic four elements, with the exception of God and Goddess invocations or evocations.

However, Aetherial spirits are naturally drawn to any act of magic, and it is often their presence interacting with the magic user's own spirit that creates a "spirit buzz," which many people experience during the performance of magic. This, in turn, elevates spiritual awareness in the magic user and is one good reason to devote a magical working to a chosen deity rather than leaving the magic open to attracting any random entity.

Dealing directly with Aetherial spirits is usually not as localised as with the other elements, with the exception of holy places. Spirit is everywhere rather than being attached to specific rocks, trees, bodies of water, or other material elements. However, it is often easier to attune to Spirit in a relaxed and uninterrupted setting. An experienced magician might well be able to "tune out" the noise of the world, even in a busy hospital emergency room in a pinch, but finding a place of quiet contemplation is much more conducive to Spirit contact.

The imagination immediately conjures images of a quiet forest or meditation room with incense and candles, but a place of quiet contemplation can take many forms. In *The Magic of Findhorn,* Paul Hawken describes how one of the founders of the Findhorn community, Eileen Caddy, used to sit quietly in the solitude of the public toilets to receive Spirit messages. Spirit does not always display glamour.

How to go about inviting or petitioning Aetherial spirits can vary. Some spirit forms can be invited into magical workings similarly to other elemental spirits as part of a ritual. Deity spirits can be petitioned through some form of prayer, as is practised by many of the world's known religions. Aetherial spirits respond easily, but whether they behave as one wishes is another matter.

Elemental spirits are all known for independence in their own unique ways. They are not forces to be controlled as one might read about in some old occult tomes but are entities who might be persuaded to be helpful if one uses the right approach. There are no guarantees. The magician who seeks to enslave a spirit entity of any sort is begging for trouble, even if they succeed.

Aetherial spirits are of the realm of Spirit itself and even less affected by human arrogance than the spirits of other elements. They will respond differently to someone who attempts to impose their own will onto them than to someone who is able to share their own spiritual essence in an ecstatic communion. Spirit works in a realm that feels like ecstatic love, almost sensual in its purity, yet innocent in its intent: love unspoiled by possession.

The world of Spirit may be sought in many ways, yet it is sometimes happened upon by accident. Many old tales tell of someone happening upon a spirit in a fairy mist or into the Land of Faery, which is known to have portals in such places as hillsides and fairy mounds. If one is attuned to Spirit, such happenstances are more likely.

Representations of Aetherial spirits are often found in homes and temples just as representations of god forms are found in churches. The world of Spirit has no physical boundaries, but the representation can form a focus or a link to the spirit form. In rare cases, statues have been known to bleed or shed tears, as if the representation actually contained the spirit.

Statues, plaques, and pictorial forms are common representations of gods, goddesses, Angels, and demons. Certain objects in nature are believed to attract or repel the comings and goings between Faery realms, such as the dobbie stones referred to earlier. Some spirits or servitors might form a close association with an object, like a piece of jewellery, thereby allowing the magic-user to directly contact the entity through the chosen object.

Purposes that might be appropriate for involving Aetherial entities would naturally be those things that deal with Spirit itself: self-transformation and guidance; the need for courage, hope, or comfort; or the invocations of qualities within ourselves that need emphasising.

Spells for these and other purposes are included in Chapter Eleven.

Folk magic that relates to Aetherial spirits tends to regard the fairies by whatever name they occur in each culture. It is a British custom to weave elder twigs into a headdress at Beltane to see spirits, and most Pagan religions regard Samhain as the time when the veil between the worlds is at its thinnest. Some believe that this allows one to communicate with loved ones who have passed on, while others believe that this thinning gives closer access to the Land of Faery.

Elder is also used to make flutes that are used to summon spirits, as well as being one of the woods used for making wands. The line between folk magic and formal ritual can become thin when dealing with Aetherial spirits. The medieval magician John Dee, for example, is well documented as dealing in Angel magic, but Angels also play a part in daily magics for those who are attuned to them (DeSalvo).

Aetherial spirits might be part of one's daily life through any form of devotion or recognition, even putting out milk for the fairies. Those who are closely attuned to Spirit tend to project an aura of calm authority and confidence. Self-mastery is behind the most effective forms of magic. It is through awareness of one's own spiritual power that a basis is formed to move into the realm of dealing with Aetherial spirits in formal ritual.

Chapter 6

FORMAL RITUAL

CONJURING SPIRITS IN RITUAL MAGIC is something most of us are familiar with, if not in our own practice, then at least from movies where such practices are sensationalised. In most Wiccan traditions, calling "guardians" is a common ritual practice.

I don't usually call quarters in my own rituals, as I identify more as a magician than with the religious side of Paganism, and my thought on the matter is, "Why should elemental spirits take that much interest in rituals performed by humans?" But I have participated in these rituals as well.

Supplication to local spirits has far-reaching tradition in many cultures ranging from Asia and the South Pacific to parts of Europe and across the American continent among Indigenous peoples. One might ask, "What is the nature of these spirits, and do they relate to the elemental spirits of an Animistic viewpoint?"

There are several different types of spirits involved in answering that question. In formal ritual magic, spirits summoned might be of an Aetherial aspect like Angels and demons, or they might be thought-form elementals (see Chapter Eight). The advantage to working with thought-forms or servitors is that they can be created to fill a specific purpose.

Some tribal cultures call the spirits of ancestors for assistance, while others might indeed seek intervention from the nature spirits we are primarily talking about. House spirits can also become participants in ritual, either on their own initiative or by invitation. Those who call quarter guardian spirits for indoor rituals might well create their own guardian spirits.

The choice of magical path or details of practices is an individual matter. I will try to apply what follows to a broad spectrum and suggest ways in which one might incorporate elemental spirits into any ritual format.

CALLING QUARTERS

While not all magical systems require calling quarters, many have some form of opening that involves forming a circle or banishing a space for the ritual. Some systems have predetermined wording for the opening and closing, which can make it difficult to incorporate additional material or to make subtle changes to accommodate an elemental invitation, particularly when doing group work.

If the magic user is working with a formula that they don't wish to change, items to represent the elemental spirits can be included among the altar decorations and magical equipment. Another possibility is to create temple spirits if a regular temple location is usually used.

To do this, an item connected with each of the elemental spirits would be kept in the appropriate quarter of the room. In most Western systems, this is North for Earth, West for Water, East for Air, and South for Fire. Aetherial spirit items would be kept on the altar itself.

There are alternative systems for the four directions. One Hereditary tradition places Earth in the South, as the land is below one's feet; Air to the North, as the sky is above; Fire in the East, where the Sun rises; but still Water to the West, where the vast ocean lies if you live in the UK. Those living on the east coast of any land mass might question this, and those living in the Southern Hemisphere sometimes reverse it all entirely!

EARTH

Items to include on the altar might include a crystal or other stone with a suitable attendant spirit, or an Earth spirit can be invited into an existing piece of equipment. A pentacle is traditional for Earth and can be made of wood, stone, or metal. Ceramic is a form of stone and is perfectly suitable. Decorative items in green and brown are also associated with Earth.

AIR

Air spirits can be effective as protective guardians as long as they are frequently invited to perform their function. To leave them unregarded for any length of time would likely result in them losing interest and the magician would have to start all over again.

As air is always all around us, Air spirits are conveniently at hand to call upon in any situation. The thought-form variety is the easiest to conjure and use for sending messages or delivering spells, but Air spirits are generally the most erratic and easily distracted, so much attention needs to be directed toward giving them focus while involving them in any magical purpose.

Items to place on the altar for an Air spell might include incense, sound recordings, a ritual flute, flowers, or anything else that contributes scent, feathers, and especially a wand.

Here we address what has become a thorny issue. The original magical equipment attributes for Air and Fire were Air as wand and Fire as sword. Many arguments have been made for the reverse of this, but the history is that in 1910, Arthur Edward Waite was writing a book on tarot and, in an effort to maintain a vow of secrecy, he reversed these two items. So, there you have it: all the tarot decks based on Waite's work are intentionally wrong.

Think about it: a sword is forged in fire and a martial instrument. The wand addresses the more cerebral side of magic, which is very much an Air attribute. Though I've heard some creative arguments for the reversed positions, the fact remains that it was and always has been an intentional deception.

Using chanting or accompanying musicians is also appropriate to Air rituals. If an Air guardian is to be invited, the magician might feel a need to focus on a specific location for the spirit. Using the wand to manifest a spirit in incense smoke is a method that goes back to medieval times and has been depicted in several sensationalistic old movies.

Creating or containing an Air temple spirit is most easily done by addressing the Air space itself, although a living room converted for magical purposes would then carry an "atmosphere" which can have drawbacks. It would also be affected by any visitors who entered the room, but if you have few visitors and don't mind freaking out intruders, this can transform even a small apartment into a spiritual place of relaxation for the inhabitants.

To keep something in the room that would hold the attention of an Air guardian, I recommend an incense burner that is used only for ritual and kept in a non-obvious place where visitors would not be likely to pick it up to admire it. Some form of daily ritual using the incense burner, even a few minutes to recognise the Air spirit, is highly recommended.

FIRE

Rituals involving Fire go back throughout recorded history and probably long before. Fire has always inspired awe and respect among ancient peoples, and this reverence for an element that represents so much raw power has only been partially lessened through modern science and understanding of the way that fire behaves.

Cultural rituals using Fire are numerous around the globe. In Britain, the tradition of hilltop bonfires still survives in some areas, although it no longer serves the purpose of a wartime warning system. Many traditions regarding Fire have survived in their original Pagan form despite widespread Christianisation.

Some traditions invoke Fire in its purification aspect as in the Christian sacrifice of lambs, which only now survives symbolically. The idea is that the Fire protects us from evil spirits, however, these are defined in any given belief system.

The energy of Fire is a consumptive force. It cleanses by consuming relentlessly until there is nothing left to consume. Just as a campfire will be fed from a fixed supply of wood, a Fire spell should have its resources—material or spiritual—predetermined and set aside so that the spell does not get out of control and consume the life force of the magician.

Midsummer bonfires, Sun god worship in all its forms, and the worship of Balder (also spelled *Baldur* or *Baldr*) from Norse origins are examples of Fire rituals and worship of Fire spirits.

On the Isle of Man on Mayday Eve, it was once the custom to burn all the gorse on the island in order to burn all witches and fairies who take refuge there after sunset (ouch!). Also on the Isle of Man, bonfires are lit on hills and blazing wheels rolled from the hilltops in representation of the legend of how the island came by its coat of arms.

The legend is that many centuries before the Christian era, the island was inhabited by fairies. A blue mist hung continually over the island, which prevented mariners from seeing or even suspecting that an island was so near as their ships passed by. This continued until a few shipwrecked sailors were stranded on shore.

As they prepared to build a fire on the beach, they heard a fearful noise that issued from the dark cloud surrounding the island. When the first spark of fire fell into their tinder box, the fog began to move up the side of the mountain, closely followed by a revolving object that resembled three legs of men joined together at the upper thigh, spread so that they resembled the spokes of a wheel. The island was thereafter visible, at least part of the time. Some legends say that the mist is actually preserved by a perpetual fire that is kept by the fairies themselves.

The word "ritual" often calls up images of a formal altar, complete with such accoutrements as a wand, sword or athame, chalice, and pentacle, as well as the formal calling of spiritual guardians or spirits. Indeed, these trappings are commonly used in some form in many ritual traditions as well as by independent practitioners of the *Arts Magical*.

The calling of spirits in some manner is well known in ritual magic, but the calling of Fire spirits, in particular, is subject to dramatic images from occult-ish B movies and Dennis Wheatley novels. The more creative magician can make good use of these theatrical mental images when introducing the element of Fire into any ritual.

Way back in the early 1990s, I witnessed a very dramatic quarter opening for Fire in a large group ritual at a private camp. The participants came from a spectrum of traditions and had been individually recruited for this ritual event. Three people were chosen to represent each of the elements and to dramatise the opening of their quarter in original ways.

When it came to opening the quarter for Fire, the trio, skyclad and painted red, jumped out suddenly, seemingly from nowhere, dancing like flames and shouting their incantation to the gods with the energy and flair that one might expect from the Fire element. It was impressive, to say the least.

Having related that, a magician can learn to stir this fiery spirit internally, without the necessity for elaborate dramatisation. A controlled and sober performance can build incredible intensity.

As with other elements, a Fire spirit can be invited into an object that is intended to represent Fire in ritual. Magical accoutrements that represent Fire might include an athame or sword, or a source of flame such as a candle or containment vessel of some description.

A representation of Fire can be kept in the appropriate quarter of a room used as a temple. Other decorations could be coloured red or other warm colours like orange and yellow. Shapes that represent wavy, flame-like movement could be taken into account when choosing items to inhabit that quarter of the room.

WATER

A standard ritual altar set-up will usually include a chalice to represent Water, but this is more often filled with wine than with water itself. Using a symbolic tool like a shell is fine. However, for a ritual specific to Water to be most effective, a source of actual water is highly recommended.

Items that have been given up by the sea can be appropriate ritual tools to represent Water. The ocean is the Great Source and the largest body of water on our planet. Shells are symbolic of the sea gods. Long spiral shells represent the God force, while rounded shells, like the cowrie shell, represent the Goddess. Holed stones found by the shore are also good representations of Water but can be difficult to find. Any item found in water that "speaks" to you might be appropriate for a Water quarter representation.

Calling the quarter for Water in a ritual that includes all the elements involves a lot of internal drama to invoke the emotional aspects of Water. Conch shells, as mentioned in the previous chapter, make excellent trumpets for announcing the opening of a ritual, though it might be overly dramatic for a private ritual when you're trying not to draw attention. Large public rituals, on the other hand, could benefit from the drama of such a calling in the Water quarter.

Usually, a simple invitation to the spirits of Water to participate in the ritual is sufficient, but an internal emotional appeal to them will bring the desired response. Without the element of emotion, a ritual easily becomes stagnant and inflexible, no more than a group of people reading words from a script. It is the element of Water that acts as a fluid medium to carry the spirit of magic forward through emotional responses of the participants. The person designated to call the quarter for Water has a rather heavy responsibility in this.

Water is an element of constant change, and it is the progressive flow of the mutable stuff of the world of Spirit that causes change to occur in accordance with will. The importance of the element of Water to any ritual is as clear as pure water itself.

If you choose to keep a representation for Water in a temple quarter, it is likely to be the West quarter decorated in shades of blue and sea green. West is the direction designated for Water in most magical systems in Western civilisation, including Hereditary witchcraft. In this, Water is consistent.

PROCEDURE

Exact wording and ritual choreography varies from one coven to another. Some make an elaborate drama of turning a group of participants in each direction. When practicing solitary, this is unnecessary. Exact wording for the call also varies, but will follow a basic formula something like:

"Hail to the guardians of the North, Lords of Earth; I do summon, call, and stir you up to witness our rites and to guard the Circle."

Followed by each direction in turn:

"Hail to the guardians of the East, Lords of Air; I do summon, call, and stir you up to witness our rites and to guard the Circle."

"Hail to the guardians of the South, Lords of Fire; I do summon, call, and stir you up to witness our rites and to guard the Circle."

"Hail to the guardians of the West, Lords of Water; I do summon, call, and stir you up to witness our rites and to guard the Circle."

To close the ritual, the guardians are dismissed back to their realms with a similar formula:

"Hail to the guardians of the North, Lords of Earth; I thank you for attending my rite, and ere you depart to your fair and lovely realms, I bid thee Hail and Farewell."

If others are participating, they would repeat, *"Hail and Farewell."* And, again, each direction in turn:

"Hail to the guardians of the East, Lords of Air; I thank you for attending my rite, and ere you depart to your fair and lovely realms, I bid thee Hail and Farewell."

"Hail to the guardians of the South, Lords of Fire; I thank you for attending my rite, and ere you depart to your fair and lovely realms, I bid thee Hail and Farewell."

"Hail to the guardians of the West, Lords of Water; I thank you for attending my rite, and ere you depart to your fair and lovely realms, I bid thee Hail and Farewell."

To incorporate the elemental spirit into the opening, you can add something like:

"And we invite (name of spirit), spirit of the crystal of Earth, to be guardian of the North in this and all our celebrations of the God and Goddess, so mote it be."

"And we invite (name of spirit), spirit of the censor of Air, to be guardian of the East in this and all our celebrations of the God and Goddess, so mote it be."

"And we invite (name of spirit), spirit of the sword of Fire, to be guardian of the South in this and all our celebrations of the God and Goddess, so mote it be."

"And we invite (name of spirit), spirit of the chalice of Water, to be guardian of the West in this and all our celebrations of the God and Goddess, so mote it be."

Another method is to have an elemental spirit dedication as part of the opening ritual that would include invitations for elementals for all the directions. Wording is an individual matter, and it must be remembered that elemental spirits respond best to spontaneity, but for the sake of an example, I offer the following:

"We invite the spirits of Earth, Air, Fire, and Water to become part of our circle, today and always, so long as this company shall gather in the name of the God and Goddess (or Lord and Lady)."

This statement can be elaborated on or kept simple. Next, whoever is leading the ritual would step to the North (or whatever direction is being used), lay hands on the crystal or other representative item, and attempt to attune to the spirit, then move deosil (clockwise) to the next position, which would be East in the standard formula, and do the same with the object representing Air, and so on through the other quarters. Others in the group follow, and each attempts to attune to each of the quarter spirits.

Once elemental spirit guardians are established through one of these methods, they can also be included in outdoor rituals by placing their representative objects in the appropriate directions in any space chosen. Alternatively, you might wish to invite local wild spirits when out of doors.

EARTH RITUALS OUT OF DOORS

Consideration must be given in any outdoor setting to the fact that you are essentially a visitor, even if you have a regular place to meet and perform your rituals. One must remember that the resident spirits are likely to have an opinion on the matter of your presence. You cannot swan into their territory and expect them to welcome you and join your ritual without question any more than you could barge into a stranger's house and invite them to join you for dinner at their table.

The first thing you should do when entering a space outdoors where you intend to perform a ritual is to ask the spirits of the place for permission. This can be done silently if you are on your own or formally in a group. Your answer will come as a feeling of rightness or wrongness about the situation.

If anyone in the group feels hostility, you must choose another place. This is where cultivating a relationship with place spirits is invaluable as an established, friendly place should pose no objection, though it is still polite to ask permission on each occasion just as you would normally ring a friend's doorbell each time you visit their home rather than barging in.

AIR RITUALS OUT OF DOORS

An Air spell performed out of doors has the potential to stir up some very strong energies. While any spell done outdoors will naturally attract the attention of wild elemental spirits, keep in mind that storms like hurricanes and tornados are powered by Air movements.

I recommend directing Air spirits to a very specific goal, such as a communication spell, and giving them very specific directions as to what contribution you had in mind for any magical working. Air spirits are the most unstable of any of the elements and unclear direction could easily get out of hand.

If you are new to working with elemental spirits in the wild, I recommend starting with the relatively stable Earth spirits. Even Fire and Water spirits are easier to contain than Air.

If you have attuned a quarter guardian for Air to an object (perhaps a censor), it can be brought along to use outdoors. If it is your intention to ask for help from Air spirits for a specific purpose, one thing to keep in mind is that outdoor rituals of any kind are open to windy conditions. Air spirits are easily excitable and are likely to respond with enthusiasm to your efforts to address them. Plan what items to include accordingly and give some thought as to how to secure them.

You can use words to try to keep the Air calm in your opening invocation with phrases like:

"In the still Air of evening, I call on the spirits of the Air to listen and to heed my words…" or a similar phrase that indicates stillness and attention.

I also recommend that the magic user get a feel for working with Air spirits indoors before attempting an outside ritual with them. It is a rare magician who can stir up a strong wind in an enclosed room!

FIRE RITUALS OUT OF DOORS

Choosing a location for an outdoor Fire ritual must include basic fire safety consideration, especially if it is to be something elaborate like a firewalk. A bonfire too close to trees, for example, would seriously upset the local Earth spirits! A sandy beach or an open field with all flammable material cleared away is good for a bonfire.

An ideal outside location for a Fire ritual might be a hot place like a desert or volcano mouth. Resident Fire spirits would certainly take an

interest, but, as with other location spirits, I recommend asking their leave to perform your ritual in their world. Also, I would hesitate to invite a volcano spirit to actually participate in the ritual and prefer a "bring your own" policy. Exciting volcanic activity brings its own hazards!

WATER RITUALS OUT OF DOORS

Once a ritual implement is established, one might wish to take it to an outdoor location in order to perform a formal ritual with the benefit of a natural source of water, or one might even wish to enter the water for the purpose of performing the ritual. Obviously, there will be practical considerations to this.

A calm source of water such as a pond can easily have an altar set up in shallow water or even laid out on a floating surface of some kind. The problem with this is that there is always a danger that the float could easily get disturbed, and all your ritual equipment could sink to the bottom!

Among the breaking waves in the ocean is no place to set up things you don't want to lose, although just above the water line is perfectly appropriate. Again, keep tides in mind and remain aware of whether they start to encroach on your ritual space! The magic user will have to decide whether it is worth bringing along such items or whether it might be preferable to call on the location spirits, combining natural magic with formal ritual. You might even seek out implements from the beach itself: a bit of driftwood for a wand, a shell to hold water, and a rock to represent Earth could be balanced by bringing only a candle to provide Fire.

As with all elements, location spirits should be asked for permission before performing a ritual in *their* place, even if it is a place you often use for this purpose or frequent for other reasons. A particularly strong ritual could be performed by bringing along your temple implements and also inviting the local spirits to join in. Water spirits are just as full of fun as other elemental spirits, although they "feel" different and can give the impression of being very deep and serious.

Remember that joy is one of the strongest emotions and can be invoked as part of an opening for a Water ritual that might include some splashing around. Again, be sure that your implements are secure or that you are prepared to go diving to recover them.

EARTH SPIRITS FOR A SPECIFIC TASK

Elemental spirits can be raised in ritual to perform a specific task or to become guardians of an ongoing task like temple spirits or protective spirits. Nature spirits already have a task in caring for their natural habitat and are not easily tamed for tasks that are only important to humans, yet in some cases, they can become very effective protective guardian spirits for a place in conjunction with our wishes.

Although using crystals for magic has come under a lot of criticism due to over-commercialisation and destructive mining techniques, they can be very effective for specific purposes (and can be obtained through reputable sources). Gemstones, both precious and semi-precious, have a long history of magical use, often correlating colour to planetary rulership.

Gemstones have an electromagnetic charge that varies from one type of stone to another, which is something a magic user can direct to a degree. It is far more effective when the magic user also appreciates the nature of the spirit of the stone and therefore seeks to work with the will of the spirit within rather than by force of their own will.

Quartz crystals have an especially strong electromagnetic charge and, as the most common colour is the clear stone, which represents purity, it is appropriate for clear-seeing or anything associated with purity of purpose. It also makes a good amplifier for other stones and works well in a grid.

Stones are not the only Earth-based material that might be set to a specific task. There is an old tradition of the wishing tree: making a wish and hanging a strip of cotton cloth on the branch of a tree. It must be cotton, no synthetics! The fabric will moulder, and the idea is that, as it disintegrates, the magic is set free to work. I find it quicker to ask the tree directly for favours.

Another method is to plant a seed or a seedling dedicated to a specific purpose. As the plant grows, the purpose unfolds. This is traditionally used for wishing blessings or protection on a child. More spells using each of the elements can be found in Chapter Eleven.

AIR SPIRITS FOR A SPECIFIC TASK

There are several possible reasons that one might wish to address Air spirits in ritual apart from calling a quarter guardian. You might want to seek inspiration, send a message to someone able to receive messages from elemental spirits, or use cerebral skills like studying or researching, for example.

The most obvious purpose for petitioning help from Air spirits is weather control. While there are limits to the influence we can have on natural weather patterns, in the grand scheme of things, moving a few clouds in a slightly different direction or calling up a breeze on a hot day doesn't interfere significantly with the natural randomness parameters of a weather pattern.

FIRE SPIRITS FOR A SPECIFIC TASK

A Fire ritual might be done with nothing but the fire itself, through stirring up the spirit of Fire through dance or, for the more practiced magic user, by stirring up strong emotions. Ideally, a Fire ritual should always be for a specific task, as Fire is far too volatile an element for just playing around.

Masking or shapeshifting rituals are associated with Fire, as they directly access the life-giving principle. Dance and dramatisation of underworld mythologies are effective methods to induce the spirit of Fire within ourselves.

Apart from creating temple guardians, purposes for evoking a Fire spirit are likely to involve some sort of definite action. Purification is one of the most basic purposes for Fire magic. As most of us know, fire can sterilise an object such as a hypodermic needle or knife that must be used in otherwise non-sterile conditions.

In agricultural communities of a more superstitious age, fires were usually lit to the windward side of fields so that the smoke passed over the corn for purification. Cattle were driven between two bonfires to keep them safe from disease.

In ritual, a magician often begins by lighting a purification incense such as dragon's blood or frankincense to purify the operation. In Alchemy, Fire represents the purification of the soul. The one drawback to purifying oneself with Fire is that one cannot immerse oneself in the element without inflicting considerable damage to oneself.

It is through the purification aspect that Fire can be employed for healing spells. A Fire spirit sent into parts of the body that are inflicted with some diseases can potentially "burn out" the affliction. The practice does have some dangers and should only be resorted to in extreme circumstances.

Any spell that is intended to cause action or change of some kind could theoretically be done with Fire, but I'd advise considering other alternatives before resorting to this most powerful and potentially dangerous of elements. If circumstances are such that Fire is deemed appropriate, set your parameters and proceed with confidence, not fear. Fire spirits can sense lack of control, which accompanies fear, and like a wild animal, they will react accordingly.

WATER SPIRITS FOR A SPECIFIC TASK

Besides cleansing, purification, fertility, healing, or anything involving the emotions, Water rituals might be used for any purpose that makes use of the subconscious. In fact, nearly any purpose that magic might be used for can be approached through Water. It is a matter of approach and attitude.

Like crystals, water carries electromagnetic energy, but water is fluid and, although it can be contained to an extent, it tends to seep or find other ways to free itself from constricting parameters. This is something to bear in mind when working with Water spirit energies.

Some purposes are very appropriate to Water rituals such as seeking pleasure, friendship, marriage, or happiness in any form. Spells for sleep, lucid dreaming, or performing psychic acts are also appropriate to Water. Sleep spells in particular benefit from the use of a Water spirit, as these spirits naturally wish to draw one into the depths of the subconscious, but caution should be exercised as this tendency could go too far and one does wish to awaken eventually.

Some people believe that water that is kept in coloured jars takes on the corresponding quality of the colour used and that drinking the water brings that quality into oneself. This can be done with ordinary tap water, but some purists believe that pure spring water is required for best effect.

Some forms of negative magic are also appropriate to Water. Cursing, for example, is something that requires a great deal of emotion. It is easy to lose control of parameters in negative magic, and for that reason alone, it is not to be done lightly. Also, any act of magic, especially one that involves Water, works through the magic user and what is sent out will also affect the spellmaker.

A simple form of sigil spell can be used for many magical purposes involving Water. If you save a piece of driftwood from a visit to the seaside, it can be taken home and a sigil drawn on it. This is a variation of the method in the previous chapter where a sigil is drawn in the sand to be washed away by the sea, but a more elaborate sigil can be constructed and carved into the driftwood. After a charging ritual, the driftwood can be returned to the sea as the tide goes out or can be destroyed in a bonfire.

The ocean is generally very co-operative in providing treasures from its depths that we can safely collect without disturbing any form of ecological balance. Inland sources of water might be less forthcoming, but it is a simple matter to take an item to a chosen source of water, wash it, and perform a dedication ritual to attune it to the source of water.

Much of the magic of Water works in the realm of symbols, just as our minds translate our subconscious thought patterns into secret messages in dreams. The use of symbols of any kind, particularly in the most abstract sense, is very appropriate to Water.

Water is the element of change, yet its basic qualities remain consistent throughout the changes. Even if conditions such as freezing or vaporising transmute water into a solid or gaseous form, when left to rest in normal conditions, it will return to its original fluid form. Water can be knocked about by tides, items entered into it, wind, or any number of external influences, yet left to rest, it will calm itself at a slow but steady rate until it is perfectly still. Water in all its forms seeks to compensate for any amount of interference, even in an environment like the ocean where interference from the Moon's pull is never-ending.

It is through learning to shape the use of emotional energy very much in the pattern of actions of natural water that the magician can learn to harness its power. To call an emotion at will or to calm one's emotions when required by circumstances are more difficult tasks than they might sound, but are inherent lessons that any magic user must learn to master if one's magic is to have any control.

AETHERIAL SPIRITS IN FORMAL RITUAL

When it comes to ritual, Aetherial entities are a completely different realm from the basic four elements. Ways in which to invoke or evoke these spirits vary widely depending on the tradition, path, system, or religious beliefs of the magic user. In Wicca or some paths of witchcraft, a calling of quarters is often followed by a call to god(s) and goddess(es), sometimes using specific names for these entities.

Conversely, in both ritual magic(k) and nature religions, a chosen deity or other Aetherial spirit might solely be invoked or evoked. To be clear, to invoke an entity is to call it into oneself, effectively allowing a temporary possession. To evoke is to call the entity hither without opening oneself up to this personal occupation. In common language, the word *invocation* is generally used for any calling or chant directed at a spiritual entity, though most often what is actually intended is technically an *evocation*.

There is a broad spectrum of practices, ranging from petitioning an entity through prayer to the Enochian calls of John Dee, which are intended to call Angelic presences. Demonic presences conjured through the erudite rites described in the *Necronomicon* or *The Goetia* are creatures of Spirit, as are the legendary denizens of the Land of Faery. We get into the area of belief here, but in calling, invoking, or evoking entities of Spirit, one should always keep in mind that, whatever you believe these spiritual essences to be, they are very powerful and not to be played with lightly.

The rituals of magical orders like the Golden Dawn and the Ordo Templi Orientis (OTO) are designed especially for dealing with some of these powerful spirit forms. However, joining a magical order is a serious business, is often not easy to do, and is not an appropriate step for everyone. Also, the quality of practice varies from one chapter to another. I recommend caution in handing over authority to any aspect in your own life to any group or organisation without assessing their actual value thoroughly.

Those who practice solitary or primarily nature-based religions can learn much about the methods of these orders and may find the information useful. (Some good source materials are listed in the bibliography.)

For purposes of this chapter, I will assume belief in all forms of Spirit. A Christian Angel is as valid to the person who works with that

spirit form as Dora Van Gelder's Devic Angels are in her hierarchical interpretation of Faery in *The Real Word of Fairies*. Individuals may interpret Spirit in different ways and imagery, but the nature of Spirit remains consistent throughout variations in perspective.

Purposes for working with Aetherial spirits might include petitioning a particular spirit entity for assistance in a personal concern in the material world or for adding strength to an act of magic. An individual or group might seek communion with spiritual entities as a way of bringing their own inner nature closer to that of Spirit. Self-transformation is one of the best-known Alchemical concepts and this is often approached through affinity with Spirit in some form.

Spirit permeates all things, but a house or temple deity or favoured form of spirits might be attracted by a representation such as a statue or pictorial image. Such an idol (idolatry) can be kept on an altar or put away between rituals, or even serve as decoration in the home or temple. In a temple where a group habitually works, there will usually be caretakers of such icons who will see to their safety.

An icon can also be transported outdoors for work closer to nature if one prefers. Those who work directly with nature spirits may choose to practice with only what nature provides, directly worshipping the trees and stones of the Earth, as well as the habitats of the other elements.

The attitude the magic user takes for evoking a spirit is likely to vary according to the nature of the entity. A magician may evoke an Angelic entity with reverence, while practitioners of some fairy traditions are more likely to call the Sidhe with a light attitude and someone calling up Goetic daemons might take a more dramatic stance.

The practices of some of these paths require specific study and dedication that exceeds the scope of this book, but again, I have included source material in the bibliography.

Much of the art of working with Aetherial spirit magic lies in using symbols and resonances. In the realm of Aether, words and images have great power. The formal structure of ritual is a medium through which words and images can be focused on intent. In the next chapter, we will look at magical correspondences and how they can be used in ritual as well as in elemental spirit magic closer to nature.

Chapter 7

CRADITIONAL SYMBOLS AND MAGICAL CORRESPONDENCES

Associations and correspondences among various things in nature are a human invention and unlikely to have much meaning to elemental spirits, but they do serve as good models for a magic user to get a feel for the interconnectedness of all things.

An elemental spirit that stirs up a strong wind might think of itself only as a spirit rather than as an Air spirit, but our association of the spirit with its medium causes a form of recognition between us and the spirit we wish to address, if that is our intent, in a way that is similar to calling someone by their name.

Elemental spirits have historically been of interest to magicians and Alchemists who recognise associations between things. One might reasonably ask what value there is in including this information in a book that is primarily about elemental spirits, but I do so because this is also a book about magic. This chapter serves as a reference that could be of use in creating your own spells, regardless of what path you follow.

Correspondences are part of what constitutes the esoteric knowledge of a magician. Though some of the information might seem "made-up" by historical magicians, they had reasons behind deciding why one thing relates to another or is associated with a specific energy.

For example, if you are choosing a stone to use in a spell to help with a material situation like finding a job, you know that you are working with the Earth element, that a green stone is appropriate for the purpose, and that this correlates with the day Friday. However, Friday is ruled by Venus, who is more appropriate to love spells, and Jupiter, who rules Thursday, is more appropriate to the purpose. As Jupiter is associated with the colour blue, the chosen stone might be a bluish-green for this particular spell, though I would choose brown for its Earthy qualities.

Those who have studied old ritual magic books like those of A.E. Waite will know that this can all get very complicated, to the point where you have to perform your spell on a specific day, at a specific phase of the Moon, and under favourable aspects of several planets at the appropriate hour.

Most magic users dealing with elemental spirits will agree with me that this degree of planning associations and correspondences is unnecessary. However, with knowledge of correspondences in general, we can get ourselves into the appropriate state of mind for magic and incorporate some correspondences that we feel are conducive to projecting our intent and communicating with the elemental spirits whom we hope to include in our spells.

With this in mind, I offer the reader some basic charts and lists that will be familiar to some already, but which are sufficiently of value to include as reminders and a central reference for those who do not wish to peruse a library full of reference books to incorporate these correspondences into their magic.

One of the most basic systems of correspondences involves assigning metals and colours to the planets as follows:

PLANETS	METALS	COLOURS
Sun	Gold	Gold, Yellow
Moon	Silver	Silver, White
Mercury	Quicksilver	Grey, Neutral
Venus	Copper	Green
Mars	Iron	Red
Jupiter	Tin	Blue
Saturn	Lead	Black

This system was created at a time when only seven planets were known to astrologers. Gemstones have also been correlated to these seven planets as follows:

PLANETS	GEMSTONES
Sun	Diamond, Topaz
Moon	Pearl, Moonstone
Mercury	Crystal Quartz, Opal
Venus	Emerald, Agate
Mars	Ruby, Any Red Stone
Jupiter	Sapphire, Amethyst, Carnelian
Saturn	Onyx, Dark Blue Sapphire

Of course, we have discovered the outer planets since this system was devised, which renders it incomplete, but simplifies the associations of planets in astrology.

ASTROLOGICAL CORRESPONDENCES

Cardinal Signs	Action, Drive, Initiative, Motivation	Aries, Cancer, Libra, Capricorn
Fixed Signs	Determination, Persistence, Stability, Self-Reliance	Taurus, Leo, Scorpio, Aquarius
Mutable Signs	Adaptability, Changeability, Flexibility, Versatility	Gemini, Virgo, Sagittarius, Pisces

Fire Signs	Inspirational	Aries, Leo, Sagittarius
Earth Signs	Physical	Taurus, Virgo, Capricorn
Air Signs	Mental	Gemini, Libra, Aquarius
Water Signs	Emotional	Cancer, Scorpio, Pisces

BASIC ATTRIBUTES OF SUN SIGN SYMBOLISM

Aries	Initiative	Libra	Balance
Taurus	Steadfastness	Scorpio	Determination, Passion
Gemini	Duality, Mental Energy	Sagittarius	Adventure
Cancer	Maternal Caring	Capricorn	Career, Personal Gain
Leo	Pride, Generosity	Aquarius	Idealism
Virgo	Organisation	Pisces	Peace, Calm Emotions

HOUSES OF THE HOROSCOPE

1 Personality and Appearance

2 Money and Possessions

3 Mental Capacities, Knowledge, Self-Expression, and Short Journeys

4 Childhood Environment

5 Children, Pleasures, Love Affairs, Risks, and Speculation

6 Health, Volunteer Work, and Services Rendered

7 Close Relationships in Marriage, Love, and Business

8 Death, Legacies, and Inheritance

9 Religious and Philosophical Views, Foreign Travel, and Dreams

10 Career, Status, Reputation, and Responsibilities

11 Friends, Social Life, Hopes, Desires, and Ambitions

12 Enemies, Secrets, the Unconscious Mind, and Limitations

ALCHEMICAL CORRESPONDENCES

Much of the concept of magical correspondences is based on the Alchemical philosophy of First Matter. This concept is based on the precept that the four elements—Fire, Air, Water, and Earth—were initially developed from First Matter.

Each of these four elements combined two of the four primary qualities that exist in all things: hot, cold, wet, and dry. Fire is hot and dry, Air is hot and wet, Water is cold and wet, and Earth is cold and dry. Hebrew magic assigns similar attributes to the four elements in the Tetragrammaton:

Yod	Fire	Hot and Dry
He	Water	Cold and Wet
Vau	Air	Hot and Wet
He	Earth	Cold and Dry

Alchemical theory accepts that everything is made of the four elements, and the differences between objects or materials are caused by the differing proportions in which the elements are combined within them. If one of the qualities of an element is altered, it turns into a different element.

When Fire (which is hot and dry) loses its heat, it becomes cold and dry and changes into Earth, becoming ash. When Water (which is cold and wet) is heated, it becomes hot and wet and changes into Air (vapour).

This theory is essential to Alchemy because it allows the possibility of transmutation. Note in modern chemistry how changing molecules in the basic structure of an atom can change the nature of the atom. Much research is ongoing to perfect a method of separating the hydrogen and oxygen molecules in common water (H_2O) to make hydrogen-based rocket fuel.

The Medieval Alchemists attributed correspondences to the basic elements for the Philosopher's Stone as follows:

Sulphur	Soul	Male	Fire
Mercury	Spirit	Male-Female	Air and Water
Salt	Body	Female	Earth

Hebrew letters come up in magic rather often and have correspondences attributed between them and tarot trumps, as well as elements, planets, and zodiac signs.

Path No.	Tarot Trumps	Element, Planet, or Zodiac Sign
1. Aleph	0. Fool	Air
2. Beth	1. Magician	Mercury
3. Gimel	2. High Priestess	Moon
4. Daleth	3. Empress	Venus
5. He	4. Emperor	Aries, Mars
6. Vau	5. Hierophant	Taurus, Venus
7. Zayin	6. Lovers	Gemini, Mercury
8. Heth	7. Chariot	Cancer, Moon
9. Teth	8. Strength	Leo, Sun
10. Yod	9. Hermit	Virgo, Mercury
11. Kaph	10. Wheel of Fortune	Jupiter
12. Lamed	11. Justice	Libra, Venus
13. Mem	12. Hanged Man	Water
14. Nun	13. Death	Scorpio, Mars
15. Samekh	14. Temperance	Sagittarius, Jupiter
16. Ayin	15. Devil	Capricorn, Saturn
17. Pe	16. Tower	Mars
18. Sade	17. Star	Aquarius, Saturn
19. Qoph	18. Moon	Pisces, Jupiter
20. Resh	19. Sun	Sun
21. Shin	20. Judgement	Fire
22. Tau	21. World	Saturn

ASSOCIATIONS BETWEEN
CREATURES, PLANTS, AND COLOURS

CREATURES	PLANTS	COLOURS
Man, Eagle	Aspen	Pale Yellow
Ape, Ibis, Swallow	Vervain, Palm	Yellow
Dog	Hazel, Almond	Blue
Dove, Sparrow, Swan	Rose, Myrtle	Emerald Green
Ram, Owl	Geranium	Scarlet
Bull	Mallow	Red-Orange
Magpie	Orchid	Orange
Crab, Turtle	Lotus	Amber
Lion	Sunflower	Greenish-Yellow
Virgin	Snowdrops, Lily	Yellowish-Green
Eagle	Oak, Poplar	Violet
Elephant	Aloe	Emerald Green
Snake, Scorpion	All Water Plants	Deep Blue
Scorpion, Wolf	Cactus	Greenish-Blue
Centaur	Rush	Blue
Goat, Ass	Thistle	Indigo
Horse, Bear, Wolf	Absinthe, Rue	Scarlet
Man, Eagle, Peacock	Coconut	Violet
Fish, Dolphin	Opium Poppy	Crimson
Lion, Sparrowhawk	Sunflower, Heliotrope	Orange
Lion	Orange-Red Poppy, Nettle	Orange-Scarlet
Crocodile	Ash, Yew, Cypress	Indigo

Our seven-day week originates from the calendar of the Babylonians, which in turn is based on a Sumerian calendar dated to the twenty-first century BC. Seven days corresponds to the time it takes for a moon to transition between each phase: full, waning half, new, and waxing half. The Roman calendar is based on the Babylonian and was further refined to the Julian calendar in 46 BC, and in 1582, the modern (Gregorian) calendar was devised ("Babylonian Calendar"). The seven planets known to Medieval magicians were named for Roman gods and goddesses, but, over time, the names of Norse gods have been added to some of the associations of the days of the week.

Day	Planet	God/ess	Colour
Sunday	Sun	Sol	Gold, Yellow
Monday	Moon	Minerva	Silver, White
Tuesday	Mars	Tiw	Red
Wednesday	Mercury	Woden	Grey
Thursday	Jupiter	Thor	Blue
Friday	Venus	Freya	Green
Saturday	Saturn	Saturnus	Black

Colour correspondences vary from one book of magic to another, but earliest sources present just two distinct systems. One is sequential, following the rainbow spectrum across the zodiac. The other is based on personality traits associated with the signs and incorporates other correspondences and associations:

Sign	Personality Colour	Sequential Colour
Aries	Bright Red	Red
Taurus	Yellow	Red-Orange
Gemini	Azure, Light Blues	Orange
Cancer	Green, Blue-Green	Amber
Leo	Orange, Gold	Greenish-Yellow
Virgo	Indigo	Yellowish-Green
Libra	Crimson	Emerald Green

Sign	Personality Colour	Sequential Colour
Scorpio	Deep Red	Greenish-Blue
Sagittarius	Purple	Blue
Capricorn	Grey	Indigo
Aquarius	Electric Blue	Violet
Pisces	Lavender	Crimson

Colour meanings are useful for all sorts of purposes. Ritual candles in particular are often chosen for colour associations.

Colour Meanings

White Protection, Purification, Peace, and Truth

Green Healing, Money, Prosperity, Luck, and Fertility

Brown Physical Objects, Healing for Animals, and Houses and Homes

Pink Emotional Love and Friendships

Red Sexual Love, Passion, Energy, Enthusiasm, and Courage

Yellow Intellect, Clairvoyance, Divination, Study, Learning, and the Mind

Purple Power, Authority, and Healing Deadly Diseases

Blue Healing the Mind, Meditation, and Tranquillity

Orange Strength, Attraction, Changes, and Luck

Black Absorption of Negativity, Destruction, Reversing Spells, and Hidden Knowledge

Trees

Certain trees are associated with Air spirits in particular. The alder is traditionally used for making whistles and flutes for summoning spirits, and the hazel and yew have been traditionally used for making wands. The hazelnut is the repository of all knowledge in Irish mythology, and the bourtree is sacred to Air spirits as it provides berries to feed birds in the winter.

Associations and symbols of any kind are representative of Air, as Air rules inspiration and the power of magic from the unconscious mind. Among the associations that affect us on this level are the vibrations of colour and the medium of writing, particularly through the use of magical alphabets. These are very important in the use of sigil magic.

Many magic users construct their own magical alphabet, but will also use a few well-known historic or magical alphabets like Runes, Theban, and Ogham.

THEBAN ALPHABET

A	B	C	D	E	F	G	H	I, J

K	L	M	N	O	P	Q	R	S

T	U, V	W	X	Y	Z	.

OGHAM CHARACTERS

B	L	F	S	N
Beith	Luis	Fearn	Saille	Nion
(Birch)	(Rowan)	(Alder)	(Willow)	(Ash)
Dec. 24 - Jan. 20	Jan. 21 - Feb. 17	Mar. 18 - Apr. 14	Apr. 15 - May 12	Feb. 18 - Mar. 17

H	D	T	C, K	Q
Huath	Dair	Tinne	Coll	Ceirt
(Hawthorn)	(Oak)	(Holly)	(Hazel)	(Apple)
May 13 - Jun. 9	Jun. 10 - Jul. 7	Jul. 8 - Aug. 4	Aug. 5 - Sept. 1	

M	G	NG	Z	R
┼	╪	≢	≣	≣
Muin	Gort	Ngéadal	Straif	Ruis
(Vine)	(Ivy)	(Reed)	(Blackthorn)	(Elder)
Sept. 2 - Sept. 29	Sept. 30 - Oct. 27	Oct. 28 - Nov. 24		Nov. 25 - Dec. 22

A	O	U	E	I
┼	╪	≢	≣	≣
Ailm	Onn	Úr	Eadhadh	Iodhadh
(Fir)	(Gorse)	(Heather)	(Poplar)	(Yew)

Runic Alphabet (Norse)

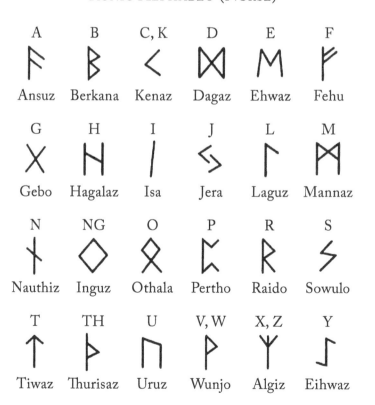

A	B	C, K	D	E	F
Ansuz	Berkana	Kenaz	Dagaz	Ehwaz	Fehu

G	H	I	J	L	M
Gebo	Hagalaz	Isa	Jera	Laguz	Mannaz

N	NG	O	P	R	S
Nauthiz	Inguz	Othala	Pertho	Raido	Sowulo

T	TH	U	V, W	X, Z	Y
Tiwaz	Thurisaz	Uruz	Wunjo	Algiz	Eihwaz

THE KABBALAH

In the construction of spells, correspondences give us material to work with, and poetry is one way to focus the intent with the use of words, which is why so many old spells use rhyme and metre in their wording.

Recognising "vibratory" relations between objects, calendar events, and celestial movements may be an entirely human perception, but systems of correspondences work in magic. So long as it brings a result, there is value in it. That is what magic is all about: results.

Fire correspondences deal with the life force. Some of the mysteries of the magical world bring Fire to mind, like the Sephiroth of the Kabbalah, which are assigned to parts of the body.

1.	Kether	Crown	Top of Head
2.	Chokhmah	Wisdom	Right Brain
3.	Binah	Understanding	Left Brain
4.	Hesed	Mercy	Right Arm
5.	Gevurah	Judgement	Left Arm
6.	Tiphereth	Beauty	Torso
7.	Netzach	Eternity	Right Leg
8.	Hod	Glory	Left Leg
9.	Yesod	Foundation	Sexual Organ
10.	Malkhut	Kingdom	Feet
	Daath	Knowledge	Mouth

There is some variation from different sources, most notably Malkhut, which in a sitting position would correlate to the base of the spine, where Kundalini (sexual) energy initiates, for a Middle Pillar working in the Chakra system.

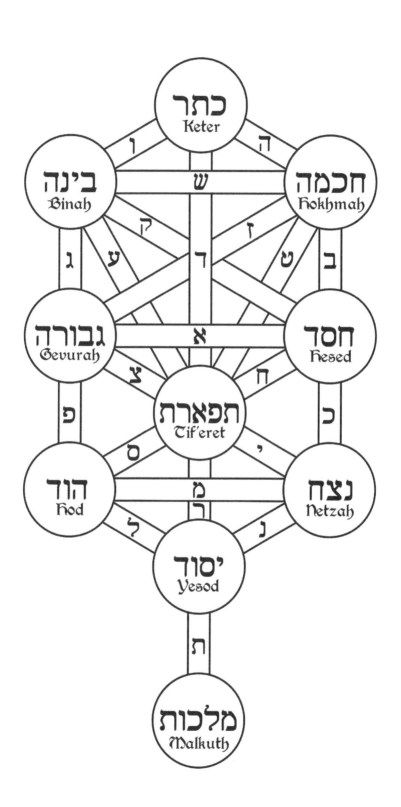

NUMEROLOGY

Numerology is an old system based on magical correspondences with numbers. The in-depth practice can get rather complicated, but the simple version that is available in a variety of books on magic is easily accessible and sufficient for our purposes.

Numbers represent progression and are useful as symbols of different energies. Understanding the properties of numbers is an important key to understanding the magic in nature, as fractal geometry has demonstrated using numbers in computer programmes to draw realistic trees, leaves, shells, and other items in nature. They are expressed in sound and colour in the form of wavelengths.

Many people fear numbers from early bad experiences in math classes, and they are better not used at all than incorrectly, but basic numerology requires nothing more complicated than a basic primary school knowledge of arithmetic.

To calculate your name number, add together the numeric value for each letter of your full name from the following chart:

1	2	3	4	5	6	7	8	9
A	B	C	D	E	F	G	H	I
J	K	L	M	N	O	P	Q	R
S	T	U	V	W	X	Y	Z	

Add together the individual digits of the resulting number until you have a single-digit result or the numbers eleven or twenty-two.

For example, Jaq D Hawkins looks like:

$$1+1+8 +4 +8+1+5+2+9+5+1= 45$$
$$4+5=9$$

Therefore, my name number is nine.

The meanings of name numbers are as follows:

ONE: Fixity of purpose and drive towards goal achievement. One-track-minded, self-assertive (sometimes even obstinate), and aggressive. Independent, do not take orders well but can be original and inventive.

Potential leaders. Resent advice and are not likely to follow it. Can be domineering.

Two: Soft, sweet-natured, quiet, tactful, and even-tempered. Love peace and harmony, and get their way through persuasion and diplomacy. Change minds easily, with a tendency to put things off. Can be deceptive.

THREE: Bold expression, versatile, and vivacious. Witty, charming, have sparkle, and are likely to succeed in life. Tend to be talented in the arts. Succeed without really trying through sheer luck and take things lightly. Spread efforts in too many directions.

FOUR: Efficient organisers, down to earth, steady, and respectable. Like routine, detail, and hard work. Can be stern and repressive. Moody. Hard-won success.

FIVE: Bright, clever, and impatient. Attracted to the unusual and bizarre. Loves travel and change in surroundings. Takes risks and is adventurous. Avoids responsibility.

SIX: Number of domesticity. Kind, balanced, and has many friends and a good home life. Loyal, idealistic, and conscientious. Long-term success through arts or teaching. Can be fussy and gossipy.

SEVEN: Number of scholars and philosophers. Natural recluse and a possible mystic. Dignified, serious, intellectual, and non-materialistic. Penetrating yet dreamy. Dislike being questioned or argued with.

EIGHT: Power, money, and material success or failure. Strong and practical. Rebellious with hard struggles. Eight is a spiritual number despite these material associations. Its symbol is a lemniscate on its side.

NINE: Mental and spiritual achievement. Idealistic, visionary, and romantic. Sympathetic and impulsive. Inspiring, strong-willed, and falls in and out of love easily.

ELEVEN: The number of revelation and for people to give their special message to the world. Subjective and live by their own inner

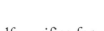

light and vision. Powerful personalities, given to self-sacrifice for their ideals.

TWENTY-TWO: Number of the spiritual master. These people are either successful, admired, and respected, or can turn to black magic or crime.

Next, add up your birth number. For example, 6th August 1987 would be:

$$6+8+1+9+8+7=39$$
$$3+9=12$$
$$1+2=3$$

Adding your name number to your birth number gives you your destiny number. Many people have made subtle changes in the form of their name to bring about a more fortuitous destiny number! Destiny number energies are:

ONE: Individuality, self-reliance, and possibly egotism

TWO: Relationships, attraction, emotion, and sympathy or antipathy

THREE: Expansions, increase, and intellect

FOUR: Realisation, possessions, and position

FIVE: Reason, logic, and domestic travel

SIX: Co-operation, marriage, reciprocity, and the arts

SEVEN: Contracts, agreements, treaties, and harmony or discord

EIGHT: Reconstruction, death, and a matter going out of one's life

NINE: Strife, enterprise, and division

Eleven and twenty-two can be interpreted from the name meaning list. One might notice that these lists correspond closely to the influences of the houses of the zodiac. It is through commonality of symbols that the workings of magic also correlate with nature and the universe.

INCENSE CORRESPONDENCES

Certain tree barks or woods have associations with magical intents when burnt. The following section includes some suggestions for making incense:

PROTECTION: Ash, bay, buckthorn, coconut, cypress, elder, gorse, hawthorn, hickory, holly, ivy, larch, mistletoe, mulberry, oak, palm, pepper tree, plum, pomegranate, quince, rose, rowan, sandalwood, wild service, wayfaring tree, witch-hazel

HEALING: Ash, aspen, bramble, horse chestnut, elder, eucalyptus, lime

INVOCATION: Alder, bamboo, buckthorn, yew

PURIFICATION: Bay, birch, bramble, broom, cedar, gum arabic (acacia), lemon, osier, tamarisk, willow

FERTILITY: Banana, birch, coconut, fig, mistletoe, oak, olive, orange, palm, pine, pomegranate, quince, willow

DIVINATION: Apple, ash, hazel, orange, poplar, rowan, witch-hazel. (Apple, ash, hazel, poplar, and rowan are also good for making runes)

LOVE: Apple, apricot, avocado, brazil, cherry, sweet chestnut, lemon, papaya, plum, prickly ash, rose, walnut, willow

PROSPERITY: Almond, horse chestnut, gorse

PLANETARY RULERSHIPS FOR INCENSE MAKING

Note that Pluto is still a planet for metaphysical purposes, regardless of the categorisations of NASA.

SUN *(self-integration):* Balsam, bay, benzoin, cashew, cedar, citron, frankincense, grapefruit, gum arabic (acacia), hickory, juniper, hemlock tree, lime, mistletoe, olibanum, orange, palm, pine, spruce, thuja, walnut, witch-hazel

MOON *(nature's rhythms, instinct, intuition, dreams):* Alder, aspen, bamboo, bergamot, broom, cassia, coconut, jasmine, lemon, linaloe, myrrh, olive, opoponax, osier, papaya, privet, sallow, sandalwood, willow

MERCURY *(communication):* Almond, ash, cassia, hazel, mace, mulberry, pecan, pistachio, pomegranate, rowan

VENUS *(unity, love, friendship):* Apple, apricot, avocado, banana, birch, bramble, cananga, cherry, damson, elder, guelder rose, hornbeam, magnolia, peach, pear, persimmon, plum, rose, rosewood, spindle, wayfaring tree, whitebeam, ylang-ylang

MARS *(action, war):* Dogwood, gorse, hawthorn, larch, pepper tree, prickly ash

JUPITER *(expansion, learning, wisdom):* Banyan, blackthorn, bo tree, cajeput, sweet chestnut, horse chestnut, clove, fig, fir, lime, linden, field maple, great maple, niaouli, nutmeg, oak, plane, tea tree

SATURN *(contraction, limitation, formation, obstacles):* Beech, buckthorn, elm, eucalyptus, holly, ivy, mimosa, poplar, quince, tamarind, tamarisk, wild service, yew

URANUS *(deviation and invention):* Cedar

NEPTUNE *(refining):* Ash

PLUTO *(transmutation):* Box and cypress

According to Dion Fortune in her novel *The Sea Priestess,* incense for the Fires of Azrael to bring insight into past lives and induce visions is made from 1 oz sandalwood chips, 1 oz crushed juniper berries, and 10 drops of cedarwood essential oil.

Other incense associations are:

- Cypress to allay grief and help heal the disabled
- Mistletoe to ward off evil
- Pine for purification
- Rose petals for healing

- Bay leaves and rowan leaves and berries to aid divination
- Gum arabic (acacia) for spirituality and purification
- Cedarwood for sweat lodges, purification, or to get rid of bad dreams

Symbols and associations to the subconscious mind are useful when dealing with skrying or dreams.

What are dreams, but symbols of our own subconscious' making? Books about dream symbolism are popular sellers, yet these subconscious symbols are unique to every person and cannot be categorised as easily as many dream dictionaries would suggest. Symbols may mean very different things to different people.

Some symbols recur frequently in different cultures. Spirals are one of the most common representations of any form of energy, including the life force, and are similar to the labyrinth designs that appear in many locations worldwide. It has often been speculated by archaeologists that these labyrinth designs represent the mysteries of life, which associates them with fertility.

Stars with varying numbers of points are also frequently found in widely diverse cultures, with great significance attached to the number of points and the specific construction of each form of star. For example, the five-pointed star used in the pentagram is representative of the five elements, including Spirit, and is also representative of man. Sometimes, the symbol appears with a drawing of a man overlaid, his arms and legs outstretched to fill the points below his head, which occupies the top point.

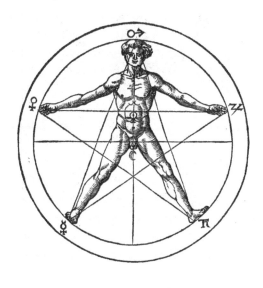

The Seal of Solomon, commonly used in Hebrew esoteric symbolism, is constructed of two triangles, one pointing upwards and the other pointing down. These triangles represent the concept of "as above, so below," which appears in many religions and magical philosophies.

Some of the most potent magic is accomplished when the magician has an abstract idea of their desires in mind and is able to leave the subconscious in control of the act of magic, allowing the symbolic work to be done within what Aleister Crowley referred to as "True Will." This allows the magic to manifest into an unconsciously decided result.

This requires a great deal of trust in oneself and in one's magic, as this sort of work is accomplished through the realm of what I call "natural chaos." Working with elemental spirits can be very chaotic because of how nature itself manifests.

Those who follow some paths of magic might recognise the names for spirits of the elements as follows:

Earth	Gnomes
Air	Sylphs
Fire	Salamanders
Water	Undines

These actually come to us from Alchemy, named by Paracelsus, though they are commonly used in various witchcraft and Wiccan traditions.

Oddly, the Celtic animal correspondences that would be more culturally akin to these systems are less often used.

NAME	ANIIMAL	CARDINAL DIRECTION
Cernunnos	Stag	East
Epona	White Mare	South
Mona	Sacred Cow	West
Artor	Great Bear	North

In this system, there is also an Aetherial association with the wolf, which leads Shamans into the otherworlds. These animals are considered to be the Guardians of Albion. The symbology might be used directly by some groups but is more often something that works on the intuitional level.

Animal spirit identification is intuitional by nature. It is known to have been used in tribal societies in many parts of the world. Unlike actual shapeshifting, which is associated with Fire, animal spirit identification is a method of accessing the subconscious by aligning one's thoughts with the nature of the chosen animal as it is understood by the Shaman, through its habits and whatever experience the Shaman has of the animal.

This clears the conscious mind and allows the more basic instincts to rise to the level of control. This might also be said of pathworking, although this is usually a guided process that turns over control to an outside entity. Both methods work with theta brain waves and both have potential for bringing forth some of the hidden aspects of ourselves that can be difficult to confront.

Semiotics is the science of signs and symbols. Apart from the representations of the elements mentioned in earlier chapters, some other symbols that are used in the construction of talismans (and for other purposes) include:

Acorn	Vigour, youthfulness, royalty, or prolonged effort preceding perfect achievement

Anchor	Hope, safe anchorage, or stability in a changing situation
Ankh	Egyptian symbol of creative power, bringing knowledge, or abundance and power
Arrowhead	Protection against evil
Bat	Health, wealth, love of virtue, long life, or happiness
Bell	Protection against evil
Caduceus (the wand of Mercury or Hermes)	Duality, balance of health, or eloquence of speech
Cornucopia	Plenty, good fortune, prosperity, and fruitfulness
Crescent	Protection from lunacy, success in love, happiness in motherhood, or the divine feminine principle
Cross (equal-armed)	Protection against evil or balanced energies
Eagle	Sharp sight, good fortune, dignity, and respect. Used to attract the favour of those in high places
Eye	All-seeing. A very powerful symbol in Egyptian magic
Fan	Authority and power, providing protection and safety when worn
Fatima's Hand	Hospitality, generosity, power, and divine providence
Frog	Egyptian symbol of life, health, and strength, particularly recovery after illness
Ladder	To overcome difficulties on the Earthly plane
Ladybird (Ladybug to Americans)	Good fortune and wealth
Lizard	Good fortune and good eyesight
Owl	Wisdom and learning
Palm	Triumph of good over temptation

Phoenix	Renewal and regeneration
Pinecone	Abundant benefits, health, power, or wealth
Salmon	Endurance, wisdom, increase, and expansion
Scarab	Creation, health, strength, and virility
Serpent	Regeneration, cycle of creation and destruction
Ship	Safe passage
Spider	"Spinning" wealth, shrewdness and foresight in business
Stork	Good weather or a birth
Vulture	Egyptian symbol for healing, power, and wisdom

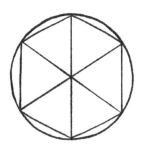

The Fryske (also known as *water witches*) are known for the symbol that still appears on many canal boats: a six-spiked wheel design. It is a religious symbol for them that attaches significance to the colours of the different spikes. Their rituals usually include the invocation of an elemental and placing of objects of appropriate colours in the appropriate directional quarter. These colours use a system that the Fryske have in common with the Druids. The correspondences are as follows:

North	Earth	Black	Winter	Midnight	New Moon
East	Air	Red	Spring	Sunrise	First Quarter
South	Fire	White	Summer	Midday	Full Moon
West	Water	Grey	Autumn	Sunset	Last Quarter

MAGIC SQUARES

Correspondences take on significant meaning when working in the world of Spirit. Spirit responds to the part of us that is of its own substance. In magic, we sometimes use a language of symbols that hold meaning to denizens of the Aetherial world because our knowledge of these systems of communication translates directly through our own spiritual essence.

Magic squares are a form of communication with the subconscious of the magician for the purpose of evocation of a specific spiritual form. They work in a pictorial sense, much like a sigil, but are based on a mathematical formation. *The Key of Solomon the King* by S.L. MacGregor Mathers is the most recognised source for extensive information on this method, but the basics are fairly simple.

A planetary square is chosen for the intended purpose, such as the square of Saturn which is:

4	9	2
3	5	7
8	1	6

Or Jupiter, which is:

4	14	15	1
9	7	6	12
5	11	10	8
16	2	3	13

In theory, the numbers in any row, including diagonally, should add up to the same total. Next, the name of a spiritual entity is chosen, and the letters worked out according to basic numerology. Then, you create a sigil for that entity by following the numbers on the planetary sigil like in a connect-the-dots puzzle. For example, Asmodeus, using the planetary square for Saturn results in:

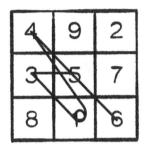 

This gives you Asmodeus' Saturn sigil, which is good for giving personal insight into one's own Saturnian nature. To use it, stare at it in meditation during the day and hour of Saturn while the Moon is waxing.

Planetary hours are worked out by assigning the planet for the day to the first hour after sunrise and continuing through the seven planets advancing one per hour. For example, if you were working on a spell for a legal situation, a strong Jupiterian energy would be beneficial, so doing the ritual on a Thursday either at the hour of dawn or another seven hours later would provide a strong Jupiterian influence.

Another useful correspondence to include here for spells performed out of doors is the traditional names of the Angels of the Four Winds, which appear on several tarot card decks and in Alchemical references:

East	Michael
West	Raphael
North	Gabriel
South	Uriel (also called Nariel)

One last correspondence I would like to include in this chapter is the Alchemical triangle:

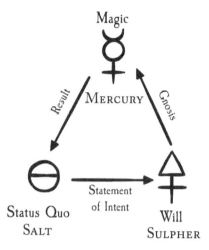

The mysteries of Alchemy are worth a book of their own, but this most basic principle works into a lot of magical symbols and practices. One of the most brilliant uses of this principle I've witnessed was in an opening and closing ritual wherein salt was sprinkled around the circle of participants to represent the current material situation.

The participants held indoor sparklers, except every third person, who held a votive candle. The sparklers were lit to release sulphur, thereby instigating change. We used charged water to represent the mercurial transmutation of events, then finished with salt again to represent new salt or the changed situation.

Correspondences can be used in many ways. You may wish to choose plants for a magical garden according to specific energies or directions, even planning a zodiac mandala with appropriate plants in each of the twelve divisions. Choosing colours or other decorative items for temple space or working with tarot for spell casting according to these associations might be desired.

Symbols—visual, audio, or stemming from any of the senses—are important to magic. They are used to access the subconscious for both ritual and divination, to align ourselves with those energies with which we are most attuned. They are also very useful in the formation of servitors, also known as thought-form elementals.

Chapter 8

Producing Element-Based Thought-Forms or Servitors

A THOUGHT-FORM ELEMENTAL is a spirit created out of the imagination of a magic user. There is an art to creating these artificial elementals, and the reader without experience of them should be made aware that there are some serious complications involved in actually exercising any control over them.

Thought-forms are essentially extensions of the soul or emotions of the magic user who creates them. However, that does not mean that the witch or magician automatically has control over them as one would have control over the movements of one's arms and legs. Thought-forms are creations of the mind and emotions, and who among us has complete control of our own thoughts and emotions?

One of the first questions to arise when discussing thought-forms is, "Are they real?"

Yes. They are real. The degree of effect they have on any given external medium is in direct relation to the amount of energy put behind their creation and sustenance, but the fact that thought-forms can have very definite effects on the material world has been proven to many an unwary soul, sometimes with very disturbing consequences.

The next question is, "Are thought-forms and servitors the same?"

Well, yes and no. The terms are often used interchangeably, but there is a subtle difference. Thought-forms are a semi-modern concept of magicians working from historical traditions where these artificial beings have been called homunculi, tulpa, and various other names.

Some forms, like the generally humanoid homunculus, require a physical "body" to be provided out of clay or some other substance. Others,

like the tulpa, exist only on the mental or astral level. Thought-forms might be used for a purpose like temple guardians and are often attached to physical objects for this purpose.

The term "servitor" came out of early nineteenth-century magic and refers to a spiritual entity created by the mind of a magician to perform a specific task, after which it is usually reabsorbed by the magician as a part of themselves.

The differences are subtle but worth noting. One might say that all servitors are thought forms, but not all thought-forms are servitors.

I cannot repeat too many times that a thought-form can and will behave independently, sometimes much to the chagrin of its own creator. The fact that magicians in certain periods of history have mistaken these elemental spirits for demons is more than the result of religious brain-washing. It is something that is easy to believe when the creatures get out of hand.

Some old tomes of magic (Mathers and Waite come to mind) insist that a magician must perform conjurations for such a creature from within a protected circle, commanding the "demon" to appear within a triangle outside of the circle in which it will remain imprisoned until released to perform its task.

The problem with conjuring an elemental in the form of a demon is that it will undoubtedly behave like one if given half a chance. This entire school of magical thought is long outdated and unnecessarily dangerous. Once you are able to accept that your thought-form is whatever you create it to be, you are better able to conjure a creature that will perform in the manner you actually had in mind.

CREATING A THOUGHT-FORM ELEMENTAL OR SERVITOR

Like most magical operations, this is best done in a ritual setting as it helps focus one's energies. A ritual should be done specifically for the purpose and not include any other matters that could distract or confuse the entity. This purpose should be very clearly thought out before you begin.

Open the ritual according to your usual practices, then focus your entire being on the purpose for your intended thought-form. If working in a group, every member of the group should be focused on the intent. It is helpful to direct focus to a specific location, either a place on the

floor where the manifestation of the spirit is desired (reminiscent of the tradition of focusing the spirit into a triangle) or a physical item. Leave room for all present to walk around the location or item, as circling around a central point creates spiral energy, which is conducive to the creation of all forms of life.

Some specific ritual suggestions will be included in Chapter Eleven, but feel free to adjust the examples to make them more personally meaningful or to create your own ritual to fit your specific purpose.

If, at any time during the ritual, you or any member of the group feels somehow "wrong" about it, the entire operation should be aborted and the ritual space thoroughly banished. This is very important. Choose your working companions wisely! In general, servitors are created by a lone magic user, though there have been exceptions. A group servitor is usually referred to as an *egregor*.

Once the entity has been created, it must be released to perform its function. This is followed by a closing and banishing as in any ritual, but in this case, the banishing should include specific banishings against residual energies forming into what one might call *fractal spirits*. These are small thought-forms that can form from the peripheral energy raised in ritual, particularly in group rituals, that can become more independent than your intended thought-form if left unregarded and free to develop in an uncontrolled manner.

Having created and released your thought-form, attention to its sustenance is now in order.

SUSTAINING A THOUGHT-FORM

Thought-form elementals exist on Aetheric energy, normally provided by their creator. Unlike their natural counterparts, they have no purpose connected to the natural world and are completely dependent on human input. However, as in nature, these artificial entities have survival instincts. Once a thought-form is created, it will generally continue to take spiritual energy from its creator until it is dissipated or reabsorbed.

The energy to sustain a single thought-form might go unnoticed, but sending armies of thought-forms off to do one's bidding could sap one's energy to depletion and lead to illness. It is always prudent to have a plan in place to reabsorb the entity (and, therefore, your own energy) once the purpose is accomplished.

If you wish to intentionally sustain your thought-form, you must effectively feed it. This is done either by replenishing its energy in repeated rituals or through continual contact with the purpose. Quarter guardians or an elemental that is created to help with divinations are good examples of relatively easy-to-feed thought-forms.

Dealing with thought-forms requires forethought and judgement. One must always keep in mind that these are not personal slaves as some old magic books might imply, but are essentially elemental spirits, much like their natural counterparts.

With that thought in place, your first action should be to decide exactly what purpose you want this elemental to serve. Does the purpose fall into specific elemental associations?

EARTH THOUGHT-FORMS OR SERVITORS

An Earth thought-form might be desired if you are performing magic for material purposes, such as money, health, or fertility. As with all things relegated to the Earth element, these purposes are rather grounded and stable and, therefore, the magically created elementals are comparatively "tame" and inclined towards stability. However, one should never take this quality for granted when dealing with any elemental spirit.

The most unreliable and potentially dangerous Earth-based purpose is money. We have all seen the old horror films that depict a magician performing a money spell for someone, usually accompanied by warnings that are summarily ignored, after which the heedless client is awarded a large sum of life insurance money because a valued loved one has just mysteriously died, or as an insurance payout after they have a life-changing accident.

This is not as far-fetched as the B-movie quality of these films might imply. *Always* be very specific when performing any sort of money spell whether or not any form of elemental is involved. You might want to specifically conjure an elemental to "influence" a job application or a specific game of chance. General money spells are inclined to follow the path of least resistance with no consideration of unwanted consequences.

By contrast, healing spells are generally safe. The only real danger involved in a healing spell is the possibility of giving too much of one's own energy or empathy to the point that the sickness or injury could rebound on the healer. This is also a consideration to keep in mind when performing fertility spells for someone else, especially for female practitioners.

From this perspective, a thought-form is a good choice for healing as it dissociates the healer from the patient, even though the elemental originates from the same source as direct healing energy, sort of like an astral firewall.

Apart from these common purposes for employing Earth thought-form elementals, there are other situations where an Earth elemental might also be usefully engaged. As well as temple guardians, Earth elementals can help when building something, making the job go well or become easier. This can also result in the elemental becoming a natural guardian of what has been built (a house or shed, for example).

Smaller projects could be anything from creating ritual implements that represent Earth to mundane objects that suit a personal hobby. As magic users, we know that a part of ourselves goes into everything that we do. To consciously send a part of ourselves into something we make or do is the most effective means possible to bring our magical selves into the operation.

AIR THOUGHT-FORMS OR SERVITORS

Setting a temple guardian for Air, even a thought-form, is most easily done through a combination of Earth and Air energies to ground it in place. A pure Air spirit cannot be contained and holding the spirit's attention long enough to befriend one is no easy task.

Air thought-forms can potentially be the most erratic of thought-form elementals. They can behave with the same limited attention span as natural Air elementals, as well as the same impersonal attitude. An undirected Air thought-form could easily do a fair imitation of a poltergeist, and, in fact, many such disturbed spirits are nothing more than unintentional thought-forms created by the inhabitants of a house, particularly pubescent girls.

This is where some of the long, drawn-out rituals of medieval magicians can be useful, as extensive adherence to ritual formulae works as a control on the parameters of conjured spirits of this nature. A great deal of thought should go into the creation of any thought-form elemental, but this is especially crucial with Air thought-forms.

Their purpose is most commonly one of communication, and it is a simple matter to give specific direction to the conjured spirit during its creation and to include subsequent dissipation upon the completion of its task.

Other purposes where an Air thought-form might be appropriate include seeking inspiration, help with exams, assistance with visualisation journeys, protection during air travel, seeking instruction or direction, divination, obtaining knowledge, discovering lost items, uncovering lies, or seeking freedom in some manner. They can also be employed to affect weather patterns, within parameters.

As with all of the elements, they can be used to form quarter guardians or to attach to a ritual implement, though Air spirits are more easily attached through the use of the ritual tool than to the implement itself. Frequent use of the item will be required to maintain the attachment, so someone who performs ritual infrequently might be better off inviting natural Air spirits into workings as needed.

Air spells can be tricky in the most innocent-seeming circumstances. For example, one would think that trying to find a lost object with help from an Air thought-form would lack inherent potential for blunders. Remember that once a thought-form is given purpose, its existence is determined by that purpose, and it will perform with a consciousness of its own.

So, what if a thought-form sets out to find a lost object that was lost far from home? Or perhaps stolen, or even destroyed? Many all-too-interesting life events could occur in the process of recovering the item, and there are no guarantees that you won't have to travel far afield to collect it. There is also a possibility that, once recovered, the object will have to be lost over and over again for the spirit to continue performing its task.

Inspiration spells are relatively harmless and potentially very valuable. However, even these should be carefully directed towards a specific goal as unbridled extremes of inspiration, if unchecked, could actually drive a person to madness.

A variation in ritual formula for creating an Air thought-form is to use incense or other smoke as the focus for manifestation of the spirit. The smoke will dissipate at the end of the ritual which acts as a natural release to set the spirit free to perform its task. Again, be sure that dissipation of the thought-form once the task is completed has been programmed in during the ritual!

Also, be sure to banish residual energies diligently after an Air thought-form ritual. Air is everywhere, and this is especially important when dealing with this element.

FIRE THOUGHT-FORMS OR SERVITORS

Certain precautions are highly recommended when constructing a Fire thought-form elemental to accommodate the naturally destructive nature of the element. Having begun on that ominous note, let me assure the reader that with proper forethought, a Fire thought-form is containable, just as much as a campfire or bonfire.

Fire, as an element, is fairly predictable compared to Water or Air and can be specifically focused just as a demolition expert can focus an explosion. The risk is minimal if one knows the behaviour pattern of the element and the proper safeguards.

The advantages of Fire thought-forms begin with pure, concentrated power. They also have a shorter life span than those of other elements. A fire begins and ends with its fuel supply. Handled well, a Fire thought-form can expend a burst of energy towards a specific purpose, then dissipate harmlessly back to its source.

Keep in mind that thought-form elementals can and will behave independently if given a chance, so a very specific purpose and direction must be established during the formation of the Fire thought-form.

For example, a general spell for change in some aspect of your life would be inappropriate for Fire, as the path of least resistance to such a change could be your home or place of work burning down. However, a more specific change can be well served through this element using the active energy inherent in the Fire element.

Another thing to keep in mind is that a thought-form begins and ends within the magic user's own energy source. Revenge or other negative energies could be very harmful when re-absorbed.

Fire servitors or thought-form elementals are appropriate for quarter guardians and for purification, but be careful the item being purified isn't consumed! They are also good for lending force to other spells and for any form of change, but again, be very specific about the nature of the change you desire.

A focus point for the formation of a Fire thought-form could be a candle flame or a small crucible. *Always* include a destiny for the spirit before it is released to perform its task. An easy method is to program it so that it is fed by the need of the intent, so that once the task is accomplished it dissipates harmlessly like any contained fire left to burn out.

One thing to note is that Fire thought-forms tend to be more visibly perceptible than other elements. This can be disconcerting to some people. Any participants in the ritual should be of an emotional disposition to deal with the unexpected, as panic could lead to loss of control of the entity.

If it is desired to sustain a Fire spirit, perhaps as a quarter guardian, it will need feeding through emotional energy. A few minutes of lighting a candle and expressing any strong emotions or driving force the caretaking magic user might feel will work, so long as it is in a controlled manner. For a protection spirit or any other long-term purpose, repeats of the original ritual are advised.

WATER THOUGHT-FORMS OR SERVITORS

Water is probably the least used of elements for the purpose of forming servitors or thought-form elementals. It isn't that there is any reason *not* to create Water thought-forms so much as that so many natural spirits of Water are generally agreeable that forming a Water servitor is seldom called for.

Of course, there are always exceptions.

The most common Water servitors would naturally be temple guardians. Natural Water spirits can easily be employed for this purpose and are either represented by an object to which the spirit attaches or by some form of container with actual Water contained in it. However, a servitor might be desirable for this purpose because not only is Water a "wild" element that tends to either evaporate or seep away easily, but it is one that can turn nasty when contained for long periods of time or go stagnant.

It can be tricky to keep a fresh Water spirit in captivity and it somehow feels wrong to do so in a way that would not apply to an element like Earth, which is stationary by nature. Air circulates naturally and Fire is ever-changing and adapts easily to containment, but Water needs refreshing.

Trying to maintain control over a Water elemental of any kind can also be tricky. Try walking across a room with a glass of water, full to the brim, and see how much control you are able to maintain. Even the most graceful person would be hard-pressed to retain every drop of water without moving very, very carefully.

This should suffice as a warning for just how easy it would be for a Water servitor to get out of control. Water can be contained, but it has a way of getting free, if only a little at a time. If it cannot get free at all, it turns bad.

Water, by its nature, never seems to be entirely under human control. Even a small quantity that might be used in ritual holds a sense of the mysterious depths of all sources of water. Creating a servitor from a source that retains this mystery can be a real balancing trick.

Many of the associations we have for Water spirits have a malevolent side, like the Water Dobbie who pretends to be helpful until it suddenly plunges its victim into a river to drown. Water spirits hold something of themselves back and the magician who deals with them can never be entirely sure of their continued co-operation.

A thought-form that would be not only of this element but created out of the deepest part of the magician's subconscious where our personal demons dwell, might just be a bit of a handful.

On the other hand, it might also be a source of ultimate power. Never underestimate the strength of Water. It can be used for hydropower with the same force that propels a tidal wave. In magic, the invasive qualities of Water can be put to good use by a competent magic user. The spirit of Water can "seep into" situations where another spirit might be prohibited entry.

With all that in mind, a decision to create a Water servitor should begin with a very specific purpose in mind and a divination of some form to determine whether the Water spirit that you create is going to decide to co-operate. A simple pendulum divination is sufficient and very appropriate, as this form of divination is closely linked to the subconscious mind of the magic user.

This is one situation where it is appropriate to perform your own divination rather than to ask someone else. It is your mind that will create the servitor. The information for the divination should come from the same source.

Water servitors might be employed for many purposes, but of those most closely associated with Water, the one that I would recommend avoiding is emotional love spells. Love spells of any kind are dodgy, but even the Fire of passion would be preferable to the absolute despair that the unbounded depths of emotion can bring.

Remember that any spell encompasses the magician performing it and getting caught up in such a spell could overwhelm the practitioner, even if the magic was being performed for someone else.

On the other hand, spells for calming the emotions can benefit from these same qualities. A cleansing spell performed on a place with use of a servitor creates a natural guardian, much as an Earth servitor employed to help construction of a building will naturally become the guardian of that building.

Conjuring a Water servitor for purposes of accessing the subconscious can be very useful, as it creates an entity with whom to consult that part of the mind directly. This is also true for servitors who assist with divinations or psychic acts. A servitor to help you attain general happiness can act as a "guardian Angel," or a really talented magic user can create a servitor that specifically exists to lull one into sleep.

I would, however, hesitate to conjure any form of servitor to assist with dreaming. Some things are meant to be accessed indirectly. One exception to this general advice would be a servitor to lend temporary help with lucid dreaming: learning to become aware that you are dreaming within the dream state to allow you to take control of the dream.

This element has the potential for spontaneity, and there might be some situations where stirring up a servitor out of a handy source of water could be useful. The matter still requires forethought, but with enough magical experience, it is possible to work out what is required within a few minutes, and the only ritual tool that is absolutely required is some water from any source, even a puddle.

In the conjuring ritual, the individual or group opens according to their regular practices, then focuses all of their consciousness on the purpose for the ritual. A container of water from whence the servitor will come should be on either the ritual altar or a central location on the floor. Note that a similar set-up can be used to petition a natural Water spirit, filling the container from the body of water the participants wish to petition.

The participant(s) will circle this container—deosil, of course—chanting a spell directed at the purpose and will literally "stir up" the servitor, utilising spiral energies in a whirlpool effect. If the water is on a table or altar, it is beneficial to splash a bit of the water in the direction one is walking to "stir the pot."

As with the other elements, any sinister feeling that affects any participant would be reason to stop immediately. It is all too easy, particularly in a group, to "stir up" something nasty from the subconscious of one of the participants that would immediately get out of control. This is to be avoided, even at the cost of the success of the spell. Another approach is always possible.

Never participate in this form of spell if you are harbouring feelings of anger in some aspect of your life. It isn't fair to the others in the group.

The dangers of residual spirits are minimal with Water, but banishing is always a good idea for clearing any stray thought-forms of the participants. Grounding is essential.

A Water servitor is perhaps the easiest to sustain out of all of the elements. Water, the element of emotions and a carrier of electric current in its physical form, is prone to transference of energy charges with very little effort.

An object that represents Water can have its resident thought-form recharged through a simple act of touching a drop of water to the object and projecting positive emotions at it.

Because of the potential for stagnation, it is a good idea to recharge Water thought-forms on some sort of a regular basis just to renew the connection to you. An item that is guarded by a thought-form and is used either in ritual or for a mundane purpose frequently is easily sustained by contact, but a Water servitor that is sent out to perform a task might need a more formal renewal.

Water thought-forms, like the other elemental thought-form entities, can and should be reabsorbed on completion or abortion of their task, with the exception of guardians. If this is anticipated, a good way to prepare for it is to include stepping into the source of water during the original ritual to create the thought-form or servitor.

Obviously, this would require a container large enough to accommodate the participant(s) stepping into it, or a wide tray to pour the water into for the ritual before returning it to a more containable vessel.

Near the finish of performing the closing spell for re-absorption, the participant(s) step into the water again, and the energy is returned to its own source.

Water thought-forms are creatures of mystery and depth, much like natural Water spirits. Complete control of their eventual actions is unlikely, and in most cases, I would recommend an eventual re-absorption or prepared evaporation of the spirit, which can be accomplished by making this a part of the original ritual.

AETHERIAL THOUGHT-FORMS
OR SERVITORS

When we move into the area of creating thought-form elementals of Spirit, the value of old knowledge becomes inestimable. The reasons for this can become all too apparent for those who delve into this area unprepared.

Those who grew up with religious indoctrination might find this area difficult as preconceived ideas of archetypal Angels, demons, and other supernatural entities are potentially problematic, and the magic user must remember that a thought-form spirit is of one's own making, a part of yourself within your own control. Maintaining that control is essential.

In nature, an elemental is spawned by the need for "being," as a spiritual entity to inhabit or care for something within their element. Thought-forms are created for "purpose," to perform a task as defined by the magic user from whom they are formed. Despite this, they can still behave independently, often to the perturbation of their creator! Any of them might get out of hand if very strict parameters are not set up for them at inception.

Too often, a fairly new magic user will read a few books—including some sensationalist novels—then decide to conjure up the most formidable servitor they can conceive of for some minor purpose. This begs for a lesson in "being careful what you wish for." A large percentage of these fail to produce anything at all as the experience level isn't yet up to the demands of the operation, but someone with a natural affinity for magic might succeed.

This can lead to a test of the magic user's nerve, wit, and defensive abilities, which might be a valuable magical lesson, but there are more desirable methods for gaining knowledge that are far less of a threat to the neophyte's (beginner's) sanity and well-being. To create a thought-form in an agreeable form is conducive to the likelihood of it performing in the manner that its creator actually had in mind.

An exception might be a protective temple guardian, where something that resembles a horrific demon from a Lovecraft or Dennis Wheatley novel could be very effective. Aetherial spirits can also be appropriate for a particularly difficult healing spell, where Angelic archetypes can be put to good use to overcome the perceived limitations of the magic user's ability alone.

For most purposes, I would recommend another elemental form appropriate to the task, and I strongly advise against using Aetherial thought-forms in any kind of prosperity spell. The ingrained attitudes we all have about material wealth are such that even a servitor of our own making could be adversely affected by subconscious guilt or feelings of what we may or may not deserve. An Earth elemental would work much better.

Aether is of Spirit and it is transmutation of one's own spirit that is most appropriate to this realm. An Aetherial thought-form might be conjured to serve as a form of guardian Angel to oversee spiritual development. Aether does not have a quarter but is appropriate to deity. Most people who work with deity representations will align with a known deity, whether it be from a chosen pantheon, mythology, or even fiction.

I've known a few magicians who choose to create their own deities, and this is where a thought-form can be useful. A physical representation of this spirit can be fashioned or provided, or it can be created in pure Spirit form within a designated space. A clear statement of intent and *very* specific intended purpose for the entity is highly recommended, as is a plan for its ultimate predestination. A banishing *before* the ritual to create it is also essential in order to avoid picking up any potentially disruptive energies.

The end banishing should also be thorough, using the full form of whatever banishing you choose. Remember that a thought-form is sustained by the Aetheric energy of its creator. It should be frequently recharged through repeated ritual so that it doesn't drain its source. This can be done through something as undemanding as lighting incense regularly to the entity's physical form.

Chapter 9

DIVINATION

METHODS CHOSEN FOR DIVINATION are a personal choice but are always subjective to some degree. Certain methods are easily associated with a specific element, while others use symbols from all of the elements in conjunction.

Whether to consult any form of elemental spirits while performing a divination is also a matter of choice. I've known tarot readers and rune masters who always consult their chosen gods to decide whether a reading should be done before even beginning to shuffle the cards or bring out the rune stones.

Divination is the use of a chosen method to tune into the higher self and one's own intuition, but some practitioners prefer to externalise their readings to consult a spiritual essence for greater objectivity. Intuition is a process that our greatest scientists still cannot manufacture or explain. No matter how far robotics experts refine artificial intelligence in machines, that elusive intuitive factor remains in the realm of organic life forms.

To some extent, elemental associations are projections. Material objects used for divination such as tarot cards, rune stones, and scrying crystals are easily associated with Earth, for example, especially those that rely on a solid system of symbols. Intuition itself is largely associated with Air, but that is the inspirational intuition of creativity. Emotional intuition takes us into the realm of Water. Divination through fire gazing can be brutal with hard facts, often lacking in the protective symbolism used in other forms of divination, while the open subjectivity of consulting Aetherial spirits can lead to misinterpretation too easily for the less experienced diviner.

Divination does not always involve spirits, yet quite often, this outside help can make the difference between the success or failure of the operation. There are times when a simple divination, using one's own natural psychic abilities, is sufficient. There are other times when one can benefit from spiritual assistance.

The choice of what method of divination to use is very much a personal one. It is generally more beneficial to learn a chosen form of divination well and use it regularly than to learn a little about several simply because they have each, in turn, become the latest New Age fad.

This doesn't mean that one cannot learn more than one method of divination, only that it is worthwhile to concentrate on a couple of specialities that work particularly well for you, as repetition of the form builds a link between the diviner and the method. This is especially true in cases of methods that involve remembering a lot of meanings unless the diviner wants to be constantly referring to a book while trying to receive psychic impressions.

DIVINATION WITH EARTH SPIRITS

In general, anything that uses materials of the Earth or the physical comes under the rulership of the Earth element: tarot and other card readings, runes, geomancy or any form that uses stones or bones, crystal gazing, I Ching or any other form that uses coins, phrenology, palmistry, reading entrails, and astrology.

Some might question whether astrology should fall here because the stars and planets are in the sky, but it is a system that not only relies on planet placements but also largely on symbols. Any system heavily reliant on easily read symbols comes under Earth. There is also the significance of gravitational pull in astrology.

Anything that involves the use of the Earth's electromagnetic energy, such as receiving visions while touching standing stones, is very much of Earth.

Divination with Earth spirits can be very satisfying or a very frustrating experience. These spirits are independent and can be very playful, yet they can also be very helpful…sometimes in ways we might find difficult to cope with.

As anyone who has studied a form of divination probably knows, divining for oneself is often difficult because it is so easy to look for what you want to hear rather than what is actually true. The divining tools will tell the truth, but our interpretation can be easily swayed by our own wishes. It is a part of human nature.

Divining with elemental spirits is then doubly frustrating because it is more difficult to escape the truths we don't wish to discover, yet the reading is likely to be much more accurate because of the spirit's objectivity.

There are two basic ways of involving Earth spirits in whatever form of divination one chooses. One is to persuade them to oversee the operation and offer guidance; the other is to actually induce them to become associated with the medium of divination.

Invoking Spiritual Guidance

Asking elemental spirits to oversee and guide a divination is a simple matter and can apply to any form of divination. All that is required is a basic meditation and request, somewhat like a prayer.

This is most effective if the method is repeated in much the same way every time or directed at the same entity (or entities) repeatedly, whether it is a nature spirit, a god(dess) form, or a thought-form elemental that is specifically attuned to seeking information on the astral plane.

The diviner might choose to invoke the spirits of a location or a specific spirit by name. Ritualistic wording can be as simple as a single sentence, such as: *"I call the spirit (name) to come to me and guide this reading, so that I may see truth in my visions."* Any specific wording that feels natural to the reader and conveys the required meaning can be used and will certainly become more effective with repeated use.

Dedicated ritual objects can connect with Earth spirits to assist with divination. I keep a necklace of clear quartz crystals with my tarot cards which I use solely during readings. It is the quartz stones that provide the Earth spirits who inspire my card readings and help to maintain my objectivity.

Whatever method of divination one chooses to practice, it is possible to either associate spirits with the medium of divination or to attune a spirit to something like a stone to keep on the table or altar during divinations. Usually, such a spirit is evoked in a basic dedication ritual for the item.

Divination methods like tarot reading and runes are well-represented in available books that the diviner might wish to study over time to learn their chosen art. A lesser-known method which I will detail here is an exception. It is called Stone Tossing.

STONE TOSSING

The method involves collecting specific gemstones to represent each planet, which are tossed onto a velvet cloth (preferably silk, but cotton will do) and read like an astrology chart.

The cloth is embroidered with an astrological wheel, divided into twelve sections with the symbol for each astrological sign embroidered in the appropriate order. This would begin at the nine o'clock position with Aries and continue around counterclockwise through the twelve signs.

Obviously, a working knowledge of astrology is necessary for this method, although a serious belief in astrology is optional as it is the symbolism represented that is used in this form of divination.

The stones that represent the planets can be rough and, therefore, cheaper than jewellery-quality stones. I actually prefer rough for this purpose.

The correspondences are as follows:

- Sun: Diamond
- Moon: Moonstone
- Mercury: Opal
- Venus: Emerald
- Mars: Ruby

- Jupiter: Amethyst
- Saturn: Sapphire
- Uranus: Chrysoberyl
- Neptune: Aquamarine
- Pluto: Onyx

Some variation is possible as long as the chosen stones are the appropriate colours. If you are unable to get a rough diamond, golden stones are recommended. Lemon tourmaline or quartz work reasonably well.

The stones are best kept in a pouch made of natural fibre (silk velvet is preferred, though cotton will do) and only brought out specifically for

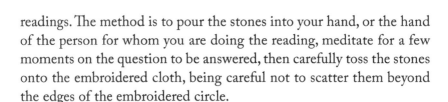

readings. The method is to pour the stones into your hand, or the hand of the person for whom you are doing the reading, meditate for a few moments on the question to be answered, then carefully toss the stones onto the embroidered cloth, being careful not to scatter them beyond the edges of the embroidered circle.

The stones are then read as planets in a horoscope, paying particular attention to aspects formed between them.

Whatever form of divination one chooses to practice, Earth spirits are the most potentially helpful assistants one can invoke because of their relatively stable nature. They are also the most reliable for telling the truth without undue confusion. It is highly recommended that one always shows them respect and consideration and remembers that they are not servants but friendly helpers to be loved and nurtured, as are any elemental spirits who choose to allow themselves to become involved with humans.

DIVINATION WITH AIR SPIRITS

Intuition itself is ruled by Air. There are many forms of divination, but those of Air rely heavily on intuition. The difficulty is that we are taught to think logically from the time we can talk, and this leads to situations where we have to make a choice when intuition and logic disagree.

It is easier to trust logic, yet those with a good sense of intuition find that, over and over again, following the intuitive course in defiance of what the logical mind suggests leads to a preferable result. Resisting the evidence of logic requires a great deal of trust that the intuitive mind will perceive that which we cannot see or measure. It requires practice and repeated success to reach a state where we automatically respond to intuition over logic in a critical situation.

Even the most empirical psychologist will recognise that the human mind receives messages and information through the perceptions of the subconscious, which may escape the notice of the conscious mind, and that some cases of apparent intuition are explainable as the mind's ability to process external information of which we are not consciously aware.

This plays a part in divination, as the medium of divination can give form to unconsciously perceived details. However, there are many times when the information cannot have come from an explainable source. In purposeful divination, we focus on insight because the nature of the act of divining is to seek information on the intuitive level. For someone who has not yet developed complete trust in their own intuition, it is easier to use a method that has definitive signs to follow, such as Augury, than something that relies entirely on intuition.

Augury, divining from the flight patterns of birds, is a very old form of divination attributed to Air. Other Air methods include cloud gazing, observing other flying creatures, and conjuring spirits in smoke. Incense smoke is frequently used for this. However, Air spirits lack the reliability of Earth spirits and, unless one is sure exactly what sort of spirit one is consulting, some caution is advised.

Ouija boards and automatic writing also come under Air divinations. Both have come under criticism for potentially attracting mischievous or even malicious spirits, though with the right approach, spirits can be left out of it entirely and the divination can come solely from the subconscious of the reader.

Conversely, an Air spirit can be invited into another form of divination (perhaps something associated with Earth for stability) to participate as inspiration or to help with seeking elusive information.

DIVINATION WITH FIRE SPIRITS

Fire gazing is a well-known divination method that goes back before written history. It is a form of scrying, helped by the dancing flames which easily form pictures to the entranced mind. As in any form of divination, the diviner must put themselves into a receptive trance and look for the pictures to form, then open their intuition to receive impressions of what they observe.

In any method of fire scrying, care must be taken not to damage the eyes. Fire gives concentrated light and the eyes can be sensitive. Looking directly into a candle flame could be more damaging than gazing over the wider expanse of a raging bonfire, or even a hearth or campfire. Sometimes unfocusing the eyes can help, as well as being conducive to trance states, which are helpful in any form of divination.

A Fire spirit can be summoned to help in many forms of divination that have other elemental associations. How often do we light a candle as part of a divination ritual or scrying session? In certain circumstances, asking the spirit of the flame to assist in the divination might be appropriate. Whatever medium is used, calling on the Fire spirit to give visions with a basic chant is very effective. A simple request for visions in relation to the question in mind will do, but address the spirit of the Fire directly, accepting it as an entity. This is a matter of respect.

Forms of Fire divination besides candle or fire gazing include scrying through the distortion of heat rising from a paved road, though for obvious reasons, this should not be done while driving! It's much better to give oneself over to this form of trance hypnosis from the passenger seat.

Dancing around a bonfire and gazing within the flames for visions is a powerful form of fire gazing. In a group divination, one person might be selected to do the scrying while others dance round the fire to raise the energy. This form of divination would be appropriate for a community facing a crisis or a group with important decisions to be made.

For ordinary purposes, a simple incantation to the spirit of a hearth fire or campfire spirit is sufficient. A candle gazing, with some sort of petition to the spirit of the flame, is sufficient for most daily purposes. Remember to seek your visions in the space just above the actual flame rather than staring into the flame itself, which can damage the retina.

The benefit of mastering the art of fire gazing is that once one learns to do it, it can generally be done as needed with any source of flame. It is an easy form to learn compared to using reflective mediums, such as crystal gazing. Fire tends to draw the attention into a natural trance with little trouble.

Fire spirits are outgoing by nature and are not inclined to keep their secrets, as are some other divinatory spirits. If anything, they can be far too brutal with hard facts, often lacking in the protective symbolism which features in many more grounded forms of divination.

There are methods of divination that involve fire in folklore and tradition. For example, there is an old tradition in Wales wherein women congregate to learn their fortune from candles that they carry. Many forms of candle divination occur in both old and new texts, using methods such as setting up candles to represent a number of choices and recognising the first candle to burn down and sputter out as the answer.

Another is to use the wax of a candle of an appropriate colour either to the element associated with the question or a planetary energy association, meditate on the question, then pour the melted wax into a glass or pottery vessel filled with cold water. Interpret the shapes that the wax forms much as you would read tea leaves, keeping subjectivity in mind.

As a general guideline in interpreting wax shapes, spirals represent renewal, circles represent fertility or completion of a goal, broken lines indicate scattered forces, and dots suggest the question is too complicated or that distractions have prevented sufficient focus.

Evoking assistance from a Fire spirit for divination would be appropriate in situations where the reader is caught up in strong emotions regarding the subject of the reading. Always be sure that the fire is in a controlled container of some sort, such as a campfire or bonfire that can be contained by removing anything flammable around the area chosen for the fire.

DIVINATION WITH WATER SPIRITS

Water is associated with the subconscious. While Air represents the intellectual and inspirational form of intuition that is associated with creativity, the emotional intuition of Water comes from within the depths of the inner mind, which still holds many mysteries, even to the world of science.

It naturally follows that forms of divination associated with Water will not only be those that use the actual element of Water, but also those that rely heavily on internal emotional perception. Methods include scrying in mirrors (including black mirrors), the sea or other bodies of water, fog, or heavy rain. Scrying by water can be something as simple as watching the reflection of the full moon on the ocean, a lake, or other watery surface. Nostradamus was known for scrying with a brass bowl filled with black ink within which he focused his visions.

Water correspondences lean towards the intuitive and may sometimes be abstract. In understanding the nature of Water spirits, we come to learn new forms of perception and insight and can rediscover the realm of instinct and precognition that still exists in other creatures of nature, both on land and in the water. The intuitive principle is more essential to our survival than we often realise.

Dowsing is one of the better-known forms of divination associated with Water. This is because it was originally used for finding underground sources of water, though in modern times, it has often been successfully used to follow energy lines or find lost objects. Variations of the traditional form of dowsing (which uses a forked hazel branch)

include using metal rods or a pendulum to find objects, or to make choices by watching its swing.

With a pendulum, the traditional indicators are either a North/South swing which means "yes" while an East/West swing means "no," or a straight line for "yes" and circles for "no." In determining the sex of an unborn child, a straight swing suggests a boy, and circles indicate a girl. Police departments in the United States have been known to employ a diviner to use a pendulum held over a map to locate lost or kidnapped children, though you would be hard-pressed to find one that will admit to it (Easter and Christensen).

The sea has been said to "whisper messages" to some people. It is an old superstition that large one-piece conch shells held to the ear contain the sound of the ocean. Scientists tell us that what we actually hear is the reverberating sound of the listener's own blood flow, yet the sound is uncannily like the ocean and will sound loudest when the sea is rough. Those who use this method have reported hearing actual words within the rushing sounds.

The methods one uses for divination are always a personal choice but bear in mind that the methods associated with Water tend to be subjective. It is all too easy to see visions or hear messages the diviner wishes to receive within these methods, and someone new to divination might find more objectivity in Earth methods, though even solid symbols can be misinterpreted if the reader is unable to be objective.

Consulting Water spirits to help with methods of divination can potentially be helpful for maintaining objectivity. Asking a Water spirit to provide clear visions or spoken messages can bring clarification. Water spirits are fairly forthcoming, though not as brutal as Fire, but they are playful in their own way and sometimes delight in shrouding information in enigmatic symbols or riddles to draw the diviner into their world of mystery.

A Water spirit, if invoked or evoked into a divination spell, will nearly always leave the diviner feeling that there is some secret or more information that has not been revealed. The cloak of mystery over any information given can leave the diviner feeling suspicious, as if they are operating without the full picture and that some important but unknown factor might be essential to proceeding wisely.

Usually, the Water spirit will have given the details which are actually needed and might, in fact, only seem to be retaining additional information when indeed there is none. It's a game they play.

CONSULTING WATER SPIRITS FOR SPIRITUAL GUIDANCE

Water, as the element of emotions, might seem an obvious choice for consulting spirits on matters of great personal importance. However, some caution is advised. Water spirits cannot help but draw one into the depths of inner conflict which might already be overwhelming.

Water makes us contemplative and, in the right circumstances, can help to clear the mind to work out issues and plans of how to go forward. Many people throughout history have sat at the edge of a pond or on the seaside, looking within the calming ripples or waves for the clarity of mind that enables one to become receptive and able to address a dilemma or contemplate the relevant aspects of a choice to be made.

A familiar spirit, perhaps the spirit of a pond or lake that is well-known to the seeker, can be beneficial and enlightening. One of my own favourite mediums is a black mirror. These are usually made from a concave glass with black woodworm paint on the back to provide the reflective surface. The mirror is washed before and after each use using fresh water, perhaps with a little vinegar mixed in to eliminate streaks.

Any source of water that is constantly renewed can be suitable for quiet contemplation. A garden fountain, for example, provides running water and is ideal for developing a familiar spirit within your own private back garden, where you're unlikely to be disturbed (apart from family members).

DIVINATION WITH AETHERIAL SPIRITS

Bringing spirits of any form into divination naturally addresses the world of Spirit or Aether. Mediumship and common prayer are direct approaches to Spirit. Aetherial divination might use items like a Ouija board or symbolic icons and symbols, but invoking a discourse with spirits, including consultation with one's own higher self, touches on the realm of Aether.

Various religions and magical disciplines provide methods for accessing Spirit. Eastern religions and most magical systems teach forms of meditation, which is good for communing with one's higher spirit. Tribal societies have been known to travel in the spirit world through the use of certain natural drugs, like peyote, used by Mexican Shamans, and some more complicated mixtures in other cultures such as the Voudon

and Santeria religions. In Western tradition, the notorious witches flying ointment provides a form of journeying through the realm of Spirit.

These mixtures are usually inaccessible to the common practitioner, and, without proper training, the complicated mixtures are subject to abuse and can even be lethal.

This is not an area for dabbling. Too often, someone without proper training will call themselves something like "the doctor" at gatherings and dispense substances with more confidence than sense, creating a very real risk for those foolish enough to trust their well-being to a stranger. If you're not working with a genuine Shaman or properly trained authority of a religion that uses these practices, you put your health at great risk.

Other methods of accessing inner Spirit more safely, besides meditation, include spinning and shaking. Quiet contemplation is perhaps the best method for accessing the higher self, which is why stillness is one of the most basic practices of any magical discipline, including martial arts.

One might choose to specifically conjure a guiding spirit to assist in divination. Aetherial forms of spirits include spirit guides, deities, or other "higher" forms of spiritual entities which can be shaped by the diviner's personal beliefs. Angels, for example, fit into some belief systems, as do natural daemons.

The diviner should be selective and learn from experience. Some spirits, like fairies, can be playful. Deities are notorious for couching answers in parables or ambiguous information. Some spirits are known to give incorrect information or to deliberately provide answers in a way that will cause distress. Whether a spirit is playful or malicious, the result is still confusion.

A guiding spirit known to the reader is best if one wishes to directly consult this realm. Some readers of methods listed under the other elements like to consult such a spirit in every reading, or, as mentioned at the beginning of this chapter, even beforehand to determine whether doing a reading at that time is suitable.

Someone who regularly visits a special place might wish to invoke or evoke the spirit of the location to guide a meditation. An invocation can be done silently, internally, or through a ritualistic invocation such as: *"I call the spirit (name, or 'of this place') to come to me and guide my thoughts and visions, and to show me the answer to (question)."*

Words are a matter of individual choice and are likely to be most effective when they express feeling rather than read by rote. However, using the same invocation repeatedly will create an affinity with the wording itself that can be very effective for recurrent use.

Attuning an object to an Aetherial spirit is a little different from doing so with spirits of the basic four elements. Religious icons or statues of deities are probably the most common form of object that will naturally attract the attention of an Aetherial spirit. Such spirits are not actually attached to the object in the way that an Earth spirit might be attached to its constituent material but are attracted to it by regular observances by a human supplicant. This applies to groupings of statues as well, such as a collection of statues of Egyptian gods or those of another pantheon.

Historical deity forms will bring with them associations created by their worshippers of the past, which should be kept in mind when invoking or evoking a deity for any purpose. This complication can be avoided by creating servitor entities with objects that do not carry associations with any familiar archetypes, but, in general, many people find that deity associations provide a stronger source of clarity, utilising the energies already put into the deity form.

Furthermore, I have personally found that a grouping of icons creates a more balanced energy than adherence to a single god form. Once upon a time, I set up an altar with the dual aspects of Sekhmet and Hathor from the Egyptian pantheon presiding. These goddesses had been instrumental in a major spell that successfully rescued my daughter from an unconscionable situation. The dual nature of Hathor's maternal aspects and Sekhmet's fierce, protective qualities combined well to accomplish the purpose.

Be sure to do your research when setting up such an altar. As Horus joined this particular altar as well as Bast, it was necessary to place a rather attractive depiction of Anubis elsewhere as Anubis and Horus do not get on well!

I lit sandalwood incense for this collection every day for a year afterwards to show appreciation for the deities' assistance with the magic performed. This also resulted in a close attunement with these deities which affected any other magic I did while that altar was intact.

The dedication of an altar or single icon can be done through formal ritual much like the invocation of the place spirit. Again, wording is a personal choice, but I would include a formal opening and closing in this situation.

The nature of Spirit is such that the boundaries between one's own spirit and an external spirit source are difficult to differentiate. Divination with a representation of deity or other spirit form is very subjective. Some might offer petitions to the icon, while others simply sit in front of the representation and wait for impressions. It is important to learn techniques for clearing the mind with this sort of divination to allow one's own thought processes to operate most efficiently and leave room for any Aetherial messages.

Basic exercises in meditation and breathing techniques are highly recommended for anyone who wishes to work with Spirit in any form.

It goes without saying that one should always show respect to elemental spirits of any kind, but this is especially true for spirits of Aether. Those who are of the realm of Spirit itself can be extremely helpful in the arts of divination (or even in giving good advice freely without having been asked), but they cannot be demanded of, and any attempt to command spirits by force is unlikely to obtain a good result, despite what some old books (mostly fantasy horror) might have to say about commanding demons to give up bits of information in response to specific arcane phrases.

This is the stuff of old black-and-white films. Real spirits are not so easily submissive to human control, and ill-conceived attempts to impose force are likely to result in nasty backlash. In the world of Spirit, there is much knowledge to be had from realising the ease with which one might gain the willing support of Spirit itself, in whatever form it might choose to manifest.

The road to Spirit, whether it is for conjuration or for seeking knowledge, will still lead to knowledge. In the practice of magic and divination, we become better able to know the unknown and sense the methods that will suit each of us best. In all methods, we must learn to trust our "sixth sense" or intuition, which are only terms for knowledge of that which we know from a spiritual understanding rather than from material facts.

The ability is there for all of us. Self-love and self-trust are the beginning of spiritual love and trust, and it is in that trust of self where divination of any form becomes a path to certain knowledge.

Chapter 10

Trees, Bird Lore, Holy Wells, and Dancing with the Fire

THE DIFFERENCE BETWEEN ELEMENTAL SPIRITS and the fairies (and other creatures of legend) can be indistinct, separated only by what happens in our world as opposed to the otherworld. Sometimes, this demarcation can also become fuzzy, and lines can get crossed.

Much wisdom can be found in folklore and history. With that in mind, some of the mostly British lore and superstition of past and present is contained herein.

TREE LORE

The tree is a universal archetypal symbol that is found in different traditions around the world. Trees are symbols of physical and spiritual nourishment, transformation and liberation, sustenance, spiritual growth, union, and fertility. Trees are used as sacred shrines and places of spiritual pilgrimage. Sacred trees are found in the Hindu, Egyptian, Sumerian, Toltec, Mayan, Norse, Celtic, Judaic, and various Shamanic traditions. The World Tree is described in the Upanishads as *a tree eternally existing, its roots aloft, its branches spreading below.*

Certain trees are considered to be sacred to fairies as well. Two or three thorn trees growing close together are a sign of fairy activity and are sometimes found hung with ribbons and rags as gifts to the fairies. Blackthorn, hazel, alder, elder, and oak are also favoured, especially if they are twisted together. Two thorns and an elder or the combination of oak, ash, and thorn are signs of fairies about.

Trees produce much of the oxygen that we breathe and, in turn, we produce carbon dioxide which trees breathe, a symbiotic relationship that we need to remember when big industries are cutting down rainforests. Japan has a tradition concerning tree spirits, generally called *Kodama*. Historically, foresters made offerings to the Kodama before cutting a tree down.

Trees have played an important role in many of the world's mythologies and religions. In many cultures and Pagan religions, trees are believed to be the homes of tree spirits, similar to the Kodama in Japan. Greek mythology refers to tree spirits as *Dryads* (in oak trees) or *Meliae* (in ash trees). The oak is especially sacred to the Druids, both historical and modern-day, and is one of the sacred Druidic three: oak, ash, and thorn.

The Tree of Life is referred to in the Old Testament and versions of it appear in other mythologies. Some equate it to the image of the World Tree, which appears in several religions and mythologies, particularly Indo-European religions, Siberian religions, and Native American religions.

Yggdrasil is the holy ash, an immense mythical tree that connects the nine worlds in Norse cosmology. Odin is said to have hung on the tree for nine days, self-sacrificed so that he could bring the wisdom of the runes to his people. In Scottish folklore, a friendly tree spirit called the *Ghillie Dhu*, helps lost children find their way home.

During the Northern Crusades, there was a common practice of building churches on the sites of sacred groves, which are groves of trees of special religious importance to a particular culture. Sacred groves were most prominent in the Ancient Near East and prehistoric Europe and were significant in cult practices of Celtic, Baltic, Germanic, Ancient Greek, Near Eastern, Roman, and Slavic polytheism. They were also used in India, Japan, and West Africa.

The trees referred to in the Bardic Tree Alphabet (Chapter Seven) hold special meanings, as do other trees in mythologies native to Europe.

ALDER: Sacred to the Druids and generally associated with protection and oracular powers, alder is associated with Bran, as he used his body to span dangerous waters. The pith is easily pushed out of green shoots to make whistles. Several shoots bound together by cordage can be trimmed to the desired length for producing a whistle to entice Air elementals. The old superstition of "whistling up the wind" began with this custom. The oily, water-resistant wood has been used extensively for underwater foundations and pilings in Venice, Italy, and in the construction of bridges.

APPLE: In Norse myth, Idunna was the keeper of the apples of immortality. Eating these kept the gods young. Apple indicates choice and is useful for love and healing magic.

ASH: A Druidic sacred tree. Wands and, historically, spears are often made of ash because of its straight grain. Ash is associated with spells requiring focus and strength of purpose, applications in magic for sea power, ocean rituals, karmic laws, magical potency, healing and health, protection, love, women's mysteries, prophetic dreams, and prosperity. Putting fresh ash leaves under your pillow is said to stimulate psychic dreams.

BEECH: Beech is concerned with ancient knowledge as revealed in old objects, places, and writings. Beech indicates guidance from the past to gain insight. At one time, beech tablets were used as writing surfaces. It's no surprise that *beech* and *book* have the same etymological origins.

BIRCH: Associated with fertility and healing magic, new beginnings, purification, protection, creativity, fertility, and birth, birch is also known as *The Lady of the Woods*. Birch is one of the first trees to grow on bare soil, and, thus, it births the entire forest. Birch twigs were once used to bestow fertility on cattle and newlyweds, and children's cradles were made from its wood. It has a wonderful vanilla smell, and nearly every part of it is edible. Its sap was an important source of sugar to Native Americans, and its bark was also used for paper, canoe hulls, and axe handles. The inner bark provides a pain reliever, and the leaves are used to treat arthritis.

BLACKTHORN: Blackthorn is used for purification, protection, grounding, and ridding the atmosphere of negative energy. It aids with inner work and in combating fear, depression, and anger. It represents the outside influences in life. The wood is used in the *cudgel shillelagh* and Blasting Stick. Its thorns are used to pierce waxen images.

ELDER: Also known as *Ellhorn*, *Elderberry*, or *Lady Elder*. The Latin name for elder, *Sambucus*, is derived from a Greek word for a wind instrument made from elder. Like alder, the pith can be removed from the small branches to make a flute. Music on flutes of elder have the same power as the wand. A tea for purifying the blood can be made from the flowers and wine from the fruit, but, in general, the tree is poisonous. Sacred to the White Lady and Midsummer Solstice, the Druids use it to both bless and curse. Standing under an elder tree at Midsummer will help you see the "little people." Elder re-grows damaged branches with ease and can root rapidly from any part. Elder indicates the mysteries of death and rebirth.

ELM: Elm is said to be the abode of fairies and is often associated with Mother or Earth Goddesses. It adds stability and grounding to a spell. Elm wood is valued for its resistance to splitting, and the inner bark is used for cordage and chair caning.

FIR: Fir represents high views of the beyond and clear visions of what is yet to be. Also known as the *Birth Tree*, the needles are burned at childbirth to bless and protect the mother and baby. Fir is a very tall, slender tree that grows in mountainous regions on upper slopes. Fir cones respond to the Sun by opening and then close when it rains.

HAWTHORN: Hawthorn is associated with protection, purification, health, prosperity, love, marriage, fertility, inner journeys, intuition, female sexuality, and fishing magic. Its leaves and blossoms are used to create tea to aid with anxiety, appetite loss, and poor circulation. The Greeks and Romans saw the hawthorn as symbolic of hope and marriage, but in medieval Europe, it was associated with witchcraft and considered unlucky. It is sacred to the fairies, and the wood from the hawthorn provides the hottest fire and wands with the greatest power.

HAZEL: Hazelwood is used to gain knowledge, wisdom, and poetic inspiration. Forked sticks are used to find water or buried treasure. Hazel is a tree that is sacred to the fey folk, and a hazel wand can be used to call the fairies. It provides shade and protection and can be made into baskets. Hazel has applications in magic done for manifestation, spirit contact, protection, prosperity, divination-dowsing, dreams, wisdom-knowledge, marriage, fertility, intelligence, or inspiration. It is sometimes called *The Tree of Immortal Wisdom*. In Celtic tradition, the Salmon of Knowledge is said to eat the nine nuts of poetic wisdom dropped into its sacred pool from the hazel tree growing beside it. Each nut eaten by the salmon becomes a spot on its skin. If outside and in need of magical protection, quickly draw a circle around yourself with a hazel branch.

HOLLY: Holly is associated with death and rebirth. Holly is also associated with magic for protection, prophesy, healing, animals, invulnerability, watchfulness, and consecration. It is said to have the ability to enhance other forms of magic. It is one of the three timbers used in the construction of chariot wheel shafts, and it was used in spear shafts for qualities of balance and directness. Holly may be used in spells having to do with sleep or rest, and to ease the passage of death.

MISTLETOE: Also known *All Heal* and *Golden Bough*. It is the most sacred tree of the Druids and rules the Winter Solstice. The berries are used in love incenses but are poisonous. Bunches of mistletoe can be hung as an all-purpose protective herb.

OAK: In general, Oak is associated with spells for protection, strength, success, stability, healing, fertility, health, money, potency, and good luck. Burning oak leaves purifies the atmosphere. The oak is frequently associated with gods of thunder and lightning, such as Zeus and Thor, as it is frequently hit by lightning during storms. Specific oak trees have also been associated with the "Wild Hunt," which is led by Herne in England and by Woden in Germany. Oak galls, known as *Serpent Eggs*, have been used in the production of ink since at least the time of the Roman Empire and are used in magical charms. Acorns gathered at night hold the greatest fertility powers and, historically, the Druids and Priestesses listened to the rustling oak leaves and the wrens in the trees for divinatory messages.

PINE: Pine is known to the Druids as one of the seven chieftain trees of the Irish. Mix the dried needles with equal parts of juniper and cedar and burn to purify the home and ritual area. The cones and nuts can be carried as a fertility charm. One can make a good magical cleansing and stimulating bath by placing pine needles in a loose-woven bag and running bath water over it. To purify and sanctify an outdoor ritual area, brush the ground with a pine branch. When made into a tea, its needles are a valuable source of vitamin C and can loosen a tight chest.

POPLAR: Poplar wood was used in the making of shields. It has the ability to resist and to shield, both literally and metaphorically. It has an association with speech, language, and the winds. The white poplar flourishes beside rivers, in marshes, and in other watery areas. The pith is star-shaped. The upper leaves are green, but the underside is silver. It is commonly referred to as the talking, whispering, and quivering tree, as the leaves move with every light breeze.

ROWAN: The rowan tree is also called mountain ash and Witchwood. It is known for aid and protection against enchantment and associated with divination, astral work, strength, protection, initiation, healing, psychic energies, working with spirits of the dead, psychic powers, personal power, and success. It is a very magical tree used for wands, rods, amulets, and spells. The berries have a tiny pentagram on them. Sticks of the rowan were used to carve runes on and it was also used in the art of metal divining. A forked rowan branch can also help find water. Rowan sprays and crosses are placed over cattle in pens and over homes for protection. The rowan was sacred to the Druids and the goddess Brigit.

WILLOW: The willow is used for enchantment, wishing, romantic love, healing, protection, fertility, magic for women, femininity, love, divination, friendship, joy, love, and peace. It is found by rivers and associated with Moon magic. Willow bark contains salicin, which is used in the treatment of rheumatic fever and various damp diseases. Catkins, which appear in early spring before the willow's leaves, attract bees to start the cycle of pollination. For a wish to be granted, ask permission of the willow, explaining your desire. Select a pliable shoot and tie a loose knot in it while expressing what you want. When the wish is fulfilled, return and untie the knot. Remember to thank the willow and leave a gift (cake is recommended).

YEW: Yew enhances magical and psychic abilities and induces visions. It represents transformation, death, rebirth, change, reincarnation, eternal life, and immortality. All parts of the tree are poisonous except the

fleshy covering of the berry. The wood or leaves were traditionally laid on graves as a reminder to the departed spirit that death was only a pause in life before rebirth. In Europe, yew wood is known for making bows, while on the northwest coast of North America, the Pacific yew (*Taxus brevifolia*) is used by various Indigenous tribes for making masks and boxes. The Irish used it to make dagger handles, bows, and wine barrels. The physical characteristics of the trees often reflect the lore that surrounds the tree itself, hence bows made from the poisonous yew as they are bringers of death.

BIRD LORE

Birds are often seen in folklore and superstition, as well as in regional stories about fairies. More than any other living creature, they are frequently depicted in both fiction and in traditional folklore as messengers either from the gods or between humans and nature spirits. In some cases, a deity or nature spirit will shapeshift into a bird.

These connections go far back in history in the stories and mythologies of many cultures. In many traditions, birds are generally symbolic of Spirit and the soul in flight. Sailors once believed that certain sea birds held the souls of drowned sailors, most notably the albatross, storm petrol, and seagull.

Seeing swans on a voyage is considered to be good luck because they allegedly never plunge beneath the waves. Some Indigenous peoples also believe that birds hold the souls of the dead, soaring freely in the sky or some version of Heaven.

Birds represent transcendence and to Alchemists, the consummation of the Great Work, as well as the transmutation of the soul. I know of a Hereditary witch family who do not eat birds—even chickens—because they believe that birds are magical messengers and will not speak to those who would eat them. Superstitions regarding hens are plentiful and easily found in popular folklore.

Shapeshifting into birds is a popular theme in stories about witches and Shamans in many cultures. The goose, the raven, and the magpie are most used in these stories. Fairy stories also include swallows, wrens, and robins among the birds that are chosen by elfin creatures as a form in which to appear to humans. In England, it is unlucky to kill a wren, except at the annual Christmas festival.

The Tuatha Dé Danann are said to appear as birds with brilliant plumage. The Welsh goddess Rhiannon had three magic birds who could raise the dead and lull the living to sleep by singing, as did the Irish goddess Clidna. Birds in fairy stories are often helpful in some manner. Most often, they bring a message, help with a rescue, or become the symbol of spiritual aspiration. They represent immortality, hope, and renewal.

The egg is also very symbolic, representing the cosmic egg of creation, the life principle, primordial chaos, the renewal of spring, resurrection, and hope. The Greek creation myth depicts the world egg surrounded by the serpent of life, Ouroboros. The egg represents the mystery of creation and beginnings, the principle of life itself.

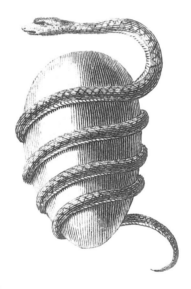

Birds are a common motif among Egyptian gods, and there is known to have been a Palaeolithic bird cult in what is now France. Birds have been used through augury for divination for centuries in many different societies.

The Phoenix is a well-known symbol of resurrection from the flames of destruction. The owl carries an association with death and is sometimes relegated the role of the bird of the underworld. The woodpecker is sacred to Zeus, Jupiter, Ares, and Mars. The hoot of an owl portended death to the Romans, and the owl was generally unlucky to Romans and Celts.

The Celtic people believed that ravens were a good omen, especially with white feathers, although supernatural ravens were a bad omen.

They believed that it was bad luck to kill one's totem bird, which seems reasonable. Celtic Shamans wore a feathered cloak for the journey to the otherworld, and Shamans from other cultures have similarly used feathers for travel into their own perception of the spirit world.

Feathers represent wisdom and knowledge, as well as transcendent power. The emblem of the Prince of Wales includes three feathers.

There are many superstitions about swans. One is that they are said to sing beautifully when they are about to die, hence the theme of the ballet *Swan Lake*. They represent beauty, grace, love, passion, and protection. Swans are known to mate for life, making them a symbol of fidelity and longevity. It is unlucky to show a dead swan to children, lest the children die too, and a swan flying against the wind portends hurricane-force winds on the way. The Greeks believed the souls of poets turned into swans.

The woodpecker is regarded as a prophetic bird with magical powers. He is the guardian of kings and trees, while the dove represents the life spirit, the soul's migration, innocence, gentleness, and peace. It is lucky to see a woodpecker on your right-hand side or for a swallow to nest under the house eaves.

It is unlucky to see one crow at a wedding, but lucky to see two. Fairies sometimes take the form of crows. A crow at the window portends death, and generally, crows and ravens are omens of death. A cock crow at night portends death, but a cock crowing in the afternoon is a warning of visitors. The early arrival of ducks promises a hard winter. The singing of a robin indicates good weather.

The first time you hear the cuckoo's call in each year portends your luck for the rest of the year; if your stomach or pockets are full, they will be so for the year. One superstition says that turning the money in your pocket over when you hear the cuckoo will attract prosperity for the year.

The kingfisher is generally good luck in Scotland. In Britain, everyone knows that the kingdom will fall if the ravens leave the Tower of London. Birds deserting their nests is unlucky.

Birds will desert a place before a disaster befalls it or become restless before earthquakes or air raids. This is actually based on fact, and it is common knowledge that domestic fowl became restless just before air raids in England during World War II. This may be down to sensitive hearing, yet there is no logical explanation, especially for rooks, who are known to desert buildings shortly before they are to be demolished.

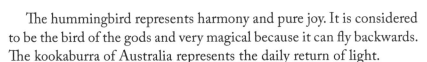

The hummingbird represents harmony and pure joy. It is considered to be the bird of the gods and very magical because it can fly backwards. The kookaburra of Australia represents the daily return of light.

In classical mythology, the harpy is a bird with a woman's head that can predict events. There are many instances of divine beings who can speak the language of birds.

HOLY WELLS

The thought of a sacred well brings forth images of magic, of spirits, and of the depths of mystery from whence all needs are fulfilled. The romanticism that exudes from the notion of deep and watery places of worship reaches into a part of the soul that transcends religion, yet also entices one into a level of emotional melding with the essence of spirituality that craves singularity. It's a personal identification with the divine that says, "This is my path and that of my people. It is sacred to us."

MYTHOLOGY AND ORIGINS OF SACRED WELLS

The origins of holy wells are often cloaked in legends. One common theme for lake worship begins as a sacred well that overflows after someone leaves the lid off. It then becomes a lake with a guardian spirit. Well spirits are most often female.

Wells are considered a reflection of, or door to, the otherworld in popular folklore, and some wells, like Sancreed in West Penwith (Cornwall), still carry these associations. Many tales of coaches vanishing into pools and wells refer to the Celtic belief in places of water as a gateway to the otherworld. Other stories of treasure that could be found at the bottom of a well or other source of contained water are symbolic of the sanctity of water itself.

There are several contenders for identification as the pool where the sword Excalibur was thrown at the end of King Arthur's life, mostly with close associations to Glastonbury. A romance known as the *Conte del Graal* recounts how the land of Logres (present English Midlands) was laid waste by an impious act of King Amangons. The tale says that he did wrong to a damsel of the well who fed travellers, and then he carried off her golden cup, thus adding injury to insult so that *"never more came damsels out of springs to comfort the wanderer."* It is said that thereafter, the grass withered, and the land became waste.

The land of Logres has associations with labyrinths, which have a Water connection and play a part of the mythology regarding the gate to the otherworld. Avalon is known to have once been surrounded by water, and the common belief is that the Tor in modern-day Glastonbury is the site of ancient Avalon. The Tor is characterised by an elaborate labyrinth design that is carved into the Earth surrounding it.

Some wells are associated with ghostly "white ladies" or well fairies. Sometimes they are named for the fairies, like Fairie's Well near Hardhorn in Lancaster, Fairy Well on Irby Heath in Cheshire, and wells of the same name in Laugharne, Carmarthen, and Fordoun Hill in Kincardine. Pixy Well or Pisky Well are popular names for wells throughout the West Country in England, and Mab Well is in Egton, North Yorkshire. It is claimed that fairies have been seen at some wells, including at Ilkley Wells in West Yorkshire.

History tells us that a lot of sacred wells come from Pagan roots, many of which were later taken over by Christians and renamed for male saints. For many sacred wells in Britain and Europe, this is true, yet it is also true that some wells actually have secular beginnings as needed sources of water for settlements. Some of these might only later have become associated with spirit worship.

History also tells us that the Celts were head-hunters. For them, the head symbolised divine power and the source of the attributes of healing, fertility, wisdom, and prophecy. Ancient Celtic well spirits or deities often originate from head cults. There is substantial evidence for a historic cult of wells throughout Britain that survives in customs like drinking from a skull kept at a well. Some of these skulls are decorated with gold. At some wells, drinking from the skull was a requirement for the magic to work. An old oak tree growing by a well might also indicate the site of an early head cult, as the oak was sacred to this culture.

Some historic wells have been lost by development over the last century or so. Not all of them have necessarily been holy or sacred wells, as many of these wells existed as boundary markers and sources of water near villages. However, water that is found in response to need has a way of becoming associated with religious munificence.

Tales are often told of wells that appear as the result of a saint who plunges his staff into the Earth in time of drought, resulting in the discovery of an underground spring that then becomes a holy well. It is thought that most of these wells were originally Pagan and discovered through dowsing, then absorbed into Christian mythology, though it is not always possible for archaeologists to determine the definite origins of a specific well.

The Pagan origins of many of the sacred wells in Britain are identified through names like "Lady Well" or "Fairy Well." *The Living Stream* by James Rattue and *Holy Places of Celtic Britain* by Mick Sharp both provide comprehensive lists of the Pagan wells in Britain for anyone who might wish to visit these sacred places.

The various religious associations with sacred or holy wells can present a varied and complicated history to the serious inquirer. The mixtures of early head cults and later Pagan customs are often combined with Christian attitudes towards holy wells that change depending on historic period as well as location.

The Roman Emperors Constantine, Valentinian, and Theodosius forbade worship of stones, trees, and fountains in an attempt to put an end to these forms of Pagan worship, yet at a time when well worship was discouraged in Rome, small Christian cults in Britain were absorbing the use of local wells or using wells of their own for baptisms.

Chapels and abbeys were built to enclose some popular wells, which, besides providing water for baptisms and other purposes, also attracted the attendance of the local populace. Some examples of these enclosed wells may be found at Dunfermline Abbey in Fife, Beverley Minster in Humberside, St. Patrick's at Aspatria, and St. Oswald's at Kirkoswald.

Historic wells of uncertain origin have been found at St. Patrick's Cathedral in Dublin, Winchester Cathedral, Wells Cathedral, Exeter Cathedral, in the crypt and foundations of York Minster, and the crypt of Glasgow Cathedral. Wells frequently appear in or near minsters. In York Minster, for example, there are two actual wells as well as at least two fonts.

The early medieval church was happy to create its own holy wells. They developed their own form of well cults and, in some cases, were willing to adopt some elements of Pagan practices regarding these wells. In the tenth century, the Bishop Cuthbert created a holy well on Inner Farne, yet the church was largely hostile to wells during that century.

Christians use water in ritual for the sacrament that admits people into the church, for baptism, and as Holy Water for blessings. Sacred vessels must be washed. Water is both a purifier and a transmitter of spiritual power. It is no surprise, then, that Christians widely adopt holy wells of other cultures.

Some examples of these assimilated wells are more easily identified than others, such as Thor's Well in Thorsas, Norway, now known as St. Thor's. Possibly the best-known healing well in Britain is Chalice Well in Glastonbury, which has both Christian and Pagan associations. After the First World War, Frederick Bligh Bond donated its wrought-iron cover as a peace offering. The cover is decorated with two circles that represent the interlocking worlds of spirit and substance. The healing waters of this well are so well-known that even King Charles has been seen allowing them to flow over an injured arm in hopes of obtaining a speedy recovery in international news.

Wishing wells came into being when religious attitudes were changing and wells were being renamed. Rather than offer a prayer to a saint, the local people would make a wish, then throw in a coin as an offering to the well spirit.

WELL CUSTOMS AND TRADITIONS

While well traditions often hold a combination of Christian and Pagan associations and common themes, each well seems to have its own unique customs. St. Maughold's Well on the Isle of Man requires the petitioner, who is seeking healing, to drink the Water, then sit in the "Saint's chair" nearby. This "chair" is a natural carved rock structure. St. Maughold's is particularly known for healing sore eyes as well as infertility.

It is not unusual for a well to be associated with a specific type of healing. The Well of Youth at Dun Iona requires those who seek healing of the youth of spirit to wash in its waters at dawn; Madron Well in Cornwall is associated with healing skin diseases and divination; St. Fillian's Pool at Tyndrum, Scotland, St. Gwenfaen's Well at Rhoscolyn, Angelsey, and St. Non's Well at Altarnun, Cornwall are all known for curing mental illness.

The Pagan legacies in well tradition become apparent through certain aspects of local customs. Traditional offerings at wells such as coins, pins, and butter are typical at fairy wells or those associated with fertility, like St. Augustine's Well at Cerne Abbas, Dorset.

Many wells—including some that have been claimed by Christian practice—still attract visitors on Pagan holidays, including Lammas (12 August, old Pagan Lugnassah), Beltane (1 May or old Celtic Beltane, 12 May), Samhain (31 October through 1 November), Imbolc (1 February), and Midsummer (21 June), as well as old Saint's Days.

Fairies are believed to still inhabit certain wells, most notably Minchmoor Well (also known as Cheese Well) in Peeblesshire. An offering must be made to the well fairy, such as a pin, a coin, or a piece of cheese. The wells in Brayton, Harphan, Holderness, and Atwick in Yorkshire and Wooler, Northumberland are also believed to be presided over by fairies or spirits.

Women who suspected their babies had been exchanged for a changeling left their babies by these wells, expecting to find their own infant in the morning. Robin Round Cap Well in East Yorkshire is reported to be haunted by a brownie. The list goes on. In France, hundreds of wells are under the tutelage of "saints" who are actually fairies disguised by Christian piety.

Healings have often been reported to have been affected at sacred wells. In one instance at Madron Well in Cornwall in 1640, the cure was witnessed by a bishop. The process for these healings generally consisted of drinking some of the water from the well and performing other rituals like walking around the well three times or drinking specifically from a designated cup or skull.

Water that had washed or been drunk from holy relics was believed to have healing powers, or water from the well itself was used for washing the affliction. Dipping heads, stones, or other objects was believed to give them magical abilities. Charm stones dipped in holy wells are still used for healing. Historians generally accept that traditional dances around the wells of England must have come from an ancient Pagan past and were probably part of a ritual associated with the well.

Stone megaliths are often found near wells and there is a belief that these have served as "guardians" for the wells. Some wells are known for spiritual rather than healing powers and their symbolism falls well into the realms of magic. Alder, oak, or hazel trees are commonly found near wells and other sources of sacred waters. Like the megaliths, they are sometimes believed to be "guardians" of the water source.

Stone circles are also found near wells including at Drumlanrig and Tullybelton. Those that have single megalithic guardians are often in

conjunction with trees, particularly alder and oak. The trees that are found near these wells are likely to be decorated with offerings. Some have old coins hammered into the bark, but these days, it is more likely to find evidence of another old custom: strips of cloth hung on the branches. These should be of natural fibre, as the tradition originates with the belief that the cloth that has bound a wound left on a sacred tree would cause the wound to heal as the cloth moulders and disintegrates.

Brightly coloured strips of cotton have become a modern-day offering for the trees that watch over sacred wells or other spiritual places. These can still be found at many wells, including Virtuous Well at Trellech, Gwent, where the strips of cloth hang from nearby hazel trees, and at Madron Well in Penzance, St. Gundred's Well (also known as St. Conan's Well) at Roche, Cornwall. St. Gundred's Well is specifically known for healing children's eyes, and St. Non's Well at St. David's, Dyfed is also known for healing children, who are dipped in the Water; their parents leave offerings of pins or pebbles.

Ritually damaged coins were given as offerings at the hot spring at Bath, near the baths complex (Roman name *Aquae Sulis*, named after the goddess Sulis, linked with Minerva and subsequently known as *Sulis Minerva*) in exchange for healings or curses, which were submitted on clay tablets.

Note that wells that require ritual circumnavigation nearly always require this to be done sunwise (clockwise or deosil). The direction is important because this reflects the movement of the Sun, which is a way of keeping in harmony with cosmic forces. It is reflected in many folk customs like stirring a pot "with the Sun." One well that is an exception to this is in Caithness, where it is customary to reverse this direction.

Wells are known for augurs. This may take the form of a well spirit who simply speaks to the petitioner, or may come in the form of a fish or worm whose behaviour determines the predictions. Sometimes a priest reads the animal's movements, but more often, it is fairly straightforward folk custom.

Odd Properties of Sacred Wells

There are tales of wells that move locations when insulted. Wells become insulted when defiled and will stop whatever power they have previously displayed. Insulting behaviour may include washing clothes in a well meant for drinking, throwing dead animals in, immersing animals in healing wells intended for humans, not following prescribed ritual, defiling trees, or allowing guardian trees to die naturally.

Some wells acquire fame because of odd properties like never freezing or never drying up. St. Andrew's Well at Kirkandrews-on-Eden in Cumbria is reputed to be *"not affected by most intense frost or the longest drought"*(Hope). Odd noises occur at some wells, including whistling sounds and drumming without benefit of human drummers. These strange sounds have been observed at Oundle in Northampton, Harphan at Humberside, and Hill Wooton in Warwick. The well at Oundle has since disappeared.

Petrifying wells that contain large quantities of mineral deposits are known for "turning objects into stone." The Dropping Well at Knaresborough, North Yorkshire is one of the better-known of these and is associated with the stories of Mother Shipton, a soothsayer and

prophetess. A few rare wells have been reported to produce substances that appear to be milk or blood. In the case of the Blood Well at Glastonbury, the red colour is the result of iron deposits.

Very rural wells are sometimes tended by women, reputed to be witches, acting as keepers of the wells. Some believe that the magic of these wells will only work with her assistance, though this often consists only of providing a drinking vessel. Many of these might only have been local residents who took it upon themselves to maintain the wells.

The healing properties of wells are something that science has attempted to explain. One theory is that iron- or sulphur-rich Waters effect cures and belief provides a psychosomatic helping hand. In Water tested from wells that do not contain these minerals, other elements that are far more subtle and something indiscernible could be responsible. No scientist will ever concede that it is simply a matter of elemental spirit magic.

The Spirit of the Well

Much of what we might expect from the attendant spirits of wells is reflected in the folklore attached to them. Their forms vary but are most often either female spirit forms or those of sacred fishes kept in holy wells. Salmon and trout were sacred fishes to the Celts, and there have been a few wells where a resident trout was held in such reverence that it was replaced if it should die. Salmon were more likely to be seen in rivers and are symbolic of the underworld, life renewed, and procreation.

Some of the fish guardians in wells have been reported to speak or to wear gold rings or chains. These fish are believed to have been of Spirit rather than flesh. Whatever the truth of this might be, there is no doubt that every well is attended by its own spirit as is any other elemental location in nature. It makes no difference whether it is a sacred pool or a constructed well, it is the Water itself that generates Spirit.

The reverence given to sacred wells will naturally affect the nature of the Water spirit, as does the calm nature of a contained source of the element. Perhaps this is why so many well spirits assume the forms of ghostly white ladies, which have religious significance both to those who follow some form of Goddess worship and to the Christians who revere their own Goddess in the form of the Virgin Mary.

DANCING WITH THE FIRE

The steady rhythm of a basic four-four drum beat pounds through the otherwise still night air. Soon, more drums join in, creating new pulses. The flames of a bonfire dance with the pure joy of being intense, as potentially creative as it could be destructive. A mood is forming among the visitors, and some begin to sway in the early cadence of dance.

They feel the need to move, almost as though they are being taken over by a spirit created through the sound and vibration of the drums, spurred on by the spirit of the bonfire.

As the dance continues, the movements become wild and abandoned, the participants completely giving themselves over to the spirit of the dance. Scientists would quote brain enzymes as the cause, but there is something more that science cannot adequately explain.

The dancers are overcome by the need to express their passion through the dance. It is not unlike the ardent spirit that possesses those who are caught up in sexual passion: a spirit of nature that can direct the human drives and take form through the movements of the human body, just as its brother Fire spirit takes form through the flame of the bonfire.

Dance inspires something in the human spirit that goes far beyond scientific explanation. It holds the rule of number, rhythm, and order. It is a demonstration of the microcosm of the greater macrocosm of the universe. Dance inspires creative genius, including Einstein, who was inspired by Russian ballet, and Wagner, who praised Beethoven's 7th Symphony as *"the apotheosis of the dance."*

Fairies have long been associated with wild dances, particularly at night. Many fairy legends speak of men who are enticed into joining the revels of the "wee folk," only to learn later that they have been dancing for more than a year without stopping or to drop dead from exhaustion because they are unable to stop dancing.

One form of magic that has been used by most primitive societies is to "dance out" the wish. Tribal cultures have historically acted out planting and harvesting to entice the gods to help crops grow. Acting out weather magic to bring rainfall or the growth of grain are still common.

Dance is also used for telling stories, passed down from one generation to the next. The Hula of Hawaiian origin is one good example of storytelling in dance that continues today. Ballet and modern dance are forms of this same art for the entertainment of modern society. Tribal dance has also been used to dance out intent for battle or in preparation for a hunt.

Dance is a natural means of inducing mystical states and even trance. In Southern India, the caste known as "Devil Dancers" dance through spinning and leaping in order to reach the degree of inspiration that is considered essential to their healing powers. A similar practice is used by Mongolian Shamans, who dance to frighten away the devils of disease who afflict their tribesmen.

Ecstatic dance is integral to the Bogomiles of Russia, as well as to the "Dancing Dervishes" of Turkey, who are well-known for their spinning dances that instigate frenzy and a deep trance state. Many forms of religious hysteria are achieved through wild dancing. Some forms of these dances include an invitation to the gods to descend spiritually into the midst of their dancing worshippers. Others are used to incite the worshippers towards some action. Fertility dances, in particular, are characterised by delirium and frenzy.

Movement brings a form of comfort to the human soul, as is demonstrated by the gentle rocking of an upset child or even an adult under stress. It brings a feeling of self-healing. In her article, "The Power of Dance: Health and Healing," Judith Lynne Hanna, Ph.D., tells us that *"dance may promote wellness by strengthening the immune system through muscular action and physiological processes. Dance conditions an individual to moderate, eliminate, or avoid tension, chronic fatigue, and other disabling conditions that result from the effect of stress"* (323).

She goes on to explain that dance involves the simultaneous use of right and left brain in an intricate sensory combination of movement, rhythm, and music that uses most, if not all, of the senses. Dance might reduce or even eliminate pain. For some people, it provides a feeling of control that minimises the sense of helplessness and fear that is related to pain.

Dance is used to induce the temporary insanity of the Bacchic or Dionysian rites. These can include outbursts of savage violence. Witchdoctors of some African tribes engage in a form of dance to "smell out" their victims. These dances awaken the full potency of nature in the same way as the agricultural gods are aroused for growing crops. The history of magical dance is known as far back as the Ancient Egyptian culture and probably predates written history in tribal cultures throughout human history.

A similar form of sympathetic magic is aroused through Greek drama. The Ancient Greeks used gesture to represent feeling, passion, and action both in drama and in religious dances associated with the cults of Apollo and Dionysus. Dance is at the heart of many ancient mysteries. Lucian says in his *Peri Orcheseos* that *"[t]here is not a single ancient mystery in which there is not dancing. Those who reveal the ancient mysteries dance them out."*

The *Geranos,* or Crane Dance, is said to have been originally performed by Theseus on his return from the Labyrinth at Crete, which was danced at the festival to Apollo in the Isle of Delos. The complex patterns of movement within the dance are supposed to represent the windings of the celebrated maze at Knossos.

Dance is closely associated with masking, often becoming a process of totemism or a connection between the living and the dead. It is used as preparation for the hunt or to commune with the gods, also represented by masked performers. The Corroboree of the Australian Aboriginal people, for example, paint their bodies with stripes resembling skeletons to represent the dead. In this culture, only the men dance for ceremonies such as initiation, conclusion of peace agreements, and purely social functions.

Dance has been used to accompany sacrifice in various cultures, such as among the Khonds of Bengal and Madras.

Ancient ritual dances survive today in folk dances of many countries. All medieval dances, according to several sources, are survivals of Pagan ritual dances. The most important relic of the dances of the Middle Ages is the Morris dance. The exact origin of Morris dancing is not known, but the word Morris is believed by some to be derived from Moorish. This would account for the black face paint used in some forms of Morris dance costuming. There is an alternative theory that it could be related to the coal industry from the Midlands of Britain, the black make-up representing the soot on the miner's faces.

Sword dancing appears in Teutonic as well as Celtic folk dance, not to mention many Eastern and Polynesian traditional dances. Lewis Spence associated sword dances generally with war dances performed in honour of a deity of strife before going out to battle.

The Longsword Dance, which occurs in the Morris tradition, has definite Sun associations as is seen at the conclusion of the performance, when the swords, locked together, are raised to show the Sunray image created by the configuration of the swords.

Some ancient Irish dances had a serpentine nature to them, like the Rinke Teampuill, or "Dance of the Temple," which was performed from left to right, but changes if a horn was blown to indicate unfavourable omens. The list of cultural and historic dances could go on and on.

Dance is magic in pure spirit form. It is alive, it is intense, and it is free. It is a fiery spirit that can be raised anytime and in any place.

Chapter 11

Example Spells and Methods

The sample spells in this chapter are meant as examples only and not as a comprehensive grimoire or Book of Shadows for elemental spirit spells. Spells of any kind are most effective when they are constructed for the specific purpose, and this applies even more so when dealing with spirit energies who respond more to the sincerity of a spell from the heart than to the reading of a script. In particular, Air spirits respond well to spontaneous creativity.

These spells are offered primarily as models and as a starting point for those who are either inexperienced in magic and not yet confident enough to construct their own spells, or for those who have learned a system that might need adapting to incorporate references to elemental spirits. Readers should develop and individualise their own spells, whether or not they start from these examples, and follow their own hearts when working magic with the spirits of the elements.

A SAMPLE OPENING RITUAL

Opening a ritual can be done in many different ways. You might choose to set up an altar, in which case you should have all of the materials you intend to use gathered and set up according to how you want them before actually beginning the spell. However, there is a tradition in magic that states the ritual is actually started by gathering these items and the shift in mind state that accompanies that process.

The items gathered might include representations of the four basic elements, representations of deity or Spirit in another form, personal items, or implements. Basic ritual equipment might include the pentacle, wand, athame or sword, and chalice, or if you're working in a more medieval magician system, you might require candles in black and white, a white wand and black wand, or other items traditional to your chosen system. A candle in a colour appropriate to your ritual intent might also grace the altar and perhaps a few candles just for light and atmosphere. If you are consulting an elemental spirit for your purpose, something to represent their element would be appropriate, like a special rock for an Earth elemental, for example.

Apart from the purpose, the procedure should also be decided in advance unless you are doing a spontaneous spell. Group rituals, in particular, need to be co-ordinated. You might wish to call quarters or the spirits as a whole, either while walking in a circle around your ritual space or while standing in one place and directing your invocation into the ritual space.

Wiccan groups tend to stand in one place and turn to face the appropriate directions for each quarter. For an elemental ritual, I suggest directing your energy to an item representing each element as you speak your invitation if you are doing a balanced ritual inviting spirits of all of the elements, or, if doing something appropriate to a single element, just to the item you wish to represent that element.

In a spontaneous ritual, this could be no more than an awareness of the natural elements surrounding you, especially if doing the ritual out of doors. An example opening for such a ritual is as follows:

"I call the spirits of the Earth, Air, Fire, and Water to come to me in love and magic, to bring me balance in the stability of Earth, the inspiration of Air, the passion of Fire, and the emotional power of Water, to aid that which I wish to do here now."

From there, you can launch into the purpose of the ritual or construct a more elaborate general opening if you feel inclined to be theatrical or feel that more is needed.

If you wish to invite the spirits of just one element for a purpose appropriate to that element, you can focus your full energy on the representation for that element and adjust your wording accordingly. For example, an Earth opening might look like:

> *"(I/we) invite the spirits of Earth to join my ritual and to give strength to the solid foundation of (my/our) purpose, even as the Earth beneath (me/us) is the solid basis of the temple of Earth and all things that come forth from it."*

Or, to incorporate the intent:

> *"(I/we) call upon the element of Earth for this ritual for (stability/ fertility/prosperity/healing) and seek within the spirit of Earth for the solid strength to accomplish (my/our) purpose."*

For Air, you may say:

> *"(I/we) invite the spirits of Air to join (my/our) ritual, to stir the creative power of inspiration and to give the spark of creation to (my/our) intent, even as the spirits of Air give this creative spark to all that lives and breathes within the temple of the Air on our shared planet."*

Another way to phrase it may be:

> *"(I/we) call upon the element of Air for this ritual for (inspiration/communication/finding a lost object) and seek within the spirit of Air for the inspiration and creative spark to accomplish (my/our) purpose."*

Direct your "fiery" emotions into your opening for a Fire invitation, regardless of the ritual purpose. Emotions such as anger, excitement, or passion will stir the required forces.

> *"(I/we) invite the spirits of Fire to join (my/our) ritual and to give vigour to the progression of the magic that I do here now, even as the Fire gives drive and purpose to the progression of life and all that exists."*

Alternatively, you might also say:

"(I/we) call upon the element of Fire for this ritual for (change/progression/retribution) and seek within the spirit of Fire for the strength and drive to accomplish (my/our) purpose."

Note that "retribution" is not the same as revenge. Magic to seek revenge is wasted energy. Retribution is more directed at seeking justice for a genuine wrong when there is something that can be corrected by it.

Two openings you might use for Water invitations, much in the same manner as the other elements, are:

"(I/we) invite the spirits of Water, of the streams, pools, and powerful oceans of the world, to join (my/our) rites and to lend the qualities of intuition, of feeling, and of conscience to (my/our) magic. Let the power of directed emotion bring productive fruition to what (I/we) do here today. Let it be so."

"(I/we) call upon the element of Water for this ritual for (cleansing/fertility/love/insight) and seek within the spirit of Water to bring the depth of intention and 'the knowing' to accomplish (my/our) purpose."

CALLING QUARTER GUARDIANS

If you wish to call quarters, there are several books in print with scripts for known traditions or you can create your own. I offer examples of wording that acknowledges the elemental spirits here, adapted from basic formulae from my experience:

"(I/we) call upon the spirits of Earth, of the trees, stones, and all things of the Earth to witness (my/our) rites and to lend their strength and stability to (my/our) magic. Let it be so." (Or "So mote it be.")

"(I/we) call upon the spirits of the Air, of the winds and storms, of the spirit of creativity, and of those things that are of the element of Air to witness (my/our) rites and to inspire (me/us) to seek the creative spark that will give (my/our) purpose form. Let it be so." (Or "So mote it be.")

"(I/we) call upon the spirits of the Fire, of Will, of change and transformation, of drive, and of the spark of life itself, to witness (my/our) rites and to lend the qualities of determination and fortitude to (my/our) magic. Let it be so." (Or "So mote it be.")

"(I/we) invite the spirits of the Water to join (my/our) ritual and to bring the qualities of sensation and empathy with the spiritual to (my/our) purpose, immersing (me/us) in the spirit of Water even as Water immerses all and flows through every crevice of its path. Let it be so." (Or "So mote it be.")

A ritual opening should always be balanced with a closing and final banishing. The purpose of a closing is to make a formal end to the ritual, after which you will want to "ground" yourself and banish any residual energies. This is very important in any form of ritual.

The wording of a closing is generally related to the wording of the opening used and, if you call spirits (whether as quarter guardians or for any other purpose), it is always a good idea to include thanks to them for whatever part they have played in your ritual. If you've used the above examples, closings to balance them are offered here:

"(I/we) thank the spirits of Earth (Air/Fire/Water) for joining (my/our) ritual and for providing strength and solid foundations to (my/our) purpose. Depart now in peace to your natural realms, until next we come together in love and magic."

Following are some examples of ways to thank Earth spirits who have assisted you in quarters:

"(I/we) thank the spirits of the Earth for joining (my/our) ritual and for providing strength and solid foundation to (my/our) purpose. Depart now in peace to your natural realms, until the next time we come together in love and magic."

"(I/we) now release the spirit of the element of Earth and thank you for your assistance in the ritual for (stability/fertility/prosperity/healing). Let the purpose be accomplished and the spirit of Earth be free and at peace."

"(I/we) thank the spirits of Earth, of the trees, stones, and all things of the Earth, for witnessing (my/our) rites and for lending their strength and stability to (my/our) magic. Let them return now to their realms, until next (I/we) call upon them for their assistance. Let it be so." (Or "So mote it be.")

Following are three examples of ways you may thank spirits of the Air for their assistance:

"(I/we) thank the spirits of the Air for joining (my/our) ritual, and for providing the creative spark of inspiration for (my/our) purpose. Depart now in peace to your natural realms, until next we come together in love and magic."

"(I/we) now release the spirits of the element of Air and thank you for your assistance in this ritual for (inspiration/communication/finding a lost object). Let the purpose be accomplished and the spirits of the Air be free and at peace."

"(I/we) thank the spirits of the Air, of the winds and storms, of the spirit of creativity, and of all those things that are of the element of Air, for witnessing (my/our) rites and for lending the qualities of inspiration and the creative spark to (my/our) magic. Let them return now to their realms until next (I/we) call upon them for their assistance. Let it be so." (Or "So mote it be.")

Following are three suggestions for phrases to thank the spirits of Fire for their assistance:

"(I/we) thank the spirits of the Fire for joining (my/our) ritual, and for providing the spark of determination to (my/our) purpose. Depart now in peace to your natural realms, until next we come together in love and magic."

"(I/we) now release the spirit of the element of Fire and thank you for your assistance in this ritual for (change/progression/retribution). Let the purpose be accomplished and the spirit of the Fire be released from this service and at peace."

"(I/we) thank the spirits of the Fire, of Will, of change and transfor-
mation, of drive, and of the spark of life itself, for witnessing (my/our)
rites and for lending the qualities of determination and fortitude to
(my/our) magic. Let them now return to their realms, until next (I/we)
call upon them for their assistance. Let it be so." (Or "So mote it be.")

The important thing to remember when summoning Water spirits
for any purpose is to feel your summoning. How you refer to the spirit
(Undine, a name of a specific Water spirit, or simply "Spirits of the Water"
or "West") is less important than the need to project the experience or
essence of Water from the emotional depths of your personal being.

"(I/we) thank the spirits of the Water for joining (my/our) ritual and
for bringing the qualities of sensation and empathy to (my/our) purpose,
for immersing (me/us) in the spirit of Water even as Water immerses
all and flows through every crevice of its path. Let them now return to
their realms in peace and tranquillity until next (I/we) require their
assistance. Let it be so." (Or "So mote it be.")

"(I/we) thank the spirits of the element of Water for this ritual (cleansing/
fertility/love/insight) and wish to remember the depth of intention and
knowing that they have brought to (my/our) purpose. (I/we) release
them now to return to their realms in peace and tranquillity until
next (I/we) require their assistance. Let it be so." (Or "So mote it be.")

"(I/we) thank the spirits of the Water, of the streams, pools, and the
powerful oceans of our world, for witnessing (my/our) rites and for
lending the qualities of intuition, of feeling, and of conscience to (my/
our) magic. Let the power of directed emotion bring productive fruition
to what (I/we) have done here today. Let it be so." (Or "So mote it be.")

THE MIDDLE BIT

For some magic users, the "middle bit" comes between the opening and
closing, while for others it encompasses the entire ritual. This is a matter
for individual choice, though I do encourage some sort of transition into
"ritual mode" as well as the importance of a final banishing.

The first step is to decide what that purpose will be. In any magic, it's highly recommended that this purpose should be very specific, with much thought given to the chosen wording, taking note of any alternate meanings that it might be possible to read into your words. Following are a few examples of spells that are related to specific elements.

EARTH ELEMENTAL SPELLS

Whether a Pagan or magician worships among the trees in a forest, builds a temple of stone, or performs magic solely within the confines of their own physical body, the basis for all magic is firmly set in some form of an Earth-based physical structure. This could even be the planet itself. Therein lies understanding of the magic of the Earth element: without a solid base, there can be no magic.

A Spell for Inviting Earth Spirits into the Garden

After opening in the chosen manner, proceed with a direct invitation.

> *"Spirits of the Earth, of the plants and flowers, the trees and rocks, (add any specific items that are included in your own garden, gesturing to each in turn), I invite you to join my garden, to help me to care for the growing things here and to bring the balance of nature to this garden and to make it a magical place, by the power of Earth, Air, Fire, and Water, so shall it be."*

Inviting a Spirit into a Stone or Other Object to Represent Earth

Apart from the pentacle you might keep for an altar implement, you might wish to invite an Earth elemental into an object for a specific purpose. Stones (and especially crystals) have their own spirits who might be persuaded to aid your purpose. Forming ritual vessels from clay and other Earthy materials has a long precedent in magic.

Carvings or other decorations can be done in advance or as part of the ritual. If you wish to decorate the object during the ritual, this is best done while stating the purpose of the object. As it may take time to carve or paint symbols on an object, the purpose can be made into a chant to repeat over and over again as you work.

One very powerful form of magic is to create a chant to state this purpose in a language that you do not normally speak, as the repetition of words that you do not consciously understand will sublimate the meaning into the most powerful part of your subconscious. Be careful with your translations, though! Getting the wording slightly wrong or using a phrase that can be interpreted differently than how you intend can lead to disaster.

Attune yourself to the chosen object, then choose a time and place where you will not be interrupted, and prepare for your ritual.

Open according to your chosen practices. If the object is complete, you need only perform the invitation at this point. Hold the object and try to feel the spirit within it. If you are trying to bring a spirit into it, issue your invitation:

> *"I call upon the element of Earth to bring forth a spirit to inhabit this (name object). Let this spirit come willingly and without reservation, to become a part of the magic of this (object), and to dedicate its existence to the purpose for which it is intended."*

I suggest specifying what this purpose is at this point, such as: *"to bring the magic of the element of Earth to my altar."*

You might want to dedicate stones or other objects to specific purposes separately using this formula or something similar. Close and banish.

HEALING

Healing spells are not meant to replace modern science, but to be used in conjunction with medical treatment.

Some healing spells come from old superstitions, employing sympathetic magic or visualisation.

To remove a disease or heal a wound, rub the afflicted area with a cut apple or potato while chanting, "Take this (disease/wound) to the heart of the fruit, let nature's healing draw forth this affliction from the root."

Dig a hole in the ground (or have one pre-dug) and bury the apple or potato as quickly as possible. As it rots, the affliction should heal.

If you are ill, find a patch of ground where you can lie comfortably either on grass or bare earth. Lie down with arms spread and mentally see your pain, anguish, or sickness sink into the ground beneath you. Sense the rhythm of the Earth pulsating in time with your own heartbeat and feel the Earth's natural healing energy rise into you. You should feel better when you are ready to get up and leave.

To rid yourself of problems plaguing you, take a handful of earth and draw a sigil representing your trouble in the dirt. Become aware of the spirit of the Earth as you do this and ask it to take this trouble from you. Mentally project all of your anguish into the symbol, then toss the dirt behind you and walk away from it. Do not turn back. Mentally thank the Earth for its healing energy as you walk away.

To make an Earth charm, tie up a small green square of cloth (cotton or silk) with some fresh soil so that none can escape. You may wish to include a special stone or a silver coin in the dirt. Carry this with you to help give you security and stability in times of trouble.

To Charge an Object

Make a ring of crystals or special stones that have attracted you enough to collect and bring home. Place the object in the centre of the circle. Trace the circle clockwise with your dominant hand, feeling the energy that connects the stones and the collective spirit of the circle.

Repeatedly chant, *"Let this (item) be infused with the energy of the Earth and with the magic of this circle."* Continue by stating what the purpose of the object shall be. Then close with, *"So shall it be."* Put the object in a safe place and ground yourself.

Knot Spells

The basic idea of a knot spell is that when you tie the knot, you're binding your intention. They can be used for many purposes including personal change, stability in some aspect of your life, to incorporate something new into your life, better luck in general, and even to promote prosperity. Always remember when dealing with elemental spirits that you must not tie a secure knot, but leave the end open!

The first step is to choose your medium: rope, cord, wire, chain, scarves, yarn; or, more pleasing to elementals, ivy or other vines (tied gently!), ribbons tied to a stone, or strips of cotton cloth tied to a strong plant or tree. Anything that can be tied has potential for use.

Construct a sentence to explain your purpose. This must take the form of a positive statement rather than something to rid yourself of, as the knots or ties will secure the subject of your statement to you.

Open the ritual with a petition to the spirit of the plant, tree, or stone you've chosen for this ritual to help bring the quality you seek into your life, then follow this with the prepared statement, repeated several times as you plait ribbons, branches, or whatever you have chosen to use.

Example wordings for different situations include:

GENERAL: *"I call upon the spirit of this (plant/stone/tree) to secure into my life this wish of my desire."*

PERSONAL CHANGE: *"I wish to breathe the fresh Air, free of the need for nicotine,"* or, *"I wish to face the world with confidence and positive thinking."* (Adapt for your chosen purpose.)

STABILITY IN SOME ASPECT OF YOUR LIFE: *"Let the spirit of this stone (or other item, though stones are good for this) infuse me with the stability of the Earth itself, of the solid foundations that I now feel the need for (purpose)."*

TO INCORPORATE SOMETHING NEW INTO YOUR LIFE: *"Let the spirit of this (stone, ivy, or other item) help me to incorporate (new influence) into my life, to feel it become a natural part of me, that I may be at peace with this new aspect of my life."* Weaving spells are generally good for this purpose.

BETTER LUCK IN GENERAL: *"Let the spirit of the Earth within this (item) bring the positive energy of better luck into my life, and let this new energy attract good things to me in every aspect of my life."*

TO PROMOTE PROSPERITY: *"I wish for the means to (live in comfort/obtain a specific item/attain a specific goal) in the world of men where these things are obtained with symbols to represent worth. Let the necessary symbols,*

called currency, come into my hands without doing harm to myself or any other person or creature of nature."

In the case of prosperity spells, it is important to specify a purpose for material gain, as well as to specify that the method by which it comes will do no harm to anyone, lest you find yourself collecting insurance payments. This is an important consideration with any magic.

The statement must be specific to the purpose as elemental spirits won't understand the concept of wealth for its own sake, and the wording must always be positive in nature.

Growing and Harvesting

Growing things—whether it is flowers, herbs, trees, or fruits and vegetables—can be a very satisfying experience in and of itself. Tuning into the nature spirits while planting and perhaps harvesting and cooking makes this experience truly magical.

While planting, remember that things you grow will be attended by Earth spirits. These will come whether or not you make the special effort to invite or recognise them, but an invitation spell will help connect you to the garden and has been known to result in better plant growth.

To harvest something you have planted, whether it's flowers to decorate your home, altar, or something you intend to eat, it is recommended that you mentally (or perhaps even verbally) explain your purpose to the plant before cutting it and ask the spirit of the plant to let no harm come to the plant itself if you are taking a part of it, like berries, or, if you are harvesting the entire plant, ask it to yield to the natural cycle of birth and death in nature, giving the life of the plant into the cycle of the food chain.

Cooking vegetables you have grown in harmony with the Earth spirits in this way is itself an act of magic. You might wish to remain aware of the spirit of the plant as you prepare and consume it, allowing it to fill you spiritually as well as physically. You might even wish to chant spells during preparation to invite the spirit of the plant to feed your spirit as it feeds your body. The words for this are best if they come from your heart rather than a prepared script.

AIR ELEMENTAL SPELLS

A SPELL FOR INVITING AIR SPIRITS INTO THE TEMPLE OR HOME

As air is with us always and Air spirits plentiful within their element, this is more of a recognition and invitation to form a connection. Begin by lighting a purification incense such as frankincense or dragon's blood, then walk throughout the home, visiting every room, and chant something like:

"I invite the spirits of the Air to share my home in peace, to bring creativity and inspired thoughts to me (and my family/housemates if applicable) and all who enter here, to reveal any who would bring deceit to this home, and to purify the Air within, that all who enter here will breathe the fresh and clear Air of Spirit."

Add or subtract phrases as appropriate to circumstances. Ideally, you should begin either in the farthest North or East point of the living space and follow a path as close to following a deosil circle as the layout permits. When you have completed the circuit by reaching your starting point again, finish by thanking the spirits of the Air for their attention. This blessing can be done alone or as part of a larger house blessing ritual which could include all elements as well as securing the perimeter.

If the blessing is for a temple space, a variation on the above might go something like:

"I call upon the spirits of the element of Air and invite them to lend their powers of inspiration and clear-seeing to this temple and the magic that will be done within it, to become a part of this place and of those who practice within it. Let clear visions of the mind prevail in all workings done here."

INVITING AN AIR SPIRIT INTO AN OBJECT TO REPRESENT AIR

This could be a wand or staff, something to decorate the altar, or an incense burner that is kept on the altar to produce smoke to represent the Air element. Whatever you choose, it is a representation of an element that cannot be pinned down entirely to a material object.

The item can be decorated. Ribbons, feathers, and bells are all appropriate for a representation of Air and are particularly attractive on a staff. If you wish to perform the ritual outdoors to allow the winds to participate, be sure to attach and secure anything like feathers that might blow away beforehand. Doing this indoors or outdoors is a matter of personal choice.

Open according to your chosen method. If the object is already decorated and ready for use, you need only perform the invitation at this point. Otherwise, you can decorate as part of the ritual. Hold the object and try to "attune" to it while moving it in some way through the air. You can wave it or trace symbols in the Air (runes or other meaningful shapes), then issue your invitation:

> *"I call upon the element of Air to bring forth a spirit to attach to this (name item). Let this spirit come willingly and without reservation to become part of the magic of this (item) and to dedicate its existence to the purpose for which it is intended."*

If the item is to be dedicated to a specific purpose—perhaps as a temple representation of the element or for an ongoing spell—state the purpose. For an altar decoration, it can be as simple as, *"to bring the magic of the element of Air to my altar."* If specific qualities of Air are desired, name those.

An item dedicated to Air must be used frequently to sustain the connection. If the item stays on a permanent altar, this is maintained through all rituals done using that altar. If the object is left unregarded for a long time, a new ritual might be required to use it effectively again.

SIGIL MAGIC

Sigil magic is a very basic method that has been used in many forms throughout history, but the method most often described by modern magicians was made known through the writings of the magician Austin Osman Spare. Spare was an artist and worked his magic very visually. He was observed on several occasions to draw a symbol on a white card, hold it to his forehead to "charge" the spell, then wait for results, which generally happened very quickly.

For more difficult operations, the spell charging was done through sexual energies. His method was to use a personal alphabet to write out his intent, then eliminate duplicate letters and draw a symbol from the remaining characters. The resulting design represented the desire to the subconscious mind of the magician.

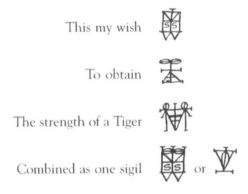

Next, the paper with the symbol drawn on it was put into a crucible made expressly for the purpose, into which he would masturbate while keeping the mind focused on the sigil. He would then bury the crucible for a period of time, then retrieve it and repeat the operation. Afterwards, the paper was destroyed, usually burnt.

Variations on Spare's methods have been popularised over time. Charging can be done through any intense emotion, and methods that magicians have used include staring at the sigil while on a roller coaster, ecstatic dance, miming the symbols, and sound sigils used by the blind. Any form of flute-like instrument is good for making patterns with music, though string or keyboard instruments can also be used.

Releasing the sigil can be done through other elements: burying it to let it moulder, releasing it into a source of water, or even creating a work of art to hang on the wall until the conscious mind stops noting it and the design is sublimated into the subconscious.

FREE ASSOCIATION

There are several ways to employ free association. This is closely related to automatic writing (see Chapter Nine). The idea of free association is to free the mind to create magic. It is the art of attaining a certain level of trance like singing spells, chanting, drumming, and other mildly hypnotic methods.

One method using writing is to write random sentences concerning your purpose around the edges of a sheet of paper, adapting the path of the writing when you come round to the beginning so that it forms a new row and begins to spiral inward. I've personally found this a very effective spell method.

In art, free association works through drawing without intent: letting your hand form lines as if by its own will as you allow your mind to wander over thoughts of your intent or desire. The resulting drawing becomes a sigil, a representation of your intent, that can be kept as a visual symbol or destroyed as in other sigil spells.

In music, free association occurs by singing, humming, or playing a musical instrument (preferably one with which you have some proficiency) randomly in a meditative state while contemplating the intent. In this way, the magician expresses the desire on a subconscious level. Different notes or riffs can cause emotional responses, and practicing this frequently may lead to developing melodies associated with spellwork to the magic user.

It is useful with any of the musical methods to determine a specific series of notes that you designate as a finish to the session with something that will break the trance and bring you back into consciously playing the music or coming to a stop. Something a little difficult to play or with a discordant note works well.

Another method of free association is done through slow body movements, similar to a form of dance or Tai Chi. It can be done in silence, with relaxed music, or with a slow, steady beat of drums. If choosing music, something that stirs a deep or intense response (often "dark" music) works well.

A Spell to Seek Inspiration

I recommend a thought-form spirit for this as it is your own creativity that you wish to tap into. Combining the attributes of Air and Earth directed at an object, perhaps a crystal, works well. The combination lends stability and allows for leaving the crystal or other object unused for periods of time without losing its "programming."

Open a ritual according to your usual method and hold the object to your "third eye" between your eyebrows. Invoke the servitor with something like:

> *"I wish to call a servitor from my deepest being, from the very wellspring of my imagination, that will inspire my imaginative and intuitive power and free the creative power within me whenever I shall have need and call. Let now this spirit inhabit this (object), forever a part of me unless and until I shall choose to take the spirit back within myself. Let it be so."*

Close the ritual as usual, banish, and ground.

A Spell to Help Pass an Exam

A slight variation of the above spell can be used to help pass exams. For this, my first choice of object would be a silver pen. (Not silver coloured, but actual silver.) Failing that, an object that can sit on a desk while an exam is taking place without drawing attention, perhaps a "lucky rock" which, if not a crystal, should at least contain some quartz. Many common stones contain quartz and can be easily identified by sparkling points within an otherwise dull surface.

Again, the spell is opened and closed according to your usual practices, but the wording would adapt to your need. This could actually be directed either at a thought-form or at a natural Air spirit. Note that you will still have to study for your exam. Either of these spells is meant to help with recall, which is much easier than tapping Akashic records for knowledge of information you haven't bothered to read.

FOR A THOUGHT-FORM: *"I wish to call a servitor from the wellsprings of all knowledge, that will inspire my own power to remember those things which I have learned or have need to know, as I carry this (object) for (name exam, time, and place). Let now this spirit inhabit this (object), to serve my purpose and to dwell within it until I shall choose to take the spirit back within myself. Let it be so."*

The formula would be repeated before each exam.

For a natural Air spirit: *"I call to the spirits of the Air, for I seek one of your kind who will come to me from the wellsprings of all knowledge, who will inspire my own power to remember those things which I have learned or have need to know, as I carry this (object) for (name exam, time, and place). Let now this spirit attach to this (object) of their free will, and to hear my call whenever I should have need. Let it be so."*

Again, you will have to petition the spirit each time you have an exam and make an effort to study the information so that the knowledge will be there in your brain to be tapped.

WEATHER MAGIC

There are many old folk customs regarding weather magic. One is to raise winds by throwing pieces of the broom tree into the air. To calm winds, burn the broom and bury the ashes. There are many more, but for our purposes, let's stick with more pragmatic methods.

To call up a cooling breeze on a hot day, look into the direction where the desired breeze would most likely come from if nature were to provide it. This is usually North in the Northern Hemisphere unless you live near a coast. Working in conjunction with the natural behaviour of the elements is always much easier than trying to force them against their natural course.

Focus on a place in the distant sky where there are few or no distractions. A patch of clear blue sky should make an easy canvas, although if there are any clouds with even a hint of colour, these can be a likely source of cooler air. Unfocus your eyes and look within the air for tiny pinpricks of moving light particles, then visualise them rushing towards you as if in a gust of wind.

Mentally "call" the Air spirits to bring the desired breeze, then release your concentration. You should get an immediate gust of air in your face. With practice, you can learn to alternate between the summoning and release, thereby keeping a steady flow of air blowing for several minutes.

If you are going somewhere and want clear weather, watch the weather report for a couple of days beforehand and study the direction that any rain clouds are following. Again, you will want to work with nature, not against it. Mentally nudge the storm systems to veer in their path to avoid your chosen area, or, if you desire rain or snow, veer them toward the desired destination.

Remember that, in nature, weather is a naturally chaotic system, and a few miles to the left or right falls within the parameters that the clouds might have drifted anyway. You are only giving it a little mental push.

FIRE ELEMENTAL SPELLS

Fire spirits require a strong sense of purpose behind any spell that is going to be effective. Emotional content should be strong and personal. Again, personalising a ritual rather than reading from a script is highly encouraged. The important thing to remember is to always put the force of your own fiery spirit behind the magic you do when you want to attract the assistance of the spirits of the Fire.

One thing to note about any Fire ritual is that incorporating some action to rouse the emotions is very conducive to attracting the interest of Fire spirits and creating the appropriate mindset for this approach. Some effective ways of accomplishing this are dancing, drumming, and stimulating music, as well as altar decorations that form a visual association with Fire.

For rituals specifically directed at the element of Fire, my personal choice for a magical element is a ritual sword. This, to me, represents the epitome of Fire and its martial energies. An athame might be used in rituals of all sorts, but I keep a sword that is used solely for Fire rituals.

This is the one element where I do not include a spell for inviting spirits into the temple. The reason should be obvious. Inviting Fire into the home is asking for trouble.

Invoking Fire spirits can significantly increase the potential for Fire to get out of control, even without an obvious physical connection. Many years ago, I read of an incident at a Pagan camp that had a strong Fire theme, including fireworks and firewalking events. During the night, a caravan caught fire for no apparent reason. No one was hurt, but the caravan and its contents were completely consumed.

Remember that Fire spirits exist just beyond the material level of ignition and can be easily attracted or enticed to manifest. This can be very useful when trying to strike a match, start a campfire, or spark an incense coal that is being unco-operative. A quick invitation to the Fire spirits can make all the difference. However, this aspect of Fire spirits should also be borne in mind in situations like a Fire-themed event.

For working with Fire elementals, I must once again emphasise the absolute necessity of thoroughly banishing the ritual space of any residual energies. One might visualise the process much like putting out a campfire. Any loose, dry leaves that might have been used for kindling could blow away and start an uncontrolled fire. These must be thoroughly cleared, and any small embers stamped out in order to eliminate any possibility of them getting loose and creating havoc.

A Note about Candles

Candles are used in many rituals, if not as a focal point, then at least as part of the altar ornaments. Usually, straight-sided or votive candles are best, in colours appropriate to the intent. Decorative spiral candles are *not* recommended unless one specifically wants to invoke spiral energies for a specific purpose.

A Spell to Invite a Fire Spirit into the Flame

This is one of the most basic rituals for working with Fire elementals. The Fire spirit already exists as soon as a flame comes into being, so the ritual forms a connection between the magic user and that Fire spirit.

Fire spirits are unique in that they exist "in potential" on a spiritual level at all times. A spark of flame brings the spirit into physical manifestation.

Open the ritual in your chosen fashion and light a candle or other controlled source of flame. While there is no danger in communicating with the Fire spirit, it may cause an emotional reaction and, if the magic user responds with fear or irrational panic, the ritual should be closed, and the space thoroughly banished immediately.

To make first contact, sit or stand in front of the source of flame and project your own spirit and consciousness into the heart of the flame, taking care not to stare too intently, as the eyes can be damaged by looking into concentrated light. This is an important safety consideration. Never stare into a candle flame, but for candle rituals, look just above the flame (and don't do so for too long). The broader expanse of a larger fire is less likely to do damage than the concentrated light of a candle flame.

The invitation is best coming from the heart, but by way of example, I offer the following:

"I invite the spirit of the Fire to come into this flame and share my purpose, to inflame my spirit with the vehemence and passion of Fire. Let our two spirits be as one, your strength be mine, my purpose be yours. Let it be so."

From there you can launch into a Fire-related ritual or simply close the ritual, having established an initial contact. If you've used a candle, the candle holder with candles replaced as needed can stay on your altar or be kept specifically for Fire-related rituals but should be considered a ritual implement and not just left as decoration.

Inviting a Fire Spirit into an Object to Represent Fire

Apart from the traditional sword or athame, an item to represent Fire on the altar might be a candle holder, an oil lamp, or even a birthday cake candle. I was fortunate to find a ceramic oil lamp at a craft fair many years ago that burns scented kerosene and looks like something right out of the tales of Aladdin. Anything that sustains a flame is a possibility.

I generally recommend bringing the object into ritual just as an ornament for some time before dedicating it to active ritual use, as this attunes the object to the user or group. When the time is right to dedicate it to its purpose, this should be done as a separate ritual apart from any other business.

The ritual can be done indoors or outdoors, but a source of flame should be present in the ritual, whether it comes from the object to be dedicated or another source. Open according to your usual methods, then issue the invitation to the Fire spirit. If possible, pass the item through a flame. If it is the source of the flame, this is not necessary.

Your words might be something like:

"(I/we) call upon the element of Fire to bring forth a spirit to inhabit this (sword/athame/vessel/implement). Let this spirit come willingly and without reservation to become a part of the magic of this (sword/athame/vessel/implement), and to dedicate its existence to the purpose for which it is intended."

I suggest specifying the purpose at this point, or including a general statement such as: *"to represent the magic of the element of Fire to my altar."*

Close and banish. There is little work required to sustain a Fire spirit as they wait "in potential" by their nature, but an item left unregarded for a long stretch of time might require re-dedication.

CLEANSING BY FIRE

The possibilities of how an item might be cleansed by fire varies according to its nature and flammability. Most ceramic or metal ritual implements can be passed through a candle flame without causing damage, though some gemstones can change colour from very little exposure to heat.

Many things that cannot tolerate direct contact can be held a little distance above a flame. Something that is subject to damage would be best served by forming a ring of votive candles and placing it safely in the centre.

Once the arrangement has been decided and the item to be cleansed placed accordingly, a simple chant is all that is required. Something like:

"I pass this (object) within the Fire of purification and ask the spirit of the flame(s) to cleanse the essence of this (object) that it may be free of all defilement. Let this (object) now be clean and pure."

A FERTILITY SPELL

There are numerous fertility spells in folklore. Many could be found through researching books and website pages on superstitions, but I will include a simple ritual here that is based on seeking the assistance of a Fire spirit.

For obvious reasons, it is best to perform such a ritual on the fertile days of a woman's cycle if this can be determined, as any magic works best with a high probability factor. Like all other health concerns, those who have medical obstructions that interfere with fertility should obtain medical treatment in conjunction with magical efforts.

This ritual can be done by a couple together or by a woman alone who wishes to conceive and will be attempting to do so within a day of the ritual, whether it is with a partner or through artificial insemination.

Open the ritual according to your usual method, making sure the ritual set-up includes a source of flame. A red candle will do, though an outdoor ritual with a bonfire or even a good campfire would be ideal. Drumming music would be beneficial as well, even if it is recorded.

Once the ritual is opened, address the Fire spirit directly, invoking the spirit of passion within the element of Fire. This is best done with body movements. If possible, dance in a way that imitates the motion of flames, and repeat a chant addressed to the flame, such as:

"(I/we) call the spirit of the Fire, the source of passion, and Will, and the universal life force. Let the womb quicken and a child be conceived. The seed (I/we) now sow, in love the fruition (I/we) receive."

Any verses you prefer are just as good, so long as the message is clear. The idea is to address the life force aspect of Fire more so than the passionate aspect. Otherwise, the result could be a particularly passionate lovemaking session that fails to fulfil the intended purpose.

Repeat the chant while circling the source of flame, building to a sense of frenzy but not exhaustion. If a couple are working together, choose a moment that feels right to sexually consummate the ritual. If a woman is working alone, build to that point but then stop and address the Fire, repeating the chant one more time, leaving a void to be fulfilled. Do not indulge in any form of release until such time as conception is to be attempted.

Close the ritual, but do not banish. This ritual is an exception to the "always banish" rule. It requires being left with an expectant feeling of unfinished business.

WATER ELEMENTAL SPELLS

Water spells must be adapted to the practitioner's inner depths of feeling. Emotion is an essential attribute for this sort of magic, and much must be spontaneously created from intuition during the actual implementation of the spell.

The magic of Water works very much on the inner levels of intuition and the subconscious Will. Forming an emotional expression of a desire cannot be achieved simply by reading a spell from a book. It must be internalised: experienced in the inner being.

An Opening for a Water Spirit Ritual

A ritual that is specifically directed at the element of Water is fairly easy to set up. The traditional magical implement for Water is the chalice, usually filled with wine in a balanced ritual that includes mention of all the elements, but for a Water ritual, I recommend filling the chalice or some other vessel with water in order to have the actual element present.

This can be ordinary tap water, which can be ritually purified, or you may wish to use water from a special source. Some magicians even visit their local Catholic church to obtain Holy Water that has been blessed by a priest, though personally, I prefer water collected from a holy well if it is available.

Alternatively, you might wish to immerse yourself in the element itself as described in Chapter Five.

More than with any other element, Water is best approached in a state of relaxation. Beginning with relaxation and breathing exercises allows you to let yourself be drawn into the depths of the Water, which is essential to this form of ritual. You might wish to use your own wording or begin with something like the opening and closing incantations offered above.

The Middle Bit

Whether the practices of opening and closing are a requirement in one's rituals or you are happy with performing the ritual without these formalities (as some would consider them), working with Water spirits lends itself easily to making a transitional period between the beginning and ending of an act of magic. Water, as I have mentioned previously, draws the human spirit into itself. Therefore, it is given that withdrawing from "ritual mode" requires a similar transitional change in consciousness.

For this reason, most Water rituals can easily be approached directly, with or without formal openings and closings, but some people will always feel more comfortable using them and that is okay too.

The following rituals can be done either way. I do, however, recommend some emphasis on grounding afterwards as the spirits of the Water are rather loath to release those who enter into their realms.

A Spell for Inviting Water
Spirits into the Home or Temple

As with Fire, inviting Water into the home or temple has the potential for destruction in the form of damp or even floods, and should be treated with reasonable caution. However, Water spirits can be safely invited in with sufficient forethought.

A good way to begin such a ritual is by cleaning the place into which the spirits are to be invited. Washing down the walls, even the ceiling, immediately associates the cleaning process with what you intend to do.

While doing this, you may wish to chant something to the effect of:

"I cleanse this room of all negative energies and thoughts and seek the purity of clean Water in all that is to be done here."

When this process is finished, the dirty water should be poured away either down a sink or into the ground outside. If you are inviting Water spirits into a garden or other outdoor location, you may wish to similarly "cleanse" the area by pouring clean water over the space from a common garden watering can.

When the cleaning is completed, set up the ritual, including a source of water. This might be anything from a small bowl to an elaborate chalice or a much larger container. It is a matter of personal preference and space availability. The ritual will be focused on this water source rather than on a candle or icon.

The water should be fresh and clean, although it is perfectly fine to draw it from a common tap or a natural source. Note that it is not required for this sort of ritual to bless the water with salt as is usually done in some ritual traditions, as the focus is specifically on the Water element. However, if you feel better doing so, feel free to "purify" the water in any way you wish.

An opening is performed in whatever manner you choose, then proceed with the invitation accordingly.

For the garden, you might say:

"Spirits of the Water, who clean and nourish all that thrives and gives environment to all of the swimming creatures of the planet, I invite you to join my garden, to moisten the roots of the plants and quench

the thirst of those creatures who dwell within this place, and to make of it a magical place, wherein the realm of emotions may be balanced and employed wisely when appropriate, by the power of Earth, Air, Fire, and Water, so shall it be."

Similarly, for an established body of water, pond, or pool:

"Spirits of the Water, who clean and nourish all that thrives and gives environment to all the swimming creatures of the planet, I invite you to join my (pond/pool/other small body of water), to embrace the lives of the creatures who live within your depths and to make of it a magical place, wherein the realm of emotions may be balanced and employed wisely when appropriate, by the power of Earth, Air, Fire, and Water, so shall it be."

This simple formula may be expanded as the magician desires. Some original wording is highly recommended in order to personalise the ritual to your specific place. This also holds with the following incantations.

To invite Water into your temple, face West as part of a ritual for all of the elements in turn, and state:

"I call upon the spirits of the element of Water and invite them to lend the qualities of balanced emotion to this temple and all that will be done within it, to become a part of this place and those who practice within it. Let them provide the wisdom to know when the power of strong emotions shall be appropriate to the magic that is done here, and also to know when detachment from those emotions must prevail. Let it be so."

A slight variation of this can be used as a house blessing as follows:

"I call upon the spirits of the element of Water and invite them to lend the qualities of balanced emotion to this home, to become a part of this place and those who live and visit within it. Let the spirit of calm and balanced emotions prevail here. Let it be so."

Having looked at invitation spells close to home, we must also consider forms for spells to invite spirits of more wild or natural places to join our rituals. As I pointed out in Chapter Five, it is important to remember that any invitation in a place of nature is being given to a spirit who is already resident of the place and might well have been so for much longer than your own lifetime. To claim a place, such as a large lake or spot of the ocean, and invite the resident Water spirits in could be compared to breezing into a stranger's house and inviting them to join you for dinner in their dining room. Some realistic consideration is in order.

The way around this awkward state of affairs is to combine asking permission to use their place with inviting them to join your ritual. An example of how to go about this is as follows:

> *"(I/we) come here to ask the spirits of the depths of this (lake/ocean/ other large body of Water) to allow (me/us) to perform this magic in your realm of Water, and to join (me/us) in its purpose, which is to (state purpose)."*

Then continue as with any other Water spell, but be sure to include thanks to the resident spirits in the closing. You might even wish to name a known spirit of the place in both opening and closing, but be sure to do your research first. Some established Water spirits—Poseidon or Neptune for the ocean, for example—can be rather powerful and independent entities to be calling up without good reason. Some lake spirits are known for taking their sacrifice. Never assume that it doesn't apply just because there hasn't been a drowning in the last hundred years. If you ask for their attention, you might well get it.

INVITING A SPIRIT INTO AN OBJECT TO REPRESENT WATER

Objects that are most frequently used to represent Water are a chalice or a shell, but other items can be used that have meaning to the magic user, particularly if they have come to you from a source of water. The item is most likely to be a solid object of some sort, assuming that the item is intended for either an altar item or to place in the West quarter of a room for general balance.

If, on the other hand, one wishes to keep a container of water to represent the element, a simple jar or vase that is kept partially full and has the water changed on a regular basis can be very effective. If one is fortunate enough to live near a holy well or other special place of water, the water could be regularly ritually committed to the garden and replaced from the source. Still, it is the container that provides a basis for the Water representation. It is something that could be carried to another location if desired.

Any of the objects can be decorated prior to or during the dedication ritual. As with any ritual, choose a time and place where you won't be interrupted and prepare for the ritual. The place may be the privacy of your own temple, or you may want to do this near or in a natural source of water. It might even be done spontaneously, having found a particularly nice shell on the beach.

Open the ritual according to your usual practices or by calling the spirit of a natural source of water if it is appropriate to the situation, but as you do so, try to feel the depths of emotion enfolding yourself and the item in a special emotional embrace that will bind you together almost as if you were a couple being bound in emotional (rather than physical) love. If appropriate, bathe the item in water and feel its texture within your hands, fondling it and making it a part of you. Then issue your invitation to the spirit of the item with something like:

"I call upon the element of Water, to bring forth a spirit to inhabit this (chalice/shell/gift of the body of water). Let this spirit come willingly and without reservation to become a part of the magic of this (chalice/shell/gift of the body of water), and to dedicate its existence to the purpose for which it is intended."

You may want to state the purpose more specifically, but be sure that if you do so, the item is forever more only used for the purpose as stated.

As with many rituals, the purpose may be infused into the item through a repeated chant, or you might feel that the dedication itself is sufficient. Close the ritual and be sure to ground yourself, especially if the ritual has been performed in a natural source of water. Refer to "Grounding After a Water Spell" at the end of this section for more details.

To Charge an Object by Water

Water conducts an electromagnetic charge, so it is ideal for charging objects in a variety of ritual practices. A very simple method of doing this is to prepare a large container of water or choose a natural source, immerse the chosen item, and stir deosil quickly in an attempt to create a whirlpool. Actually forming a whirlpool can be hard to accomplish, but it can be done, though it isn't strictly necessary for the purpose. The swirling motion of the water will suffice.

For maximum effect, have the container in a position where you can walk around it, not having to bend over too far to immerse the item and circle it deosil while chanting the purpose of the ritual. The deosil direction is appropriate to all purposes, even the most nefarious, as it reflects the natural movement of the Earth's energies. This, of course, is reversed in the Southern Hemisphere.

A simple chant can accompany the motion. Perhaps you'll use a repetition of the intent, or something like:

> *"I charge this (item) by Water and release its magic to flow through the ways of the Aether to its ultimate destination."*

Some practicality must be considered when using this method. A sigil on paper or parchment will become soaked and ink may run. This can be incorporated into the ritual, running ink substituting for burning the sigil, or it may be that you will need to allow the item to dry before proceeding with the release of the energy. A sigil spell done by Earth and Water, for example, could finish with burying the sigil.

A stone or other solid object is unlikely to suffer any ill effects from water unless it is a type of stone that reacts badly to getting wet (especially an opal which is, ironically, ideal for representing Water within the gemstone and crystal spectrum of magical stones). If you use a stone for a ritual charging in water, be sure not to drop it as this would seriously disrupt the "flow."

An item can also be anointed with water, perhaps from a sacred source, or purified during the ritual. This is the method I would *cautiously* choose to charge an opal if I was to dedicate it to the Water quarter or any Water ritual purpose, as some opals can lose their colour if they get wet.

Again, the wetness would need to dry on a paper or cloth item if it needs to be subsequently burned, but it would make no difference to an item that was to be buried instead of decomposing over time. Releasing a spell can take many forms and may involve any combination of the elements.

Evoking a Water Spirit
Out of the Depths

This might be something you would wish to do in the opening of a very powerful ritual, but be careful what you wish for! Water spirits of the depths have been known by such names as Poseidon, Neptune, Leviathan, and even Nessie. Whether you wish to acknowledge that some of them have been looked upon as gods or god forms is a matter of personal belief, but they are very powerful images, in any case, and are often associated with destructive storms or disappearances into the depths.

It is just as appropriate to use the method in local lakes, ponds, or other sources of water, but the most powerful aspect of the guardian spirit of the Water might well be just as potentially dangerous as the more widely known examples.

Let us not forget Cthulhu, from the fictional universe of H.P. Lovecraft. To stand at the shore of an ocean and invoke a powerful entity known for destruction might stir a lot of power into your ritual, but the ocean is full of creatures I'd personally be reluctant to try to invoke up onto the beach to tangle with.

On that ominous note, the evocation is actually frighteningly simple. The only part that might require some practice for less experienced magic users is the act of projecting one's being into the source of water sufficiently for the purpose.

Obviously, this invocation is only really appropriate to a natural source of water. Invoking the most deep and powerful spiritual guardian of a bucket of water freshly drawn and sitting in your living room just doesn't have the impact or the sense of ancient power that can be evoked from a dark pool, a hundred-year-old river or pond, or another natural place of water.

First, choose your source of water. Unless you are, by nature, extremely calm in a crisis and experienced in emergency banishings, take a magically experienced friend along to the chosen source, if only to monitor the situation for water safety and help with anything that might "come up." As much as it would be more effective to immerse oneself in the water for this evocation, I would recommend that you sit or stand by the side of the source for this one. Water is treacherous at the best of times, and concentration on ritual doesn't mix well with water safety, even without consideration of potentially enveloping spirits whom you are actively calling up. If your source is the seaside, I recommend standing beyond the water line. Waves can be unpredictable.

You may wish to set up an altar and perform an opening, or you may wish to let the calming effects of the water source serve as preparation and launch directly into the evocation, using it as an opening with the intent of imploring the Water spirit to perform some service for you.

Do not do this without a specific purpose, and always have a banishing ready! Water spirits can be very temperamental.

Having chosen your place, position, and choice of opening, begin by mentally projecting your being into the water (not the surface, but the deepest depths that you are able to visualise and beyond to the realm of sightless perception).

Feel the water around you, as if you were submerged within its comforting depths, embraced by its smooth and cleansing currents. This is the tricky bit.

Maintain a sense of grounding where you stand or sit while projecting yourself into the water in this manner, then begin your evocation, which may be something like:

"I call you, (name optional), spirit of the depths of this (pool/lake/sea/ body of water) to come to me from within your watery depths, that I may ask of your assistance for my purpose."

From this point, you might wish to state the purpose, or if there is no immediately detectable *presence*, you might wish to continue with the evocation, continually imploring the spirit to come to your aid.

It is important that you insist on the spirit coming to you rather than giving in to any impulse to go to it within the water source, while also remembering that this is the spirit's place and that you are an intruder. It is also important to remember that Water spirits are historically known for demanding their sacrifices. Bringing along something to offer to the fishes; fish food from a pet store, in small amounts that won't cloud the watery environment, is always a good idea. Also, keep in mind that this is no time to go for a swim. The friend you brought along should have strict instructions to prevent you from entering the water at any cost.

Once the spirit has manifested in some form, visible or not, it is likely to create a feeling of foreboding. This is not a task for the faint-hearted. It should be immediately asked for the favour intended and some form of offering dispersed with perhaps additional offerings promised for later when the purpose is accomplished. Do not offer meat in any form at any time.

Having made your request and offerings, begin closing by sending the creature back to its realm without personally banishing it, which might go something like this:

> *"Return now to the depths of your watery realm and consider my purpose, until next we meet when I shall bring to you the promised offering."*

Then immediately ground yourself, banish any residual spirits, and leave the place immediately.

To Sustain a Water Spirit

Sustaining a Water spirit for a specific purpose, as with the other elements, is largely accomplished by repeated contact. However, a spirit who has been called from a specific source of water can also be fairly easily re-evoked after a considerable amount of time if it is a constant water source, such as a natural lake, pond, or ocean.

Water holds memory, just as the ever-changing drops of water hold the form of the lake, pool, or any other source of water. Even the rushing water of a river, constantly replenished with new water, somehow holds the form of that specific body of water. The boundaries might vary slightly over time, but the basic path or form remains much the same (barring human interference).

All that is required to evoke a spirit of such a place is to basically repeat the original ritual, perhaps slightly changing the words to accommodate the fact that you are recalling a known spirit.

A Water spirit who has been dedicated to an object, such as a chalice, also remains constant but is best given frequent "drinks" of whatever is normally poured into the chalice, lest the spirit dry up too far and become ineffective. A chalice that is used in frequent rituals, perhaps monthly during the full moon, is naturally provided for during these regular ritual practices. An object that is used less frequently might benefit from some sort of observance to maintain contact with its element.

Something like a shell can benefit from regular ritual baths. All it takes is a few minutes to immerse the object into ordinary water taken from the tap (although water collected from a nearby natural source is better) and to perform a simple observance. While bathing the object, quiet your mind and allow your consciousness to flow into the water as in other Water rituals already described. Feel the presence of the spirit of the object and speak words such as the following:

"(I/we) commit this (object) to the element of Water to cleanse it of all negative energies which it might encounter, and to renew the fresh and clear spirit of Water within its source."

More may be added according to your personal experience and interpretation of the object, but this covers the basic intent. Handle the object gently and kiss it with reverence when it is removed from the Water, perhaps adding something like:

"(I/we) now return this (object) to its place of rest, until (I/we) shall again require the properties of the Water spirit who dwells within. Let it be so."

SIMPLE FOLK SPELLS AND OTHER MAGIC

Folk spells involving the use of Water are many and varied throughout the cultures of the world, but the basic themes remain essentially constant. Water represents cleansing, purification, sustenance of a vital life force, and, perhaps most importantly, the portal to the otherworld. The dark mysteries of the deep are a vital element in many Water spells.

Some spells will involve either washing or bathing something in water, while others will require throwing something into the watery realm. Still others depend on the magic user's ability to attune to the element itself or the spirit within, to use the medium of emotion to call qualities (usually in their calming aspect) of Water into themselves.

Any of the spells included in this volume may be freely adapted to incorporate personal innovations and the reader is strongly encouraged to do this with Water spells in particular.

Impromptu Water spells, performed on the spur of the moment and created from just a basic formula, can be very effective. The essential ingredient in any of these spells is to put oneself fully into it on the emotional level, recognising that the format of the spell only serves as a medium of expression and transmission for channelling spiritual energies.

HEALING WITH WATER SPIRITS

Naturally, any healing spell performed with Water spirits is likely to invoke the cleansing and purifying aspects of Water to clear away the affliction. Care should be taken to assess the wisdom of using the actual element depending on the situation. An open wound might be either cleansed or infected through the use of water. Fevers can be cooled or made worse with its use. Common sense must prevail over any decisions taken on the actual use of water.

However, calling the spirits of Water from a nearby source doesn't have to include pouring liquid on an unwitting patient. The spiritual cleansing can take place with or without actually getting wet. The details of spells should vary according to the actual sickness or injury, but a basic formula might go as follows.

Collect a large bowl of water from a natural spring or other source, evoking the natural place spirit into the water for assistance. The evocation can be worded something like:

> *"I call upon the spirits of this (spring/river/pond/other body of water) in the cleansing aspect of Water, to come with me now and cleanse away the (illness) that afflicts (name of patient) and promise to bring back that which is not used or evaporated, that it may be purified through your own natural resources."*

If the patient is close to you, you can refer to them by that relationship—my husband, my daughter, my grandmother, or others—but still include the person's name. The familiarity forms a closer bond between healer and patient, which can make a significant difference to the effectiveness of any healing. For this reason, you might want to use "my friend" to refer to someone you do not know well.

This also applies to healing animals, although in some cases, it might be appropriate to refer to a related god or goddess, such as referring to a horse as a "child of Epona" or a cat as a "descendant of Bast." Again, including the animal's name (if known) forms a closer connection.

The water must be transported to the patient after collection, if using some form as part of your ritual, preferably without spilling it or speaking to anyone if possible (an old superstition). If speaking is unavoidable, keep it short and return the focus of your attention to the task at hand. It may be practical to transport using a container with a lid and transfer the water to the ritual bowl, chalice, or other container.

When all is prepared, proceed with a continuation of the spell that was spoken at the water source. If practical, bathe the wound, the forehead of the afflicted person, or the affected areas of the body, keeping in mind that water from natural sources could have contaminants that would adversely affect open wounds. In this case, a symbolic "washing" with a dry sponge could be preferable. Perform your incantation, which might go something like:

> *"Let the spirits of the Water wash away this (illness/infection/injury) and allow (name) to be whole again, to heal, and become strong."*

Add detail to address the specific circumstances of the affliction, perhaps adding a wish for a specific eventual outcome. For example, you might wish for someone with a leg injury to run freely and swim again (remembering that you are dealing with Water spirits who can appreciate the pure joy of swimming), or for someone with a debilitating illness to grow as strong as Poseidon or some other figure from mythology or a preferred pantheon.

A short incantation can be repeated several times while bathing the appropriate area, or if using actual water is inappropriate, the bowl of water can be kept close to the bedside and the spiritual essence evoked by a slight adaptation, such as:

> *"I call the spirits of the (river/spring/other body of water) to come forth from their watery abode and to cleanse (name) of this affliction..."* Continue with a detailed description of the problem and a wish for a specific result.

After the spell has been performed with the patient, the promise to return to the source must be kept if such a promise was made. The remaining water can be transported as it was brought and then must be poured back to its source with thanks given to the Water spirits for their assistance. As with any outdoor ritual, an offering should be left.

If the illness was directed into the water, pour it on nearby earth so that nature can purify it of the disease before the moisture rejoins the source of water.

A Fertility Spell

Fertility spells are most often associated with either Earth or Fire, yet Water can play a part in a gentler form of fertility magic by way of watering the planted seed in sympathic magic or creating life from the primordial soup. This can be incorporated into a spell that encompasses all of the elements, or approached separately by someone who might wish to avoid invoking Fire energies for whatever reason.

A Water spell might also be appropriate in cases of artificial insemination, where the process is physically accomplished through the transference of fluids that bypass the Fires of passion.

For a Water fertility spell to have any effect, the essential components for fertilisation must be present through artificial or natural means. Specifically, for human reproduction, sperm must meet egg, or, for more agricultural fertility, seed must be planted in earth and watered.

In Paganism of all sorts, the link between the Earth and Water is strong, and it is historically the act of human reproduction that is used to symbolise fertility for the benefit of crop growth. While this can easily be continued in modern times even with birth control methods in common use, it is well to remember that this practice comes from a time when producing children frequently was considered desirable and that modern birth control methods can fail. Magic always rebounds on the user to some extent. If it is your garden that you want to fertilise and not your family that you wish to increase, using magic of any kind for this purpose could be very risky.

However, if the intent is to produce offspring, a proper fertility spell performed in the fields might well be just what is needed to benefit from the reverse of the symbolism that our ancestors intended.

Whether in an open field or the privacy of one's own house or temple, the evocation of Water spirits in a fertility spell would take form much like watering your own private garden. As part of a spell that includes other elements, the Water portion would require a reference such as: *"May the spirits of the Water bless and nourish the seed that is planted, that it may grow to fruition…"* continuing with a direction for a specific result such as, *"…and bringing forth the child (or specifically son or daughter) whom (I/we) desire"* or *"…and bring forth an abundance of (name crop), for which (I/we) have planted the seed this day."*

As a separate Water spell, using the symbolism of life evolving from the sea is very effective. Belief in this version of scientific theory is optional, as with any symbolic system in magic. Any symbolism can be used separately from actual belief, whether it is in a god form, a theory of science, or a concept of physics. The magical method was called "free belief" by Austin Osman Spare, who was pivotal in teaching a form of magic that uses belief, real or temporary, to produce results (Spare).

One way of employing the symbolism required for this purpose is to open a ritual according to your chosen methods near a body of water that is appropriate for submersion (i.e., clean, of a temperature that isn't going to cause hypothermia, and free of underwater hazards). The prospective mother enters the water, bathing freely and getting thoroughly wet. The incantation to the Water spirits can be done by the woman herself, or performed by a priest, priestess, or group by the waterside. Ideally, if the ritual were to be officiated by the prospective father of the desired child, the ritual could be consummated with lovemaking if sufficient privacy is available. In semi-public places, a camping tent would prevent getting arrested for public indecency.

Incorporating creative spiral energies is appropriate for this ritual and can be accomplished by the woman turning herself in the water, deosil as always, as the ritual progresses. She can be fertilised by her partner within a twelve-hour time frame before the ritual if this is most workable and should be on the fertile days of her individual cycle, which is usually two weeks after the onset of the previous menstruation but can be more accurately determined by taking her temperature daily. The release of the egg will make her average temperature rise by a full degree Fahrenheit. The incantation itself might go something like this:

"From the depths of the Waters of creation, (I/we) call the spirits of the Water to witness the beginning of a new life, of creation itself, as (I/we) seek to bring forth a child of the Water, a (son or daughter)

sought through love and longing, and through the infinite power of the primordial sea do (I/we) seek the magical child whom (I/we) desire this day."

As the woman emerges from the water, a group in particular might wish to continue with a chant such as:

"Life from Water, creation to be, primordial matter, life from the sea."

The chant doesn't have to carry a distinct message but only abstract symbolism delivered through simple rhyme. This one lends itself easily to a circle dance around the prospective mother. Give the woman a large towel and close the ritual as desired.

One note on gender and partners: it is a biological reality that only those who are assigned female at birth, with a uterus and ovaries, can carry a child unless some obstruction to the process exists. A woman can choose to have a child with a partner or to have a child on her own. I don't preach morality or ethics, that is for the individual to determine for themselves. It's possible that science may try womb transplants to allow transgender women to reproduce someday. In that situation, a ritual like the above might help.

Also, she needn't be skyclad if it might cause issues in the situation. A loose shift is perfectly appropriate, or even ordinary swimwear if the fertilisation occurs separately from the ritual.

A Water Meditation

Water is very conducive to meditation by its very nature and can be useful in active, as well as passive, meditation. Passive meditation is that which is first taught in many Eastern philosophies. One sits in a comfortable position and clears the mind, a more difficult process than it sounds. Most people will find, at first, that the constant stream of internal dialogue interferes, as well as stray thoughts.

With practice, one learns to push the internal thoughts aside and return to focus, normally done either with a visual symbol in mind or a mantra, which is a repeated phrase. It can also be done by concentrating on counting to four for the breathing cycle: breathing in to the count of four, stopping for another count of four, then breathing out to the count of four. Stopping for another count of four before starting the next breath is good if you're able. If you feel a strong need to breathe, then breathe!

A way of using the element of Water for passive meditation is to visualise moving water—a river or gently crashing ocean waves—as a focal point. For some, it might be possible to focus on a still source of water such as an imaginary pond. This is a little more challenging as you have to build the pond in your mind. Alternatively, you might remember a real lake or pond, or, if you have been in the vicinity of an inspiring river, that might work best for you.

An active meditation is one where some purpose is achieved through an internal action, such as a psychodrama where the source of water actively cleanses something (possibly something that represents an aspect of one's life). For the more active imagination, Water might also take form in the mind to create things you wish to bring into your life, perhaps using a symbol like a water spout to deliver a representation of the desire into the meditator's mind's eye. Note the creative process in the previous fertility spell!

The possibilities for this meditation method are only limited by imagination. The key to success, however, lies in first mastering passive meditation, which allows the mind to begin from a place of clarity and calm.

CHARGING A DRIFTWOOD SIGIL

I mentioned in Chapter Six that a sigil could be drawn on a piece of driftwood and returned to the sea as a spontaneous spell using natural materials at hand. Obviously, this could also be done with planning, but I was using it as an example of spontaneous magic.

There is some value in creating the symbol itself, carving it on the wood, and managing to get the tide to take it out to sea if the tide is going out and chooses to co-operate. If you live near an ocean or are visiting for a few days on holiday, becoming familiar with the tides is highly recommended. This is not just for safety reasons, but because attuning to these rhythms has spiritual balancing effects.

If you are doing the spell spontaneously and the tide is in flow rather than ebb, the ocean isn't likely to co-operate with the intent to send the sigil out to sea. However, the intensity of the magic put into the sigil construction and charging is more important than the eventual fate of the piece of wood. Plus, if you're staying by the sea for at least a day, you can come back at ebb to release your sigil to the elements.

Much of the magical energy is created by the construction of the sigil itself, as well as the act of carving out the symbol, which takes more work than just drawing it (although this can also be done if you've gone out without a pocketknife, possibly using charcoal that has also washed up on the beach). More can be done through a charging.

One form of charging the driftwood sigil that can be done on a public beach without drawing undue attention to oneself is through an active meditation, as described above.

Construct your sigil, apply it on the driftwood, and sit comfortably high enough above the tideline to save yourself any wet surprises, closing your eyes and listening to the sounds of the crashing waves. Visualise them, but do not worry about accuracy. Allow yourself to drift into the ocean of your mind. Once you reach a state of calm non-distraction, visualise your desire as accomplished, perhaps with a fantasy action of the ocean waves in Fantasia-like imagery, keeping aware of the Water spirit intelligence behind your imaginary waves.

If you are in a very public place, you may wish to stop there, but if you are away from people or unconcerned about their curiosity, now would be a good time to verbally petition the Water spirits for assistance with the task. Wording would have to be decided on the spot, relying on sincerity more than perfect metre. Be sure your words are precise and reflect your exact desire. In any magic, leaving room for alternate interpretations can lead to trouble.

Finish with an instruction to take this desire to the heart of whatever ocean deity or other entity you choose, or to the spirits of the Water in general, then open your eyes. If the tide is at flow, you might wish to come back later when it is at ebb and repeat the finish before consigning your driftwood back to the sea. Throw the driftwood as far out to the receding tide as you can and walk away without looking back. Don't worry about the sigil's eventual destination. Ground yourself thoroughly, as is appropriate from a Water spirit ritual.

Cleansing and Purification Spells

Cleansing spells have an obvious connection with Water. The same basic symbolism (the washing away of something) can be applied to many situations and ritual formats.

In a purification spell, the washing away applies to things like negative energies, distracting thoughts before a ritual, or some aspect of a person's life that makes them feel in some way "unclean." A spell can be constructed specifically for this purpose, or it can form the beginning of a ritual for another purpose, purifying the participant(s) in preparation.

In some traditional forms of magic, this occurs by the participant(s) having a bath before beginning the actual ritual, although the bath itself is considered to be ritualistic preparation. The main difference between this bath and any other for washing one's body is an internal attitude of purification.

More overt ritual can also be performed during a preparatory bath. For example, you could pour a container of water over your head while saying something like:

> *"I call upon the spirits of the Water to cleanse me of all negativity and concerns of mundane matter as I prepare for the ritual to come."*

This same procedure could also form a specific cleansing or purification ritual, by mention of that which the participant wishes to wash away. The exact words would need to be specific to the purpose.

Within a ritual space, pouring water over the head while intoning a spell for cleansing or purification is a very old practice that far predates the Christian baptisms that also use this formula. Again, the exact wording must be specific to the purpose, but the participant(s) might wish to begin with something like:

> *"(I/we) call upon the spirits of the Water to cleanse (name if performing ritual for someone else, otherwise, me) and to wash away (fill in as appropriate), sending these things into the Earth that they may be cleansed and purified through the natural process that cleanses all things. Let (me/him/her/them) arise now refreshed and renewed, freed forever from these things that (I/he/she/they) leave(s) behind. Let it be so." (Or "So mote it be.")*

A Spell to Seek Marriage or a Partner

Be careful what you wish for. That is my first advice in this area of magic. Marriage or partnership with someone is too often perceived as a goal in itself rather than a result of an already-formed relationship that develops to this stage. If the seeker wishes to perform a ritual to result in marriage with a specific person already known, I strongly advise leaving magic out of it. Forcing a union in a relationship that isn't naturally developing that way is begging for unhappy results. Work on the relationship itself instead.

On the other hand, an unattached person seeking a partner might well benefit from a little magical "push" toward meeting the right person if it is done carefully and with substantial forethought. The key is to avoid too many specifics and cast the net wide enough to be brought to the attention of someone who will bring happiness and fulfilment to your life rather than to try to fit some unsuspecting person into a preconceived mould.

Like any spell, this would be performed with a ritual opening and closing, but what happens between will make all the difference. Keeping in mind that Water uses emotions, this is actually an appropriate element to use to bring satisfaction to the emotional side of your life.

By way of example, an ex-partner of mine (with whom I'm still friends) once performed a ritual to attract someone with an interest we share. He met me. However, the relationship was not destined to endure. We grew in different directions and eventually parted. For his next try, he did a ritual to attract someone who would bring him happiness as a life partner, he met the woman who became his wife and lived happily ever after.

A Spell to Seek Happiness

Happiness can be a difficult thing to define. However, most people are aware of whether or not they are generally happy. Someone who is miserable much of the time usually has to look at the various aspects of their life to find the reason, but this is less commonly done that one might think. Apart from clinical depression, which often has causes within the chemistry of the brain, misery is largely an attitude. All too often, people muddle along in unfulfilling lives because of habits that they have never questioned or feel they cannot escape.

These may include an unhappy relationship, an unfulfilling job, a lack of either partner or employment, dissatisfaction with their current location and—increasingly these days—with the actions of political leaders, or many other subtle aspects to their current circumstances.

A spell to bring general happiness must begin with a definition of what is needed to achieve this happiness. For this, the Water meditation earlier in this chapter can be useful. Set up a large, preferably clear glass bowl of freshly drawn water. Place a single floating candle, preferably blue, in the centre of the water. You may wish to anoint the candle with an essential oil in a scent you find calming.

Sit in a comfortable position, making sure that you don't cross legs or anything that might "go to sleep" during the ritual meditation. You can decide for yourself whether this is best done on the floor or with a chair at a table where you can place the bowl of water. Be sure that the bowl is close enough to reach, yet far enough that you won't light your hair on fire if your head sinks forward as you relax. Also, leave sufficient room around the bowl or table that you can walk around it comfortably.

Begin with a passive meditation to clear the mind, followed by an active meditation to seek what you desire. Command whatever visualisation of Water you use to convey (with some clarity) what your heart's desire is. The third stage of the ritual will be to invoke the assistance of the Water spirits to achieve your newly defined goals. You might also wish to petition their assistance in the first and second stages of the meditation.

To do this, you should begin with some form of relaxation exercise, then light the floating candle as you invoke the calming aspects of the Water spirits in the bowl. Settle into a comfortable position with palms facing upwards after lighting the candle. You can choose your own words, or use the following:

> *"Water spirits calm and deep,*
> *Help me clear my mind to sleep,*
> *And in the depths of soul assess,*
> *My true desire for happiness."*

Great poetry is not required. Something with meaning for what you wish to accomplish is.

Clear the mind, allowing yourself to sink into a hypnotic-like state, but without actually falling asleep. This might take a few minutes or longer, so don't try to rush yourself. When you feel that you have cleared your mind as far as you are able, proceed to the second stage.

You could potentially find it difficult to speak at this point, but clarity of speech is not important. Focus on the bowl of water, with eyes open or closed as you prefer, and ask the Water spirits to reflect your own desires back to you. Again, you can use your own words or the following:

> *"Spirits of the Water now help me see,*
> *My own True Will and the path to find*
> *To move forward to the goals that will satisfy me*
> *And leave unhappiness of the past far behind."*

Continue to be aware of the Water element as you consciously examine the various aspects of your life—home, job, relationships, and so on—and assess your satisfaction with each area of your life individually. Take your time and consciously work out what would be necessary for each aspect to make you happy, but try to remain realistic.

Telling yourself that all of your problems would end if you won the lottery won't get you very far, but working out a plan to get a job, get ahead in a current job, or start a business can be done with deeper insight into the vast pool of possibilities that actually exist but are so often overlooked.

By the same token, wishing for an admired celebrity to drop into your life and become your partner is rather low on the probability scale, but examining how to either repair a current relationship or how to go about seeking a new one can easily set you on the path to accomplishing the goal.

Even little things like how to go about breaking bad habits or getting around to things you want to do but keep putting off can now be examined and planned out. The depths of Water are a thoughtful and insightful realm where the largest and smallest problems that plague us often become so easily resolved if we are able to put into practice our own plans formulated in that realm.

Once all aspects of your life have been examined and plans made for changes, the third, activating stage of the ritual will help both your own resolve to implement plans and the positive energies that will make things fall into place in the way that magic has a way of doing.

When you feel that you have finished assessing all that needs changing, stand up with eyes open and address the candle flame, remaining aware that it floats in water. Using your own words or those that follow, begin to chant in your original position, then begin circling the bowl in a deosil direction slowly, gaining speed (in relation to available space), and allow the words to dissolve into a repeated chant:

> *"Activate now my true desire*
> *Spirits of the Water, and of Fire*
> *Open the way and help me see*
> *Opportunities endless to me."*

Repeat the first two lines over and over until you feel you have exhausted the power of the chant. Stop in your original position and close the ritual by your chosen method.

A SPELL TO BRING SLEEP

Everybody has the occasional sleepless night, but some have chronic insomnia or the stress of temporary difficulties over a period of time that cause sleeplessness.

The first thing to try when having difficulty sleeping is relaxation exercises. Probably the best known of these comes to us from the practice of yoga. It is a matter of relaxing each part of the body in turn, beginning with the toes, travelling up until you reach the head muscles, and finishing up with the throat, which will have some tension from practicing methodical breathing.

There are two variations of the method. One is to tense each muscle and then consciously relax it. The other, which is often used in hypnosis techniques, is to take a deep breath and "breathe into" each muscle in turn, intentionally allowing them to relax. Either method can be enhanced by using Water visualisations as described in this chapter under "A Water Meditation."

There are times when relaxation techniques alone will not quiet the internal dialogue that comes with things that play on our minds. At these times, something more is required. The best solution, of course, is to resolve the problem causing the stress, but this isn't always possible in the short term. The following spell might help to divert the focus of your thoughts, though the root cause of the difficulty will still need to be addressed in the light of day.

Place a bowl of freshly drawn water next to your bed, preferably a fairly large glass bowl on a bedside table. Lie on your back and begin with one of the relaxation techniques as described, including a Water visualisation. When you have completed this, petition the Water spirits slowly and carefully with your internal voice to take you into the depths of sleep.

As you hear the words with your mind's ear, visualise yourself sinking into whatever water source was used during the relaxation exercise, going deeper and deeper into the realm of the subconscious. You may use your own words or those that follow, but use caution in the choice of words as you do not wish to be taken so deeply into sleep that you fail to reawaken. A "return clause" as is included in the example is highly recommended:

> *"Water spirits, take me deep*
> *Into your world where I might sleep.*
> *Let my cares all drift away*
> *'Till my return by light of day.*
>
> *Deeper still we seek to rest*
> *Let mind be clear to seek it best*
> *In the depths of sleep and dreams*
> *Let all be well, go deep and dream."*

Repeat the chant in internal dialogue, continuing to visualise your Watery descent and concentrating on steady, deep breathing. Push aside any intrusive thoughts. It might be necessary to repeat the chant a few more times, always internally and with an awareness of the bowl of water at your side.

On awakening in the morning, thanks should be given to the spirits of this bowl of water, and perhaps some of the water splashed into the face to break the spell and promote waking.

A SPELL TO PROMOTE LUCID DREAMING

Lucid dreaming is what happens when you become aware that you are dreaming and begin to take control of your dream, making things happen as you will them. This is a useful tool for dealing with inner conflicts that cause stressful dreams, allowing the dreamer to address a symbolic representation of the cause of the conflict within the dream context.

Often this will take the form of overcoming a monster or other bogey that represents the cause of internal stress. It isn't unusual to battle the dream environment itself, which represents circumstances outside of the dreamer's direct control.

Dreams are very much a part of the world of emotions and, therefore, the realm of Water spirits. A Water spirit spell to promote lucid dreaming could be combined with a sleep spell or done separately for those who have no trouble sleeping. Either way, the suggested spell below is very similar to the sleep spell with a little variation.

As with the spell to bring sleep, place a bowl of freshly drawn water next to your bed. Lie in a comfortable position and begin a relaxation technique to help take you to the threshold of sleep. Include a Water visualisation with this. When you have completed this stage, petition the Water spirits to take you into the depths of sleep as described in the sleeping spell, but use different wording to incorporate the intent for lucid dreaming. For example:

> *"In deep subconscious sleep and dreams*
> *Water spirits, help me see*
> *To be aware within my dream*
> *And walk the sleep paths consciously."*

As in the sleeping spell, repeat the chant in internal dialogue, continuing to visualise yourself sinking into a Watery source, but seek within your awareness of the bowl of water at your side an awareness of yourself (that which constitutes the consciousness of *you)*. Don't concentrate on this too hard though, or it might prevent sleep in favour of deep philosophical thoughts.

It may be necessary to practice over several nights to get the feel for the right amount of self-awareness. Like many things, lucid dreaming becomes easier with practice.

Don't forget that thanks should be given to the spirits of the bowl of water on awakening, regardless of results. If you have not been successful, petition to try again the next night and save the bowl of water for the purpose. Water can be saved this way for up to three nights, then must be changed.

Do not blame the Water spirits if you have not been successful yet. Elemental spirits should *never* be addressed in blame or anger, even though they may sometimes be slow to respond to our requests. It is not unusual for them to test us: to wait and see what we will do if they don't respond or to see if perhaps we might succeed without their interference.

Too often, we humans are quick to seek spiritual assistance and neglect to tap into the magical sources within ourselves, and spiritual helpers can become bored with this overly dependent attitude, which is interpreted as plain laziness.

WATER SPIRIT DIVINATIONS AND A
SPELL TO ASSIST IN PSYCHIC ACTS

There are many methods by which we might attempt to access the depths of the subconscious where psychic perception occurs. Techniques of scrying—automatic writing, directly accessing the Akashic records, and so on—are many and varied, but all of them can benefit from assistance from Water spirits.

The element of Water is of course closely associated with the subconscious. Water itself is used frequently as a scrying element. Just having a source of Water nearby while performing a spell easily affects the whole atmosphere of the working. Similarly, performing a psychic act in the vicinity of Water naturally inspires psychic energy and draws the level of the mind into the hidden realms.

The obvious next step is to directly petition the spirits of the Water to assist in that which comes naturally, perhaps in some situations taking some precautions to avoid sinking too deeply.

First of all, you will need to choose a method for what it is you want to do. It might be a meditative session, a divination, or possibly even a direct scrying of a water surface. It might be a spell that requires going into psychic perception. Choose a place to perform the act that is either near a natural source of water or where you can produce a contained source.

Sitting in your living room with a large bowl of water may be sufficient, or you might wish to perform your ritual next to a waterfall, pond, river, or beach where the power of water is easily perceptible. A bowl of water is very much under the control of the practitioner, something that comes from the subconscious mind, while a wild source is beyond that conscious control and can have a more profound effect, taking us away into the deeper realms by their close proximity alone.

This is another situation, however, where I do not recommend immersing oneself in the water unless you are working with a partner or group and have someone in charge of monitoring the water safety situation. The subconscious is clearly linked to sleep and as one is drawn deeper and deeper into the altered state of psychic perception, it would be far too easy to continue to sink…literally! Don't forget the tendency of river and lake spirits to periodically claim their drowned victims.

Having set up your intent and location, you will only have to petition the Water spirits and proceed with the chosen divination method. Words from your own heart are always recommended and should be tailored to your specific intent and method, but the following example will suffice as a general guideline:

> *"In depths of mind, to clearly see,*
> *Bring the images now to me*
> *Water spirits to me show*
> *The things that I now wish to know."*

Yes, this sounds really hokey, but that's the point; it doesn't have to be great poetry. Elemental spirits respond to the rhythm of verse itself.

From a general opening like the above, the specific needs of the divination can be added in mediocre verse and will be just as effective as great poetry would be for the purpose. The important thing is that the words must reflect the emotions involved and the specifics and feeling of the intent. Then, having evoked the assistance of the Water spirits, carry on with whatever divination method you have chosen.

Spawning a Water Thought-Form Elemental

As is explained in Chapter Eight, thought-forms are potentially chaotic spirits who are best dealt with under very controlled conditions, most often created in an indoor temple rather than a natural setting. There are exceptions to this general idea of course, but Water thought-forms or servitors can be twice as "slippery" as any other sort, and I don't recommend calling up a Water thought-form from a natural source of Water to any but the most experienced magicians.

One would think that something spawned from one's own spirit would be relatively safe and easily controlled, but remember that Water is the realm of emotions, an area where we often have less command than we imagine. Also, remember the nature of the Water element, to split and combine so that, in a place where two water sources converge, none can say whether a random sample would belong to one source or the other.

Similarly, a Water thought-form created in a natural setting that includes a source of water will be as much a part of the water source as of its creator. The internal discipline required to keep such an entity focused on a specific intent rather than "leaking" its way into mischief is no laughing matter.

Having dispensed with the dire warnings, a Water thought-form can be very useful for certain tasks, particularly for help in divination in a different way than the natural Water spirits whom one might consult as explained in the previous section. Calling up a thought-form from the bowl of water could provide the necessary objectivity that is required for subjective divination methods.

Paradoxically, I suggest collecting the water from a natural source for this purpose, as it is preferable to using tap water. There is a stronger life force present in water that is collected from ponds, rivers, or the sea, and it will form natural parameters from having been collected into a container. Tap water is involved in a process of shifting from one place to another and has a feeling of mobility to it as a result. Establishing containment is an important aspect of dealing with thought-forms of any kind, but especially with Water.

Having set up your altar as desired and provided a container of water, open your ritual in the way that you choose. The container of water should be positioned so that you can easily walk around it. Creating a Water servitor is similar to those of the other elements: you walk deosil around the container as you state your intent and purpose, but interact with the water by keeping your right hand (rather than a wand) just above the surface, allowing yourself to feel the transference of energies between yourself and the natural Water spirits who inhabit this water.

This is the same for those who are left-handed, as to change would result in walking widdershins, which is definitely *not* recommended for this purpose. The only exception is for those who live in the Southern Hemisphere, where spiral energies run in the reverse direction.

The spirit you are creating will be of yourself, but the natural elementals may choose to join in or to stay out of the way. Either way, the parameters of this thought-form will be unstable, so the more specific you can be in giving instructions, the better. Don't forget to provide for re-absorption after the task is completed. This is important!

Begin as with any thought-form: *"I wish to create a servitor for the purpose of..."* then continue with the specific purpose, such as, *"allowing me to see objectively as I read my tarot cards to determine whether I should (specify intent of reading)."*

Remembering that we are dealing with the realm of the subconscious and emotions, the purpose should be very specific. With a little imagination, the reader might see the potential for influencing any number of situations where subjectivity is involved, such as a job interview, but the ethics involved in deciding how far to go in influencing the opinions of other people is an immensely complicated issue in itself. I suggest leaning towards caution in this area. Such ethics exist to keep things from going very wrong.

Repeat your specific purpose as many times as it takes while continuing to circle your container of water, until the feeling of built-up energy is intense and you feel that it is time to release the thought-form to perform its purpose.

Releasing a Water thought-form requires an act of bringing it out of its element. An easy method for this is to suddenly change your motions while circling the container, using your left hand to pass your wand into the right which has been interacting with the water, visualising the formation of a growing waterspout as you command the spirit to go forth and do its work:

> *"Go now, servitor, and perform this task (specify task again). Then return again to this place of Water, that we may blend again in harmony. Let it be so."*

Close the ritual and ground yourself.

You will need to save this container of water for re-absorption. Keep it safe from spillage. If you were able to obtain a suitable container that also has a lid, all the better!

Once the purpose is fulfilled, re-open the ritual in the same way as before, using the same water. Following the same formula as closely as possible, re-create the ritual but change your words slightly:

> *"I now recall the servitor whom I have created for the purpose of (state purpose exactly as before) to this source of water. Let it now be re-absorbed into its source and let it dissipate within my spirit with the calm of an undisturbed pond. Let it be so."*

It is rather effective to actually dip your hand into the water at the point where you are commanding it to be re-absorbed into its source, thereby forming the physical connection that was separated in the formation of the servitor.

It should be apparent that the purpose should have been thought out carefully before beginning, as anything that has been sent out is going to be re-absorbed directly into one's own being. It is necessary to do this as residual spirits are very chaotic and Water spirits are most proficient at getting into things where you would rather they did not. Close the ritual as before and do a thorough grounding.

Grounding After a Water Spell

Earlier in this chapter, we noted the value of sending residual energies after a ritual into the Earth and lowering internal energies by eating something sweet. The most important thing to remember when grounding after a Water ritual is to make the transition from Water to Earth, especially if you have been immersed in a natural source. When you have returned to land and have finished closing the ritual, direct all energy into the Earth and include a transitional phrase in your grounding chant such as:

> *"From Water to Earth,*
> *I stand firm on the ground of my making,*
> *And ask the Earth (or Gaia) to cleanse my spirit*

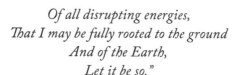

Of all disrupting energies,
That I may be fully rooted to the ground
And of the Earth,
Let it be so."

Rest and feast.

After any magic, it is strongly advised to lower your natural energies by eating something sweet, preferably with natural grain. Oats are ideal, which makes a great excuse for indulging in homemade flapjack or oatmeal cookies, as they are made from oats and sweetened with sugar or honey.

AETHER

By now, the reader will likely have noticed that these example spells have focused on the four basic elements, excluding Aether. The realm of Spirit works as a gestalt of the combined elements and is affected by the beliefs of the magic user.

For most purposes, working with Aetherial spirits is done through common prayer or petition, either to the idea of the entity or to a physical representation, such as a picture or statue.

One exception is forming a thought-form spirit from the magic user's own spirit.

One's expectations can have a significant influence on control and direction of such a thought-form. Confidence is good, but always have a good banishing spell ready. Having done my duty with dire warnings again, let us get on with method.

The first thing to do is to think out your purpose. Could a different form of elemental spirit serve it better, perhaps? Purposes appropriate to Aether might include self-transformation, finding one's way through a dilemma, dealing with philosophical questions, or some forms of healing, as well as for perusing the Akashic records for esoteric knowledge.

The method is similar to Air thought-forms: choose either a space on the floor for manifestation or a physical object in which to house your thought-form. A small bottle can be used for a Djinn-like spirit.

Open the ritual in your usual manner and state your purpose very specifically:

"I wish to create a servitor for the purpose of (state purpose)."

Be sure to include careful attention to every detail. You may wish to follow this with a charging, perhaps with a sigil, dance magic, or any number of representative actions that apply to your intent.

Circle the manifestation point and chant your purpose, perhaps incorporating dance, song, or drumming. Infuse the rite with your own spirit, allowing yourself to let go and "become" the extant spirit as well as maintaining a sense of yourself. A feeling of elation usually accompanies this form of self-release.

Then, halt the proceedings and feel yourself as separate from the created spirit while continuing to infuse it with energy. Release it with a one-time command to go forth and accomplish its purpose, stating once again what that is as you do so. Close the ritual, ground, and banish.

As part of this ritual, you must include a command to return to the place prepared for the spirit's manifestation. To re-absorb the energy back into yourself, repeat the ritual, changing the release command to one to become one with your spirit again.

Needless to say, if the servitor was sent out for a nefarious purpose, this could go horribly wrong. The alternative is to include a command for the spirit to dissipate once the purpose is accomplished, but I recommend doing this infrequently as it means a loss of some of your energy, rather like giving blood. Allowing recovery time would be wise.

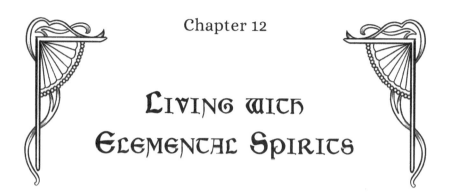

Chapter 12

Living with Elemental Spirits

THE CYCLE OF DEATH AND REBIRTH is reflected regularly in nature. Flowers die in winter, only to be reborn in the spring. Natural "disasters" like fires and hurricanes clear areas of the earth, only to be followed by new growth.

The Earth spirits who participate in some versions of this natural cycle, such as earthquakes and landslides, are very much a part of this cycle and generally don't mean us harm, but the magical renewal of life must continue.

Therein lies the explanation for human interest in elemental spirits. We, as humans, are ever drawn to the magic of nature and to understanding the natural laws that are at the heart of our ability to perform our magic.

In general, humankind has largely forgotten the connection we have to the natural world. Our artificial constructs and involvement in imaginary worlds, such as the stock market and world economy, have taken over the collective thinking of a large percentage of the world's population. We have forgotten that we, too, are a part of the magic of the natural world.

When we become aware of the nature of elemental spirits, we reawaken ourselves to a part of ourselves that we no longer learn from one generation to the next as a matter of course. It is up to more recent generations to remember the elemental spirits and to teach our children to respect the fairies in the garden as well as the more powerful forces in nature.

Those of us who are drawn to the world of magic owe it to ourselves to learn about the nature of Spirit. It is our own spiritual nature that draws us into magic to begin with. Magic is a natural part of Spirit and in turn, spirits are attracted to magic and can be of great benefit in many of our magical operations.

Friendly spirits are valuable friends to have, and the Earth spirits are the most stable and enduring of all spiritual helpers. If we treat them with respect, we can often find that qualities like health, prosperity, and general good fortune will come to us organically.

Working with Air spirits can be a double-edged sword. On one hand, they can be very agreeable and protective spirits. On the other, they can be callous and unreliable, and might change from one to the other at any time without warning.

An inherent quality of Air is change. Change comes from movement, as does inspiration. Air spirits are constantly in motion of one sort or another, and drawing their attention can result in becoming the target of pranks (or worse) if one offends them or fails to fulfil their expectations.

Air spirits, like magic itself, work within a delicate balance of influences that can change direction with a wisp of a breeze or in the subtle vibration of a stray thought.

Similarly, Fire can be friend or foe. Death and renewal take on a new dimension with Fire spirits whose nature is destruction of the old to make room for the new. Like the Phoenix that is destroyed in the fire only to be reborn, the purifying transmutation of Fire is a cycle of cleansing and new possibilities.

The Fire spirits who become harbingers of destruction do so not out of malice, but because it is part of their character. Lightning strikes a tree or sap pops in dry conditions and creates a forest fire, and the forest is cleansed of old, dead wood. New shoots soon follow. Animals flee the raging fire, but some do not escape. Yet more will always breed. Nature can be cruel in its impersonality.

Fire spirits need not be feared, only respected. Used wisely, it is a friendly element that brings warmth and light as well as immense power. Used wantonly, it can turn suddenly into the force of destruction.

Becoming aware of the disposition of Fire spirits can give us the ability to contain our dealings with them (within reasonable parameters). To ignore or abandon them out of fear would mean cheating ourselves of an integral part of the inherent balance of the elemental world.

Without the drives and passions of Fire, we would only stagnate in mediocrity. The ecstasy of gnosis and the power to send forth one's Will are mechanisms of the life force and therefore of Fire. The Divine Light, in whatever form, is much of what separates humans from other animals.

Water spirits affect our lives as constantly, as do Air spirits. It is an element that is always present and always a part of us. This alone creates the imperative that we must work with them rather than try to deny them.

Emotions are a natural part of the human psyche. Those who reject their own emotional potential, usually as a result of having suffered through some form of severe emotional pain or trauma, quickly become less human, less magical, and much more prone to some forms of negative energy.

The magic user can apply the positive energies of love and passion, the drive behind anger, or even the spiritual "high" that accompanies the elation of success to both life and magic. While the stronger emotions require some parameters through the disciplines of magic in order to avoid getting totally out of control, all of the emotions have the capacity for being put to constructive use.

Water spirits, though they are potentially as destructive as the floods and tsunamis that demonstrate the pure force of water, are also essentially calm creatures who can be as co-operative as the currents we create for ourselves when we go for a swim in a calm pool or lake.

Despite the tendency of Water to entice one into its depths, it is an affectionate element. The Water spirits are sensual and intimate in the way that a friendly cat might show affection when it seems to attempt to *become* a part of the human object of its attention, trying to surround the larger human with its small but ever-convoluting body.

The gentle cleansing power of Water is very different from the more violent cleansing that comes from Fire. The spirits of Water are, in essence, calm, yet are not to be trifled with. The slightest outside influence can change their gentle disposition into a raging tempest. Tales tell of creatures of the Water who attack ships or entice swimmers to their deaths, as well as those who give freely of gifts and advice, or even magical favours.

Dealing with Water spirits requires an adaptability that obliges us to exercise some degree of command over our more turbulent emotions in accordance with our intuition. It is the spirit of our sixth sense that will lead us to the spirits of the Water, but it is down to us to learn the art of remaining in a calm frame of mind when dealing with them. We have the ability to allow ourselves to be drawn into the depths of the world of Water spirits without completely abandoning ourselves to their whims and mercies.

Friendly Water spirits might be the most valuable allies we have in times of personal trouble. They can and will assist freely in divinations and all other purposes that are associated with Water, yet we must remember to approach them with calm and not despair when we seek counsel from the spirits of the Water.

Spirit permeates our life, regardless of our beliefs or what form they might take. There is far more to Spirit than belief alone. It cannot be measured or dissected. Some of us have learned that belief can actually shape reality, not just perception. This is one of the mysteries of magic.

The limits of magic are like the limits of the spiritual realm: unknowable. The Aetherial spirits within our perceptions may vary according to each individual's understanding of their nature, such is the very nature of Spirit.

The magic in nature is accessible through many paths, yet has a consistency that can be understood with an open mind and an open heart. Knowing the Aetherial spirits, whether we understand them as projections of inner Spirit or as separate entities in whatever form, awakens our own magical potential.

The realm of Spirit creates the magic of life and of hope, enthusiasm, and endurance. Pure Spirit is intoxicating in its absolute clarity, and the immersion into the world of Spirit transforms us, melding the nature of our own spirits within the force of nature and magic.

Whatever form of practice we choose to employ in addressing the elemental spirits, communing with them brings a powerful dimension to our magical toolbox. For those of us who maintain an awareness of them in our daily lives, they become nothing short of treasured allies.

BIBLIOGRAPHY AND RECOMMENDED READING

Aburrow, Yvonne. *Auguries and Omens: The Magical Lore of Birds*. Capall Bann Publishing, 1993.

Alexander, Marc. *British Folklore, Myths and Legends*. George Weidenfeld & Nicolson, 1982.

Alli, Antero. *Angel Tech: A Modern Shaman's Guide to Reality Selection*. Falcon Press, 1988.

Arrowsmith, Nancy. *A Field Guide to the Little People*. MacMillan London, 1977.

Blackburn, Simon. *The Oxford Dictionary of Philosophy*. Oxford University Press, 2016.

Bord, Janet and Colin Bord. *Sacred Waters*. Granada Publishing, 1985.

—. *The Secret Country*. Granada Publishing, 1978.

Briggs, Katherine. *Abbey Lubbers, Banshees & Bogarts*. Kestrel Books, 1979.

—. *The Vanishing People*. B.T. Batsford, 1978.

Britannica, The Editors of Encyclopaedia. "Babylonian Calendar." *Encyclopaedia Britannica*, 10 Feb. 2021, https://www.britannica.com/science/Babylonian-calendar. Accessed 6 November 2023.

Brown, Frank A. "Persistent Activity Rhythms in the Oyster." *American Journal of Physiology-Legacy Content*, 1954, https://doi.org/10.1152/ajplegacy.1954.178.3.510. Accessed 6 Nov. 2023.

Cavendish, Richard. *The Magical Arts*. Arkana Paperbacks, 1984.

Coghlan, Ronan. *Handbook of Fairies*. Capall Bann Publishing, 1998.

Cunningham, Scott. *Earth Power*. Llewellyn Publications, 1984.

Daniels, Cora Linn, and C. M. Stevans. *Encyclopaedia of Superstitions, Folklore, and the Occult Sciences of the World*, Volume 2. University Press of the Pacific, 2003.

de Troyes, Chrétien. *Conte del Graal (Perceval, or, The Story of the Grail)*. University of Georgia Press, 2011.

de Valéra, Sinéad. *Fairy Tales of Ireland*. Four Square Books, 1967.

DeSalvo, John. *Lost Art of Enochian Magic: Angels, Invocations, and the Secrets Revealed to Dr. John Dee*. Destiny Books, 2010.

Dickens, Charles. *David Copperfield*. Penguin Publishing Group, 2004.

Dukes, Ramsey. *SSOTBME: An Essay on Magic*. Nigel Grey-Turner, 1979.

Easter, Michael A. and Angi M. Christensen. "Forensic Spotlight: Dousing for Human Remains—Considerations for Investigators." *FBI Law Enforcement Bulletin*, 11 Jan. 2022, https://leb.fbi.gov/spotlights/forensic-spotlight-dowsing-for-human-remains-considerations-for-investigators. Accessed 6 Nov. 2023.

Easwaran, Eknath. *The Upanishads*. Nilgiri Press, 2019.

Evans-Wentz, W.Y. *The Fairy Faith in Celtic Countries*. Citadel Press, 1990.

Flowers, Stephen. *Original Magic*. Inner Traditions, 2017.

Fortune, Dion. *The Sea Priestess*. Weiser Books, 2003.

Foss, Michael. *Folk Tales of the British Isles*. GPS, 1977.

Fries, Jan. *Visual Magic*. Mandrake of Oxford, 1992.

Froud, Brian, and Alan Lee. *Faeries*. Bantam Books, 1978.

Gale, Jack. *Goddesses, Guardians & Groves: Awakening the Spirit of the Land*. Capall Bann Publishing, 1996.

Grant, Kenneth. *Images and Oracles of Austin Osman Spare*. Frederick Muller, 1975.

Graves, Robert. *The White Goddess*. Faber & Faber, 1961.

Graves, Tom. *Dowsing*. Granada Publishing, 1980.

Hadingham, Evan. *Circles and Standing Stones*. William Heinemann, 1976.

Haggar, Nicholas. *The Fire and the Stones*. Element Books, 1991.

Hawken, Paul. *The Magic of Findhorn*. Souvenier Press, 1975.

Hawkins, Jaq D. *Approaching the Elements Directly*. Kia Press, 2002.

—. *Spirits of the Earth*. Capall Bann Publishing, 1998.

—. *Spirits of the Air*. Capall Bann Publishing, 1998.

—. *Spirits of the Fire*. Capall Bann Publishing, 1999.

—. *Spirits of the Water*. Capall Bann Publishing, 2000.

—. *Spirits of the Aether*. Capall Bann Publishing, 2001.

Heselton, Phillip. *Mirrors of Magic: Evoking the Spirit of the Dewponds*. Capall Bann Publishing, 1997.

—. *Secret Places of the Goddess*. Capall Bann Publishing, 1996.

Hill, Douglas. *The Illustrated Faerie Queen*. Newsweek Books, 1980.

Hitching, Francis. *Earth Magic*. Picador/Pan Books, 1977.

Hope, Robert Charles. *The Legendary Lore of the Holy Wells of England: Including Rivers, Lakes, Fountains and Springs*. Llanerch, 1893.

Hughes, Ted. *River*. Faber and Faber, 1983.

Johnson, Samuel. Preface. *The Plays of William Shakespeare, With Notes*. By William Shakespeare. J. and R. Tonson et al., 1765.

Jones, Evan John and Doreen Valiente. *Witchcraft: A Tradition Renewed*. Robert Hale, 1990.

Jones, Gwyn and Thomas. *The Mabinogion*. Dragon's Dream B.V., 1982.

Knowles, Elizabeth. The Oxford Dictionary of Phrase and Fable. OUP Oxford, 2006.

Lineman, Rose and Jan Popelka. *Compendium of Astrology*. Para Research, 1984.

MacGregor, Alastair. *The Peat-Fire Flame*. The Moray Press, 1937.

MacLellan, Gordon. *Talking to the Earth*. Capall Bann Publishing, 1996.

MacManus, D.A. *The Middle Kingdom*. Maz Parish & Co., 1959.

Mathers, S. L. MacGregor. *The Key of Solomon the King*. Red Wheel Weiser, 2016.

McLean, Adam. *A Treatise on Angel Magic*. Phanes Press, 1990.

Mitchell, John. *Megalithomania*. Thames & Hudson, 1982.

Moore, A.W. *The Folklore of the Isle of Man*. 1891. Llanerch Publishers, 1994.

Morris, Ruth and Frank. *Scottish Healing Wells*. The Alethea Press, 1982.

Mullin, Kay. *Wondrous Land: The Faery Faith of Ireland*. Capall Bann Publishing, 1997.

Potts, Marc. *The Mythology of the Mermaid and Her Kin*. Capall Bann Publishing, 2000.

Rattue, James. *The Living Stream: Holy Wells in Historical Context*. The Boydell Press, 1995.

Rogers, Jesse. *Common Sense Paganism*. Lulu Press, 2012.

Roob, Alexander. *Alchemy & Mysticism*. Taschen, 1997.

Samuel, Geoffrey, Hamish Gregor and Elizabeth Stutchbury. *Tantra and Popular Religion in Tibet*. Crescent Printing Works, 1994.

Sepharial. *A Manual of Occultism*. Rider & Company, 1972.

Sharp, Mick. *Holy Places of Celtic Britain*. Blandford, 1997.

Skelton, Robin. *Talismanic Magic*. Samuel Weiser, 1985.

Spare, Austin Osman. *The Book of Pleasure: The Psychology of Ecstasy*. CreateSpace Independent Publishing Platform, 2018.

Spence, Lewis. *British Fairy Origins*. The Aquarian Press, Ltd., 1946.

—. Myth and Ritual in Dance, Game and Rhyme. Watts & Co., 1947.

The Tibetan Book of the Dead: First Complete Translation. Translated by Gyurme Dorje, edited by Graham Coleman and Thupten Jinpa. Penguin Books Limited, 2008.

Thoreau, Henry David. *Walden; or, Life in the Woods.* Ticknor and Fields, 1854.

Thorsson, Edred. *The Book of Ogham.* Llewellyn Publications, 1992.

Van Gelder, Dora. *The Real World of Fairies.* Quest, 1977.

Vinci, Leo. *Talismans, Amulets and Charms.* Regency Press, 1977.

Waite, A.E. *The Book of Ceremonial Magic.* Rider & Company, 1911.

Wildberg, Christian. *John Philoponus' Criticism of Aristotle's Theory of Aether.* Walter De Gruyter, 1988.